Catching the Light

KAREN POWELL

Harbour Books Ltd
20 Castlegate
York YO1 9RP
www.harbourbooks.co.uk
Represented in Great Britain & Ireland by
Signature Book Services
First published in Great Britain by
Harbour Books 2005
This edition published by Harbour Books 2006

A catalogue record for this book is
available from the British Library.

ISBN 13: 978 1905128 04 4
ISBN 10: 1905128 04 5

Typeset by Antony Gray
Printed and bound in Finland by WS Bookwell

PART ONE

CHAPTER 1

I am a girl who loves to be alone. Lottie, the silly creature, can't do it. My sister, though she is thirteen and older than me by two whole years and a bit, cannot even spend a quiet half-hour in her room, reading or playing, without rushing back down the stairs to check where the rest of us are. Mummy says she must have skipped a stage growing up, that, at a certain age, a baby believes someone disappearing from view no longer exists. I can see how this might make a tiny baby cry out loud, what a scary idea it is, but what I love are the little pockets of aloneness that come my way now that I am getting bigger and can be trusted not to answer the door to strangers or set fire to the house or myself.

Today I enjoy the silence that falls as the slam of the door disappears into the thick walls of the cottage and the cushions and heavy curtains that cover the hard stone of our house, and then I run to the window to make sure that they are really leaving. Yes, there they go, followed by their short shadows on the hot pavement: Mummy, upright as always, despite the heat, Lottie looking pale-faced and miserable at the thought of having to buy shoes for her new school, her straight hair already lank though she washed it this morning – kneeling down with her head over the bath and yelping because the water from the shower attachment either scalds you or makes your skull ache with the cold. Mummy's mouth is moving, telling off Lottie, perhaps, for her sulkiness. They will walk to the Market Square and then catch the bus into Braxtable,

Mummy never having learnt to drive because, she says, in London one always took taxis or the tube and that she is too old to learn now. Her arm is linked through Lottie's and she walks fast with her head up. Nothing could stop her progress you know; if a mountain should suddenly appear in front of her, she would simply march over it without a hint of surprise. But then everyone in London walks that way. I remember this from the last time we went to stay with Aunt Harriet before they found cancer making itself at home in her bones and took her away to be fixed: all those people pushing themselves forward, eyes straight ahead, bodies moving through places without ever noticing them. Once I overheard Sandra Mills and Mrs Harvey talking about my mother in Kentons, the local supermarket, where Mummy refuses to shop unless she really has to, disliking the dusty looking shelves loaded with tinned vegetables and packet soups and the freezers with misted-up windows stacked with boxes of breadcrumbed or battered things – what she calls 'war-time food'.

'The girls are sweet,' said Mrs Harvey, who runs the launderette in the centre of town and whose husband says he's disabled and never does a day's work if he can help it.

'Oh yes,' said Sandra Mills without enthusiasm. She drops her eyelashes that are heavy and clumped with the black stuff that Mummy puts on with a little brush, and then lifts them again as if it is a big effort to do so. Her neck is a yellowish colour below the edge of her make-up, as though she has never seen sunlight since the day she began to work in Kentons. I am fascinated by her face, never see her without having the urge to reach for her jaw-line, where the peachy-pink mask comes to an end, to see if I can pinch it with the tips of my fingers, peel the whole lot off in one go like a magician. Sandra babysits for us every now and then because she and her boyfriend Roy are saving up to get married and every little helps. I once heard Mummy say to Harry she's not altogether happy about leaving us with someone with an IQ lower than mine and Lottie's put together, but how else would they get to see a play or an exhibition? (Later, when I ask her what an IQ is, she looks embarrassed for a second, and then smiles and shakes her head at me for listening to their conversation.)

'And *she's* nice enough, I suppose,' says Sandra, and then adds, 'a bit snooty though.'

Then they spot me and start talking loudly about something else and I pay meekly for my bag of butterscotch and smile and say thank you as if I'd heard nothing at all. That night, ashamed of my cowardice, I lie in bed practising all the clever mean things I will say if it happens again, see myself marching out of the shop afterwards like a queen and two mouths wide with wonder.

Watching Mummy now, marching along the street, I can understand why you might think of her like this. The pride she takes in the way she looks – never leaving the house without having her hair drawn up into a neat pleat and her make-up carefully applied – cannot help but make her seem a little bit royal. And though she is always polite, greeting anyone she meets and stopping to talk if necessary, I can see how she might make you feel that you have taken up a piece of her time that she did not want to give you. Now glee rises within me as she and Lottie disappear out of sight and the street is empty again. What to do with these few precious hours?

I race upstairs and, because it is at the top of the stairs and because I am not thinking, I go into my room first, which is no longer mine though I have left some of my things there. Then I turn around and go to Lottie's room instead, where Mummy has made up the foldaway bed in which I am to sleep until the end of the holidays. I ignore this for now, lie down on Lottie's bed instead, pushing my head into the pillow and wondering what it must be like to be her, with limbs that stretch almost to the foot of the bed.

Then I jump up and go to the cupboard where she keeps her things, take out the doll dressed in Welsh national costume which Harry brought back from Snowdon for her and which I am not allowed to touch because it is not really a doll. Snowed On. A good name for a mountain, I decide, as I twirl the red-cheeked doll around on the bed for a minute, making her dance. Then I check to see if her arms move and if she is wearing knickers before carefully putting her back where I found her.

In Mummy's room there are thin curtains at the window, which lift and fall in the breeze. The walls are a deep pink and the bed is covered with a thick cream bedspread. Our cleaner will not come till Monday but this room, like the rest of the house, is always neat and well ordered. Mummy's perfume still hangs in the air and the blue satin dressing-gown that came all the way from Paris is draped over the bedstead. The photograph of my father is back out again, I notice, and I pick it up from where it stands among the creams and perfumes and brushes on Mummy's dressing-table and stare down at it, trying to conjure up feelings that won't come because it is hard to believe that this slightly fuzzy image, this flat thing, was ever filled out with blood and a real pumping heart. The thought of blood reminds me of what Mummy told me about the other day and I suddenly feel shut in by this room. I spray myself quickly with Mummy's perfume and dab my nose with her powder puff, and then skip back down the stairs into the dark hallway that runs down the middle of the cottage. Then, an idea coming to me, I walk along the hallway and push open the back door.

The air is thick with summer. It closes round me as I step from the shadow of the house and on to the narrow lawn, which is losing its greenness despite Mummy's work with the sprinkler these last weeks. Here, in her garden, is the only time you will ever see Mummy looking untidy. She loves the digging and hoeing and pruning and weeding. It is how Harry first saw her – last autumn when he knocked at the front door and no one answered and he came through the back gate to fix the guttering – all flushed from the cold, her hair falling out from the clip that holds it at the back of her neck, about to drop a great big armful of prunings into the wheelbarrow that Lottie and I were fighting over. She always looks younger and prettier when she is happy and she is always happy when she is working in the garden. Harry is her boyfriend, by the way. (Her *boyfriend!* If I keep saying this over and over again I can make Lottie stop being upset about it, can cross my eyes and make my voice go high until her mouth begins to twitch and both of us explode with laughter and it takes her a few minutes to remember to be annoyed with me again.) Grown-up people with children are not supposed to have boyfriends, but Mummy and Harry are not married and we have seen them kissing, so this is what he must be. Harry is the reason why our father's photograph keeps disappearing.

As I step into the garden, the flower borders rear up at me on either side like waves. The purply-grey acanthus – I can hear Mummy's voice, telling me the correct Latin names of the plants as I pass among them – still stand tall at the back of each border, their tough leaves bearing the heat, and the open faces of those plants that look like daisies and whose name I can never remember push up from the cracked earth wherever they are planted in the garden, but the heads of the more dainty arching flowers are starting to droop now, as if anxious to sink back down into the cool earth again. Fat bees heave themselves lazily from flower to flower, sleepy in the heat, their humming electrifying the air. I watch my sunburned feet moving across the lawn as if I am looking down at them through the clear blue water of a swimming pool (not the muddy green of the sea, which I can hear, faintly, in the distance). This heat does not worry me too much, though adults give little moans every time they step out into it, wondering out loud if it will ever end and dabbing at brows that can't possibly have broken into a sweat so quickly. I like the way the skin on my arms and legs deepens another shade each day, check the change before the bathroom mirror each evening, pushing up the arms and the hem of my T-shirt to see the paleness beneath. In the hot artificial light, my limbs look as if they have been grafted on to someone else's body.

I stop for a moment on the lawn and slide the toes of one foot down over the heel of the other, trying to ease off the strap of my white leather sandal. It would, of course, be easier to bend down and undo the buckle in the normal way but I don't, even though the tight leather strap drags painfully across my skin, unwilling to break the contract I have made with myself, one of the little challenges I set myself each day. My days are full of these contracts and now my nights too. This week I vowed not to sleep before two a.m. for seven full nights and I have spent each of these nights glaring fiercely at the red glow of my digital alarm clock, a devil's eye in the dark, willing my eyes not to close until the right time. This morning, the last day of the test, I felt almost tearful with tiredness when Mummy called me to come down for breakfast. Even so, I am thrilled that I have not failed.

The sandal scrapes free and I flip it into the air. It lands in a knot of herbs, which have grown looser and messier as summer's gone on, and the air is suddenly full of the scent of basil. I do not bother to fetch the sandal from where it has bruised the caterpillar-green ears of the herb, which are almost see-through if you hold them up to the light. I remove the second sandal in the same way, enjoying the way my tiered cotton skirt flies up to display its broderie anglaise hem as I launch the shoe across the lawn. I've had to pester Mummy for weeks to sew in this hem, because all the girls at school have them and sometimes she forgets her promises. I am thankful that I will not have to wear a uniform like Lottie's – which is hanging stiffly in her wardrobe in the room we will be sharing until the end of the holidays – for another few years. I hate the idea of being locked inside that rigid blazer and grey scratchy-looking socks. To tell the truth, I do not really believe the day will come when I will find myself in that uniform: in the vast stretch of the next two years something must surely happen to prevent such a thing. You see I am sure that something – a something that I cannot put into words – protects me from anything unpleasant. 'Deliver us from evil,' we recite each school morning and these words make me shiver deliciously though I have no clear picture of what form evil might take, am only able to conjure up the shadow figure with a dagger in its hand on the front cover of a book about Jack the Ripper I once found in the library.

I feel the dry prickle of the rougher grass beneath my bare feet as I skip towards the plum tree near the grey stone wall at the bottom of the garden where Mummy allows it to run wild, 'to encourage the butterflies'. Last year it rained almost all summer and though there was lots of fruit, many of the plums had split before they could be picked. But this year every branch is straining under rows of firm egg-shaped fruit, each rosy-yellow plum waiting for a hand to mould itself around it. I realise that I should have brought the china mixing bowl from the kitchen to fill, but will not waste time by returning for it now, instead will lay the plums on the ground as I pick them, nesting each in the grass, and then gather them up in my skirt, holding the hem up to keep them from falling.

If I gather quickly and don't get distracted by woodlice or ladybirds or bright-faced daisies wanting to be picked and threaded into long, fragile necklaces and tiaras, there will still be time to find the recipe in Mummy's folder, cook and tidy up before she and Lottie come from town. It's true that when I suggested making something as a kind of welcome for our visitors tomorrow Mummy said not to go to any trouble – had actually seemed annoyed by the suggestion – but I can't help thinking that she'll be pleased anyway when she returns to the smell of the plums cooking and sees their gluey purple juice bubbled up through the crumble. I reach up and begin to take the fruit from the tree, laying each plum carefully on the ground. A scattering of fruit has fallen from the branches already and I watch the wasps buzzing round the splits in the broken flesh. One whines past my ear and I bat it away, noticing as I lay my own harvest on the grass, how the fruit seems to have soaked up the sunlight so it looks like it's lit from the inside.

Soon there are at least twenty plums around my feet, enough, once they have been split in two and had their stones prised out, to fill the deep ceramic pie dish Mummy keeps in the dresser. It feels much hotter than when I first came outside and I notice that I am breathing more heavily. In the heat, this small task of stretching, picking and bending takes out more from your body than usual, like running through water. I can feel blood throbbing through my tummy and I stop, hold my hand there, imagining the swirl of blood like a red sun in the dark of my body.

I crouch down and begin to fill my lap with the fruit, watch a wasp enjoying the clear pink juice of a damaged plum that lies a foot away from me. I promised myself that I would not waste any of the fruit, but I am suddenly thirsty and can't stop myself from lifting one of the plums from my lap to my mouth. I use my front teeth to tear back a little patch of skin, exposing the flesh beneath, hesitate for a second, and then take a huge bite. Sweet juice spurts into my mouth and down my throat. It trickles down my chin and falls in a shower of drops to the grass where another wasp swoops in to share it. I eat greedily with my eyes closed, pulling the flesh cleanly away from the stone with my teeth, then flicking the stone away into the grass when I have finished. I should stop now but still my hand closes around another plum. I lift it to my mouth, push my teeth through the skin, this time keeping my eyes open. I glance down to admire the clean bite I have taken and the creamy maggot in the centre of the plum uncurls itself and nods blindly at me, the sudden intruder. The shock makes me reel inside but I do not move for a long second, just stare at my hand. Then breath forces itself into my lungs and out again in a shriek that rises from somewhere deep in my stomach and I am on my feet, fruit tumbling from my skirts, as my arm springs back and catapults the plum away across the garden, no thought, no aim, just *away*.

It lands, smashing against the grey stone wall and dropping into the long grass beneath, leaving a damp mess of shattered fruit on the wall. I sink to my knees then, eyes never leaving the wall. I am panting and I force my breathing to slow, push down a sob that wants to escape, then wipe the moisture from my face that is sweat not tears.

CHAPTER 2

'Kate! Are you asleep?' Without waiting for a reply, Lottie slides in beside me, wriggling beneath the thin sheet that is all the covering you need these nights and making the metal legs of the foldaway bed squeak.

'What is it?' I reply, though I know already. Lottie cannot hide her feelings: her body gives her away every time. She lies rigidly beside me now and if somebody were to switch on the light, I know exactly how she would look: face frozen, eyes wide and scared, and for a second I feel a flash of irritation, a desire to be really mean.

'I wish they weren't coming tomorrow,' she says in a shaky voice. The small voice doesn't match the length of the body beside me – Lottie's legs and arms have got noticeably longer this summer and she draws attention away from this whenever possible, pulling in her too-large feet beneath her bottom when she sits on the sofa or yanking her bony knees up to her chest and pulling them in with her arms. Her limbs, stick-like in her school uniform, which Mummy insisted she try on this afternoon, have become another thing she resents. They have betrayed her with their change. I, on the other hand, pay no attention to the solid, straight lines of my own body most of the time, though I do feel a rush of pride when my muscles pull me through the branches of a tree or when I sprint along the beach, the bones in my feet pushing me off the firm sand at the water's edge until I feel as though I am about to take flight.

'It's only for a few weeks. Just till school time,' I reply. 'And it's only Josie really. Daniel's too old to play with girls our age,' I add, using Mummy's words or something like them to give my own weight. I awake often to Lottie's shape in my doorway, skinny in the white cotton nightie that is too short for her. Now that we are sharing her room she has even less distance to travel. I play the role of grown-up in these night-time talks until Lottie feels better and then the following day she will act as if the conversation has never taken place and find me as annoying and babyish as ever. I am not sure when this routine became fixed, when it was agreed that I, even though I am younger, must always be the one to comfort – the idea seems to have taken root without my noticing it and I am not always comfortable with this. There are times when I feel dizzy with the responsibility that falls upon me in these moments of night when it is just me and Lottie, and the whole world of paths to choose from and fears to be overcome seem to push down on me, but it is too late to question now.

'But we hardly know them!' She waits a moment, then adds, 'I don't see why they can't stay on with their mother.'

'Oh Lottie . . . !' I was rolling towards the edge of sleep a moment ago, but Lottie has destroyed the moment. There is something determined about my sister's misery; it will not be ignored. Now I force myself awake again. 'You know why! It wouldn't be fair to Harry. Not when he's been expecting to see them. Mummy says we should think about all the things *he* does for *us*.' She says nothing but her thin body does not relax. 'Anyway,' I add. 'I don't know why you and Mummy have to be so . . . ' I stare up at the ceiling, trying to bring the right word to the surface, 'so curmudgeonly about it,' I finish triumphantly, smiling to myself in the dark. It is not really the right word, doesn't describe the mood I have noticed in recent days, but I read it in a book last week and it is so satisfying to get out of your mouth, like a heavy carpet unrolling, that I can't resist using it.

'We're not!' retorts Lottie and she sighs in irritation, as if it is me and not her that is keeping us awake. I know better though. About them being curmudgeonly, that is.

Mummy was cheerful enough when she first explained to us about the lease on Harry's rented house not being continued: 'He's been so looking forward to having them with him for the whole month, you see . . . These weekends here and there are simply inadequate, no time at all. I told him that you girls would be more than happy to help out.' And she pauses, eyes telling us to agree, and I rush to say yes, ask too many questions to cover Lottie's silence. She needn't think she fooled me though: whenever she talks about the visit her body goes as tight as my sister's. Perhaps she dislikes the thought of the extra work involved, forgetting that we will be out of the house most of the time. As for Harry, well, he apologises about the inconvenience whenever he has the chance till we are rather tired of telling him that we don't mind at all. Privately, I am hoping that the others being here will alter things, persuade Lottie that a younger sister is not always an irritation.

'It will be fine,' I say. Then I turn over, my feet seeking a patch of cool between the hot, rough cotton of my sheets. A minute or so later I feel Lottie going back to her own bed.

Let me tell you a secret: I wish Harry was my father. I say it's a secret but once I told Lottie and made her furious. She pushed me away and told me that it wasn't Daddy's fault he died or that I am too stupid to remember anything about him. And, she said, Mummy would never get married to anyone else, she was sure of it. Perhaps I am very wicked but I don't know how to be loyal to someone whose shape and smell I cannot make come to life, even when I stare and stare at his photograph and will them to come to me. I just know that when Harry started coming round to our house I felt different. I am not saying that we were unhappy before he walked through the back gate last year, but we are a quiet family, not given to big bursts of talking over the dinner table or in the living-room where we sit in the evenings: me reading or scribbling in one of my little notebooks; Mummy choosing things from her gardening catalogues or, occasionally, doing paperwork from the charity shop in the High Street where she works part-time; Lottie sitting at the table with her homework, during term-time, or jammed into an armchair, staring out of the window or lost in a magazine. And though Mummy sometimes talks about growing up in London, where it seems she did nothing but go to parties or the theatre or the ballet or restaurants, none of this seems to have anything to do with her now. But when Harry breezes in after work some nights, windswept from a walk along the beach and smelling of oil-paint, something comes in with him and everyone seems to wake up: Mummy will pour a glass of wine for each of them, and we laugh more and louder – even Lottie when she forgets to sulk. Something about him makes us more of a family than we are when he is not here.

Today, when our visitors are coming, we talk less than usual over breakfast, and as the morning drags past, we each go off to our own places in the house. Mummy is in the kitchen, draining potatoes in a cloud of steam, and she makes it clear that she does not want company. Lottie is lying, bored, on the sofa staring at the television screen, as she has been for the past two hours. The curtains are closed to keep out the glare of the sun and the sounds of a cartoon fill the room. Though I'm sure she is not really watching it, I have given up trying to draw her out by suggesting we play on the beach or go to the rec and am sitting in a chair on the patio attempting to read. But the sun is glaring on to the pages and for once I cannot concentrate on *Swallows and Amazons*, which Harry bought for me last week and that I love with passion already. I drop the book into my lap and think that it is as though the air in the house has shifted to make way for the newcomers and we are feeling that they are here before they arrive. I wish they would hurry up and come because even I, who have been most excited about the visitors, am not comfortable in these last hours before they come.

Then, suddenly, Harry is hallooing at us through the door and they are here and the house is full of voices and suitcases being bumped through doors and cold drinks being offered and I scamper down the hallway from the garden and stand on the edge of it all, struck by shyness for a moment, but edging forwards all the same till Harry throws an arm around my shoulder and draws me into the thick of it.

'Josie, Daniel. You remember Katie, don't you? The baby of the household.' He drops into his pirate voice and announces, 'otherwise known as Captain Nancy Blackett, Amazon Pirate and Terror of the Seas!'

'Who?' says Josie, staring at me. Harry is referring to my favourite character in my new book, but doesn't explain himself any further, just puts his hands under my armpits, picks me up and twirls me round so fast that my stomach flips and my eyes go all blurry and I feel sure we will topple over. Everyone scatters in alarm and I shriek until Harry stops and places me giggling and dizzy back down on solid ground. Mummy shakes her head at him and Lottie rolls her eyes as if his play-acting is somehow my fault, but I do not mind this or being picked out as the youngest because when Harry talks about me he has something in his voice that tells me I am special. He introduces Lottie again, though he does not put his arm around her shoulder or tease her in the same way. It is not a snub just politeness with him. Lottie does not like to be touched and Harry would hate to upset her. My sister and I say hello to Daniel and Josie, who seem much bigger than they did last Christmas when we first met them, and then Mummy takes them into the kitchen for drinks and I, feeling more awkward than I had thought I would, offer to help Harry with the suitcases.

'Thanks, kitten,' he says, grinning at me. 'Can you manage the little one?' he asks. 'That's Josie's.'

'Of course,' I say, though when I lift it, it is heavier than it looks. I climb the stairs after Harry, drop Josie's case just inside the door to my room and then wait for him as he takes the other case up the narrow staircase to the attic room where Daniel is to sleep. Then I follow him as he takes the largest of the cases into Mummy's room. He places it down in the centre of the lilac rug and looks around, taking in the room, though it is hardly new to him. Sunlight crosses the room at this time, a buttery slice falling on to the bedspread and the dressing-table where my father's photo no longer stands. I wonder if Mummy has placed it beneath her underwear in the top drawer or whether she has put it away for good now Harry is here for more than just one night. We are, of course, used to him being here by now: 'Harry will be staying for the occasional night from now on,' Mummy said one morning last winter, then carried on making breakfast in a way that told us that the subject was closed, but now I have a sudden vision of the two of them messing up the perfect surface of the bed tonight. Then I imagine them lying stiffly apart, arms pinned to their sides like two silly mummies, their bodies slotted into the envelope of sheets, bare shoulders sticking out. I find myself uneasy in this room for the second time in several days.

'I'll fetch the other bits,' I say quickly and trot down to gather up the little pile of shoes and jumpers, books and an orange football left at the foot of the stairs.

Mummy serves out plates of roast chicken and potatoes at the kitchen table, sending people into the right chairs and telling them to serve themselves with vegetables from the large white dishes in the centre of the table. She is cool in the heat of the day and I realise that I could never say to her what I said to Lottie, about wanting Harry to be my dad. Not that she would be angry if I did. More disappointed, I think. You see, for someone who loves paintings and plays and books, she is strangely disapproving of anything but the here and now.

When we begin to eat, the clinking of cutlery seems too loud and people concentrate hard on their plates, but then Harry begins talking to Mummy about an exhibition in Canterbury they should visit and a little later Mummy asks first Daniel and then Josie about their schools and how they spent the first half of their holidays. She is very good at times like this, clever at making people she hardly knows feel comfortable. Sometimes I wonder if this is what is left over from her London life. Lottie is sitting beside Josie, looking unhappy and saying nothing, while I nip in and out of the conversation, too timid to introduce any subject myself, but tacking a sentence on now and then so that no one forgets I am here. Between this and eating, I cast secret glances at the newcomers.

Daniel looks nearly the same as he did when we first met him at Harry's house last Christmas, only taller and a little broader. His blond hair has been bleached into streaks by the sun and his arms and face are deeply tanned from playing so much football over the summer. He knows some of the boys in Broadgate already, he says, is hoping to get a team together to keep up practice. He wants a motorbike too, just as soon as he can get one, but his mother isn't keen ('I must say, I can understand why,' says Mummy, nodding her head sympathetically) even though he's too young to ride it yet and just wants to take it apart and rebuild it. Daniel is polite and talks in a quiet voice and he surprises you by throwing in long words, like 'apprehensive', when you're not expecting them.

But it is to Josie that my eyes keep returning. Last Christmas, when I first met her, she had joined the mulled-wine-and-mince-pie party at Harry's house for only half an hour before disappearing upstairs again, but in the short time she'd been in the room, I couldn't stop sneaking glances at her because she looked . . . well . . . *odd*. Even in the orangey light of the open fire that Harry had lit, her skin looked bluish-white, like cold milk, and her hair, which was long and pulled tightly back from her large forehead with an Alice band, was also white so that only the sharp blue of her eyes stood out from her face. She looked like someone who has been caught in the flashlight of a camera and you simply couldn't help staring at her as she stood in the doorway.

'Unfortunate looking child,' Mummy murmured in the taxi on the way back home.

Now she looks different. The first thing I noticed in the hallway was how tall she has grown, but though she is almost as thin as Lottie, she looks softer somehow. Her hair has been chopped to jaw length, with a deep fringe that covers her forehead and there are darker chunks in it now. Her lashes and brows are no longer white. Something on her cheeks and around her brows gives her face some colour. She is still far from pretty, I decide, yet there is something about her that makes you want to look at her as much as you ever did, but no longer just out of curiosity. She talks more now, chatting as easily as Harry does and speaking to Mummy almost as if she were her equal. If this annoys Mummy, she does not show it. Daniel, sitting on one side of his sister, takes little notice of her chatter, concentrating on his food for the most part. Lottie, sitting on the other side of her, says less and less.

'Well this is fun, isn't it?' says Harry, noticing her silence. 'Everyone together like this.' But Lottie just shoots him a stinging look.

After a time I grow impatient with everyone dawdling over their food. The crumble I made yesterday has been warming through in the oven while we eat our chicken and

I am going to bring it to the table with a jug of chilled cream. Because of the effect it might have upon everyone, Mummy has forbidden me to repeat my story about the maggot. This is a pity for I would have liked the chance to impress everyone with my horror story, indeed, had rushed to tell Mummy about it the minute she and Lottie returned, but she was too busy chivvying Lottie into her uniform to respond with anything more than a 'poor you!'

'Would you like to fetch the pudding now, Kate?' she asks at last as she begins clearing dishes from the table. I skip from my chair, bringing plates and spoons for everyone, then the jug of cream from the fridge.

'This should be a treat,' says Harry, rubbing his hands in anticipation.

'It's supposed to be a kind of welcome present,' I say, turning to Josie and Daniel and smiling. 'And I know it's your favourite too,' I say to Harry, wanting to be nice to him to make up for Lottie, who keeps rolling her eyes at all his jokes and won't be jollied out of her black mood, no matter how hard he tries.

'Thanks, sweetie,' says Harry. 'You're the best.' Daniel returns my smile, but Josie says nothing, just stares at her father and then at me again. I put on Mummy's oven-gloves and bend down to take the crumble carefully from the oven. When I turn round again, I am surprised to see Josie whispering something to Lottie but I concentrate on setting the crumble down on the metal trivet in the centre of the table. Then Mummy dishes out the pudding for everyone except Lottie who decides that she doesn't eat plums. She sits in silence while everyone else begins and soon I am receiving compliments from nearly everyone around the table. I am pleased with this, of course, but their praise is not enough. I do this all the time: build myself up too much about things. I hide my disappointment by putting my head down and working away at my plate until I am finished. Then I push it away with a clatter, which makes Mummy frown at me.

I glance around the table in case anyone should feel moved to compliment me again. This time it is Lottie who is turning to Josie and I wonder again what they have found to talk about and I am struck by a sudden urge to gain Josie's attention for myself, want to say something to make her take notice of me instead of Lottie who never likes attention anyway. I search around for a full minute, but when I finally speak, the sentence that comes out of my mouth seems to belong to someone else.

'I do hope you'll make yourself at home in my room, Josie,' I say stiffly, sounding like a character from one of the Jane Austen programmes Mummy enjoys when she watches television. Lottie gives a snort and Josie giggles. I blush as everyone else smiles at my stupidity, even Harry.

'Actually,' says Josie, talking to Mummy, not to me, 'we were just wondering if Lottie and I could sleep in the same room, instead of me being on my own?'

'Oh,' Mummy pauses, looking slightly taken aback. She is not used to having her arrangements questioned. 'Well . . . I did consider organising things that way in the beginning, but I thought you might like some privacy and Kate's room . . .'

'Really, I'd much rather share with Lottie,' says Josie. And though her tone is polite, there is a determination there, the same determination that I always sense beneath my mother's words.

On hearing Josie's words, Mummy hesitates again, looks at Lottie who nods happily, then, without bothering even to look in my direction, says, 'Well, I suppose if that's what you both want . . .'

And so it is settled.

CHAPTER 3

We don't believe in God in this house, so it comes as a surprise when Harry takes Josie and Daniel off to church early next morning. They don't have far to go: the street that leads to Broadgate's Catholic church is almost opposite where our house stands (at the far end of town where the High Street narrows into a single lane). We say goodbye without any comment, as if church-going is a regular happening around here and not something that makes us feel uncomfortable in our skins, then clear away the breakfast things, waiting for someone else to say something. As usual Lottie breaks first, saying she didn't know Harry was a Catholic, and Mummy says no, he isn't, but Theresa, who is Daniel and Josie's mother, is, and so they have to go, even when they are away from home.

'How funny,' says Lottie for whom God belongs only in school assembly. I copy her puzzled look and Mummy says something as she wipes down the cooker – more to herself than us – about supposing she can understand the appeal of religion, and then we are done with it.

Nobody knows about me and God. He is my secret. I used to make deals with Him, but Mrs Gibson, our headmistress, says you shouldn't do this and so I have stopped. Instead, I read bits from my illustrated pocket Bible (bought for fifty pence in the second-hand bookshop and hidden under my mattress) and try to think good things about everyone I have encountered during the day, even if they were mean or rude or smelt a bit peculiar, hoping that if I keep on reading a little more day after day I will be able to work myself up to a state of holiness. I can't help but wonder though how all that endless begatting is supposed to inspire anyone. Before I am allowed to sleep, I get down to my knees and make sure that I pray for everyone and in the right order: for Mummy, for Lottie, for Harry, for dead Daddy, for all my teachers and my friends at school and the other people I know and all the people I don't know, especially those in *the Third World* and for all the trees and biscuits and books God has given us. I do this every night without fail, even if I do find it a bit funny that He wants praising all the time like Lottie, and then I say a sing-song Amen but only inside my head because I would die of embarrassment if anyone heard me. When the moon is full, I like to draw back my curtains and kneel there in my white nightie, all saintly, but when I really want something, am not just running through the usual lists – like that time when I said a terrible word to Lottie and she threatened to tell Mummy – I don't bother with all this and just lie beneath the covers and recite what I want. I am going to be a nun if I can't find anyone I want to marry when I grow up, though I haven't yet worked out how I will keep this from Mummy and Lottie – who will think it silly – when the time comes.

I look at Daniel and Josie carefully when they return an hour later, checking them for signs of goodness, which I think might show itself as an aura or even a halo above them. More than anything, I envy them being able to get inside a church that way for though Mummy has taken us to Canterbury Cathedral on several occasions, where we have stood and gazed up into its dizzy tallness, I am longing to go to a proper service, just to see what goes on in that secret world. I could never get away with it though, not while we are living here. Someone would be bound to notice me and mention it to Mummy. I have thought of disguising myself, so that the whole church wonders about the mysterious figure dressed in black who leaves just before the end of the service each Sunday, but the only disguises I know how to get hold of are the false moustaches and werewolf masks in the toyshop in Braxtable, so my plans have come to nothing. To my disappointment, there's nothing noticeably different about either Josie or Daniel when they return, and, since Harry is going to work for a couple of hours, Mummy sends us out to show them around Broadgate while she cooks lunch, which is the usual roast even though, as I point out, we had one yesterday.

The house where Harry used to live, until the lease went wrong, is in Moreland Bay, which lies around the headland at the other end of our village. Though Josie and Daniel might have visited Broadgate before, they would have played mostly in Moreland Bay and gone into Braxtable, the larger town lying just inland, for shopping and things like that. It feels important that I am with them when they see, properly, where we live, so when Lottie shyly suggests we go into town, I buckle my sandals quickly and only stop to stuff a small ball and a packet of sweets into the pocket of my dress in case we should need them. I follow the three of them down the hallway and we step out into a blank, hot Sunday where the air is empty of everything except the occasional slam of a car door and revving of an engine or the on-and-on barking of a dog in the distance. We walk in a straggly line towards where the High Street proper begins – Daniel just in front, Lottie and Josie in a pair behind him, talking in whispers again, and me at the back. Lottie stops us to point out the doctor's surgery where our father used to work, as she does to everyone who visits, and then we continue past the pub and the terraced cottages and rows of shuttered shops until the High Street widens into the Market Square. Here I point out the Anglican church with the bit missing on the side of the tower where it got hit by a German bomb in The Wartime. The church ladies are forever baking cakes to raise money for its repair but nothing ever seems to get done and sometimes I think it would be quicker to block up the hole with all that cake mixture they keep churning out. Josie kicks at the sand-coloured stone around the door of the church and yawns and then Daniel spots a couple of lads he recognises on the other side of the square and crosses to talk to them while we stand around and look at nothing and Josie blows fat pink bubbles of gum. Daniel comes running back a minute later to tell us that they're going to the rec, farther along the High Street by the school, to play football, that he'll be back at lunchtime.

'Oh, Dan!!' Josie wails as he sprints off again, shielding her eyes and squinting into the sun, 'can't we come?' But he doesn't seem to hear her. We see him joining his friends and a minute later they are out of sight. Josie scowls, blows another enormous bubble, which she bursts with her finger and then packs back into her mouth. 'We should follow them,' she says, and suddenly scoots across the road herself, between the cars which are parked on the market site today, towards the war memorial that stands right in the middle of the square. We watch her as, instead of continuing onwards in the direction that Daniel and his friends went, she clambers up on to the base of the memorial, then stands up and turns to wave to us: a tall figure against the blue sky, dressed in a green T-shirt with cap sleeves, jeans and scuffed plimsolls – the same outfit she wore to church this morning which shocked me when I saw it because I thought you were meant to dress up for God. Her boyish clothes somehow make her look even more grown-up than us, like an American teenager, though I have never met one in Broadgate, only seen them on TV on Saturday evenings. I feel stupid in my gingham sundress and prim white sandals.

We are about to cross the road to join Josie when a group of girls, aged about thirteen or fourteen, appear from the other side of the memorial where they must have been sitting. They stare up at Josie as they walk past her on their way to the High Street, but instead of looking away as Lottie or I would have done, Josie places her hands on her hips and glares at them until one by one they drop their gazes. Then the tallest of them says something to the others, which makes them snigger and look back over their shoulders.

'Want to come here and say that?' Josie hollers after them, her hands on either side of her mouth. The tall girl glances back and I recognise her as Samantha Jones who used to come to the house and play with Lottie until Mummy moved us to The Abbey, a private school in Braxtable, because she said we weren't being stretched. I had a funny vision, when she said this, of classrooms full of racks and other instruments of torture, but when I mentioned it to Lottie she looked at me as if I was an idiot. Samantha Jones turns right around and holds Josie's stare for a good twenty seconds and then thinks better of it. She tosses her hair, which has been twisted into thin plaits, and stalks off with her friends, her wedge heels clacking over the cobbles.

'You'll know me next time!!' calls Josie and then laughs loudly and this time they just keep going. 'Silly cows,' says Josie, leaping down in front of us as we join her and planting her feet firmly on the concrete, like a gymnast.

'Yes,' agrees Lottie. 'They hate us,' she adds, looking scared. It's an exaggeration though. It's more a habit on their part, to remind us that we're outsiders.

'They won't bother you now,' Josie assures her and we stare at her in admiration.

'I'm not afraid of them anyway,' I say, folding my arms over my chest and scowling fiercely, but it is obvious that neither Josie nor Lottie is taken in.

'I'm bored,' Josie announces. She gives a great sigh and perches on the edge of the memorial. 'I hate these small towns!' she says, with a sweep of her hand. 'There's never anything to do.'

I look at her, puzzled, because I have never thought of Broadgate as being big or small or as a good place or a bad place to live. It just is. And Josie hasn't seen the half of it yet. I am about to tell her about the rock-pools, and the fishing boats in the brand new little harbour beyond our house, and the derelict presbytery, the priest's house, by the Catholic church with the old air-raid shelter in its orchard, and the café farther along from here that opens every day except Sunday which sells milkshakes and Knickerbocker Glories and has a one-armed bandit and a pool table you can play on if the bigger boys aren't around, when Lottie speaks out.

'I hate it here too,' she says in a voice that makes me stare at her. 'Mummy only came because Daddy's father had the practice here.' This is true. And the fact that we have been on the point of leaving Broadgate for as long as I can remember, even though Mummy puts us into schools and tends her garden and keeps up with the house in fits and starts. Josie looks at Lottie through narrow eyes.

'What if your mum marries my dad though?' She stretches her arms above her head towards the sky and spits her bubble gum on to the bonnet of a car. 'I reckon you won't leave then. I can't see Dad shifting himself from here now. He's too bloody lazy.'

'No he's not!' I snap, angry on Harry's behalf. Josie ignores me.

'They won't get married,' says Lottie setting her mouth in a firm line, 'it wouldn't be . . . right.' There is a silence for a moment. A shiver seems to run beneath the surface of Lottie's skin, like a wave, and she looks as if she's about to cry, and then Josie slips an arm through hers and whispers something in her ear and before I have realised what they are doing, they are off, squeezing between the parked cars and crossing the road without a word to me.

'Where are you going?' I call. I am used to Lottie being cross with me, but she will usually put up with me rather than be on her own. Yet now she doesn't even look round. Josie does though and when she sees that I am crossing the road behind them, she takes hold of Lottie's arm again and the two of them break into a run, back along the High Street the way we came.

'Wait for me!' I shout. 'Please!' Then, seeing that they have no intention of doing so, I start to run myself, begin to pound after them along the hot, hard pavement, praying that the open toes in my sandals will not trip me. But though I force my legs to do their best, it soon becomes clear that I am never going to catch up with Josie, or even Lottie, who usually hates any kind of exercise but is managing today to push herself into an awkward sprint. I watch as the two of them crash into Mrs Harvey and her husband coming out of their daughter's cottage, almost knocking Mr Harvey's walking stick out of his hand. After staggering about a bit more than need be, he steadies himself and I hear Mrs Harvey's voice rising, but rather than stopping to apologise, Josie looks over her shoulder, sticks out her tongue and she and Lottie carry on running. My sister gives a hysterical, almost frightened kind of laugh that I have never heard before, as if the act of running has let out something wild in her.

My legs are tiring already, but even though I said I love to be alone I hate the idea of being *left* alone, so I ignore Mrs Harvey too, dodging her as we meet and pretending not to hear whatever she is saying about having a word with our mother. I spot Josie and Lottie turning off into one of the small side streets that wind down towards the beach and I tear after them, but as I approach the side street, I suddenly drop to a walk. Anger and something close to tears rises up in me and when I turn the corner and see the two of them at the far end of the street, walking now, I have to stop myself from yelling something at Lottie about what Mummy says, about looking after me at all times, in case Josie should think I am more of a nuisance than she already does. I continue to follow them, though I pretend I'm just strolling now, looking at the flowers in the little front gardens that I pass and stopping to stroke the hot rough fur of a black cat stretched out in the sun on the pavement, in case either of them should turn around and think that I care. They turn left at the end of the street – heading towards the boat-houses, I realise. When I next see them, they are sitting on the wall opposite Harry's place, watching him at work and, it seems, waiting for me.

'Come on, slowcoach!' says Josie, when I reach them. Her tone is friendly enough and I am glad now that I did not cry or do anything stupid. 'Been busy, Dad?' she says, going over to where he is standing and hanging an arm across his shoulders.

'Not terribly,' says Harry, frowning to himself as he finishes the little bit he's working on. 'Two coachloads passed this morning, but no takers.'

Harry is an artist. He came to Broadgate to paint pictures which he sells from this converted boat-shed he shares with a pale young woman with long mud-coloured hair called Maia, who sells knobbly pots and ashtrays the same colour as her hair, and an elderly lady who paints delicate pictures on seashells. When the tourist season finishes he does odd jobs around the town: decorating, clearing gardens, mending fences and gutters, which is how he met us. After that first time, Mummy hired him again, once to redecorate her bedroom and another time to paint the front of the house. Both jobs had needed doing for some time, but she always hesitates before beginning any household jobs because, as I said, we won't be staying in the house for much longer.

Harry stands back from his work and smiles at us. 'Think I'll finish for the day at lunchtime.'

'Really?' says Josie, with a little leap of excitement which makes her look younger than she is for a second. 'Can we go to the caves this afternoon? Please, Dad?'

Harry shakes his head. 'Tide'll be up by then. I'll take you later in the week perhaps.'

'Yeah,' says Josie, looking disappointed.

A party of middle-aged women, dresses of ice-cream pink, mauve and yellow, is approaching.

'Shove off now, kids,' says Harry in a friendly voice, 'and don't forget lunch at one.'

I would have liked to stay to keep Harry company. He often lets me do this because I don't bother him. I love to sit quietly among the grown-ups on an old wooden chair, busy with the book I am reading at the time, though I am always ready to jump up and watch someone's stall for them if they need to pop out for a while. Sometimes I watch Harry as he works. I like to watch the careful mixing of colours and the quick strokes he uses, in case I ever change my mind about being a nun and decide to be a painter instead. Mummy once said that Harry is too relaxed for his own good and when I asked her what she meant, she smiled and said she suspects Harry may have wasted his talent. She is wrong though. Harry is a brilliant artist. Every picture he paints is as good as a photograph: you can pick out all the buildings that you know and they are all in the right places and painted in exactly the right shade. I tell him this, to cheer him up one day when business is slow, and he hesitates for a moment, then laughs and said that's what the tourists go for. I am secretly hoping that he might start to include real figures in his paintings, not just outlines in the distance, and have taken to leaving my book sometimes and wandering about on the beach in front of the boat-house on the off chance that I may inspire him. There is no chance of this today though: it is clear that three children will be nothing but a nuisance. The women amble around the boat-shed, ooh-ing and aah-ing at each other as if they have never seen a pot or a painting before and we escape by sliding off the wall and on to the beach, the shingle crunching as our feet sink into it.

'Rock-pools?' says Lottie with a shrug, indicating the far end of the bay, where the cliffs begin to rise towards Moreland Point. A slap of wind catches at us then and Lottie is off again, running across the shingle, out towards the firm sand that edges the sea, as if the wind has magically got into those thin legs.

'Come on then,' says Josie to me, and we follow, this time jogging at a pace I can manage.

Rock-pools are wasted on Josie and Lottie. On a hot day like this I love to take off my shoes and crouch as still as can be, just back from the edge of one of the little pools, making sure that my shadow does not cast itself across the shallow, warm water. If you stay like this for long enough, ignoring the cramping feeling behind your knees and just enjoying the sun turning you the same temperature as the sand beneath your feet and the air against your skin, and watch very carefully, you may be rewarded by a little movement: a crab's long curved claw, emerging from a shell perhaps, or the pale flicker of a shrimp. Today there is nothing to see except the little red storms of anemones and the cone-like limpets clinging to the rocks, because Josie and Lottie have rolled up the legs of their jeans and are too busy splashing and squealing to listen when I try to tell them that you have to keep quiet and still if you want to see anything. I try to teach them what I've learned from a library book, that limpets actually attach themselves to the rocks by a kind of muscular foot, but neither of them pays any attention to me.

Some boys are fishing on the rocks farther out and one of them shouts at us to be quiet, though they seem to be more interested in watching Josie who, having bellowed at them to mind their own business, is whooping as she leaps from rock to rock, balancing herself precariously on the slimy sea-green surfaces. Incredibly, she spots a crab in one of the pools (perhaps it is old or half-asleep) and she reaches down and scoops it up, then chases after Lottie with it. Lottie, who never draws attention to herself if she can help it, is shrieking and laughing all at the same time and the boys on the rocks make no pretence of fishing now.

'Please don't hurt it!' I protest, worried for the crab, which has pulled its legs up towards it body to protect itself. Lottie is on her back on the shingle, giggling hysterically and kicking out at Josie, who is trying to thrust the crab into her face. She does this several more times, then, when I tug at her arm, tosses the crab to one side.

'Have it then,' she says, dropping down beside a panting Lottie. I pick up the crab, which has landed on its back, and carry it as gently as I can back to the deepest rock-pool, talking softly to it under my breath. With my free hand I lift the hem of my dress up high and tuck it back on itself into the waistband and then step down into the water. I release the crab and as I do so I slip on some weed and sit right back into a puddle on the rocks behind me, which makes Josie and Lottie howl with laughter. I am used to getting wet so I take no notice, just hop out of the pool, peel off my wet knickers and stuff them into the gingham patch-pocket on my dress. The boys on the rocks cat-call and Lottie sits up then and hisses at me, 'For goodness sake, Kate!! – sounding like Mummy for a second.

'Look at her, showing herself off to boys!' says Josie and there is something in her voice that makes me feel as though I have done something very wrong. I pull my dress down quickly and pretend to be busy watching the crab.

When I turn round next, Josie is trying to clamber up the lower face of the cliff, which climbs sharply behind the rock-pools at this point, though there are pathways running around the cliffs and into Moreland Bay just down from where we are playing. She scrambles up fairly well, but as she pulls herself up some shale comes loose and starts to patter down on to the rocks beneath.

'Be careful!' calls Lottie, sounding alarmed.

'It's easy!' returns Josie. After a minute, she squirms her way round on to a little ledge and perches there.

'Coming, Lottie?' she calls. I look at Lottie, knowing that she won't dare. She can't even climb a tree properly. But though I can see her body stiffening with fear, Lottie astonishes me by walking straight to the base of the cliff. She feels for a handhold, then, very slowly begins to climb up towards Josie.

'You can do it!' encourages Josie from above. 'Just keep going!' Lottie says nothing, but she does just that, her body moving over the rock-face uncertainly, as though it has found itself suddenly pinned there. From time to time she pauses, but never looks down before continuing the climb. When she nears the ledge, Josie leans over and stretches down a hand to help her up the last few feet and eventually Lottie makes it, though she nearly loses her balance when she has to turn her body around to sit on the ledge. Even from where I am standing, I can see she looks pale.

'Kate won't be able to do it,' she shouts down in a trembly sort of voice.

'Nah,' agrees Josie, swinging her feet and kicking loose some more shale.

'Yes I can!' I insist. 'If I wanted to,' I add, hoping that they won't insist on my proving it. I have no fear of heights and will happily shin up the sturdy branches of the horse chestnuts in the old presbytery, but I don't like the look of the shale wall in front of me, which might trick you at any moment by slipping off another layer.

'Shame you can't manage it,' calls Josie. 'I was just going to tell Lottie a secret.'

'What?' I call, tipping back my head.

'A secret!'

'What kind of secret?'

'You'll never know, will you?' mocks Josie.

'Come back down and tell me then,' I plead. Though I keep many secrets of my own, I think it is unfair that other people should have them. My voice contains as much bravery as I can manage, but this is one thing I cannot bear.

'Nope. If you want to hear it, you'll have to come up here, won't you?' taunts Josie. 'It's something I heard my mum saying. About you.'

'What is it?'

'Not telling.'

That decides it. I stretch up, seeking out Lottie's first handhold. It is a deep notch in the rock, cool and damp despite the midday heat and I slide my hand into it and pull myself up. I glance upwards but all I can see are two pairs of legs and feet dangling a long, frightening way above me, and the cliff-face leaning in towards me at an odd angle. I look over to where the boys were fishing but they have gone now. For a second the whole world seems to lurch.

'You don't have to do it,' Lottie calls down. She is worried now, for she knows she will be blamed if anything happens to me.

'She'll never make it anyway,' says Josie, just loud enough for me to hear. Something hardens in me and I take a deep breath and pull myself up again. My fingers are already numb with the pressure of my grip and I can feel a kind of trembling in the pit of my stomach. Several more heaves and I am gaining height, though I do not dare look down. Then a voice beneath me almost startles me into losing my grip.

'What the hell are you lot doing?'

'Nothing,' I squeak, keeping very still, not daring to look down at Harry. He sounds angry.

'Come back down at once,' he orders, 'before you fall.' My left handhold suddenly crumbles between my fingers and I am grasping nothing. I give a squawk of terror and claw at the cliff-face and by pure luck find another rock at which to grab. I look down at the ground then and a horrible weakness runs through my limbs. I can't help beginning to cry.

'All right, all right,' says Harry, his voice gentler now. 'Just keep very still for a moment.' This is easy. I am frozen on this cliff-face and could not move now if I tried. In fact I may be here for ever. I can hear Harry climbing up beneath me, his breathing coming closer, and I have the feeling that if he tries to prise so much as one of my fingers loose from my handhold I will scream and flail about and we will both be in a heap at the bottom of this cliff. The tears are dripping down my chin now, darkening the grey rock where they fall. I stare at these splodges as if there is nothing else in this world and then Harry has me in his arms and I am clinging to him instead and in a matter of seconds we are back on the ground again. I sink my head against Harry's chest and feel my lungs heaving.

'It's OK, sweetheart, you're fine. Everything's OK,' repeats Harry.

When my legs regain their strength I lift up my head and see that Lottie and Josie have slithered back down and are standing beside us, looking sheepish. I feel better now, but I can't resist forcing out another couple of sobs to pay them back.

'Bloody stupid thing to do,' Harry is saying angrily to Josie. 'Bad enough you two climbing up there, but you should know better than to let Kate do it! You can see how loose this stuff is,' and he aims a kick at the base of the rock. Josie says nothing though her face is flushed. She looks straight at him, though not in a defiant way. 'I thought I could trust you and now I've had to shut up the stall to come haring across here! What were you thinking of?' The anger is leaking out of his voice now, and when he next speaks, he has turned back into the old Harry. 'Well . . . no harm done, I suppose. Come on,' he says and though he is looking at Josie still, he reaches out with a paint-spattered hand and ruffles my hair. 'We might as well all head back for lunch now.' He turns back across the shingle towards the boat-sheds, expecting us to follow him. Lottie glares, and though she daren't say anything to me in his hearing, she gives me a spiteful little nudge with her elbow. Josie's face is still scarlet but she remains silent, just watches Harry walking away from us, and then she turns to me and looks at me with such hatred in those cold blue eyes that, for the first time in my life, I feel utterly ashamed of myself.

CHAPTER 4

People say Mummy never stops, but I know better. She can be perfectly still sometimes and I want to be with her most when she is like this, when I find her sitting in the garden at twilight, breathing in the scent of the tobacco plants she grows beneath the kitchen window or admiring the white roses which glow against the dusk. Then, when her day's work is done, she has space for me in her lap, at least before I get too heavy (sometimes, though, she has such a dreamy look about her that I'm not really sure she knows who is sitting there). And it is when she is like this, I think, that Harry likes her best too. Often I find them sitting in the garden or the living-room about this time of night, drinking wine and talking quietly, sometimes about local stuff, the charity shop or Harry's work, but more often about paintings or other countries. Then Mummy's voice sounds different, sort of yearning and happy at the same time. I like to slide off her lap after a while, down on to the floor where I lean up against the hardness of Harry's shins and listen to them talk: Harry using his hands as well as his voice to describe something called a fresco which he saw in a church when he was travelling around Italy ('if he'd only bother to paint the way he talks!' said Mummy to Aunt Harriet before they gave up trying to fix her crumbling bones), and Mummy talking about Venice, which I have seen in a book, and Rome, where they ride in chariots, and somewhere called Florence, the name of which she says like a prayer, saying maybe when the girls are a little older. She reaches out and strokes my face, but still as if I'm hardly there, says poor Peter was always too tied up with his patients to go away for any length of time.

But something has gone wrong with Mummy now Daniel and Josie are here. Our cleaning lady let us down again and Mummy, suddenly losing patience, announced that she would manage by herself from now on. Now she is too busy to pull me on to her lap or to drink wine with Harry in the evenings. She begins the housework early each morning, before the full heat of the day sets in (earlier still on the days she is due at the charity shop), vacuuming and dusting and polishing, and then pulling shoes and coats and tennis rackets and balls out of cupboards and sorting them into piles to be sold at the shop and piles that need putting away again. She scrubs down paintwork and doorsteps, cleans out the oven, washes rugs and curtains and cushion covers. Yesterday, when I asked her why housework made her so cross, I thought that she was going to shout at me. Mummy never shouts. Instead she pushed her face into a new shape and told me to go outside to play.

*   *   *

Harry has noticed now. He says she'll drop dead in this heat if she's not careful.

'It needs taking in hand,' she insists, but still she rejects Harry's offers of help, looking at the house as if it is a naughty child as Harry is talking. Then she is off again, with no time to talk to me or to look at the starfish I crammed into a jam-jar and brought home from the rock-pools, stopping only to make meals that are bigger than you could ever want in this weather and then washing and drying huge piles of plates and pots and pans and refusing any help. One night, halfway through my prayers, I remember the way Mummy looked at me just before she didn't shout, and I am suddenly convinced that it is me Mummy is angry with, and not the poor, scrubbed house, and then I get frightened because Harry must be right and she *will* die of exhaustion if she doesn't stop, just like Daddy did. The next morning I stick to my night-time promise to God and offer to give up a whole day's play in order to help her. I do this with a real sense of giving, since last night's worries seem silly by daylight. What's more I can't resist announcing at the breakfast table what I'm going to do in order that my good works have an audience. Mummy, who approves of domestic things and is always ready for company if you are prepared to learn the right way to roll pastry or to peg out washing, only frowns.

'You should be making the most of your holidays,' she says as though she is accusing me of something.

'But I *want* to help,' I insist.

'Thank you, but no, Katie,' she says. 'I've enough to do without hordes of children under my feet.' I stare at her, about to reply that I have never been a horde before and that she ought to be more grateful, but then she is talking in perfectly friendly tones to Daniel about a school project of his ('such a lovely boy', I heard her say to Margaret, her friend in London, on the telephone last night) and Harry is saying something about taking the afternoon off tomorrow and no, Josie, not to go to Moreland Bay, and so my goodness and its rejection are lost in suggestions for tomorrow and the clatter of cutlery being cleared away.

We are going to have a picnic on the beach because Harry has borrowed a small sailing dinghy from his friend Ron and is going to teach me to sail. Actually, he is going to teach all of us to sail, but, as I am keen to point out, it wouldn't have happened if it hadn't been for me and for *Swallows and Amazons*. Lottie and I have played around in rowing boats from time to time, but I have become fixated on the idea of learning to sail ever since I began reading about the Lakes and camping on Wild Cat Island and leading lights and midnight races. Harry saw me reading *Sailing for Beginners*, which I found in the library, and mentioned that he'd done a bit of sailing himself and now, because he likes people to be happy, he has borrowed a boat and says that the Mud-Coloured Girl who makes the pots has agreed to watch the paintings for a while. The paintings are more likely to sell when customers can see the artist at work, but I don't remind Harry of this. Mummy looks agitated when Harry first suggests a picnic, casts her eye around the kitchen as if seeking out the merest speck of dust that might prevent her from coming, but in the morning she takes us by bus into Braxtable where she and I buy picnic food from the new delicatessen in the High Street and Lottie and Josie go off to look at nail polish in Boots.

'Ah, civilisation!' sighs Mummy as she steps into the delicatessen, where the air is kept cold by a machine, and takes a wicker basket from a pile by the door. She spends a few minutes picking up bottles of oil and vinegar and packages of dried-up things as if they are precious jewels. Then she concentrates on the picnic. She chooses from a heap of cheeses beneath the glass counter, then gets the assistant to cut thin slices from a ham which is the colour of dried blood and streaked with fat, like dots of cream.

'This shop always reminds me of Paris,' she says, adding long sticks of bread and some paté to her basket, and I think that it is just as well Harry isn't with us because she is talking about her honeymoon and has fallen into that other world where she says things without thinking who else is there. We walk through an arch to another bit of the shop, which has wooden counters and bare walls, and buy a tart, covered with overlapping slices of shiny apple, and some éclairs, which she saw me gazing at.

*　　*　　*

'Somebody's birthday?' sniffs Sandra Mills, outside Kentons, looking at our smart carriers and the ribboned cake boxes.

'Not that I'm aware of,' replies Mummy in a crisp tone and Sandra takes the warning and adds, 'Looks like being another hot one!' in a jollier tone, just in case Mummy doesn't ask her to babysit any more.

Sandra turns back to what she was doing, arranging pears that are on the point of shrivelling on to emerald-green grass matting. Josie looks at me and Lottie and somehow turns her own face into Sandra's, putting her head on one side, just as Sandra does, then opening her eyes wide and emptying them of any intelligence. She lets her jaw hang slackly, then, checking first that Mummy isn't looking, flicks two fingers at Sandra's back. I can't help giggling.

*   *   *

'Come on then, girls!' calls Mummy and Josie comes down the stairs followed by Lottie. They have been putting on make-up and are splaying out newly painted nails in front of them – Josie's crimson, Lottie's pale pink. Mummy says they must still carry something though, so Daniel takes the hamper and the rest of us carry blankets, sun umbrella and all our other beach things down to a cove next to the harbour, just beyond our house. Harry has chosen this one because it is sheltered from the stronger winds by a long stretch of rocks. I run down to the end of the jetty, waiting for Harry to bring the dinghy round from its usual mooring in the new harbour. Eventually he comes into view.

'Land ahoy!' sings out Harry, across the water.

The boat approaches the jetty where there are heavy metal rings for mooring and Harry brings it in with only a small bump, hollers at me to fetch him a bottle of rum, and then throws the rope to me, which I catch first time. He tosses a life-jacket on to the jetty before stepping up out of the boat and checking I have moored it properly, then he goes off to help Daniel who is setting up a windbreak on the beach – though it is hardly needed – leaving Lottie, Josie and me to inspect the boat (with strict instructions not to get into it unless we wish to be made to walk the plank).

I am a little disappointed at first: I had looked forward

45

to a 'proper' boat, like the *Swallow* or the *Amazon*, made of creaking wood, with a mainsail of canvas and a little jib-sheet, but this is Tizer-orange and float-shaped, with the shallowest of dips in the centre where you sit. But when Harry comes striding back along the jetty, he says it is the perfect boat to learn in because it is so simple and he shows us the centre-board and the mainsheet and the tiller; then he starts to explain with his hands about how the wind works (I know already because I studied my book under the covers last night, until Mummy came in and took my torch away).

'Oh, come on, Dad,' interrupts Josie, impatient to begin. 'We'll pick it up as we go along.'

'As you like,' says Harry, giving up with a shrug. 'But don't blame me if the wind gets up and you cop a few duckings. Now, who's coming out first? She can only take two at a time.'

'Me,' I say quietly, urgently. I have thought of nothing else since Harry suggested borrowing the boat.

'Take me! Take me!' yells Josie, shouldering her way past me. 'And then Lottie next! We could go round to the main beach, and even round Moreland Point to see if we can see the old house and the caves!'

'Absolutely not,' says Harry firmly. 'We're staying right here where it's sheltered.'

'Daniel can go before me,' says Lottie, looking suspiciously at the lightly rippled water around the jetty as if she's expecting it to rear up into a tidal wave at any moment.

'Come on then, Jose,' says Harry easily. He hands her the life-jacket and shows her how to put it on, and then hops down into the boat before turning to help her down. She seats herself and then, once the two of them have shifted around a bit and the boat has steadied itself again, looks up at me with those sharp blue eyes of hers as if she knows she has taken something valuable from me. I turn and walk back down the jetty to the beach, where I do not join Mummy and Daniel but sit at the edge of the water with my knees drawn up under my chin and watch as Harry and Josie, wobbling a little to begin with, set off across the bay in the gentle breeze.

Daniel, quietly, persuades Lottie to go in place of him. She blushes crimson at this, as though he has said something embarrassing, and then swaps places with Josie. She sails as she does everything else – as though she fears her bones might break. A gust of wind carries a whimper from her across the water and though I cannot see her properly from where I am sitting, I know she will be biting her lip. Mummy has spread out a blanket and is leaning up against a rock, shading her eyes with one hand and holding a book in the other. She does not look in my direction or out across the bay, even when Harry calls to her. Daniel has brought his fishing-rod with him and while Lottie takes her turn, he shows me how he baits hooks with the maggots that he takes from a Tupperware bowl. After watching Lottie for a minute, Josie comes back down the jetty to boast about her sailing and shrieks when she sees what we are doing. She refuses to touch the wriggling maggots, but despite the plum incident I am determined to be as brave as an Amazon Pirate and force myself to pick up a fat beige one and push a hook through its squirming body. I beam with pleasure when Daniel congratulates me, and then again when he tells me that he'd rather fish than sail today, that it's my turn after Lottie. I smile gratefully at him as he picks up his fishing tackle with his strong hands and heads off towards the rocks, his blond hair catching the sun.

'I'll come and help you afterwards!' I call to him.

Josie gets up from where she has been squatting and says something under her breath.

'What?' I say, not hearing her properly.

'Stop bothering him,' she says evenly.

I start to explain that Daniel will need a good helper if he is to catch anything worthwhile, but before I can finish she has walked off down the beach. I sit very still for a minute, my eyes fixed on Lottie as she pulls herself shakily back up on to the jetty. Then Mummy is standing up and calling us for lunch and my turn to sail must wait until we have eaten.

I say little over lunch because, despite the lovely picnic and the hot sunshine, I can tell that Mummy is not happy. Nobody else seems to sense it though. Harry is as jokey as usual, teasing Josie about nearly capsizing the boat, though I'd only noticed a slight shudder from where I'd been sitting. There is a giddy edge to his clowning today, because of the sailing, and eventually Mummy tells him off because he is distracting us from eating and Josie says, 'Calm down, Dad!' in a way that makes her sound more like a wife than a daughter.

I concentrate on working my way through a piece of French bread and pâté while Josie talks in that grown-up way of hers to Mummy, who is smiling at whatever she has said, for Josie is a good mimic of other people and has a way of putting things that is very funny. I wonder if Mummy has noticed that Josie will not stay at a table when it is only me sitting there and that she finds a way of not hearing anything I say. I must have done something to make Josie dislike me in the short time she has been here and it is no wonder then that Mummy is angry with me because we are all supposed to be trying very hard to get along with each other. My mouth feels dry all of a sudden and I refuse an éclair, then throw the remains of my bread to a nearby seagull who gives me an alarmed look and then gobbles it down.

'Coming for a sail, Mary?' says Harry, ' – after Katie, of course,' he adds hurriedly, seeing me glare at him.

'I don't think so,' says Mummy.

I am sailing at last! At first, Harry shows me how to reach

across the bay with the boat at right angles to the wind, which is blowing lightly in towards the shore, and I have to concentrate so hard on steering and keeping the weight of my body in the right place and adjusting the sail and ducking down when we change direction (or 'go about' as Harry calls it) that I stop worrying about Mummy and whether Josie is talking to her about me, like a grown-up, while I am out here.

'Good, good,' encourages Harry. After half an hour or so of going back and forth across the bay, he looks out towards the entrance to the cove. 'The wind's picking up a bit now,' he says. 'Want to try beating into it?'

'Yes!' I say eagerly, though I can't quite remember what this means, and Harry shows me how to steer the boat round and pull in the mainsheet until the sail suddenly snaps and the boat tips beneath us and begins to whizz across the wavelets.

Harry leans over and steadies my hand on the tiller. 'Let out the sheet a touch,' he instructs me and I do as he says, feeling the boat right itself a little and then we are moving along much faster than before and the boat is rearing up as we meet bigger waves and the water is fizzing and foaming beneath us and slapping at the hull. 'Lean out with me!' says Harry and I do, and we let the weight of our bodies balance the pull of the sail. 'That's it!' calls Harry, 'Now remember to keep an eye on that sail. Don't try to come in too close to the wind just yet.'

'Aye, aye,' I mouth. Harry glances over towards the rocks where Daniel is an outline against the sky.

'Changing tack now. Ready about!' he calls, putting his hand over mine on the tiller. We duck down and scramble to the other side of the boat as the boom flips over above our heads and then we are off again, nipping across the water with the power of the wind surging up through our bodies.

'Enjoying it?' calls Harry, grinning at me.

'Fantastic!' I yell and then I have to stop talking because

the wind really is getting stronger and Harry is no longer telling me what to do but leaving it up to me to watch the sail and to adjust the steering and move my weight around and I am biting down on my lip, just like Lottie does, and frowning with concentration. Then we go about again and this time everything comes together and I know exactly what I should do and what the boat wants of me, as if it is part of my own body. We skim the surface of the water and a dash of spray lifts in front of us and curves through the air like a glittery rainbow and catches me in the face. I give a whoop of excitement, loving the tug of the mainsail and the firm pull of the tiller in my hand.

'You've got it!' shouts Harry and I know that he is right and pride suddenly pushes up in my chest as if I am about to cry.

We beat all the way across the bay, waving to Daniel who is making his way back towards the others, and then Harry looks up at the sky and points to a splodge of dark clouds on the horizon.

'Enough for today, captain!' he calls, and he takes the tiller from my hand. 'Better let me take us back in,' he shouts, 'running with the wind can be a bit tricky.' He turns the boat back towards the land, letting out the sail. The wind lifts us and we fly back towards the shore, with Harry keeping the boat at a slight angle to stop the wind from catching the wrong side of the sail, which could make the boom whip across unexpectedly. We duck as Harry brings us in towards the jetty with a neat turn.

My legs are weak with excitement as I step back on to land again but I tear along the creaking jetty to where we left Lottie and Josie practising handstands and cartwheels by the water's edge. Now they are sitting quietly, Lottie drawing pictures in the sand with a stick and Josie with her knees pulled up in front of her, examining the varnish on her toes.

'Did you see us? Did you see how fast we were going? It

was brilliant! You really pick up the wind when you go farther out,' I gabble and I can tell that Lottie is impressed for once because of the way she is looking at me.

'Our Katie's a bit of a natural!' says Harry, coming up behind me. 'Did you notice how she kept trimming that sail Josie? Makes all the difference, you see.' And then he looks closely at Lottie and holds out a hand to her, saying: 'You look done in, my girl.' I look at my sister again and see that he's right: the blusher Lottie has dabbed on her sharp cheek bones stands out like war-paint on her white face. Unusually, she allows Harry to take her hand and pull her to her feet. 'Let's go and help your mother pack up,' he says, 'and then you lot can head home.' He looks up at the sky, which is getting darker by the minute. 'I want to get the boat back round to the harbour before the rain comes.

It is just me, Josie and the storm-heavy air. Seeing Mummy glance over at us, and fizzing inside with the success of my first sail, I feel the urge to try to put things right with Josie.

'Your dad's right, you know,' I say, squatting down next to her. 'It really does make a difference. When we . . . '

'Just fuck off,' hisses Josie. Her hands shoot out and she digs long red nails deep into my skin. I stifle a cry, of shock more than of pain, and wrench my arm away. 'Spoilt little bitch,' she says, jumping to her feet. Then she runs up the beach and joins the others. For a moment the striped windbreak and the hamper and the little group of figures holding the corners of a blanket seems to freeze into a picture that doesn't include me. Red stripes, like claw marks, are rising already on my forearm.

*   *   *

I am lying in bed, my muscles already beginning to ache from today's sailing. I cannot concentrate on my book because of Josie and Lottie whispering in the other bed-room. Do you know how it feels to be hated? When I say hated, I don't just mean ignored. I am used to this at school, because sometimes I say things without thinking or become so caught up in a game we are playing that I forget there are other ways from mine. I am learning where I belong though: I am not one of those popular girls like Hannah Williamson who is as mean as can be and still everyone wants to be her friend; nor am I one of those sad creatures like Tess Young who, as far as I can remember, has never done any harm to anyone and yet is tormented and shunned as if she had some particularly revolting skin disease. There is something awful about the way Tess tries to move her clumsy body around the school without drawing attention to herself, and as someone who believes in God I should feel more sorry for her than I do but, unfortunately, she makes my skin prickle and I avoid her in case she mistakes the odd smile as an offer of friendship.

Somewhere, right in the middle between Hannah and Tess, is me. In that other world that exists inside my head, I remain Captain Nancy Blackett (leader of the Amazon Pirates, Terror of the Seas) or someone wonderfully brave and good like the heroine of *What Katy Did*, but my school report just says I am a well-liked girl, and I have a small, but, I think, loyal group of friends. I am learning to be more careful about what I say and do because if no one will sit next to you in lessons or if you are left alone in the playground for a day it is the loneliest feeling in the world.

Though I am no longer allowed into her room now that she and Josie are sharing, Lottie does not hate me. There is something between us that can make the two of us collapse in giggles together, when nobody else, not even Josie, understands. That will never change. I don't know how I know this but I do. I know it as surely as I know that Josie hates me.

CHAPTER 5

Lottie is ill. 'Period pains,' announces Mummy, coming down to the kitchen. Daniel picks up his motorbike magazine and studies the cover but you can't stop Mummy talking like this: she likes things to be called by their correct names. Lottie says this is because she has been a doctor's wife.

'Should someone be at home with her?' asks Harry looking a little anxious because he really ought to back selling paintings at the boat-house today.

'No, no. She's had some painkillers. She needs to be left alone to sleep it off,' says Mummy. 'I've popped her into my room because the curtains keep it cooler in there. Besides,' she adds, 'Judith's on holiday so I can't very well take a day off.' I think about reminding her that it doesn't matter whether she goes to the shop or not since she doesn't get paid for it, that even if she did we don't need it because of grandfather's money. Then I think better of it. 'And I don't think you'd be much use to her,' Mummy finishes, and Harry agrees and says nothing about my mother saying 'my room' not ours.

I slip upstairs to see Lottie. She is lying in my mother's darkened room on her side with her knees pulled up to her body. She looks lost in the double bed, adrift in a sea of bedding, which is crumpled up all around her. Just as I enter the room she gives a little moan to herself and wriggles around, repositioning herself on her stomach. This turns out to be unhelpful and she rolls back to her original position.

'You OK, Lot?' I say, sitting on the end of the bed. Her

face emerges from the sheets and I see that she is white to the lips.

'No—ooo', she moans. 'Feel sick.'

'Can I get you anything? A drink of water?' I say, putting my hand out to her. It is the sort of thing Mummy would say and I am copying her because I don't know what else to say about this pain that grips Lottie every month. Mummy says not to worry about it, that I may have an easier time, but I'm yet to be convinced it will happen at all. I do know that I trust my body to be good and strong and not to turn on itself like this.

Lottie gives another moan. She is looking at me but it as if she sees me through a fog. Then she bats my hand away and rolls herself over and up on to all fours, her skinny bottom up in the air, then sinks back on to her heels. There is a small dried bloodstain on the back of her white nightie. She reminds me of that young fox we once found in the road, dragging its broken body towards the under-growth until Harry lifted it up and carried it into the woods before returning to the house to fetch a heavy spade. Seeing that my little voice will not reach through Lottie's pain, I tiptoe out, promising to come back later. The pain-killers must be strong ones for when I check on her again ten minutes later she is sleeping.

'Can I go fishing with Marcus later, Dad?' calls Daniel from the phone in the hallway. Harry shouts back yes but he should get his schoolwork done first.

'Take me too!' demands Josie, when Daniel comes back to the breakfast table.

'Sorry, no girls,' says Dan. Josie shoots him a look and carries on eating her toast. 'Want to do something?' she says a minute later. Nobody answers and after a moment the thought arrives that she is talking to me! I look up from the book in surprise and then suspicion, but there is nothing mean in her face, just a questioning look. The marks from her nails are still on my skin and it would be a fine thing to draw myself up grandly and refuse, but Mummy has stopped straightening her crisp workdress and is looking at me, looking as if she wants me to say yes. The house is as scrubbed as ever, but she seems a little less angry than yesterday and I must not spoil this. But more than this, more than anything else, I can't stop myself wanting to be with Josie. All my pride cannot prevent my wanting to enter that world of whispers and looks and delicious jokes at night-time that she and Lottie share.

'Yes,' I say, laying down my book. 'Why not?' Mummy smiles at me for the first time in days.

'So, Josie, you're taking care of Kate today?' It isn't really a question but an instruction.

'Yeah, yeah,' says Josie, as if her father's request is too boring for words. Mummy goes upstairs to look in on Lottie and then comes down to say goodbye. Harry follows her out into the hallway and I wait for her to squawk or for one of those laughs that are just for Harry, but I hear the front door closing behind her and today there is nothing.

'Right, to work I suppose,' says Harry quietly when he comes back in to rinse out his coffee cup. Josie looks at his old jeans and unshaven face.

'Aren't you going to tidy yourself up first?' she asks. I have never met Josie's mother but I think Josie must sound like her now.

'No need,' says Harry, rubbing the stubble on his chin and grinning, 'it's what the punters expect of an artist.' He pronounces 'artist' in an actor's type of voice and strikes a pose, gazing out of the window with his hand clutched to his heart. I giggle, but Josie just looks at him with something unkind in her sharp blue eyes. Then he picks up his bag and says goodbye and suddenly she flings herself around his neck and covers his cheek with kisses.

*　　*　　*

'There's never anything to do around here,' complains Josie after we have messed around on the swings and climbing frame in the recreation ground and then wandered back to the Market Square again. She is dressed in her drainpipe jeans and plimsolls again, and a tight white T-shirt, and she walks in a way that lets you know she is scared of nothing. We pass Samantha Jones and two of her followers standing at the bus-stop and she and Josie look at one another carefully for a second, as if they are teetering on the edge of something awful, and then the tension slips out of the air.

'All right?'

'Yeah, all right,'

I nod my own greeting to the other girls as coolly as possible. The younger of the two ignores me and the other one, a fat fair-haired creature, just widens her eyes at me. They don't dare say anything though because of Josie. Unlike Josie I am not in the least bored, simply because I am allowed to walk next to her today. But I cannot allow myself to relax too much; Lottie will almost certainly be better later and I need to find a way of impressing Josie before the two of them have the chance to shut me out again. What's more I want Mummy to see that I can put right whatever it is in me that Josie disliked in the beginning, whatever it was that might prevent us – me, Mummy, Harry, Josie, Lottie and Dan – from sticking together. I imagine the six of us stacked up like one of those human pyramids at the circus with me wobbling on top, almost making the whole thing collapse. I run through the things I can do to keep Josie entertained, knowing that she will not want to play horses or girl detectives or the other games we play at school; or *Swallows and Amazons* or any of the adventures that normally take place inside my head.

'Have you been to the old presbytery yet?' I ask.

'What's a presbytery?' demands Josie.

'Lottie hasn't taken you there?' I say, acting surprised because I know full well that my sister avoids the waste ground where the old presbytery used to stand before they knocked it down and built a new one with orange bricks and plastic windows, right next door to the Catholic church. Lottie doesn't like it because the rough boys hang around there, throwing stones at each other or at rows of bottles on the walls and shouting rude things at girls who pass by. And anyway, we are not supposed to go there. But there are trees to climb and dens to make and an apple orchard to explore where donkeys used to live when the presbytery was still standing. And because Lottie is scared to go, all this is mine to lay before Josie!

'We'll need to go and fetch my torch from the house,' I say, unable to stop myself bobbing about in excitement though this always irritates Mummy when she sees me doing it. 'There's an air-raid shelter. A *haunted* one!'

Josie raises her pencilled-in eyebrows.

'Who says it's haunted?'

'Everyone.'

She nods her approval.

*   *   *

I am delighted with myself because Josie is having a good time. She likes the wildness of this place, sheltered from adult eyes, as much as I do – I can tell by the way she breaks into a run as soon as we have eased our way beneath the rusting barbed-wire fencing that surrounds the site, clambered over an old stone wall and dropped down into the long dry grass. She gives a whoop that echoes back from the distant boundary wall and then begins leaping over nettle patches and the roots of great trees that snake out across the pathways trodden through the undergrowth. I follow in her footsteps until we reach the pit at the centre of the site where the old presbytery itself used to stand until the bulldozers and excavators came in and tore it down. We teeter on the edge, one on either side of a deep rut which has been worn by boys riding their motorbikes up and down the pit, then let our feet run away with us down its steep sides to the bottom, trying to keep up enough momentum to take us back up the far side. We only make it halfway before we have to use our hands, scrambling up the rough chalky surface and grasping at the weeds that have already grown over the earth's white scar. Then we climb over a small fence, snagging our clothes and our hair on brambles as we do so, and I show Josie the orchard that lies on the other side. We eat a few of the sour, hard little apples that still grow there, then pick some dusty looking black-berries from the bushes and use them to paint our lips a deep, vampire purple. I want to collect some to take home but Josie has spotted the remains of a tree house in the crook of one of the trees that overhang the orchard and she starts climbing up through the branches to investigate.

'Just an old platform!' she calls to me and settles herself down there. I follow her up straight away, wanting her to see that my tears on the cliff-face were out of character. It is harder work that I expect it to be and Josie has to stick out a hand to haul me up the last few feet. I heave myself on to the platform, the rough planks sticking painfully into my stomach as I do so, and then flip over and lie panting on my back. Josie laughs at me and I lean up against the rough bark of the tree and get my breath back while Josie kneels up and points and says she can see the roof of our house, over there towards the sea where the sky turns smoky blue. It is not our house because the chimney is all wrong but I pretend that she is right all the same. Then she pulls a handful of leaves from the tree and starts tearing back the green flesh to the veins while I stare up at the leaves flickering dreamily against the sunlit sky.

'I reckon my dad and your mum are going to break up soon.'

'What?' I say, shocked awake.

'I reckon they will. They've hardly done it at all since we came to stay, you know.'

'Done what?'

Josie stares at me, and then lets her features drop into her dumb, Sandra Mills face. '*It*,' she says. 'You know, sex.'

'Oh.'

I know all about sex because Mummy once heard Lottie saying something to me about it and decided it was time. The talk we had was very clear and quite interesting and I have a book that shows a woman cut in half with a baby curled up like a snail in her tummy. But what Josie is saying doesn't make sense to me, so I say nothing.

She tears off another handful of leaves and then continues. 'I'm always hearing *my* mum and her boyfriend. They think I'm asleep, think they can do all the thrashing around and puffing and panting they want,' she gives a laugh. 'Once I even peeped round the door and saw them at it.'

I stare up at the leaves, needing Josie to slow down. To start with, the 'thrashing around' she is talking about cannot be right. It has nothing to do with the way I imagined it, which I have understood to involve next to no movement on anyone's part – something akin to sliding a key into a lock and then removing it straight away before going about one's day. And what does any of this have to do with Harry and Mummy anyway?

'You don't mean,' I hesitate for a second, wary of inviting Josie's mockery, 'that Mummy and . . . your dad have done . . . *that* before? That they do . . . ?'

Josie stares at me.

'Don't you know *anything*?' she demands. 'Of course they do, you idiot! All grown-ups do. Daniel nearly did once with a girl he met when we were on holiday but she wouldn't let him at the last moment.'

'How do you know . . . ?'

'One of his friends told me.'

But again, all this is racing too far ahead for me.

'But,' I say slowly, 'Mummy and Harry don't want to have a baby – they would have told us if they did – so why would they need . . . ?' My voice trails off. This is how I have imagined it. Something that Mummy did many, many years ago because she and Daddy wanted to have babies. Almost like a business arrangement that you made with the man, an appointment to be kept.

'You really *don't* know anything, do you?' says Josie, half pityingly, half scornfully.

'So you're saying,' I try again, 'that my mum and my dad and *your* mum and dad . . . '

Josie sighs.

'And everyone's mum and dad and people who hardly know each other sometimes,' she supplies, 'they're all At It.'

'But if not for babies, why then?' I ask, beginning to feel tearful.

'Because,' pronounces Josie, 'they can't stop themselves.'

'I don't believe you,' I say, my voice suddenly stronger. I know for sure that Mummy has never done anything in her life because she couldn't stop herself. Josie laughs again.

'Well what *do* you think they do when they're in bed together? Read each other fairy stories?'

'No!' I snap. Somehow I know that they do not just lie side by side in that bed in which Lottie lies sleeping at this very moment, know that Harry being my mother's boy-friend means more than this. I remember a dream I had about an older boy in the village where we lay down on the ground together and cuddled each other very hard and yet I cannot imagine Mummy submitting to the indignity of that other thing, of thrashing around, unless it was for a very good reason. But even as I tell myself this, I am thinking about the squawks in the hallway, the laughs that she keeps for Harry.

'Anyway my dad was doing it with everyone when he was married to my mum,' says Josie lazily, flicking a leaf skeleton into the air and leaning over to watch it twirl towards the ground. I stare at her. This is too much.

'I don't believe anything you say,' I say and I slide myself off the platform and slither back down the tree. Josie calls, 'You'll see,' to me. After a minute, I hear her following me down. She has to run to catch up with me because I am walking away as fast as I can.

'Show me this air-raid shelter you were on about then?' she asks and I am torn between feeling furious with her for telling lies and wanting her to see the air-raid shelter in case the woman who dresses all in white and is only seen when there is a full moon decides to show up early. Some older boys are jumping from the boundary wall on to a rope swing they have suspended from an oak tree. They whistle at us as we pass.

'Nice tits!' calls one with a shaved head and no shirt, and instead of looking as if she wants to pull her head back into her body like a tortoise, as Lottie would do, Josie stands up straighter, pushes her chest out in her white T-shirt and looks directly at the boys.

'Thanks,' she calls with a smirk and a toss of her white hair, then, 'Come on,' to me. I hand her the little torch I have been carrying in my pocket and lead her in the direction of the air-raid shelter which you wouldn't find unless you were looking for it because it is behind a tree and weeds hang down over the top of the entrance, which is just an archway in a small bank of earth. Somebody has tried to block it since I was last here and then been disturbed or had their work undone by others: boulders have been pushed around the foot of the doorway and several lengths of wood are hanging by nails from one side of the entrance. We clamber over the boulders and duck beneath the weeds and then Josie leads the way down the dark stairway, pretending to jump back in terror as she reaches the bottom, just to frighten me. She disappears inside the shelter and then her head pokes out again.

'You coming then?'

I nod, unwilling to admit that I have never been all the way down into the shelter before, only shone my torch down the steps and peered in. I steel myself and follow her, leaving the bright sunlight behind, until I am standing next to her in the entrance to the shelter itself. I screw up my eyes, straining to see in the darkness. Josie is shining the torch around and its feeble yellow cone of light illuminates the walls and ceiling of a room that seems to be constructed from something like corrugated iron and is much smaller than I had imagined it to be. The torch picks out an old wooden chair with a broken back, a pile of bottles and cans in one corner, a pink blanket and what look like the remains of a fire on the floor. The air is a dark solid block, musty and unmoved. I venture a step inside.

'Looks like someone lives down here,' says Josie's voice, coming at me suddenly like a train out of the darkness. 'Or some*thing*,' she says. Then she sniffs the air. 'Smells like whatever it was died down here too.' Both of us jump violently at a crash from above, like stone dropping on stone, and then we both scamper out to the bottom of the steps to see the tunnel of daylight above us being blocked out with branches. Someone makes a ghost noise and then a pair of hands drops another boulder in the doorway.

'It's those boys,' says Josie. 'They're shutting us in.' Something catches in my throat. The rotting smell in the air seems to thicken as though I have moved closer to its source and suddenly I want to gag. A sound, animal-like, escapes from me before I can stop it. 'Don't worry about it,' says Josie calmly, shining the torch at me and pulling her arm free from my grip. 'They'll get bored and unblock it again in a few minutes.' She turns, with the torch, back into the shelter again, leaving me in the narrow tunnel with the darkness closing down on me, branch by branch, and that thing again, tightening my throat and pushing up through my chest. I look for Josie and see only a glimmer of white hair or white skin in the blackness and then I find myself at the top of the stairs, beating at those branches that are stopping me from breathing and tearing with the strength of madness at the hands that try to press more down on me and moments later I am free and on my knees gasping in sweet, clean air and the boys are running away and laughing. Josie is standing behind me.

'That smell . . . ' I explain when my breathing returns to normal, 'and I don't like being shut in like that.' Josie gives me a strange look, then is distracted by a shout from the boys, who have returned to their perch on the boundary wall.

'What?' she calls.

'Come over here!' shouts the boy with no shirt. He is hanging from a branch now and you can see the muscles on his tanned arms standing out like brown cables. He drops to the ground and Josie wanders over, her thumbs crooked in the loops of her jeans, taking all the time in the world as if she just happens to be passing that way. I stay right where I am, hating those boys for their laughter and their brutish sunburnt bodies.

'Let's go,' orders Josie, returning a minute later, and I follow her along a pathway through the dry grass which hooks on my bare legs, then through a gap in the boundary wall and back out under the barbed-wire fence.

The house is quiet when we return. Daniel's school books sit in a neat pile on the kitchen table and we find Lottie asleep still in Mummy's bedroom. Her arms are thrown out from her body now and she is breathing evenly.

We make brick-like sandwiches in the kitchen and take them up to my bedroom. It is the first time Josie has been in there and I wish now that I had put all my babyish soft toys up in the loft, as Mummy had suggested at the beginning of the holidays. 'Poor Lottie,' I say.

'She'll be all right,' says Josie, sweeping teddies and

rabbits and owls on to the floor to make room for herself to sit. 'I never have any trouble,' she adds and looks down at her own body smugly. She eats her sandwich quickly, then jumps up from the bed again. 'Right. Time to get ready.'

'For what?'

'Going out.'

'Oh.' I wait for her to explain, but she is walking through into her room, pulling her T-shirt over her head as she goes. I follow her. 'Where?'

'To meet Simon.'

'Who's Simon?' I ask as Josie unbuttons her jeans and starts pushing them down over her narrow hips. She sits on the bed and unpeels each of her legs from the tight denim, then throws the jeans on the floor.

'The boy from the presbytery, stupid. I said we'd meet him and the others at the White Horse.' She gets up off the bed, heading for the bathroom this time.

'But . . . ' I have no desire to see Simon and his friends again, but more importantly, I know that I cannot go into a pub. 'I'm too young though. Aren't I?' I say this uncertainly, because sometimes Josie doesn't seem to be aware of rules. She turns on the hot tap in the bath, takes down Mummy's bottle of lavender bath salts, then looks at me.

'You'll be OK,' she decides. 'We'll have to sit outside but with a bit of make-up on you might pass for fourteen. If anyone asks, just lie about your age. You'd better have a birthdate ready.' She bends over the bath again. I am scared now. I am growing taller these holidays but I know that there is little hope that anyone could mistake me for a fourteen-year-old. But I daren't ask any more questions just now because Josie already thinks I am a baby who knows nothing. Instead I try to think of the year in which I would have been born if I was fourteen but panic is scrambling all the numbers in my head. If I just had a piece of paper I could collect my thoughts, write down the years in reverse order, and work it out that way, but Josie will think I am even more stupid if I start scribbling notes for myself. I'll just have to hope that I can work it out on the way to the White Horse. As I tell myself this I understand that Josie really is going to force me to go through with this plan whether I want to or not and something heavy and hard settles in the pit of my stomach. We are going to get into terrible trouble over this. Or rather I am, because Josie always seems to slide her way out of bother.

'What if someone sees us?' I ask, wondering if I can plant some seeds of doubt in Josie's mind.

'They won't, it's out on the Moreland Road,' says Josie, unhooking her bra and turning to me, 'and Dad and his friends drink in the Ropemaker's' Arms.' Her breasts fall from her bra, pale and surprisingly heavy against her wiry frame. I have been proud of my own firm flatness, have pitied Lottie these last few months for the tender, almost painful looking appearance of her chest, but as Josie stands in front of the bathroom mirror, running her hands admiringly over her breasts and then down over her waist to where her hips wing out, the straight lines of my own body seem suddenly silly and inadequate. She turns again, wriggles out of her knickers and slips down into the foam.

'What are you going to do with your hair?' she demands from under the dryer. She is sitting cross-legged on the floor in Lottie's room in front of a mirror that she has propped up against the bed. Using a professional looking circular brush, which she took from my mother's room, she is drying a section of her hair at a time, winding it around the brush then pointing the drier at it for a minute until it turns from the colour of wet sand back to white-blonde. Then she draws the brush out, leaving a perfect upwards flick of hair. I pull at a strand of my own hair that hangs heavy and straight to my shoulders. There is nothing to be done with it.

'I think I'll leave it as it is,' I say as casually as I can manage. I have changed into my jeans and borrowed a white shirt from Lottie's wardrobe which is too big for me. Josie has a small see-through make-up bag by her feet. 'Can I borrow some of your make-up?' I ask, hoping that Josie will offer to help me, but she has finished her hair now and is leaning forwards into the mirror, tweezing out hairs from her pale eyebrows. I take a sea-green and a bright blue eyeshadow out of the bag and go into the bathroom where I apply a stripe of each to my eyelids. I blink at myself in the mirror. The effect is startling.

'What do you think?' I ask, going back into the bedroom.

Josie gives me a curt nod and then sets about pencilling in her eyebrows.

*   *   *

I do not want to be walking down the High Street exposed to all eyes by the white glare of the midday sun. Mrs Harvey's daughter, Gina, comes out of her house pushing her new baby in its pram. I would like to stop and admire this baby because I have been waiting for it to arrive all summer, fascinated by the way Gina's belly has been swelling and swelling until she resembled a fat ripe fig about to burst out of the purple maternity dress which was the only thing she could fit into in the last few weeks. What's more, Gina is always kind to us and slips us money for sweets when Mummy isn't looking, but Josie is striding along rapidly and seems in no mood for stopping, so I just mumble a hello. Gina looks puzzled, and a little hurt, and I promise myself that I will make a fuss of the baby next time, pretend that I hadn't noticed the pram before.

Mrs Harvey is coming out behind Gina, carrying a baby's changing-bag and a parasol for the pram. She frowns when she sees me: 'You're looking very gaudy today, Katherine,' she calls after me, disapprovingly, 'has your mother seen you like that?' And I laugh uncertainly, as if she has told a mild joke, and increase my pace.

'Nosy old bag,' says Josie when we are barely out of earshot. 'Oh shit, here's Dan,'

'Where are you two going?' asks Daniel, eyeing our made-up faces suspiciously as he steps out of the fishing-tackle shop with a margarine pot in his hand. I wonder if he can feel the vibration of all those maggots writhing around inside.

'To the White Horse,' I say and Josie's elbow finds my ribs.

'You *are* joking,' says Daniel to Josie, not to me, which is just as well since I find it hard to look into his brown, open face now I know about that thrashing-around thing. All the time that Daniel is fishing or doing his schoolwork or talking to Mummy he must be thinking about it, wanting to do it because he can't stop himself.

'Maybe,' says Josie, with a shrug. I notice that she isn't meeting Dan's eye either.

'Don't you dare Josie,' warns Daniel, taking hold of her arm. 'Remember what Dad said? About looking after Kate?' Love rushes up inside me. I might not be able to look into his face but I do want to throw my arms around him, to be taken home to safety.

'All right!' says Josie angrily, shaking off Daniel's hand. 'We're just going up to the rec, actually.'

Daniel lifts a finger at her. 'I mean it, Josie,' he says, but he doesn't make us go home with him, just continues on his way with his maggots.

The White Horse is a long way from the High Street. To get there you have to go to the far end of Broadgate, past the recreation ground and the local school, then make your way through the alleyways between the council houses on the edge of town and skirt the small industrial estate until you are on the main road that runs from Broadgate round to Moreland Bay. Once you are past the petrol station there is nothing apart from a few houses for half a mile or so until you reach the edge of Moreland itself and here, right beside the road, you'll find a square modern pub built of yellowy bricks, surrounded by a car park, no beer garden, no hanging baskets. I only know where it is because the Mud-Coloured Girl's boyfriend is in a band and Harry gave him and his drum-kit a lift there one night.

But, long before we have reached the industrial estate, Josie has ceased talking to me.

'What are the others called?' I ask brightly though the heat of the pavement is passing through the soles of my shoes and my head is beginning to ache with squinting into the sun. I must not give Josie an excuse to start hating me again.

'What others?' she says, through tightening lips.

'The other boys. Simon's friends.'

'I don't know.'

We turn into an alleyway, stepping over the mosaic of green glass that glitters on the concrete, and walk in silence for another minute, past garages, all painted in an unpleasant shade of bright blue, and long, threadbare gardens.

'How old is Simon?' I try again.

Josie gives an incredulous little laugh. 'How should I know?'

She retreats into silence again and when I glance at her out of the corner of my eye I see that her face is set and sullen. We cross a road and enter another alleyway.

'What are you going to drink?' she asks suddenly.

'Huh?'

'At the p–u–b,' she says slowly, as though I am retarded.

'The same as you,' I say quickly, but Josie shoos that idea away with an irritable wave of her hand and I feel fear rising in me again. Not only do I have no idea yet of the year in which I am supposed to have been born, but I do not know what you are supposed to drink in a pub if you are pretending to be fourteen. It does not occur to me that I could order lemonade or a Coca-Cola or that I should leave it up to Josie or one of the older boys to go inside and fetch drinks. I have a sudden vision of myself standing in front of a bar, like the one in the Ropemaker's Arms where Harry took me once when he was mending the toilets there, faced by all those pumps and the shelves of bottles arranged behind and all of them blurring and jingling at me.

'Beer?' I try, thinking of what Harry drinks when it's hot, but Josie just gives that hard little laugh again and I know that this is the wrong answer. 'Well, I don't know then!' I say, a whine beginning to rise in my voice, though I try to push it down. 'If you won't help me, how should I know . . . ?'

We walk on, though I can't stop my feet from dragging now. Two more alleyways and then the diamond-wired fencing that surrounds the industrial estate is in sight. Josie comes to a halt.

'Well there's no point then, is there?' she says.

'What do you mean?' I ask, hope beginning to worm inside of me in spite of myself.

'If you don't even know what you're drinking we might as well not go,' she says. There is contempt in her voice and I am ashamed, ashamed of my stupidity, ashamed because I cannot work out when I was born, but still I want to go home more than anything in this world.

I can't help it. I am joyful now that we are going in the other direction, and though Josie is still silent, I find myself chattering on about school and Gina's tummy and the trick we played on Sandra Mills last time she babysat for us. Josie responds with silence or nods you can hardly see and walks faster and faster until I am almost trotting to keep up with her. Just as we near home, she suddenly stops dead and spins rounds on me,

'No wonder your mother hates you!' she snaps. I gaze at her.

'What do you mean?' I ask.

'You heard!' she says and for a moment she looks as if she wants to hit me but she flings the strap of her little bag over her shoulder and stalks off.

For a second I watch her go, absorbing the shock of what she has just said to me, feeling as if she really did strike me. Then I bolt after her, trying to get in front of her to force her to stop. 'Why did you say that?' I demand, when eventually I manage this. I am skipping backwards now because Josie will not drop her speed.

'Because it's true,' she says, fixing me with her sharp blue eyes.

'But she doesn't!' I splutter. 'Why should she?'

'Because of everything,' says Josie in a flat tone, still walking straight at me. 'Lottie will hate you too when I decide to tell her.'

'What? What am I supposed to have done?' I plead.

'I'm not telling you,' says Josie. 'Not yet.'

And I remember the day at the rock-pools, Josie's taunting voice dropping down at me from the sky: *I was just going to tell Lottie a secret.* Then, *'Something I heard my mother saying about you.'*

'Please,' I say. Secrets are what I have. They are not for other people. 'Please tell me.' But Josie has seen Lottie at the kitchen window and pushes straight past me. I follow her into the house, make to go into the kitchen but the door slams in my face. Instead, I go slowly up the stairs to my bedroom, where I stand in front of my mirror for a long time, trying to see what it is in me that makes Josie and Mummy hate me, but all I see is a round, stupidly young face looking back at me and no answers in my peacock-painted eyes.

CHAPTER 6

'Not eating today, pumpkin?' says Harry, glancing at me across the table.

I nod my head and then begin scraping violently at my plate with my fork, just to show him that I am and to stop Mummy looking at me like that because she spent all after-noon preparing the meal. Harry often calls me pumpkin but today it makes me angry. There seems to be some insult lurking there that I resent, sitting here opposite Josie's easy leanness and my sister's newly stretched limbs. I leave the table without asking if I may.

All the time that I'm wondering about Josie's secret and what it is I have done to make Mummy hate me (yet hide it with smiles that do not fit her face), I am harbouring a secret of my own: my body is beginning to betray me. Josie points out one day how clumsy I am, says it gets on her nerves, and now I realise she is right, for every time I reach for a glass of water or walk across a room to pick up a book, I feel her watching me or hear her whispering to Lottie and I become aware of the awkwardness of my movements, as if my muscles have forgotten how to work together. She says the way I chew my food is funny too, that I never stop eating and do I know that I will grow fat as a pig if I carry on eating like that? I keep my head down when I sit at the table so as not to offend her or the rest of the family but when I try to eat, it is as if my mouth doesn't know what to do any more and swallowing a dry mass of food starts to feel like an unnatural thing to do. I stay in my bedroom more, away from the eyes of others, but even when I try to read I cannot escape Josie for she has made me see that I am too clumsy and stupid ever to be Nancy Blackett, Terror of the Seas. After a while, my books are abandoned and I spend time in front of the mirror at my little dressing-table, examining myself up close, until I begin to understand what Josie sees and have to turn away in disgust because surely I *am* too fat and my face is all wrong: chubby and too babyish with its big cow-brown eyes.

And then, on certain joyous days, she gives me another chance and I am allowed into Lottie's room for beauty parties, when the two of them lie on their beds with towels round their shoulders and I have to put slices of cucumber or cold teabags on their eyes to make them clear and sparkling, or splodge lumps of mashed banana, oats and honey from a bowl on to their faces, making sure the porridgey mess doesn't slide straight off and on to the pillow. Sometimes I receive a whispered summons and scramble into bed next to my sister when we should all be asleep, to hear about the adventures Josie and Dan used to have together at the old house in Moreland Bay and thrillingly scary stories about the caves in the bay and the ghost of a drowned little girl that haunts them. Then I forget how unhappy I have been, because Josie has the power to make everything feel better in an instant. She invents a new entertainment called the Dying Game where I have to pretend to faint and she and Lottie kneel down on the carpet beside me and check my pulse and listen for my heartbeat. When they decide that they can find neither of these vital signs, I am lifted by my arms and legs and bundled into the wooden toybox that they have emptied and dragged through from my own room. Then Josie conducts a solemn service at one end of my coffin and Lottie, wrapped in Mummy's black evening shawl, pretends to weep. Since the day when the two of them tiptoed out of the room and ran off into the garden to play without me, leaving me lying in the box, I insist that the lid is placed at an angle so there is a slice of light at the edge of the darkness and, if I open one eye slightly, I can peep through my lashes and see what they are up to.

*   *   *

It seems that the way I speak is peculiar now. Today, Josie is unable to understand me when I tell her that Mummy had gone into town to buy a new blouse.

'Blowis?' she says, screwing up her face.

'No, blouse,' I correct her.

'What's a "blars"?'

'I said blouse.'

'Blows?'

'No,' I say, desperately. 'BLOUSE, you know, something you wear!'

'I don't know *what* you're on about,' says Josie and stalks off and I am ashamed of being such an idiot because all morning, until this point, she had been friends with me. She often is, but I always manage to say something that makes her despise me and feel that she cannot bear to be with me any more. She is trying to help me, gives me chance after chance, and I am so stupid that I never seem to learn what it is that ruins everything until it is too late and I cannot put that shameful thing back into the place where it should be concealed. It should be a comfort that Josie will leave soon but it isn't because everything that she knows about me she will take with her and always know it and because what she has taught me about myself has a life of its own now as well, like one of those virus things I read about, doubling itself up over and over inside me.

*   *   *

I know how it is with a secret: the more someone wants to prise it away from you the more determined you become to hold it up close to your body. With Lottie, it's easy: all you have to do is pretend not to care for half a minute and it comes tumbling out of her mouth in a torrent if she isn't already wearing it on her face. But Josie is not Lottie and despite my knowledge of the science of secrecy I cannot stop myself from trying to get information out of her whenever she seems to be putting up with my company. She knocks me back every time with a laugh or a taunt or, at best, another clue that tells me nothing.

'How does it feel to be so wicked?' she asks me one day, regarding me with genuine curiosity. Another day, just after she and Daniel have returned from mass: 'Do you believe in hell, Kate?'

Once I grew tearful with the frustration of it and threatened to go straight to Mummy and ask her what it is that I have done, but Josie merely laughed and said I could if I wanted to, but then my mother would have to send me away. I don't know where I would go if I wasn't here, but that night I picture myself walking along the big road towards Canterbury with a bundle of my things on my back, like Dick Whittington, then huddling down in a cold, damp ditch beneath the stars. I lie in bed, aching for Mummy even before I have left, knowing that I must never, never ask her the question.

'Ask her about *that*,' says Josie one day in the garden when we are collecting plums from the tree.

'What?' I ask, trying to cup too many plums in my hands at once and then dropping them all with a series of dull thuds.

Josie rolls her eyes at my clumsiness. 'This,' she says, tapping with her toe on a small concrete oblong in the grass which Mummy has almost hidden with a collection of pots planted with grasses and ferns.

'What about it?'

'Looks like something might have been here before,' says Josie. She walks the edge of the oblong in pigeon steps, her eyes on her feet. 'A playhouse, maybe? Or *something else*,' she adds significantly, and then refuses to say another word on the subject.

'Mummy, what used to be at the end of the garden?' I ask that evening after dinner. 'Where the pots are now,' I add, and then realise straight away that once again I have done something very bad because Mummy's face sort of freezes above her book and a deep flush rises on her neck. She looks directly at Harry who is sitting across the living-room from her and whose newspaper has suddenly stopped crackling.

'Nothing,' she says calmly. 'Just an old greenhouse. Why do you ask?'

'Oh,' I say, 'I thought it might have been a playhouse or a shed . . .' I feel something else. Lottie's eyes are burning into me, signalling something to me that I do not understand. 'I just wondered, that's all . . .'

'The Cézanne Exhibition opens next week,' interrupts Harry, turning his newspaper around to show Mummy and pointing to a quarter-page advert. Josie never looks up from the *Jackie* magazine she is reading, but there is a little smile on her lips.

*   *   *

The bloodstain on my knickers jolts me. It is small and darkly red at the edges and I know exactly what it is, but Mummy said that it was unlikely to come for another year or so. Immediately I want to cry, as if someone has deliberately wounded me, and even as the thought occurs to me, a sharp pain knifes my stomach, followed by a slow, dragging, downward sensation, as if my body is trying to return itself to the earth. I crouch over while it lasts, then stand up and, after a moment's thought, slip first my jeans and then my knickers off. I scrunch up some toilet paper and push it between my legs before hurriedly pulling my jeans on again. Mummy said to tell her as soon as it happens but she doesn't have time to talk any more. I could tell Lottie, but she would be bound to tell Josie. Instead I go to the small cloakroom basin, take the bar of white soap from the dish there, run the hot water, and begin scrubbing the blood out of my knickers with my fingers. The water and the soap turn pink but the patch refuses to budge, the edges still standing out in the harsh electric light that fills the room like an accusation. I wring out as much water as possible, hesitate for a moment, then bundle the sodden knickers into the pocket of my jeans. Then I slide out of the cloakroom and tiptoe upstairs like a criminal. In my bedroom I sit on the edge of the bed with the wet knickers in my hands and look all around me. Eventually I settle upon the pyjama case that Lottie bought me last Christmas – a fat, furry blue cat with oversized paws and a mean grin – as the safest place. I unzip its belly, put my hand in and pull out my pyjamas and put them next to my pillow. I conceal my newest secret within the cat's tummy, zip it up and then take the creature and stuff it into the darkness at the very back of my wardrobe.

CHAPTER 7

Mummy comes upstairs again and says that was Sandra Mills telephoning to say she can't come after all because she keeps being sick and there's that stomach bug going around. I hear Harry give a snort and say more likely up the duff by that throwback fiancé of hers and Mummy shushing him because I am playing in my room across the landing and Lottie and Josie are in the bathroom.

'So that's today ruined,' says Mummy. I hear pillows being thumped and then the rustle of the duvet – which Mummy throws back as soon as she gets out of bed each morning so as to air the bed properly – and the catch in Mummy's breath as she pulls it back into place.

'Not necessarily. I mean, Dan and the girls are hardly babies any more,' says Harry. 'They're more than capable of looking after Katie between them. It's no different from when we're both at work.'

'Oh, but it is,' insists Mummy. 'We're close at hand then if they should need us.' Her hands will be working over the thick cotton of the bedspread now: smooth, smooth, smooth, turn back the top section to show the duvet beneath. 'And it's too short notice to find another babysitter now.'

'They'll be fine,' says Harry. 'We'll be back by late afternoon anyway.' Mummy doesn't answer and after a moment Harry says in a low voice, 'I thought you were keen to see this exhibition, Mary.'

'I am . . . ' says Mummy. Her voice doesn't agree with her words and both Harry and I are waiting for the 'but'. 'But school starts soon. We could wait till then.'

'The tickets are for today,' Harry reminds her and there is something in his voice that makes me leave my book and creep over towards my door. Peeping around it, I can see Harry standing with just a towel wrapped round his waist and a pair of socks in his hands.

'Well, what can I do?' says Mummy. Plump, plump go the cushions that sit on the chair in the corner of the room. 'I've plenty to do here and it's hardly life and death, is it?'

'I'm aware of that,' says Harry evenly and because he is so polite I know that they are really having an argument now.

'Apart from anything else, I'm not sure I'm very happy about leaving the girls. Katie seems . . . ' In my eagerness not to miss anything that is said, I must have edged too far because Harry suddenly spots me and the door of Mummy's bedroom is pushed shut with a bang. A few minutes later it opens again and Harry comes striding along the landing, fully dressed now. He passes my room and thuds down the stairs into the kitchen.

Mummy comes down and stands in the kitchen doorway. She is wearing her London clothes. Harry, who is in the middle of making coffee, keeps his back to her though he must have heard her on the stairs. Then he has a quick glance towards the doorway and I see his shoulders relax and he turns right around then, walks across the room and drops a kiss on to the tip of Mummy's nose.

Josie and Lottie are looking through the catalogue, each spending an imaginary hundred pounds. I am sitting in the window seat behind them, trying to read *Pigeon Post*, but finding it hard to concentrate while they are choosing négligés for themselves.

'That!'

'That.'

'I *love* that.' And the jabbing of fingers as they turn the flimsy pages.

I have the curtain pulled halfway across to conceal me ('like a little Jane Eyre!' says Mummy as she pops her head around to say goodbye). Daniel finishes his phone call to Marcus and Josie begins pestering him the instant he comes back in from the hallway.

'Where are you going, Dan?'

'Don't know yet.'

'Can we come with you?'

'No.'

'Oh wwwhhhy?'

'I've told you before, Jose. You make too much noise. It scares the fish away.'

'We won't, will we, Lottie?' Lottie shakes her head, tongue-tied, as usual, in Daniel's presence. 'We promise we won't bother you. We'll just play around on the rocks and stuff.'

'Well why do you want to come then? You can do that anywhere.'

'It's not the same,' says Josie. 'You never want me around, Dan,' and her face grows heavy with sulkiness. Daniel spreads his hands in apology and then looks over to Harry who has just come into the room and is waiting to say something.

'Better let them come this time, eh, Dan?' says Harry. 'Just for today while Mary and I are in town. Katie's a bit little to be left on her own.'

'OK, Dad,' says Daniel easily. He is always like this with grown-ups.

'Happy now?' says Harry, grinning at Josie and Lottie. My sister nods her thanks, but Josie stares down at the catalogue, punishing Harry for forgetting that he was supposed to be spending the day with her as he'd promised last week. 'Just make sure you don't bother the lads. And don't go too far away from them, please.'

'Make up your mind,' says Josie rudely.

'What are you doing hiding behind there, minx!' says Harry, whipping back the curtain. He slides his hands beneath my armpits and lifts me off the window seat, then tosses me up into the air as if I am not as fat as a pig. My book thumps to the floor and I let out a giggle, the sound of which is shocking to me because I have not laughed for days now. Lottie gives a groan of annoyance and Mummy says they'll miss the train if they don't go now. Josie doesn't soften towards her father even when he ruffles her hair in farewell.

*   *   *

'*She's* not coming.'

I have followed Josie and Lottie out of the front door, not through any desire to be with them but because of what Harry said. Dan and Marcus have already started off ahead of us and I can see their fishing-rods poking up above the hedges as they walk.

'Doesn't she have to?' says Lottie uncertainly.

'No. She's a pain.'

I say nothing, just look down at the toes of my sandals, noticing how the stitching has pulled loose in a couple of places and how the white leather is scuffed grey here and there. A solitary ant gleams in the hot sun, its black beaded body making its way across the cracked paving, heaving aloft what looks like a crumb between its spindly front legs. Like carrying a boulder from here to the other end of town.

'But didn't your dad say . . . ?' I can tell that Lottie doesn't want to go against Josie but it is not in her nature to disobey an adult.

'Fuck him,' says Josie. She stamps her foot and then screws up her eyes and looks into the distance.

'I don't think we can leave her here,' says Lottie, beginning to breathe more loudly as she always does when she is nervous. 'It's just that Mummy . . . our mother would be really angry with me . . . Couldn't she come with us?' I look at her and her eyes catch on me and for a moment I almost believe that she loves me.

'All right,' says Josie shortly. 'If she must.' We set off in single file down the path.

*   *   *

There are two paths running around Moreland Point to the next bay. A lower one which starts from our beach and is little more than a track across the rocks, and a wider path, dug out from the rock-face, which begins alongside the last house in Broadgate and runs all the way round to Moreland Bay until you go down some steps and it turns into a road. We use the lower path to catch up with Dan and Marcus who have already stepped off it and keep disappearing among the rocks as they search for the best spot for fishing. Eventually we see their heads bobbing into view halfway out on a spit, Dan's blond hair standing against the grey-black rocks.

Everyone in town says the weather is going to break soon, surely can't go on like this, but the air drags at your limbs today and even this close to the water you can hardly breathe. We are all puffing by the time we reach Dan and Marcus, who are sitting on a rock jutting out over the water preparing their equipment. We watch for a little while, then Josie, showing off because Marcus is there, insists that Dan lets her fish first, so he shows her how to cast and she does as she is told and manages quite nicely, the line whizzing out across the water and the float landing with a plop in the water which is an oily green today, little waves sloshing into the hollow beneath our rock. Predictably, Josie soon grows tired of sitting staring at the orange float and of Marcus, who is more interested in talking to Daniel about bait than paying attention to her.

'Here, you have a go,' she says, thrusting the fishing-rod towards Lottie, who takes it gingerly as if she's expecting to be immediately wrenched out to sea by a sea monster.

'Nothing's happening,' she says after five minutes or so and Daniel and Marcus look at each other in quiet exasperation. Daniel takes the rod from her and she and Josie start scouting around for somewhere to paddle. They return after a short time to collect some of the food Mummy left for us this morning, which we packed up into several carrier bags.

'We're going over there,' announces Josie, 'and we don't want to be disturbed, thank you.'

'Good,' says Daniel, grinning at Marcus.

I am not particularly hungry but I take a sandwich for myself and then wedge my body into a sun-warmed crevice in the rocks. The boys chat quietly and take little notice of me, but half an hour or so later, when Marcus's float suddenly disappears in the water, Daniel brings the fish he has caught to show me. I stare in fascination at the moss-green body, a metallic arch in the sunlight, and look straight into the fish's alarmed eye before it is returned to the water. I watch them for a little longer but nothing else happens and then the sound of Josie and Lottie fooling around in the distance seems to drift away and I fall asleep.

Daniel's shadow wakes me.

'Do you want to have a go? We forgot all about lunch and we're starving now,' he says, and he holds out the fishing-rod to me.

'Can I really?' I say, honoured that I am to be trusted in this way. 'I don't know how to cast though.'

'I'll show you,' says Daniel.

I am sitting very, very still, watching the float and holding the rod firmly but not so tightly that I cannot feel the light vibrations that run through it. I refuse to be distracted by Josie and Lottie's giggles and shrieks when they eventually tumble back over the rocks, nor by Josie's loud announce-ment that you can spot the old house from where they've been sitting. I just keep my eyes on that fluorescent orange float swaying lazily on the surface of the water. When it disappears it takes a moment for me to believe it. Then I squeal: 'I've got something!'

Daniel throws down the remains of his sandwich and is with me, half-squatting by my side as he puts his hands over mine and then jerks the rod sharply upwards.

'That's it!' he says. 'Got it. Now, start reeling in!' And again, with his hands over mine, he shows me what to do and before we know it a fat little silver fish is twisting and glittering on the end of the line. We land it together and everyone gathers round while Daniel lifts it up and eases the hook out of its rosebud lip. He shows it to me and I cannot stop grinning with delight and pride, then to Lottie, who feels obliged to come closer. She gives a scream as the gasping fish opens its mouth wider and out pops another tiny fish.

'Oh, that's disgusting!' she says, backing away with her hand covering her mouth as if she is about to be sick.

'It's only a tiddler itself,' says Josie dismissively. 'Might as well chuck 'em both back.'

'At least I caught something,' I find myself saying and am immediately scared by my own bravery because I have made it a rule to say nothing that might annoy her.

Daniel shows me my fat little fish again, before releasing it, and the little one, back into the sea. There is a gleam beneath the surface, and then they are swallowed up by the water again.

'How much longer do we have to stay here?' says Josie to her brother.

'You don't *have* to stay at all,' says Daniel. 'I told you you'd be bored.'

'Remember what Dad said,' Josie reminds him. Daniel looks at his watch and then at the sea.

'We'll be another hour, two at the most because of the tide. Why don't you go back to the beach and we'll pick you up on our way back?' Josie looks annoyed at first and about to argue, but then she seems to change her mind.

OK,' she says.

'Katie can stay with us if she wants,' says Daniel. 'At least she understands about keeping quiet.'

I grin at him, proud of myself, then see the look of fury on Josie's face and stop.

'No, she'd better come with us,' she says and she orders me up with her hand. I should refuse to go, because I would much rather stay here with Daniel and Marcus and because I know that Josie only wants to take me away from her brother, but something makes me get to my feet all the same. Till now I had been quite sure that there was nothing left to try for, but once again I have got things wrong, because even now hope has its hook in me and I cannot stop myself from being reeled in again.

'We're not going to the beach,' says Josie as soon as we are out of Daniel's hearing.

'Oh?' says Lottie. 'Then where?'

'Not telling,' says Josie, and she is off, leaping over the rocks. We scramble after her until we reach the narrow pathway at the bottom of the cliff where she is waiting for us, but as soon as we come close, she runs off again, not towards the beach but in the other direction.

'If we don't bother she'll come back in a minute,' I say.

'Yes,' says Lottie, but we follow her anyway, around the cliff-path, where she waits for us until we are nearly in reach and then tears off again, laughing to herself.

When we finally catch up with her, some ten minutes later, she has cleared the rocks and is lying on the sand at the very beginning of Moreland Bay. She smirks at us as we approach, both of us panting in the heat.

'Ready now?' she says, then jumps to her feet and starts marching off down the beach.

'I thought you said we weren't allowed to go as far as your old house,' says Lottie, looking into the distance and scampering along behind her.

'We're not going there,' says Josie. She does not drop her pace, but heads away from the water now until we are standing in the shadow of the cliffs which rear up behind this part of the beach. 'We're going there.'

'Where?' Lottie peers to where Josie is pointing. 'I can't see anything.' Josie pulls her to one side, so that her view is altered and I move with her: concealed by a jut of rock is a narrow crevice which stretches up the cliff to about the height of a man. A trickle of rocks runs out from it across the sand.

'Oh, Josie, no!' protests Lottie. 'I hate caves. There might be bats in there.'

'Don't be daft,' says Josie.

'I'm not afraid of bats,' I say truthfully.

'We've got to go in now we're here,' says Josie and she takes a shrinking Lottie by the arm and steers her towards the entrance to the caves. I follow, holding on to the back of Lottie's shirt so as not to lose her in the darkness that comes down on us almost instantly when we squeeze inside.

'I don't like it,' I hear Lottie saying in front of me.

'Just shut up a minute,' says Josie, 'and let your eyes adjust.' We stand still for a minute or two and the flat darkness begins to have shape. I move farther inside the cave, away from the entrance. The air smells the way I imagine death in the next room to smell. From somewhere above our heads, natural light is entering and soon I can see that we have entered a domed cavern. I reach out and touch the wall nearest to me, which is slimy – water dripping down it from somewhere.

'Follow me,' commands Josie and she moves towards the far wall. 'It's here somewhere,' she says.

'What? What are you looking for?' I can hear the shrill edge in my sister's words.

'The entrance to the next cave. There's a whole series of them leading off from this one, you know. Dad brought me and Dan here one day.'

'But we haven't a torch,' says Lottie. 'And we might get lost. Let's just go back to the boys again.' Already she is yearning for living air and the shriek of seagulls.

'In a minute,' says Josie impatiently. 'Let's just crawl through here to the next cave. If we hold on to each other we can't get lost, can we?'

'Come on, Lottie!' I say. Though I do not like the darkness or the smell any more than she does I cannot pass up the opportunity to impress Josie. 'Don't be a baby.'

So Josie goes first and we all crouch down and begin to crawl through the damp hole that Josie has located, which turns out not to be a hole but a tunnel. I can see nothing at all now, can only hear the shuffle of Josie and Lottie in front of me and then a little moan of fear from my sister. I have a sudden fear of my own, that something will grab my feet from behind and my armpits begin to prickle with sweat.

'I don't like it, Josie,' says Lottie with a sob hovering in her voice 'Really, I don't. Can we go back?' Thankfully we emerge into the next cave and can stand upright again, though it is much smaller than the first. Once more there is a little light from somewhere above us.

'Can you feel it yet?' says Josie, when we are all standing upright again.

'What?' says Lottie. I can hear her breath, shallow in her chest.

'I felt it as soon as I came here,' says Josie mysteriously.

'What do you mean?!' says Lottie in a tight little voice. 'Felt what?'

'There's something about these caves,' says Josie. 'Something bad.'

'Shut up!' says Lottie.

Josie laughs loudly. 'Can you see the entrance to the next one?' She points to a patch of deeper blackness at ground level on the wall opposite us.

'I'm not going through there,' says Lottie firmly.

'Ssshh,' Josie hisses suddenly. 'What was that?'

'What?' Though I can hardly see my sister in the dark I can feel her body tensing.

'That noise.'

'What noise – what are you talking about?' barks Lottie.

'There it goes again,' says Josie, ignoring my sister's question. We all listen but I can hear nothing except the dripping of water.

'Where?' says Lottie.

'Close by. Coming closer now. Can't you hear it? It sounds like . . . '

'Like what?'

'Like . . . *crying* . . . ' Josie drops her voice to a loud whisper and even though I am almost convinced that she is lying, a little trickle of sweat runs down my back. 'Maybe it's the little drowned girl. Maybe she's looking for her mother again.' And to demonstrate Josie gives an eerie little cry herself.

Lottie lets out a scream of terror and I feel her pushing past me and scrabbling down on the floor for the hole through which we have just come.

Josie bursts out laughing. 'I'm only kidding!' she calls after her in a normal voice again, but Lottie is gone, back towards warm sand and sunlight and sea-washed air.

'I'm not afraid of ghosts,' I say quickly, proud that I have managed to hold on to my nerve.

'You don't say?' says Josie. 'Well you should be. You of all people.'

It is her voice that warns me more than her words. She is going to make me pay for answering her back earlier and for winning Daniel's approval.

'Why?' I ask, hearing the fear that threads through my voice.

'Because of what you did.'

'What did I do?' I ask in a low determined voice. I must have it this time.

'Made your mother hate you,' she says confusingly because

I don't know what this has to do with being frightened of ghosts and yet I feel I am reaching towards the very thing she has been hiding from me all these weeks.

'Do you really think she does?' I ask, and then hate myself for allowing her the pleasure of confirming it.

'Of course.'

Suddenly I am fired with anger and resentment for all the times she has taunted me with this, for all the times she has drawn me in and then pushed me away again since she came to our house, for all the things she has made me know that I didn't want to know and all the things she has kept from me.

'Well, Lottie doesn't hate me, no matter what she says in front of you,' I say defiantly. 'And your dad loves me!'

A hand reaches out of the darkness and grabs at me, twists my hair until I can't help but yell out. 'Does he now?' spits Josie, her mouth next to my ear. 'Well that just shows how stupid he is then, doesn't it? He should be careful around you.'

'He doesn't have to be careful,' I say, struggling to free myself. 'Get off me!'

'Don't you want to know why?' She is taunting me again.

'I haven't done anything!' I cry.

'He should be careful in case you try to kill *him* as well,' she hisses, 'just like you killed *your* dad!'

I wrench away from her, leaving a clump of hair in her hand though I feel no pain

' You're just lying again! You lie about everything!'

'Ask your mum then,' says Josie. 'Ask her about your dad's greenhouse again. Did you see her face last time you asked her?' She laughs. 'Ask about the time she went away for a whole week with Lottie and it was just you and your father . . . ' In the blackness I see the photograph of my father that no longer sits on Mummy's dressing-table, try to push myself into the picture alongside him. 'About how your father got ill when the two of you were in his greenhouse together but he could have been saved if you hadn't just sat there and watched him die . . . ' I am lagging behind here, still trying to fit myself in, next to my father's flat image. 'And how you sat there day after day until your mum and Lottie came back home again and found you next to your dad's body. It was the hottest summer ever until this one, they say.' She pauses then comes up close again and whispers gleefully in my ear, 'Can you imagine the smell of him? And the flies and the *maggots*?'

I am on the ground. The damp is coming up through my jeans already, sucking the heat out of my body.

'Let's go,' says Josie, her voice suddenly returning to normal. I shake my head and then remember that she cannot see me.

'No.'

'You have to.'

'No.'

Josie's hand comes at me, either to strike me or to take hold of me. I am too quick for her though, am rabbiting through the short tunnel into another cave before she can reach me.

'Suit yourself,' she shouts through to me and her voice echoes around me. 'I'm not coming to get you, so you'll have to find your own way back.' She waits for a moment. I hear some movement and then no more.

*   *   *

There is no light. Here the darkness presses in on you. You could hold your arm out in front of you, stretch a leg, and peer. Nothing disturbs the thick blackness. Good: I fold myself in again. Here I can stay and not be. I crave my mother – feel that if I could just taste her skin, I would sink my teeth into her flesh and make her be a part of me again – but I must not think. Then I might cry and Lord knows there is enough crying in here already: the little girl is sobbing all around me, her broken voice rebounding off the walls of this cavern and driving into my ears. I cover them and wish she would go away: I do not want icy hands grabbing me like that girl in the story Mummy likes, who lived up on the moors and drove people crazy with her tap, tap, tapping at windows. How long have I been crouched here now? An hour? A day? It is hard to know with nothing all around you, nothing you are anchored to, and the crying, crying going on in your ears. Here is nothing. A place where there are bad things, she said. Where I belong then. Damp rotting air. Your body starts to eat itself eventually, will become the same temperature as the rock and sand then slide into it. There are no flies in here though. What happens to your flesh then, if no maggots? They were good enough for my father, did their job well, it seems. The noise is too much now and I would strangle the little brat myself if only I could see her. If only to stop the crying.

*   *   *

My feet are wet. The crying is fading away, drowned by the sound of water. Not the constant drip-drip of wall-slime but something else, something more, but I am too cold and dazed to think about it. Then a different kind of wetness comes, a quick warm flood in my knickers. The bleeding, which I thought had stopped, is coming again: something alive and moving that jolts me awake. I feel down to the floor. Cold bubbling foam runs between my fingers. A message in this dead darkness. I thought that I would stay here for ever, but now, no. Not here with the ghost of the crying girl always in my ears and the warm blood coming. I must pull my body out of this niche where I have hidden from Josie, if she comes looking, and from myself, and shake life into my muscles. I stand up, stretch my arms and legs, then drop to my knees and feel at the rock until I find the entrance to the tunnel. Inside it the water is high, swishing and gurgling madly through the narrow space like in a washing machine. I crawl through, and manage to get out into the second cave, where I stand upright, shin deep in water now. The entrance to the big cavern, the very first one Josie brought us into, should be right there. I am sure of it. But the light from above seems weaker now and though I drop to my knees and grope at the rock-face it will not let me into it. Fear is making me blind, idiotic, just like Josie says. Think, think. I hear myself, mewing with fear, like a stupid kitten. Water is rising fast now. Must make a circuit of the entire cave, map it out with my hands, like Braille. Words spill out of my mouth like that little fish from the mouth of the other: *Please, God, please help me.*

I do not want to die, not here, in a flooded cave, bobbing about blindly like in one of those snow-shakers you get at Christmas. Mouth open, fish in and out. Eyes eaten by crabs. Let me find my way out and I will never be bad again even if I can't help it. I will find a way. Mustn't bargain though. The water is higher now. Have I gone the whole way round yet? How to know when? Have I gone past the entrance to the cave where I was before? It is hard to know with water fizzing and hissing at me. You can't hear yourself think, Mummy says sometimes.

Please, God.

Wrong. All wrong. I don't know now where I started. There must be some other way. Has to be. Up to the light? Too high. No way to get there and my legs are too cold to try now. Easier to stop and let it come.

Please, God. Save me.

I am getting tired now and that girl is starting again. I would strangle her if she weren't already . . .

'Kate!'

Someone? The ghost girl? The water feels like icy hands on my legs. No. That voice was too big to belong to a whining ghost.

'Kate!'

A real voice! It comes again. A flood of light falls on the

rock-face, like the pictures in my Bible with the light of God streaming through the clouds and everyone down below awestruck and afraid.

Help me.

There is splashing now and the light moves around the rock-face and then finds me. Daniel peers down at me, then grasps me by the shoulders, shakes me. 'Why didn't you answer?'

I blink into the light. 'Where did you find a torch?' I ask stupidly.

'Marcus has it for night-fishing,' says Daniel. 'Come on.' And he takes my hand and pulls me with him, straight to the tunnel that I have been searching for all this time. 'Pretty wet in here,' he says calmly, flashing the torch down to show me the black foam that is swirling from the entrance. 'I'll go first and take the force of the water and you're to follow directly behind me. Do you understand?' Daniel shines the light into my face. 'Katie!' he shouts. 'Wake up! Do you understand what I said?'

'Yes.'

The water wants to play with me, to take me in its jaws and toss me around, like a hound with a stick. I stay close to Daniel's feet as they move forward in front of me, just as he told me to, until we reach the end of the tunnel. Then Daniel pushes himself into the first cave and his hand reaches down for me. Strong fingers close around mine and even before I am on my feet again I can see a slice of golden sunlight floating in front of us, and I know that I am saved.

Outside again, Daniel orders me to climb up on to a small ledge in the cliff-face and I let myself down on to his shoulders, because we still have to wade through the water that is coming up past his knees now. He puts his hands up and grasps mine to hold me steady and then we set off, Daniel striding through the waves and me swaying along like a maharaja high up on an elephant. Farther down the beach I can make out figures standing beneath the sea wall. In front of them is a great mirror of water where the beach should be. As we come closer the figures start twitching, like puppets with invisible strings. The one nearest, knee-deep in water, looks like Harry, and then another one of them that turns out to be Mummy starts moving, passing Harry and coming towards us in a kind of running motion through the water, though the weight of it makes it difficult. I wonder if she realises that her best linen dress will be ruined by the sea water. I watch her clumsy coming from my perch above the world, wishing that she wouldn't run so quickly and spoil everything because I am beginning to enjoy our royal progress across the water and anyone can see that I have already been saved. Soon she is upon us though, splashing more than necessary and dragging down on my clothes, then punishing my bones in her grip. Somehow we are back on that last strip of dry sand and Mummy is pushing Harry away from me and he, in turn, is hugging Daniel and then shouting at him for tearing off like that when help was on its way. Mummy is running her fingers over my skin and peering into my face, searching for something, and Lottie is there too, crying and saying something over and over again, about thinking I'd taken the other path home, that she didn't know. Marcus stands a few paces back, watching all this but not taking part. Suddenly Mummy is finished with me, releases me into a heap on the sand and I watch as she strides, bare feet and wet linen dress, to where Josie is standing: a tall figure beneath the sea wall, apart from the chaos. Harry is going too, but not quickly enough. I watch my mother's hand rising through the air and then it falls, ringing out as it lands on Josie's pale cheek.

PART TWO

CHAPTER 8

I lie, face down in the half-light, listening to the repetitive roar of the ocean, trying to let my muscles unfurl like waves stretching out across a beach. It is no good though: there is something all wrong about that shriek of seagulls in the background, something desolate and unnerving. I find myself waiting for it, and for the cold scrunch of water sifting madly, blindly, through shingle every thirty seconds or so, instead of doing what I am supposed to be doing, which is relaxing as much as I can.

I have no qualms about the nakedness of my body – it is still lean and firm enough to bear inspection in stronger light than this – nor about being touched by a stranger (there is something impersonal about it which pleases me in a way) but I have done this several times before now and I can't help thinking that it is wasted on me. Marina, the young girl who is taking care of me today, is doing her best, drawing down a thick white towel to cover my legs when she finishes working on them, then tiptoeing round the table on unshod feet to begin on my shoulders. The music changes to some kind of breathy panpipe incantation that conjures up Peruvian mountains and ponchos and dumb-eyed goats, and for one terrible moment a wave of hysteria rises in my chest. Marina notices nothing though, begins pushing her small fingers into the wings of muscle across my back, smoothing warm lavender-scented oil into my skin. Already I can feel myself starting to resist, becoming aware of the ticking of my wrist-watch, which I have forgotten to remove, close to my ear, and an ache in my neck from lying in one position for too long. The ticking gets louder the more I try to ignore it and I wonder how many more minutes I have to lie here pretending to be adrift in sixty pounds' worth of dreamful ease. I try to breathe more deeply, to force the appropriate mood and overcome the sudden urge I have for a cigarette.

Ting!!

I am just thinking about tonight when I realise Marina is standing over me with a little bell, signalling the end of my 'journey' (as the blurb on the spa's literature refers to this particular treatment).

'How was that?' she enquires gently.

'Oh *wonderful*,' I say, swallowing a giggle at the bell, and blinking as though I am coming up out of sleep.

'You looked as though you'd drifted off a few times there,' says Marina.

'Yes, almost certainly,' I say, hopping off the bed in relief and heading for my robe, which is slung over the back of a wicker chair, before she has had time to tiptoe out discreetly.

There is long rectangular pond filled with Koi carp in the centre of the relaxation area. I sit beside it and wait for Eleanor outside the treatment rooms for a few minutes, but more New Age music is being piped through speakers in the roof above me and there is something obscene about the pond, the way the muscular bodies of the carp boil at its surface, their great fleshy mouths groping sightlessly at the surface for food or oxygen or whatever it is they are seeking. Instead, I wander across to the swimming pool, which is deep and blue and almost empty at this time of the afternoon. (Eleanor insisted that we should come today – Friday – because she said she couldn't bear to spend her entire birthday at work, and I have not bothered to mention that, for me, this means losing a whole day's pay.) I glance around for her again but she has still not emerged from her Balinese mud ritual – or whatever bizarre thing she's having done to herself – so I leave my robe on one of the wooden-slatted loungers, spaced at intervals beneath the colonnade that runs around three sides of the pool, and stand over the water, among the white, reflected columns.

I hover on my toes for a moment, then tip myself forward and push off with my feet, letting myself fall down through the glassy surface until the blue-mosaic tiled bottom of the pool rears up in front of my face. Then I strike out with my arms and legs, maintaining my depth and relishing the power of my body as I pull myself through the water, which bubbles and fizzes in my ears, turns my hair to undulating seaweed, and pushes up beneath me, wanting to return me to my own element. I make it all the way to the far wall and then back again before the will of the water and my need for oxygen win, and I crash up through the surface, gasping for air.

'Aren't you supposed to be relaxing?' demands Eleanor, standing over me in her robe.

'Are you done?' I say. 'How was it?'

'Bliss,' she says, squeezing her eyes shut and smiling beatifically. I can see a smear of dried mud under her chin. 'We should come here again for my hen weekend.' She waits for me to pull myself up out of the water, and then we go across to the bar – which serves no alcohol – and sit among drifts of white-robed business types on sofas. We read magazines and drink green tea and Eleanor keeps stretching and casting serene smiles at me or into the air, while I feel a kind of enervated dissatisfied lethargy settling over me, which only disperses when it is, at last, time to leave.

*   *   *

Cave is not a cave at all but a restaurant in a cellar. More a wine bar than a restaurant actually, and David, Eleanor's prospective fiancé, and Adam, my current boyfriend, have joined us to celebrate Eleanor's birthday. David is breaking off from assuring Eleanor that no, she does not look discernibly older today, to fill our glasses with something expensive, and then he interrupts Adam, who is complaining about a client, to propose a toast.

'Here's to Ellie, then. Happy birthday, darling!' he says and kisses her on the lips. We all raise our glasses to her and intone appropriately, though I refuse to call her Ellie.

'So,' says Adam, after glancing around at some new arrivals at the table next to ours with his usual air of ennui, 'are you going to tell us about your suburban weekend?'

'Oh,' says Eleanor with a sigh. 'Rather grim, as expected. I've really *no* idea why Gill invited us . . . '

And we are off, dissecting the wedding of one of Eleanor's old schoolfriends and all the other weddings we have ever attended and bickering gently over certain points. I speak when it is expected of me. I help myself to more of the red, studying its ruby luminescence as I swish it around my glass, and relishing the woody dryness it leaves as it passes over my tongue, slides round the meagre amount of food I have eaten and straight into my bloodstream, where it mixes with the cocktail I drank earlier. My semi-drunkenness compounds the pleasure. Fragments of the conversation settle on me like snowflakes, and then it shifts direction, to Eleanor and David themselves and whether they will ever get round to buying an engagement ring or, indeed, to moving in together. Adam nudges me, then starts teasing Eleanor about the whistle-stop wedding David has planned for the two of them, and Eleanor says she doesn't care, that she couldn't bear all that fuss and nonsense. Food disappears and plates are clattered away by a surly-mouthed waitress. I light a cigarette and watch the smoke rise up, web-grey, a delicate, beautiful skein stretching itself across the low, arched roof of the restaurant.

'You'll be married in church though, won't you?' I ask, thinking of Eleanor quietly slipping out from our halls of residence each Sunday morning, hoping that nobody would notice.

'Well . . . no,' she says, looking at David in a way that invites him to speak for both of them. He covers her hand with his.

'It's just not for us,' he says, settling the matter. And then we are back to pulling apart the most recent wedding again.

I drift like the smoke, removed from the moment. Four figures enclosed in a box on a street in a semi-fashionable part of London. Laughter at the right moments. Clinking of glasses. Always the same, though I could move different figures in and out of the scene. Archness born out of boredom. Me as bad as anyone. David is pulling himself up in lawyerly fashion now. I half-listen as he starts to enumerate his objections to church weddings, wonder whether I am still hungry and why it is that Eleanor feels the need to nod in agreement at everything David says, as if all his utterances were universal truths. Perhaps it is the afternoon of enforced relaxation that has made me so irritable this evening.

'Anyone for dessert?' says Adam, managing to grope my leg under the table at the same time as flapping a menu in my face.

We split the bill down the middle and walk with Adam to his architectural practice around the corner, where he has a project to be completed.

'Sorry,' he says ruefully to me, and then kisses me goodbye as nonchalantly as he can manage.

David, Eleanor and I flag down a cab and then we drive across Albert Bridge and through Chelsea, towards David's flat first, because he is flying to Scotland in the morning and has to make an early start. Next we head north, towards the flat Eleanor shares with someone or other from work.

'Thanks for a lovely birthday,' sighs Eleanor, yawning contentedly.

'What?' I say, turning to her with eyes widened from staring into the violet dusk that is slotting itself between the flat-fronted office buildings and brightly lit store windows outside. The skies in London always suggest something tantalising – something perfect you might be able to reach if you could climb as high as the highest building or just keep driving past all the obstructions – hold more promise than any unblemished landscape.

'For coming today.' Then, when the taxi comes to a halt some minutes later: 'Sure you won't come in for a drink with me and Cally?'

I shake my head and drop a kiss on her offered cheek. Then I have the taxi take me back across town where I let myself in and have sex with her almost-fiancé.

CHAPTER 9

The phone is ringing. I check the incoming number to see who it is and then ignore it. I don't have time for my sister Lottie and her indistinct unhappinesses. Besides, she should realise that people have to get to work in the mornings. I grab my coat and bag and leave, knowing that there is no chance of Helena, the girl who owns the flat and from whom I rent my room, answering on my behalf, since her job never seems to require her to rise before ten.

I do not need to leave this early, but I like the city at this time of day: sleepy-eyed commuters sitting quietly at their crosswords or lost in private thought, cocooned by the yellow light and the vestiges of bed-warmth as the tube rocks them through the darkness. I read for a few minutes, then let my mind drift until the right number of stops have passed. At South Kensington I join the stream of people heading towards the stairs and a minute later we all emerge, mole-like, into the chill, slow-brightening air of a London morning. I stop to buy an espresso from the station kiosk where bundles of newspapers thud, paper-cold, on to the counter, then walk briskly, feeling the blood beginning to move around my body, towards the offices of Demeter, the medium-sized publishing house where I have been working for the past four months. And all around me, as I make my way through the slow beginning roar of traffic, dodging the black cabs that swing round corners like fat purposeful beetles, awnings are being unrolled and shop-fronts unmuzzled and chairs clattered down on to soap- sudded pavements. I push open Demeter's heavy glass entrance door, nod to the receptionist and take the lift to the fourth floor, where I switch on the overhead lights and my computer and printer. Then, in the soothing thrum of machinery, I begin work.

'Somebody sleep here last night?' says Paul Davies, Demeter's head of contracts, glancing at my in-tray as he elbows the door open. He is clutching a cardboard takeaway coffee cup in one hand and a paper bag of something greasy in the other. The smell of bacon and hot cheese turns my stomach this early in the day, but I return his smile briefly without taking my eyes from the computer screen, privately berating myself because it is only just gone eight a.m. and I have already completed two contracts. It is not wise to draw too much attention to oneself: I should know by now that there is a balance to be kept between conscientiousness and anonymity.

I am the world's best temp. Or so they say only half-jokingly at Opus Employment Services, with whom I am contracted. After university I travelled in fits and starts because that's what people seemed to do and then, because I needed work, I took a job with an exclusive travel company in Mayfair before realising that I didn't care about other people's holidays. After this I worked at various things but nothing seemed to sit well with me, and every time I felt myself being sucked into the fabric of an organisation, becoming part of the team as they liked to put it, I would be overcome with panic, as though something in me was being shrunk-to-fit. The minute the offer of employment came through the letterbox – other possibilities, other versions of me seemed to be extinguished then and there. Feeling the vaguest of ambitions to do something useful, I talked myself on to a law course, but after a time I couldn't force myself even to appear interested and I abandoned the course two thirds of the way through. A month later I walked into the offices of Opus and since then I have never been out of work. I am able to make enough money to live on without feeling that I am being shaped into something I do not want to be.

The reason why I am considered so good at what I do is because I don't care. I am always punctual and perfectly dressed, I work fast and efficiently until an assignment is completed, and never need to be told anything twice, but I care nothing for personal popularity or office politics. I will not make endless cups of coffee, laugh at anyone's poor jokes, no matter how senior they may be, volunteer myself for tasks that nobody else wants to do or try to make friends with anyone. None of that. The odd thing is that this aloofness seems to impress people more than any frantic attempts to infiltrate an office structure, and after a few days on a fresh assignment I am treated with a new respect. Less fortunately, I am also rarely left alone. You can sit quietly at your desk and the world becomes intrigued by you, starts pressing invitations to lunch or to the pub after work or to office parties upon you. Occasionally I will accept, because there are times when I would rather have people around me than not, but I never show gratitude. When my contract finishes I invariably return to Opus with another excellent reference and promises of further work in the future.

This morning passes quickly enough. Girls drift in to their desks, some pale and irritable, resentful of being forced from their beds to earn a living on this morning when the first hint of autumn is beginning to chill the air, others sweet and loquacious even at this hour. Tempers amalgamate as the hours pass – cups of coffee, the gentle patter of keyboards and the trilling of phones gradually bringing everyone to the same pitch. The odd jag of a crisis rises up and then dies off to save us from tedium. Though it is

clearly pointless in the scheme of things, there is no deny-
ing the satisfaction of completing my tasks and the
steadily increasing stack of papers in my out-tray has a
soothing effect on me. It is hardly challenging, the work I
am given, but it requires a degree of concentration and I
like the way it takes up a certain space in my mind.

I am just about to take this morning's contracts through for
checking when my phone rings.

'Can I see you tonight?' says David.

'Yes.' I reply curtly, because he knows I don't like private
calls at work and because it is too risky, him calling here.
'I'll come to you at about seven.' I never invite him to my
flat.

'Yup, seven's good.' He sounds edgy, as if he's just come
off the phone to Eleanor.

Just before midday, Paul Davies calls me into his office and
offers me a full-time position with Demeter. It is my own
fault because my initial contract here was for two weeks
(and I only took this because Eleanor, who works downstairs in Children's Fiction, recommended me without
asking me first), but then I allowed myself to be persuaded
to cover on reception and after that in this department and
now people think that I belong here. I thank Paul for the
offer and inform him that, unfortunately, I will be leaving
when my current contract finishes at the end of the week.
Then I go out to lunch early in order to avoid Eleanor.

Here is something else I enjoy about the way I work: the
pleasure of being randomly dropped into new territory,
these solitary hours in the middle of the day when I can
learn the textures and patterns of another pocket of this
city in which I live. (And I like the solidity of pavements
beneath my feet, the civilisation of shops and restaurants
and museums, much more than the countryside with its

big, brutal skies, where all that foliage creeping around your legs and the lunatic whine of insects could make you mad.) Today, among the arrogant mews and the shiny black railings of Chelsea, I discover a street full of rare-book and antique dealers and then come unexpectedly upon a small island of shops, like a wealthy village centre, comprising a *pâtisserie*, a Japanese restaurant, an upmarket butcher's shop with a window full of game, a shop selling wooden toys and a greengrocer's. I do not usually bother to eat until the evening, but I am hungry today, so I wait my turn in the *pâtisserie*, behind women in layers of cashmere and discreet jewellery queuing for *tartes aux pommes* and loaves of rustic-looking bread, and buy a smoked-salmon bagel before heading back to the office.

*   *   *

'I can't do this any more,' he says, running his hands through his hair in a parody of despair. One side of it stays on end while the other flops down again, giving him a ludicrously lop-sided appearance. That, and the tragic expression, means I have to restrain a giggle.

'Not even just the once? The taxi cost me a fortune.'

'I'm serious, Kate! I mean, what the fuck are we doing here?' He spreads his hands out as if expecting the answer to drop from above. 'I'm supposed to be engaged for Christ's sake!'

'I know that,' I remind him. David drops down into a chair.

'And Adam's a mate, and you and Ellie go way back . . . ' He looks up at me sorrowfully. 'I just can't.'

'OK,' I say, equably. I pat his arm as if I am comforting a small child. 'We don't have to then.' It's what he wanted me to say, the reason he asked me to come here, ostensibly, but now he's not sure. I can see that arriving in his eyes as I gather up my things and make to go.

'I need a fag,' he says with a sigh, putting his words

between me and the door and offering me a cigarette, which I decide I may as well take. 'What a fucking mess, Kate. I don't know how all this happened.'

'We–ell, you got very drunk and I got a little bit drunk and I made a mistake and so did you.'

He doesn't like that. He wants it to stop all right – or, at least, he thinks he does – but he doesn't want to be my mistake.

'No, no, it wasn't a mistake . . . ' he says, lighting my cigarette for me, and then his own. 'At the time it was . . . '

'All right,' I say out of pity for him. 'But that was then.' I drag lightly on my cigarette as he slumps down into a leather armchair, his hands flopping down by his sides like dead fish.

'I mean, you *know* what I think of you, Kate, we've always had fun together . . . And you're so beautiful, it's hard . . . '

I am not beautiful. I have flashes of prettiness when I am animated, but people make the mistake of thinking I am beautiful because I dress so well – a legacy from my mother – and because I don't seem to require reassurances.

'Go and see Eleanor,' I say kindly. His shirt is rumpled up over his belly and I think with a certain detachment that I will miss the skin stretching over the arch of his rib cage and the clean lines of his body that have demanded nothing more of me than a physical response. 'Take her out to dinner. Or on holiday or something.' Then I leave.

It is dark when I come out of the tube station and a boisterous wind is stirring up the leaves on the pavement. Rain begins to spatter down. I stop to buy a newspaper and some wine from the shop, then walk the three streets to where I live. The beggar is sitting under the arch of the bridge at the beginning of my road. Sometimes you hear the sound of his tin whistle, high and tuneless, before you see him, but tonight he is curled forwards, gazing down at the pavement. Normally I cross the road to avoid him or walk straight past, but tonight I feel in my pocket for change and I drop a few coins into the plastic bowl sitting in front of him. The sound of them falling rouses him and he jerks his head up and stares at me with wild, unfocused eyes. There are sores around his mouth.

'There you go,' I say fatuously, his appearance startling me into speech because I am sure that the last time I saw him he didn't look that bad. He mumbles something at me and I walk on quickly before I can be snagged by his madness.

Helena is out, probably at one of her bizarre country-and-western evenings. Generally, I do not like unplanned evenings alone, but I pour myself some wine, have a hot bath, and then, out of a sense of duty, return my sister's third call. She answers after four or five rings, then talks for half an hour or so. Imagining her in her house (which is just like a child's picture with its four doll's-house windows, neat fenced-in lawn and one or two obligatory splodges of trees), I listen as best I can, and make her see – without upsetting her too much – that nobody in their right mind would have an affair with her husband.

CHAPTER 10

'Please don't worry, I am used to killing people.'

She would flinch if I said this out loud, though I would perhaps say 'things', not 'people', to soften the truth. I would like to protect her, you see, this middle-aged woman with the tired face who has made sure the apricot walls of her office are decorated with watercolour prints and that the chairs are softly cushioned, who guesses what I am about to do, yet still looks at me with kindness. On the other hand, I am still not sure I believe in the existence of this new thing, any more than I believed in my father when I was a child and he nothing more than a flat image in an old photograph, so I say nothing. Sheila – for this, she tells me, is her name – glances down at the notes on her lap.

'The doctor says you are around seven weeks, Kate,' she says and my mind automatically starts making calculations – who, when – though it hardly matters, 'so you still have a little time to think about what you want to do. I can arrange for further counselling for you – or for you and your partner – if you feel it would help in any way . . . ' She puts her notes down on the table, folds her hands together, then looks at me. Sunlight is shining through the blinds on to her face and I can see the faint blue outlines of her contact lenses shifting across slightly bloodshot eyes as she blinks. I have an urge then to reach across, to squeeze one of her hands that look older than the rest of her body – from years of washing and cleaning for children and a husband perhaps – this woman who has a whole existence outside of this place but still comes to work to sort out the messes of people like me.

'I have no partner. And there's no question of continuing, I'm afraid,' I say, repeating the exact words I used in the doctor's surgery in order to be referred here in the first place. I could tell her more, explain that someone like me is not to be trusted with another life, but though I turn the word over in my mind, trying to give it some weight – life, *life* – I cannot invest it with any kind of resonance. She understands enough though and gives me a sweet, sorrowful smile. Then we both consult our diaries.

Nearly everyone is kind here. Only the last person I see in this anonymous three-storey building off Oxford Street, a slim young woman dressed in black who wearily runs through the 'procedure', shows any signs of contempt for me and I am happy to accept this as my due. I too would find it almost intolerable, working here on this conveyor belt of mistakes, naïve hopes and plain stupidity. The Asian doctor who examined me when I first arrived and pronounced on my condition was positively jolly.

'So then, now you understand that you are young and healthy and fertile,' he said with a smile and a wag of his chubby brown finger as I got up off the couch. He is pleased with this, as if he is giving me a prize. 'And you will be sure to use proper contraception once this is over!' I return his smile and try to look grateful, knowing it is pointless to explain that he is wrong, that though my body functions well enough, moves me where I need to go, sleeps when it should, it has never given me any warning that something young and warm could spring to life within it. Here, between the hard bow of my hips, is no place for anything tender to house itself and I cannot help feeling that my body has made a mistake, allowing the soft, curled, prawn-like thing all the evidence insists is here to attach itself, to pretend it has something to do with me. I dressed quickly behind the screen as the attendant nurse ripped the paper cover from the couch with a swift, practised hand, in preparation for the next patient.

'I don't know what else to say to you,' I explain once again to Adam. Ten days ago, finally, I brought our relationship to an end and now I am beginning to resent him for the way he keeps drawing me to the telephone, all his lofty detachment and flippancy vanished now as he eagerly spills out his latest take on the break-up of our relationship, as if he believes that by persistent application he will eventually light upon a solution that will drop us right back where we were. I am not quite courageous enough yet to tell him that he is wasting his time: that we are not one of his projects at work, capable of being restored or redeveloped, but at least the bout of flu from which I am supposed to be suffering keeps him from bothering me in person.

My body has realised what it has done and is trying to rid itself of the parasite. Morning sickness begins to bubble in the pit of my stomach as soon as I wake each day, building up in increasingly violent waves until I can no longer ignore it and find myself running to the bathroom and on my knees over the toilet, retching up thin bitter liquids until my head, and the muscles of my abdomen, ache. My entire body strains in this process, as though it is trying to flush out body cells and not just the contents of my stomach. I ring the girls at Opus and tell them that I will not be available for work for at least a week and that I will contact them as soon as I am better. I am slightly shamed by this weakness because I am never ill. Still, the sickness is endurable, a secret difficulty that will soon be dealt with, and it has the advantage of keeping Eleanor at bay, as well as Adam. I stay in bed each morning till the worst has passed, then shower and dress, read a little – though I rarely manage to finish a book these days – watch television and once or twice telephone my mother because she can be trusted to talk about lunches and theatre trips with her shoal of friends and not to ask personal questions. I ignore Lottie's calls since she has a habit of sensing when something is amiss and pouncing upon it with a little too much glee, as if other people's troubles have the potential to balance out her own. Helena passes through from time to time, on her way to or from work, but since we have no more in common than usual, we speak only briefly, and she displays no signs of having heard my retchings from the bathroom or any curiosity about my increased presence around the place. I pity Helena's wealthy parents who, I am sure, only bought her this very expensive two-bedroom flat in the hope that their oddball daughter might find a friend to share it with, not banking on Helena deliberately seeking out someone like me.

*　　*　　*

It could be a waiting-room in a doctor's surgery: the same magazines, the same sad-looking pot plants and dusty venetian blinds at the windows. Mothers sit next to mute daughters, their voices brave and determinedly cheery. We are not ashamed is what they really want to say. Most of her friends too if you believe the statistics, they would add. A few men are here, holding hands with pale girlfriends. They look nervous or sheepish and the rest of the room, single women mostly, eyes them half in sympathy, half in disapproval. You are the reasons why, their looks say. At least you came though. I sit alone and read my newspaper while I wait. One by one we are taken up to a ward.

*　　*　　*

The girl in the next bed is crying as they bring her back. A nurse pulls a curtain around her, comforts her, but the crying doesn't stop.

'Is it over?' she keeps asking and the nurse talks to her in soft, reassuring tones.

'All over now. Try to rest,' I hear the nurse say before leaving the room at last. I drift back to sleep then and wake next to see a male doctor standing at the end of my bed.

'Your baby was nine weeks old,' he informs me in brusque tones, consulting his clipboard. 'The operation was successful.' I think I may be still half dazed from the anaesthetic or perhaps his clinical delivery sets a factual tone because I almost find myself enquiring what happened to the body. The thought of his expression, had I done so, makes me almost laugh out loud. He moves on to each of the other three beds in the room and imparts similar information.

*   *   *

The crying goes on and on behind the curtain, a full-blown sobbing, unrestrained and mucous-thick, like a child's. I remember her from the waiting-room. She has the face of a child. If I had the energy I would tell her to shut up.

*   *   *

The next morning I ache a little but the sickness is marvellously gone. I drink coffee for the first time in weeks and feel quietly jubilant. I do not take part in the slightly hysterical exchanges in the breakfast-room, but it is easy to see that among some of the girls relief fuels the hilarity. After breakfast we are sent to pack our overnight bags and then each of us is summoned to see another doctor.

'You should rest for the next couple of days,' advises the young Asian woman behind the desk. 'There will be someone at home with you? Just in case there are any complications.'

'Yes,' I lie. 'Thank you.'

'See you again,' calls one of the girls as I leave the ward, and then clamps her hand over her mouth and giggles, realising what she has said.

I am attached to nothing and nothing is attached to me. Without work to order my days, without the sickness and the knowledge of what is to come, it is just me and my bleeding body. I spend a couple of days at home, taking walks along the High Street to buy a paper and to the park behind the tube station. Here I sit for a while and look up at the trees, their leaves fiery against an electric-blue autumn sky, and think how city life buffers you from the seasons for the most part, how they come to be little more than an extra layer of clothing or an umbrella telescoped inside your workbag. I suppose I ought to be troubled by the mothers pushing their doughy-faced infants in buggies towards the swings and the bright red climbing frame, yet I cannot feel that they have anything to do with me. Another day passes in this way, then, feeling that I may disappear completely if I stay here, I ring Opus and demand some work.

*　　*　　*

Helena comes out of her bedroom as I push open the front door and motions towards the living-room.

'Someone through there to see you,' she says in an accusing tone because, by tacit agreement, we do not encourage guests here. I notice that she has a new pair of orange-fringed cowboy boots, which make her already large feet look like ocean-going liners bedecked with bunting, and some kind of weird, hessian poncho that I haven't seen her wearing before. Upbeat country music is twanging from behind her bedroom door and one of the liners is jigging away in time to it. She may well be on her way to line-dancing class or whatever it is she does on Wednesday evenings. I look at the new clothes again and wonder if she has finally found herself a boyfriend. Then I glance towards the living-room, hoping that Adam hasn't arrived to plead with me. Several days of work in a merchant bank across town, involving two tube changes and a mile long walk there and back, have tired me more than I had anticipated.

*　　*　　*

Eleanor is standing with her back to me as I enter the room. Even so I know something is wrong because the air around her is charged. She hears me enter, waits for a moment, then swings round. Her face is swollen with crying.

'How could you do it?' she says, walking towards me. I take a step backwards as she jabs a finger into my breastbone. 'I just want to know, that's all. How could you do that to me?' And all I can think is that, as usual, she can think of nothing original to say.

David has told her everything. Guilt, apparently. Clearing out the past. I wish that Eleanor would just content herself with filling the room with her words, the pitch of her voice rising and falling as she elucidates her opinions of me, of David, of me again, because I understand that it is my place to absorb these. She deserves that. But she keeps demanding answers, answers that I cannot give because the questions have never arisen before and even now – though I can quite see how they might matter to Eleanor – mean very little to me. Sometimes she loses pace, flops down on a chair, seemingly exhausted, and then she is up on her feet again, pacing the room, wanting to know if I ever thought, even for just one minute, about what I was doing to her, whether I deliberately set out to destroy her and if I am satisfied with what I have done? And what about Adam? What he will say when he knows? Because he will have to know. I understand that, don't I? I make no real attempt to answer since I do not know what she wants me to say and because, it seems to me, she needs to go through this process of dropping down in chairs, of pacing the floor and pointing fingers in my face, of turning her face away and sobbing, in order to achieve some kind of catharsis. I am not sure yet if she might attack me physically.

'I'm sorry,' I say from time to time because it seems fitting, but after a few minutes this proves too much for her.

'Stop it!' she screams at me, pushing her face in towards mine. 'Stop fucking apologising all the time! As if it could make any difference after what you've done!'

I feel blood moving between my legs again and for a moment I consider telling her about it, letting her know that a payment of sorts has been exacted, but when it comes to it I cannot bring myself to dissemble about what is, after all, nothing more than an emptiness within me, so I say nothing.

Eleanor stares at me, hard, as if she is seeing something in me that she has never noticed before.

'Do you know what, Kate?' she says, wonderment in her tone. 'All this time I've thought of you as my friend – my best friend in fact – and now I'm not sure that you ever even liked me.'

'Yes I did . . . I do . . . ' I say. *As much as anyone.*

She changes tack again.

'So come on, you've yet to enlighten me. When did all this start? When exactly did you decide that you wanted my fiancé so badly that it was worth sacrificing our friendship? At university? That long ago? It's just that I'm interested, you see . . . '

'I don't want him,' I interrupt.

'Oh really? So it was just a bit of fun, was it?' she snarls. 'Or were you trying to punish me for something?' Her voice quavers and I see that I will probably have to try harder.

'No,' I say slowly, 'nothing like that. We'd both had too much to drink and . . . ' There is no point is saying that I do not understand this irreplaceability of people, how one person, removed, can bring this much pain to another. That to me, they are just faces that move in and out of the picture.

'And what?'

'And after it happened once there seemed little point in stopping,' I say baldly. I could also mention my own boyfriend, Adam, and his part in it. How, for all his urbanity, he was closing in on me, wrapping his emotions and his needs around me until I could no longer bear to be alone with him. Panic is not an excuse she is likely to accept. She gives an incredulous laugh.

'You really don't get it, do you? I mean, what exactly is the *matter* with you, Kate? Does anything or anyone in your life mean anything to you?' Again I say nothing, but this time she requires no response from me. 'You know,' she says, marching over to the window and staring down at the street below, 'now I think about it, there *is* something peculiar about you.' She pauses and turns to me again, but I do not help her out. 'I mean, look at the way you *live*,' she motions round at the room which is bare of any symbol of personal taste. 'You can't stay in a job for more than five minutes and who, exactly, are your friends, apart from me? Oh, sure,' she says, as if I have argued the point, 'you've heaps of acquaintances and you always manage to have plenty of men hanging round you, but nothing actually seems to *connect* with you.' I watch her mind working around this, thinking that it is a pity that Eleanor is becoming more interesting, or at least more perceptive, just at the end of our friendship. Then she returns to her earlier theme. 'I still can't believe that you would do this!' she says, shaking her head to illustrate the point. 'To do it to Adam is bad enough. But to *me*. To your best friend. And all you can do is stand there and say sorry, as if that was enough! As if that is any kind of reparation for the damage you've done!'

Warm blood again, stickiness, the tail end of life. I am heavy with fatigue now, but it doesn't prevent irritation surging in me as Eleanor starts gulping back tears again. Suddenly, I want answers too. I would like to ask her what it is that makes her believe I am her best friend, why she had to follow me around at university, leeching off my popularity, and why, without any encouragement from me, she sought me out when she came to work in London. Why too she is surprised that I should sleep with her fiancé when it was common knowledge that I spent a good part of my college life in bed with the married members of the academic staff, behaviour she found amusing enough at the time. Still I say nothing. I watch her as she drops her head into her hands again and she begins to sob in earnest.

'Oh, Jesus, what is wrong with you?' she shrieks, flinging her head up again. 'Why don't you do something instead of just standing there?'

'What do you want me to do?' I ask.

'How the hell should I know?' she yells, and she rakes at her hair in frustration. 'But any normal person might try to comfort me, put their arms around me or *something*!'

'But you wouldn't let me,' I say reasonably.

'Of course I wouldn't, you fucking idiot, but you could at least try! Try just one damn thing to show that this means anything to you, to prove you'd actually like to salvage something from this mess you've made, instead of just standing there with that blank look on your face!'

'You're right,' I say. 'I'm sorry, Eleanor . . . '

'Ellie,' she hisses. 'Everybody calls me Ellie in case you hadn't noticed.' She looks as if she wants to hit me but I risk continuing because I am alert to the way this might begin to turn. I must not let her force me to continue this relationship between us in whatever warped form it might now take.

'I'm sorry but I'm simply not good at friendships . . . '

'Or relationships,' she adds spitefully.

'Or those,' I agree.

'And what about Adam?' she asks irrelevantly. 'Just because you've dumped him it doesn't mean he shouldn't know what was going on all the time you were together.'

'Fine,' I say wearily. 'Do whatever you feel you need to do.'

'Oh no you don't, Kate!' she says and she laughs again, a long, stagey laugh, devoid of humour. 'Don't you dare try to cast *me* in the role of wrongdoer here!'

'I'm not,' I say as evenly as possible. 'I do understand how you feel and I probably am a useless friend – I really don't like the responsibility of other people . . . '

'There's no "probably" about it,' explodes Eleanor.

'Well, all right,' I agree, beginning to lose patience. 'But I don't know what you want from me. All I can say is sorry.'

'And you expect to keep me as a friend? After all this?' She is staring at me again, searching for emotions – regret, grief – in my expression. She wants to see them there because, for all she says to the contrary, it might mean we have a future. Try as I may, I cannot put them there.

'No,' I say quietly.

'I give up,' she says, trying to muster up a hard tone as she picks up her coat from the back of the chair where she flung it earlier. She swings round again. 'You know, I'm trying to remember what I liked about you, Kate, and strangely enough I can't think of anything. Oh, you're good company, I suppose, and that's always made you attractive on the surface, but when it really comes down to it, what is there?' I wait. 'I'm going now,' she says and still I can see that she wants me to stop her, still she believes that if I would only try, there would be some way we could work around my defective character. 'And,' she says, watching me, 'let me make this very clear, I don't ever want to hear from you again. Have you got that?'

'Yes.'

She gives a sob of disbelief as she slams the door shut, and I listen to her footsteps clattering down the stairs before I go to the bathroom to clean up the blood that is starting to seep down my legs. 'Stand by yeeerr man!' warbles Tammy Wynette from behind Helena's door.

*　　*　　*

The phone is ringing when I get home from the last day on the merchant-bank assignment. I have switched off my mobile because Eleanor, and now Adam, have more to say to me each day and then more again, and whatever I offer them, it is never enough to dull their hunger for the facts or their need to wring a little more contrition out of me. I cannot stop this phone from ringing though, because Helena and I share the line. It rings and rings as I hang up my coat and bag and shake the rain from my hair. I go to check the incoming number, thinking that it is time the two of them took their unassuageable pain elsewhere. It is Lottie.

'Hello?' I say, picking up the receiver.

'It's me. Daniel's dead,' says my sister.

'Who's Daniel?' I say.

CHAPTER 11

My mother insists on collecting me in a taxi, which takes us from my flat to Victoria Station. Here we buy coffee and wait for Lottie to arrive from her doll's house in the suburbs. She arrives fifteen minutes late, a thin figure wrapped in a long black coat, her legs beneath her A-line skirt still as skinny as a child's and looking wholly inadequate to support an adult's frame. She peers anxiously around the coffee shop as if expecting to be attacked by a stranger at any moment – despite having spent most of her teenage years in London, Lottie has never felt at home here – and then descends on us with a look of relief, jabbering about getting the children to school and Brian being in a foul mood because he didn't have a shirt ironed before she has even sat down at our table. She kisses us both then blinks at the range of coffee available and orders a cup of tea instead. My mother, smartly dressed in a slim-fitting black wool suit with her silver-grey hair taken up in a smooth chignon, sips her espresso and looks at Lottie with love and at the same time an air of disbelief, as though she finds it incomprehensible that this nervous, angular creature whose hair is already escaping from the black plastic combs which sit over her ears like ugly seashells, could have taken anything from her own body. Lottie drinks her tea, still talking all the time. Then we walk to our platform, our heels clipping smartly over the vast concourse, and board a train for Bromley.

'It's just so awful,' says Lottie for about the twentieth time. 'I just keep thinking about his wife. And those poor little twins losing their daddy at that age. Just dreadful. If anything were to happen to Brian . . . ' She squeezes her eyes shut, pushing the image away.

My mother is looking out of the grimy window as the density of the city starts to open itself out around the neat green spaces and gardens of London's suburbs. 'They would be about the same age Katie was when your father died,' she muses. The train swerves on to a new line with a rattle and at the same time my nerve-ends flare, suddenly sensitised – because though my mother sometimes talks about my father's life, I cannot remember her approaching the subject of his death before. 'Such a very brutal way to go though,' she continues, returning to Daniel. 'You have so little protection on a motorbike, don't you? He always did love them, of course, but when one thinks of the damage that might be inflicted . . . '

'Don't,' shudders Lottie, 'I can't bear to think about it.'

'At least Peter still looked like himself,' my mother goes on. 'Not like poor Harriet. All those months of pain obliterated her, even before she died. In fact,' she says with a little smile, 'I kept expecting them to tell me that they'd got it wrong with your father, to say that actually he was only sleeping.' She thinks for a moment. 'You see, Peter once told me himself that that's a common reaction among relatives, so all the time I was thinking one thing, I had another more rational voice disputing it.' Lottie and I look at each other in puzzlement because this is not the way my mother talks, but they say that funerals can do this: crack people open so that you can see what lies beneath the surface. Our mother pauses, lost in inwardness for a minute. Then she gives a laugh. 'His hair was too tidy though. He was forever running his hands through it when he was worried or tired, which was most of the time.' Lottie is nodding now, remembering, her eyes filling with pain as they so readily do. 'The nurse had laid him out and though I tried to help – really wanted to help – she was terribly strict and wouldn't let me and she'd used Brylcreem or something like it to plaster his hair down which made him look rather ludicrous, as if his head was too small for his body. Well,' she says confidingly, 'the minute she'd gone off, I nipped back into the room and mussed his hair up a bit.' Lottie looks horrified at this but despite the disquiet I feel I have a sudden rush of warmth for my mother, for the impulsive, girlish naughtiness, the lovingness, of that gesture. Then I wonder how you go about removing maggots from a rotting body. Some kind of jet-wash arrangement perhaps. A scene from the television screen comes to me: riot police aiming water cannons into a crowd that suddenly loses its solid homogeneity, breaks up into bodies as light as air, twisting and writhing helplessly on their ropes of water. Our train is sucked into a dark tunnel then spat out the other side into the sunshine again. We ease to a halt.

'Bromley South. This is Bromley South,' announces a nasal voice. 'Change here for Swanley, St Mary's Cray . . . '

'A taxi from here, I think,' decides my mother, leading the way off the train and down the platform with her brisk bobbing walk.

I am still not sure why I am in the back of this taxi, veering through the streets of a town I don't know towards the funeral of someone I hardly remember. Life should be settling to some kind of equilibrium again, with the structure of work to soothe and reorder me, and no more Adam and Eleanor and David pushing themselves into every corner of my day, but now I am being pulled out of my element and forced into a place where I do not want to be. I did my best to escape, but Lottie, who can hardly believe that she has to remind me who Daniel is, or was – a sign, I think, of how few people have passed through her life since then and how many through mine – shrills down the phone at me until I give up and call my mother, hoping for her support. To my surprise, she too insists that all of us must attend, that Harry would expect it. I protest that I had no idea she'd kept in contact with Harry all these years, that she has never so much as mentioned it to me, but my words stream over her surface.

We drive through a town centre, past the end of a high street, where I can see a shop full of Halloween masks and fat plastic pumpkins and the awnings of a street market, then out past rows of large Victorian terraced houses which eventually fall away on either side of us into bay-fronted 1930s houses which in turn give way to new estates with wide curving roads, trim rectangles and triangles of grass and coniferous landscaping.

'Looks like home,' says Lottie. 'It's funny to think this is where Daniel and Josie grew up. Do you know, I always thought they lived somewhere incredibly cosmopolitan from the way Josie used to talk about it.' Lottie looks troubled suddenly, as if she shouldn't have mentioned Josie's name in front of me, starts to rattle on about how Louise, her eldest, is given to the same sort of flights of imagination, how only last week she invented an entire incident at school . . .

'You did say the Catholic church?' interrupts the taxi driver and my mother nods her assent. A few minutes later the taxi slows as we pass a small parade with shops and then we turn off the main road and stop opposite a church set up on a bank on one side of the road. St Michael's is built of toy bricks and red tiles and sits on a mat of grass, the bright unnatural green of advertisements for lawn fertiliser. A yellow crucifix hangs above a set of swing doors that would look more in keeping if this were the entrance to a library. I pay the taxi driver before my mother has the chance to get her purse out and then we make our way up the steps, our coats billowing in the lively breeze, three thin black witches against the emerald green.

The organ plays dolorous music and the pews begin to fill with people I do not recognise. I gaze up at the gold crucifix above the altar, the one object of beauty among all this fresh paint and blond wood, drawn by the contrast between the body of Christ, which is twisted in pain, the muscles of his arms and thighs straining against his fate, and the serenity of his expression. Then I hear a single set of footsteps and turn to see Harry walking down the aisle. I had wondered if I would recognise him, but now I see that this was a ridiculous thought because Harry still looks exactly like Harry except that his hair is shorter and thickly streaked with grey. He stops to greet people on the way down the aisle, shaking a hand here, accepting a hug there; then he sees my mother and as he strides towards her something collapses in his face, as if the underlying structure has suddenly been whisked away. He goes straight to my mother's arms, burying his face in her shoulder.

'Mary, Mary,' I hear him murmur, then, 'my boy,' and my mother rocks him gently and says: 'All right, all right,' as she would to soothe a child, until Harry has recovered enough to lift his head again.

'Lottie,' he says, managing a stricken smile. 'Look at you,' he shakes his head in wonderment that my sister might have continued to grow up in his absence and reaches out his hands to her.

She grasps them for a second and, with tears already overspilling, says: 'I'm so, so sorry, Harry,' and he nods his thanks, acknowledging everything else that cannot be said.

'Thank you so much for coming,' he says in heartfelt tones, and then he sees me for the first time. 'And Katie. My Katie, too.' His features are dissolving again and then I find his arms around me, enveloping me in a way that I suddenly remember so well. 'Oh, it's such a long time since I saw you,' he says, 'such a long time.' And then I understand that he *is* a different man now, that the embrace isn't quite as it would have been then, for though Harry's frame is as broad and lean as ever, all the strength has gone out of it. I cannot know whether this has been a gradual process or whether it has been a matter of days. He makes an awkward little movement towards the front of the church and says something about seeing us after the service; then he walks down the remainder of the aisle and takes his seat in a pew on our side of the church.

'Oh, poor Harry,' says Lottie, wiping her eyes on a ragged piece of tissue. 'I can't bear it.' Then she nudges me. 'Here's Josie.'

I steady myself before turning, then am startled when I do so and find Josie is almost level with us. She doesn't see us as she passes, but continues towards the front of the church on the arm of an older woman who, from the resemblance between them, I take to be her mother. Behind them comes a stocky man in a pinstriped suit. I cannot help but stare at Josie's profile as she takes her place and examines the order of service. Her hair is no longer that extraordinary shade of white-blonde, has darkened now by several shades. She wears it cut into feathers around her face, which is as pale as ever, though I can see that her skin has lost the milky quality it once had, sits more thinly over her bones now. As a girl she had hovered somewhere between beauty and peculiarity; now she has settled into plainness.

Lottie nudges me again and informs me in a whisper that Josie and her husband, the man in the pinstripes, cannot have children.

'How on earth do you know these things?' I demand crossly, irritated by her ability to switch from tears to tittle-tattle so swiftly.

'Harry told Mummy. Although, apparently, he and Josie haven't spoken in years. This must be Daniel's wife, the little woman with the two children just coming in now . . .'

'Shut up,' I say as the organ begins to play more loudly. Everyone rises.

I worry for the men and boys carrying the coffin because I am not sure that they are up to it. One of them, a boy of no more than sixteen or so, is crying uncontrollably. His shoulders heave spasmodically, which must surely put a strain on the rest of the party and I fret about whether he can see where he is going through all these tears. They move forward in spurts, with uncertain slow-motion strides, each foot hanging in the air for a second as if feeling for a foothold, and then connecting with the floor once more. The coffin jerks as they progress slowly down the aisle and I think about all the weight they must carry. A wreath of waxen white lilies shivers on top of the coffin and it is a relief when they finally place their load before the altar and move away to their seats. Someone steps forward and places something on top of the coffin.

'Oh God!' says Lottie, beginning to sob into her tissue. I strain around the head of the person in front of me so that I can see: the landscape frame displays a head-and-shoulders shot of a smiling Daniel, taken, I imagine, when he was younger, since his blond hair falls almost to his shoulders and around his face in tendrils, like those around the face of the Christ figure above him. Only now do I believe that it is Daniel lying in that coffin with the lid shut down over his face and his eyes – open? No they close them – his eyes closed for ever. I wonder what they have dressed him in and whether his hair – still golden? – fans out over that bizarre cushiony satin they use to line coffins. Then I think how cold his body must be in this suddenly cold church where my hands feel icy even within my gloves and how it would feel if just for one moment you could see yourself raised up on that plinth with everyone you have ever known come to take a look at you, to wind up your time on this earth.

The service begins. Hymns start and end; people move

forward to speak – mostly of Daniel as a husband, a father, a colleague – then are absorbed into the congregation again. 'Good', 'kind', 'gentle', 'unassuming' are words that reach me again and again and then slip away. I try to listen but I know nothing about the adult Daniel and my eyes keep wandering: to the woman he married, whose small frame looks ill-equipped for the rigours of single motherhood, to the fair-haired twins who are wriggling beside her, to Harry who is weeping freely and to Josie whose eyes do not leave the coffin. Though it is a warm day outside, the chill within this church seems to be crawling up through the earth, sucking the heat out of my feet and travelling up the bones of my legs. I stare up at Jesus, at that face that endures all pain, and will myself to ignore the cold. Lottie cries beside me, a constant, easy flow of tears, while my mother stands quite still, wiping the occasional tear from the corner of her eye with a delicate linen handkerchief.

The priest is talking now.

' . . . Good . . . '

'kind . . . '

'loving . . . '

Then he is talking more about love, God's love, the love of Jesus, the love all of us had for Daniel which will never die so Daniel himself can never die, which is patently untrue because he is lying right there for anyone to see, all boxed up for burial, yet something in the priest's words reaches me and I find myself wanting to believe him, to believe that we might just be the summation of all the love we have given and received and that this endures; wanting to push away the idea that persists in me of long, dark nothingness. And though I am now so cold I can barely think, I am remembering the small thing that lived in the dark within me and died unnamed, unloved by me, or anyone. And as everyone rises to their feet to sing I am thinking about a dark cave and the saltiness of water, of light coming and a hand reaching out for me, and how the light that came to the thing inside me was a treacherous light, a bright tunnel towards death, with no soft voices and loving hands waiting.

Lottie's hand squeezes my arm sympathetically and she whispers: 'Are you OK, Kate?'

I nod and brush her away.

The hymn finishes and everyone sits down while the priest talks again and busies himself about something at the altar. I watch Josie. She never moves her eyes from the coffin and I am struck by her statue-like quality. Suddenly she does move though and I realise then that all around me people are shuffling along their pews and out into the aisle where they are forming a queue down towards the coffin. My body is numb but I get to my feet and push clumsily past Lottie and my mother, taking no notice of their murmurs, just hearing a voice in my head, 'Daniel, my Daniel,' and needing to go to him, to offer him my hand, pull him out of the dark horror of that coffin which they have pushed down so heartlessly over his good, kind face. The people in front of me don't move fast enough and I have to restrain myself, stop myself from shouldering through the crowd, past Daniel's wife, past his mother, past Josie, to reach Daniel, yet when I finally reach the front of the queue I find that people are not approaching the coffin at all but turning to the left instead, and I do just as they do and walk towards the priest who holds something up to my lips. I open my mouth, like a dumb goldfish, to take a thin, papery wafer, which I move over my teeth uncertainly, and then someone else lifts up a cup to me and I sip the warm, vinegary liquid, most of which dries on my tongue, just a trickle of it sliding down my throat.

I turn then, defeated, knowing that I have failed Daniel and walk back to the far end of our pew and rejoin my mother, who is looking at me and shaking her head, and Lottie, who is rocking with silent, inexplicable laughter.

I drift in and out of the rest of the service, no longer looking at the coffin but at those around me. Daniel's children are becoming restless and fretful and an older woman ushers them out of the church. Harry has stopped crying but is leaning over, supporting himself on the pew in front of him. I observe my mother and Lottie during a prayer, noting that Lottie bends her head and closes her eyes piously, though I know full well she has never attended church since her children were christened, while my mother folds her hands together but keeps her eyes open and her gaze forwards, a small smile on her face as if she is tolerant of yet mildly amused by the folly taking place around her. Then my eyes are drawn to the pews on the other side of the church and I see that though her husband has merely dropped his head in prayer, Josie is right down on her knees, her hands clasped together and lifted to the sky, and her voice, intoning the words of the prayer, is rising above everyone else's. Fervour emanates from every angle of her body and I am shocked and a little embarrassed by it, this very public display of devotion. Then the priest hovers over the coffin for a minute and after this the men close in around it again, lifting its bulk with a more practised air this time, and Daniel's moment is over.

'What was so bloody funny?' I demand as we leave the church and disperse into little groups on the grass, while Daniel's family take their places in the great black cars that are waiting to carry them the three hundred yards to the cemetery. The wind has dropped now and I would like to turn my face up to the sunshine, to drink in its warmth.

'You, you idiot!' says Lottie. 'Going up for communion like that!'

'I wasn't,' I say in confusion because I cannot say precisely what it was that drew me up that aisle.

'Yes, I must say I wasn't aware that you'd converted to Catholicism,' says my mother with a chuckle.

'Converted from what?' I say, using pedantry to draw

attention away from my mistake. 'Surely you have to convert *from* something? You can't convert from nothing. That's what we are, aren't we? Nothing?'

'Yes, you're right, of course,' says my mother in a placatory tone, though I can see that she is still amused. I am unreasonably angry with her all of a sudden, perhaps because I had not wanted to come in the first place.

'And how, exactly, am I supposed to know what I should or shouldn't do in church? It's not as though we ever had the opportunity . . . ' I go on, aware that I am managing to combine pomposity with petulance. 'I'm not even sure whether I'm supposed to be standing or sitting half of the time!'

'Oh, come on, Kate,' says Lottie, 'you have to admit that it's funny. Susie, my next-door neighbour, had to go through months of instruction before . . . ' She is trying not to laugh again.

'And it didn't occur to either of you to stop me?' I say, trying to summon up some dignity.

'Well, how should we know you were proposing to hotfoot it up the aisle like Sister Wendy?' says my mother and she and Lottie collapse into fits of unseemly giggles.

They bury Daniel in the earth and then Harry approaches us. I watch him coming, his face grey with fatigue, and remember how I once wanted this person I now barely know to fill the blank left by my father.

'You'll all come back for a while? We're at Theresa's house because Dan's . . . ' he grimaces, then continues, ' . . . Jenny's house is too small for all this crowd.' My mother hesitates but Daniel's mother, who is standing near by, overhears the conversation and turns to us.

'Hello, Mary,' she says and she reaches out to take my mother's hand. 'Thank you for coming. You're more than welcome to come back for a drink and something to eat. And the girls, of course,' she says turning to Lottie and me.

Her face looks exhausted with life but still she smiles at us. 'You know, Daniel often used to speak of that summer he spent with you at the seaside,' she says to my mother. 'How much he enjoyed it.'

'He was a lovely boy,' says my mother with quiet conviction. 'And I'm so sorry,' and her other hand encloses Theresa's, mother to mother.

'Josie doesn't seems to have changed much,' observes Lottie in the taxi to the house.

'No,' says my mother. 'She still looks hard as nails.'

'That's not very kind,' reproves Lottie. 'Especially in the circumstances.'

'No,' agrees my mother. 'I notice she couldn't bring herself to talk to Harry though.'

'Yes, you'd think, wouldn't you?'

'Indeed. I'm not sure what it is they quarrelled about, but, as you say, now would be the time to put an end to it. I do hope she doesn't try to speak to me at the house.' My mother takes out her powder compact, flicks up the little mirror and checks her appearance. 'It's a terrible thing to say about a child, but I never could bring myself to like Josie.' She looks at me. 'Even before all that business with you.' I nod and look away, out of the taxi window, because, once again, we are on new ground and I am not prepared for it. 'And after all,' ponders my mother, dabbing at her nose with the powder puff, 'I don't suppose she can help being so ugly.'

'Mummy!' says Lottie in horror. The taxi flings us all together as it takes a tight corner and we burst out laughing.

Theresa's house is large and guests settle themselves in various rooms, distant relatives greeting one another and conversation settling on more mundane subjects now that the funeral is over. People begin to laugh without looking guilty, though from time to time someone will begin to reminisce about Daniel and others will join in, eager to contribute their piece to the picture of his life. The oddity of it strikes me as I listen, how we can only be contained in a narrative when we are dead. Only then can others clap their hands together and say about us, 'So, that's that!' and walk around our entire circumference, mapping us out without any surprises. We accept a glass of wine apiece and eat a little food, because it is expected of us more than because any of us is hungry, and, after Lottie has had a covert glance at the train timetable, agree among ourselves to stay for an hour.

I feel ill at ease here, though Harry keeps pressing drinks on us and everyone is friendly enough. Daniel's children are running round our feet, letting off energy, and our very presence here begins to feel sham. It becomes clearer to me by the minute that we knew almost nothing about the man whose burial we have just witnessed. I remember that I have some cigarettes in my bag and feel a sudden urge to smoke, but when I look around the room for an ashtray I cannot see one. Indeed, it seems unlikely that I will find one anywhere in this pristine house. I can, however, see a patio door at the far end of the next room, opening out on to a long lawned garden.

'I'm just going out for a cigarette,' I announce and, leaving my mother to listen to Lottie, who is bemoaning the fact that Brian refused to come today, make my way through to the next room which is busy with people helping themselves to desserts at the buffet table. I am just about to step out into the garden when Josie walks in at the patio door, coming in from the garden herself. I start, despite having wondered, from the moment I realised I would have to attend this funeral, what I might say to Josie if we came face to face, whether pity and decency would override any childish desire for revenge and I would be able offer her my sympathies in a genuine spirit. Now both of us pause and meet each other's gaze warily. Nothing comes to me. I realise then that I have no words with which to address this adult Josie. The past is not to be got at or rearranged in this way. She nods briefly and I manage a smile of sorts and we pass on.

An hour later, my mother, Lottie and I are on the train, returning to London. I leave them at Victoria, Lottie looking exhausted now, and take the tube home. As it rattles northwards I watch my bright reflection in the window and push thoughts of Daniel away from me, burying him for the second time in one day.

CHAPTER 12

Helena knocks on my door and then comes in, right inside, instead of poking her head round the door and then withdrawing it as soon as possible. She wants to tell me that she has, as I suspected, met someone.

'Oh,' I say slowly, for though it is only seven o clock in the evening, I was half asleep a moment ago. I put the book that has fallen on to my chest to one side and sit up properly. 'That's good.'

'Yeah,' mumbles Helena and then she adds that, by the way, would I mind moving out. 'Sorry about that, but you know . . . ' she frowns through her glasses then spreads her hands in explication and kicks at the skirting board. I can see that this level of articulacy is fast draining her resources.

'But won't – I'm sorry, you haven't told me his name yet . . . '

'Joe.'

'Won't Joe want to see where it is that you live? Before both of you take such a decision?' I ask, raising the kind of sisterly concerns that have never had any place in my relationship with Helena.

'Oh, he's been here loads of times,' says Helena airily, and then, seeing me staring at her, flushes. 'Just lunch-hours,' she explains. 'He closes up when they're not busy.'

'Right,' I say, not bothering with 'what' and 'who'.

'I can see how people might think it's a bit sudden,' she says, and for the first time since I have known her, her face shows signs of animation, 'but I think he might be The One.'

The Only One, I have to stop myself saying, and then Helena actually comes right across the room and perches on the end of my bed as if we have this kind of intimate female chat all the time and starts telling me all about Joe and how he runs a country-and-western music shop in Clapham and how twenty-five years isn't such a huge age gap and now that they've found each other they don't want to waste any more time. I take little notice of any of the details, being more concerned with removing her from my room.

'Helena!' I have to interrupt when she shows no sign of abating. 'Please don't explain any more. I quite understand.' She stops mid-flow.

'Oh. Is two weeks notice all right then?'

'Two weeks!' I protest. 'That doesn't give me a great deal of time to find somewhere else!' But, it seems, Joe has already given notice on his own flat and will be moving in here, come what may, two weeks tomorrow. I can, of course, stay for a few weeks longer, just so long as I don't mind sharing. 'Fine,' I say, holding up my hands. 'I'll be out in two weeks.'

'Cheers,' says Helena. She gets off my bed at last and edges towards the door looking shamefaced, as though suddenly aware that she has breached our unspoken etiquette (which indeed she has). 'Thanks a lot then.'

I lie in bed that night staring at the walls and thinking that it would take a matter of an hour to remove all traces of my presence from here. I did not realise how much I needed this bare-walled flat until now, how, though it belongs to Helena, it has come to seem integral to me, to the quiet space at the centre of me, unsullied by other people and their untidy desires and expectations. My acts of acquaintanceship and the occasional intimacies that my body demands have always taken place on other people's territory, so that I could remove myself whenever necessary. Here, I need not speak or be spoken to, and the thought of sharing a house or a flat with people who might want to weave me into the fabric of their own lives fills me with horror.

On Tuesday, I buy the local paper and work my way through the list of rooms to let, circling those that may be suitable, but work becomes busier than usual and the days pass and then it is the end of the week. It seems unlikely that any of the rooms I have marked will still be free, so I throw the paper in the bin with the thought that I will be more efficient in my search next week.

Helena is away for the weekend – a wedding or something in Scotland. I have been invited to a party, but as the time approaches I feel less and less inclined to go. The weather has turned viciously cold and, though I normally enjoy the ritual of coming home from work and transforming myself for the evening, the thought of actually leaving the flat daunts me for some reason. I go through the motions of preparing myself, but when I am ready, I cannot bring myself to pick up the phone and call for a taxi. I sit down instead on the edge of my bed, trying to gauge where this feeling comes from.

After a minute, I lose patience with myself, get up and cross to the mirror, where I examine my appearance. I have had an expensive and rather beautiful haircut recently and my red dress and heels look good. I have lost weight in the last few weeks and as a consequence my legs look coltish, but though the thermostat in the flat is turned up to its highest level, my face looks pinched and I realise that I am chilled through. Sharp little pains are jabbing between my shoulder blades and into the small of my back. I give a shiver and realise that I am sickening for something. It is with a sense of relief, of pleasurable anticipation almost, that I take off my clothes and my make-up and go to the airing cupboard where I pull out a pair of fleecy pyjamas

Eleanor bought me one Christmas, which I have never worn. I get into these quickly and then drag my duvet through to the living-room. My plan is to keep warm and watch television – one of those banal quiz shows perhaps, the kind that we were never allowed to watch as children and which I only ever glimpse on my way out in normal circumstances – but when I point the remote control at the television, the screen flickers for a second, then makes a peculiar sound, a kind of dangerous electrical fizz, and then goes black. I stare at it for a minute, already feeling incapable of doing anything about it, and then, aware of a cold draught working its way into my cocoon, I pull the duvet more tightly around me. My head is beginning to ache now and a wave of tiredness hits me. I cannot bring myself to move again, even to fetch a book or a newspaper, so I lie still and gaze at the bare walls until I fall asleep.

For the rest of the weekend, I hardly move from here. The phone rings five or six times, various people wanting me to call them back, but only Lottie leaves a proper message. Apparently I haven't called her for ages and she's been thinking that I didn't seem quite right at the funeral, so she's just ringing to make sure that I am. In reality she will be wanting to talk about Brian, about how he is failing to satisfy the great big want of her, and, though I have never been able to perceive any of Brian's attractions – am, in all honesty, repulsed by his blunt bloke-ish humour and thickening middle-management body – I do pity him at times, because, for all her veneer of normality, Lottie remains a strange, complex creature and I wonder if anyone could give her what she needs. You could pour all of yourself into her and, in turn, allow her to insinuate herself into every corner of your being and still it would not be enough. I try not to trouble myself about her unfathomable wants right now though, because my head is aching badly.

*   *   *

They are coming again, as I lie here sliding in and out of sleep, only more bizarre now, skewed by the fever, the kind of dreams that have been waiting for me in the dark for many nights now because I can't seem to stop thinking about Daniel lying down there in the cold ground and even when I am at work find myself staring at nothing and wondering about the mechanics of death, about how quickly a body starts to rot and what blood smells like when it is incinerated. They say your brain is layered like an onion inside and any great impact – I see a car pulling out from the side-road and driving right through Daniel's flesh – makes those layers spin around inside your skull, severing all the connections between them so that everything that you have stored up in there – the sum total of all your memories and loves and fears and all the images that you have filed away – is lost in an instant. But how does something go to nothing? It troubles me because it does not seem to obey the laws of energy.

On Sunday, I feel a little better. I read a brochure that my mother sent me, about the Florentine Art Exhibition at the National, and then get up to take a bath. This alone exhausts me and my head is throbbing painfully by the time I have finished. I collapse back on to the sofa and within minutes I feel sleep washing over me.

I am at Daniel's funeral again, except that it is taking place not in a church but in a vast, pillared room and in the middle of the room is his body, in a glass case, like Snow White's coffin. Eleanor is on the other side of the room, giving an interview to a television crew and sitting beside her is Sandra Mills, the girl who used to babysit for us when we lived in Broadgate. She is chewing gum and on her lap are two enormous babies, grotesquely chunky and muscular like Renaissance cherubim. One of them is vomiting copiously but no one takes any notice. Then everyone else is gone and the room is in semi-darkness and I am aware that the great wooden doors at the far end of the room are locked. Cautiously, I approach the glass case, but when I come closer I see that there has been some mistake because the body curled up inside is not Daniel's at all but that of a tiny, shrunken creature with shiny bronze skin stretched tightly over its knobbly spine, like the mummy I saw at the British Museum when I was a child. I lean over the case to take a closer look and a little wizened claw of a hand flies up at me, pawing blindly at the air in some kind of spasm, and I barrel up out of sleep drenched in sweat and with my heart battering against the wall of my chest. Eventually my breathing slows. Dusk has fallen outside.

The next morning I am up and on my way to work before Helena, who returned late last night, has woken. This is my second week with the North-West London Examination Board. I have worked here several times before, though not in this particular department. The work is easy enough – all I am required to do is to convert various examiners' reports into a standard format – but the offices are open-plan here and I am unlucky enough to have a photocopier situated directly adjacent to my desk. Normally this would not trouble me, but I seem to be more sensitive to noise than usual and sometimes, when people are laughing and joking around me or the photocopier is incessantly whining into action and chugging out papers, the noise gets inside my head and pushes everything else aside so that I cannot remember what it is I am supposed to be doing.

One of the girls has left a Post-it note on my phone asking me to return a call to Opus. I am feeling exhausted after the journey here and I wonder if I have made a mistake coming in at all today. I sit down and call the number immediately.

'Marian? It's Kate here. Kate Matheson.'

'Oh, *hi*, Kate, thanks so much for calling back,' says

Marian. I can hear her scrabbling with papers at the other end of the phone. 'Kate, I just wanted a quick *word* with you, just to check that everything's OK really.'

'What do you mean?' I ask guardedly, because Marian is sounding too chummy for good news. I hear her take a deep breath and then she sighs and tells me that something has been mentioned, that she wouldn't normally bother me halfway through a contract because, as she always tells clients, I'm one of her most reliable . . .

'What is it I've done?' I ask.

'We–ell, what they're saying, which I must say surprises me, is that they think your work could be a little quicker,' says Marian. 'And they feel that the accuracy isn't quite there, that perhaps you're not picking up on things as quickly as they'd like.' I am silent for a second, hot with mortification. The work I have been given is so simple that a school-leaver ought to be able to do it.

'I'm sorry,' I manage eventually and for one horrendous moment I think I might cry because whenever anyone has questioned the way I work – implied perhaps that I am wasting my education – I have extolled the easy freedom of it and then hinted that when the right moment arrives I will, of course, apply myself to something more demanding. And now this. The humiliation of being told I have not managed to function at this most basic of levels.

'No, no,' says Marian hurriedly, 'I wasn't ringing to criticise, you know me better than that, Kate. It just seemed so unlikely that I wanted to check with you. I mean, it's unheard of for anyone to find your work wanting, so I thought maybe you were unhappy with the situation there . . . ' Both of us know that the Examination Board is one of the agency's best clients and that Opus cannot afford to upset them, so I apologise again and manage something about having been ill, still feeling ill in fact, and when Marian suggests that I take the rest of week off, because she can easily send someone else in my place, I agree straight away. She says she has nothing for next week at present but promises to call me if anything comes in. As soon as we are finished I leave my desk, thankful that the rest of the girls are still chatting around the coffee machine at the other end of the corridor, then say goodbye to the receptionist as cheerfully as possible on my way out, as if my departure at ten minutes past nine in the morning is nothing to be remarked upon.

There is a problem on the tube and after waiting for some time I give up and stand all the way on a packed bus that stops everywhere and takes for ever. When I finally reach home I am weak with fatigue and feeling bullied by the roar of traffic and pavements full of people who keep coming at me. The door of the flat closes behind me and I stand there for a second, letting the silence wash over me like cool water. Then, from Helena's room I hear the sound of laughter and my eye is drawn to an object on the side table that stands in the hallway. It is a large Stetson. I go straight to my room where I strip off my work clothes and get back into the pyjamas. Then I get into bed and pull the duvet up high so that it covers my ears. I wait for sleep to come.

When I awake, the afternoon is drawing in and Helena and The Stetson have left. I check the phone for messages, but, probably because I have stopped returning calls, nobody has rung for me. There is a note on the kitchen table.

Any luck with finding a room yet?
Helena

Sleeping during the day like that was a bad idea because I spend all night in a kind of semi-trance, acutely aware of being nowhere near the edge of sleep yet not quite capable of getting up and reading a book or something else that might distract me from the whirring of my brain. I do not quite dream, but bad thoughts pass

143

through my head with the unpleasant vividness of dreams: a moment of childhood humiliation relived; sudden, overwhelming guilt for the time I joined in bullying a girl at secondary school; a lecturer at university who responded to my attempts to eclipse his wife with barely concealed distaste. Everything floats through untouchably, not processed and made more bearable by reason. A bleak dawn comes on the horizon at last, bloody red clouds torn by the wind, and I feel so ill and exhausted now – no longer, I think, because of the virus, but just in myself – that my bones feel like they might break. I huddle myself up against the bad feelings and eventually fall asleep as the rest of the world is stirring.

I awake with a jolt, then get up and dress quickly because it is late and I am anxious to be out of the flat. Reason tells me that I must do something to take a hold of myself, so I walk to the newsagent's, then to a nearby coffee shop where I force myself to start working through this week's adverts for shared houses. I mark half a dozen of the more neutrally worded ones – those that don't rattle on about bubbly personalities and easy-going atmospheres – but though I sit and stare at the paper for some time and have my mobile ready in my hand, I cannot bring myself to dial any of the numbers. Instead I order another coffee and look through the adverts for self-contained flats that I cannot afford, allowing myself to imagine a clean white space waiting for me, somewhere within these lines of grimy typeface. But only one advert in this section fits my budget and this has clearly been placed in the wrong column. It is a terse few words strung together at the bottom of the page:

Single bedsit, no DSS, no pets, suit prof. female.

A tube stop is mentioned – the next one along the line from here – and a telephone number. I have not been aware of harbouring any special affection for this area of London where I have found myself for the last few years, but now, seeing this advert, I have a sudden yearning to maintain contact with it. This, plus an absolute shrinking from the thought of sharing a house with other people, means that I pick up my phone and make an appointment to view the bedsit this afternoon. I spend the remaining time walking around the High Street and the local market, moving from coffee shop to coffee shop, not wanting to return to the flat in case Helena and The Stetson turn up there. By three-thirty I am suddenly desperately tired and would like, more than anything, to sleep, but this would only invite all the bad thoughts back in, so I make myself walk to the tube station, skirting our beggar, who is crouched to one side of the entrance today instead of in his usual spot under the bridge at the end of our road. He has a thick woollen hat pulled down over his face but he has recovered enough since I last saw him to be playing his tin whistle again.

Twenty minutes later, I am looking around the bedsit, accompanied by Patrick, a furtive looking man with brown curly hair and a brown nylon suit, who appears to have extended his aesthetic tastes to the décor of this Victorian house, the hallways of which are all carpeted and curtained in brown and decorated with a nubbly beige paper. The bedsit itself is on the top floor and has one window, which looks straight out on to the side wall of the next property, a sloping roof and a skylight. The floor is divided into two sections, one of which is covered in more of the brown carpet and the other, at the kitchen end of the room, in brown lino with a tile design. An orange curtain hangs lopsidedly at the window and the whole place is, admittedly, utterly depressing, but it is clean enough and tucked away at the top of the house, away from other tenants. I can afford it too, so I sign the flimsy piece of paper that is the tenancy agreement and promise to return tomorrow with cash for my deposit.

It is dark when I step out into the street again and the stars are far out of reach above the tops of the trees which are dotted at intervals along the pavement. I walk back towards the main road, where cars and brightly lit buses are easing forward in fits and starts as the rush hour begins. At the end of the street I turn left towards the tube station, and it is then that I notice the church on the corner. I wonder how I could have missed it before, for though it is set back from the road and built of some kind of dark stone that has sponged up all the traffic fumes and grime of London, it is an imposing structure and its grounds take up the entire corner plot. A light is glowing in its porchway and, feeling that I cannot face going back to the flat yet, I walk up the pathway towards the carved entrance.

When I reach it, I see that the wooden door into the church itself is closed and I hesitate, remembering that churches have to lock their doors to prevent theft these days and not wanting to be seen to be trying my luck, but then there is the thud of footsteps on the other side and the door opens from the inside. A middle-aged woman comes out, followed by a line of chattering children in blue blazers.

'Quietly now, please!' orders the woman, then, 'Sorry!' to me for blocking my way. She chivvies along the last small boy, who is holding a loaf of bread almost as big as his head, in advance of a group of adults, probably the mothers and fathers. I wait until they are all gone, then slip inside.

It is much larger on the inside than I had anticipated. Lights are low in the nave, but my eye is drawn to the little chapels on either side, which are illuminated by shelves of candles flickering at their entrances. I walk towards the nearest one which is more brightly lit than all the others and where a table stands. On it are ten or more shoeboxes, each of which has been covered with paper and then decorated, in a child's hand, with pictures of leaves in autumn shades of red and gold, of nuts and berries and, on one, of an alarmingly ferocious squirrel. Each box contains a little selection of offerings: apples, pears, oranges, a packet of biscuits here, a shop-bought cake and a tin of salmon there. In the middle of the table stands a shiny golden wheatsheaf of bread.

'Harvest Festival,' confirms a voice, making me start. I turn to see a young priest behind me. 'The Salvation Army are collecting the boxes first thing tomorrow,' he explains in an apologetic tone and I realise that he thinks I have sought out this particular chapel to worship, that I might be put out by this temporary arrangement.

'Oh no, it's fine,' I say quickly. 'I'm not . . . ' I make some vague gesture with my hands. 'I'm just . . . looking around,' I say, then feel embarrassed by my clumsy phrasing, which makes me sound like a browser in a shoe shop.

'Of course,' says the priest with a smile and a nod. A minute later I hear the wooden door closing with a heavy clunk and I am alone.

I feel more at ease now because the priest seems to have given me permission to be here. I wander up the nave and into each of the chapels on the right hand side of the church, stopping to read inscriptions like a dutiful tourist: a memorial to the men who died in the Great War, another to those who fell in the Second World War; tombs of people who have been slotted into the walls – presumably because they were important to the church – but whose names mean nothing to me. I return then to the chapel where the children have been celebrating their Harvest Festival, to look again at the stained-glass window above it, which is rather beautiful and which I had been admiring before the priest distracted my attention. I gaze up at it for a minute and as I do so something from the children's table of produce reaches me, a certain smell perhaps, some essence of the past because I feel a wave of sharp, almost painful nostalgia breaking over me and I am remembering the hall of my primary school, the precise aroma of it and the odd way it absorbed the echoes of a hundred pairs of plimsolls, a trestle table at the front also piled up with shoeboxes, this time filled with dusty tins of baked beans and evaporated milk, with blocks of jelly and packet desserts. I look at the little display and the lovingly painted boxes and I suddenly wonder what we are left with when we throw off these annual rituals, childish or otherwise, that pattern our lives, and whether the blankness we are left with is liberation or just a loss.

I move away, over to the left hand side of the church, and only then does it occurs to me that this cannot be a Catholic church because there are no confessional boxes. It is a shame because I would have liked to take a better look at one and now would have been a good time, with nobody here to observe me. All I know about the act of confession has been gleaned from literature or the odd television drama and the idea of popping into one of those wooden phone booths and dialling up God – or, at least, his appointed intermediary – to ask for his opinion has always struck me as a weirdly medieval practice. And, though every Catholic church is clearly equipped for it, I am still not quite sure I believe that it happens. Today though, as I sit in a pew in the dimly lit nave of this empty church, it presents itself in another way. It comes to me that you might approach confession not as a judicial procedure to be endured, as an act of passivity, but as a way of speaking out loud what you are, of hearing how it sounds to your own ears – because it is easy to keep tucking things away, not giving them a name or a shape. And I wonder how cathartic this might be, whether every-thing could be simplified and tidied away if you could just make yourself hear the words with which you, yourself, have just filled the air, actually feel the reverberations of your deeds around you.

A bell strikes somewhere nearby and its doleful tone calls to mind the tolling on the day of Daniel's funeral. I would like to do something for him while I am here, a gesture of some sort, but despite the emptiness of the church I still feel exposed beneath the arch of this nave, so I move across to one of the little chapels instead and stand by the iron railing. There are ways of going about things in church but I can only remember the Lord's Prayer from my schooldays and I cannot bring myself to say this, even in my head, because it seems to have nothing to do with either me or Daniel and if God is anywhere I cannot expect Him to listen to a mere formula. If I am to pray at all I should be starting out with a Dear God, but there is something faintly ludicrous about it, as if I am issuing a lunch invitation. I think of Josie at the funeral, down on her knees, fervently offering herself up in front of everyone, and I am about to abandon the idea of a formal appeal altogether when I see a sign by the candle stand.

A CANDLE IS A PRAYER
(A donation of twenty pence is suggested)

This is something I can manage. I unzip my bag, take out my purse and, finding a twenty-pence piece in the change, drop it into the black metal box attached to the candle stand. Then I take one of the little nightlights from the cardboard box on the floor beside the stand and hold it to another which is already alight. Nothing happens for a second, and then the flame begins to move, wick to wick, and my candle is burning. Carefully, I place it in the middle of the stand, and as the slender bright flame takes hold, I look up at the little statue of Jesus on the altar and softly, in my head, I say, 'Watch over him.' I smile, stand for a moment, watching Daniel's flame burning strong and upright and then something – something that is both within and without me – makes me reach for my purse again, searching for another twenty-pence piece, which I drop, like the previous one, into the slot. I take another candle from the box and I am holding my breath as I stretch my hand towards Daniel's candle. I wait for a sign. The flame leaps up, almost immediately, and I place this second candle next to Daniel's with the words, whispered now: 'Watch over him.' My throat is dry and I can barely swallow, knowing that Jesus's black eyes are watching me from the altar. 'Or her.' I wait. The bell is silent. That is all.

Then I feel it: a falling away of something that has been pressing down on me, and next, an excitement, almost unbearable, flares up in me. And suddenly I don't want to stop. If this works – and it seems to – then I must keep going. My hand goes into my bag again, starts scrabbling madly for my purse. I grab it and start sifting through the change for another twenty-pence piece. I cannot find one so I give up and just snatch up the biggest, brightest coin I can see, but as I do so I hear the heavy door of the church open and then the entrance to the nave floods with prosaic light. I turn to see two women dressed in navy-blue tabards, one of them carrying a plastic box with cleaning products in it.

'Oh!' says the elder of the two, noticing me by the chapel. It is she who has switched on the light. 'I beg your pardon dear, we thought everyone had gone home.'

'Oh no, go ahead,' I say and I step back from the candle stand and smile brightly at them. They return my smile but seem to look at me quizzically too, as if they can sense I have been doing something strange, here in the half-light of the chapel. 'I was just leaving anyway,' I explain as I drop my father's coin back into the pocket of my coat, damned if I'm going to waste a two-pound coin on someone I can't even remember.

I take the tube home, then walk the few streets back towards the flat. In the distance someone is setting off fireworks, even though Bonfire Night is still a few weeks off. I watch the cold coloured stars falling away in a desolate night sky and, out of nowhere, loneliness rushes in on me. I let it come, feeling the textures of it, relishing it almost because it is tinged with elation too. I walk faster then, thinking that I must ring Lottie as soon as I get home because I have let her think that I do not care about her. I do not know what words I will use to show her otherwise but I am sure they will come because somehow goodness has found its way inside me tonight. Our beggar is walking towards me as I pass under the railway bridge. He is swaying slightly and he seems to have lost his hat during the day for his shaggy hair falls in clumps around his face and shoulders now. I could cross the road without appearing to be deliberately avoiding him, but the two-pound coin is still in my pocket and I would like to share something of my lonely elation with someone, if only for a moment or two. I slow down, reach into my pocket and find the coin and then hold it out to him but he doesn't see because he never looks up, just keeps walking right at me until he cannot help but see my feet in front of his. He makes to walk round me then but at that same moment the smell of him reaches me – stale urine and unwashed clothes – and I change my mind about giving him the money and try to sidestep him in the same direction.

'Sorry,' I say in my friendliest tones, moving aside again to unblock his pathway.

Some kind of mad noise escapes from him, a growl almost, and then he lifts his head and the black, enraged eyes of Jesus stare straight into mine.

'Cunt,' he says.

Something in me breaks.

CHAPTER 13

It is Helena and The Stetson who call my mother because I was crying for her, she tells me much later, sobbing like a little child. They went right into my room and found my address book and then telephoned her and she came straight away and took over with the calm efficiency of a doctor's wife, knowing just what needed to be done. And it is to the graceful rooms of her garden flat that I come when the hospital has finally finished with me, here that I spend a quiet Christmas and the early months of the new year, walking in the park beneath trees that stand like skeletons against the grey sky, and beginning to read again. My mother continues her life as normal, busy with her part-time work in a local art gallery, her lunches and theatre trips with friends (who treat me with careful kindness yet clearly view me as another species), but she continues to monitor me with a quiet vigilance. I am calm now, almost happy at times, though my world is so small. It is enough for a winter.

*   *   *

My mother never asks what happened to me and after a time I stop steeling myself for when she does, remembering that it is not her way. Her love arrives in other forms: a beautifully cooked meal to reawaken my appetite, a theatre programme to read or a new hardback she has seen reviewed. I accept everything she offers but ask nothing of anyone else, for my skin still feels new and tender and I do not want the world to touch me. Lottie calls every few days and there is the occasional phonecall or e-mail from someone

I knew before, which I never return. One day Helena rings to see how I am and to invite me to her wedding in the autumn. I find myself surprisingly moved by this.

*   *   *

March rushes in, wet and windy, and we keep the fire lit in the living-room most days. Then one morning I awake and spring has arrived. The air has a new, pellucid quality, as if you have just blinked and the soft green buds on the trees and the spikes of grass, dew-wet, in the park have been pulled into sharper focus. Birds sing jubilantly, clowning in the trees above my head, and I return to the flat from my walk feeling unsettled, unable to concentrate on my book or anything else for the rest of the day until night closes in and I feel safe again.

*   *   *

My mother must notice the restlessness that has invaded me because a few days later she asks me whether I have thought about what I am going to do next. I am startled by the directness of the question because till now we have just let the days unroll themselves and not questioned how I am to fill them until they have arrived on the doorstep, and even then we have divided them up into manageable, invalid-like portions: a walk in the morning, a doctor's appointment in the early afternoon.

'I haven't decided,' I say, suddenly tremulous.

My mother helps herself to salad and says nothing and I begin to think the conversation is finished, but then she continues: 'Only I've been thinking you could have the old house. Just until you're completely well again.' I ponder her words for a moment until I understand that she is talking about our old cottage in Broadgate. 'It's not a long-term solution, of course,' she continues, 'and I don't suppose you'd want to be there for more than a few months, but I wondered whether some sea air might do you good . . . ' I smile inadvertently at her idea of a rest cure, thinking how Jane Austen-ish she can be at times. 'The house has been empty for months now – it seems to be harder and harder to find suitable tenants these days – and Harry's just had it repainted after . . . '

'What's Harry got to do with it?' I ask, puzzled.

'He handles the tenancies for me. I thought you knew that.'

'No. You never mentioned it. Didn't you have an agency or something, I seem to remember?' Fretfulness enters my voice. My mother is trying to help me, but I feel as if once again I am about to be ousted from a safe place.

'Yes, but they were hopeless and eventually Harry offered to look after the house for me. He used to do the repairs as well, though now he's so busy with the shop . . . '

'What shop?' I say, growing resentful that she has never thought to share any of this information with me before now.

'Didn't you know that he has his own shop now, a little gallery? It's just on the High Street apparently.' She responds to my ignorance with surprise, as if she's expected me to have absorbed these facts by some kind of osmosis.

'You've never visited then?'

'Oh no,' she says shaking her head. Shaking off the past.

'But I have to get back to work. To pay you some rent for all these months for a start.'

'Don't be ridiculous,' says my mother. 'Who else is supposed to look after you if I don't?' She surveys me with a critical eye. 'I really can't see you being fit enough for work just yet, but I quite understand that you wouldn't want to stay here for ever.'

The last few months seem to have eroded any vestiges of pride. I want to say that of course I do, that I am far too fragile to be allowed out into the world again.

'You've your grandfather's money if you want it, you

know,' she continues. 'Why not give yourself a few more months, just to be sure that you're quite well again?'

'I thought the money was supposed to be for when, and if, I get married?'

My mother gives a dismissive wave of her hand. 'Well, yes, but it's at my discretion and I think now is as good a time as any. I believe your grandfather would have understood. He had a breakdown himself, you know.'

'Really?' I know very little about my mother's father other than that he was a surgeon at the hospital where my mother also worked as a secretary when she left school, and where she met my father when he was a junior doctor; and that he inherited money from his mother's side. 'Why? What happened to him?'

'Oh, I don't know exactly,' says my mother. 'These things weren't discussed so much then. I just remember visiting him in some dreadful old place with high walls and lots of locked doors. It was my mother that pulled him through in the end. She was utterly indomitable, you know, decided that they weren't helping him in there and so she brought him home and simply wouldn't let him give up on himself.' She lays down her knife and fork and sips at a glass of wine. 'It's not as if I need the rent for the old house, you know. As it happens, I'd been thinking about selling it altogether – I'm not really sure why I've kept it all these years – and Harry would be close by if you needed anything . . .'

'I'll think about it,' I say.

My mother is right. I can no longer hide here under low winter skies. The evenings begin to stretch themselves out and spring is pricking at my skin every day, prodding at something in me that does not want to awaken but cannot help itself. In the park, the folded shoots of hostas are pushing their way up through the ground, pink and exposed. I do not know where else I should be, but I have used up all the comfort that is to be found here. I take a tube journey down to the river one day, stand on the Embankment and look along the river as far as I can see. In my mind's eye I see beyond its curves to where the river widens, the water spreading itself out and the banks retreating farther and farther. I open my mouth, feel the wind on my tongue, imagine the clean, sour taste of salt air.

PART THREE

CHAPTER 14

I cannot hear the sea when I come out of the station. I have
no memory of being able to do so in the past, but this has
not prevented me from imagining it that way. Two seagulls
circle above me and my suitcase, their cries echoing
mournfully across a vast, blue bowl of sky, and I remember
how much I disliked them, how, as a child, I was repulsed
by their big muscular looking bodies and pitiless eyes.

The Market Square and High Street look exactly the
same until you get up close and realise that Broadgate has
reinvented itself. My mother tells me that it has become
fashionable with Londoners in recent times – that there
was a feature in one of the Sunday supplements a few weeks
ago, about the beach huts being sold at extortionate prices
to be used as weekend retreats – and you can see the
evidence of this already. Here, where the hardware store
used to be on the corner of the Market Square, is a shop
selling expensive yachting clothes, a full-page spread from a
lifestyle magazine displayed among the chunky-knit jumpers in the window and a model of a sailing boat tacking
towards the rolled-up linen trouser-legs of a blank-faced
male mannequin. And as I walk along the High Street I
pass a wine bar, then a delicatessen where, I think, the
launderette used to be, its window displaying white dishes
filled with marinated olives like glossy black eggs, dried
hams and salamis, and a bowl of buffalo mozzarellas
swimming in their milky bath, then a sandwich bar, several
bistros with chalked-up menus displaying seafood specials,
a vegetarian café and a Thai restaurant. The second-hand

bookshop is still a bookshop but the trestle tables outside are gone and the old windows have been replaced with heavy plate glass that gleams in the spring sunshine. The exterior has been freshly painted in sea-blue and a selection of recent literary fiction is displayed against a deeper blue silk background in the window. I do not see Harry's gallery anywhere on this stretch of the High Street and then I recall my mother saying something about its being next to the charity shop where she used to work, in the stretch of High Street beyond the Market Square.

Remnants of the old Broadgate remain though: the woolshop still has the kind of window display I remember from my childhood: two hand-knitted cardigans, one in sugar pink, the other in primrose, pinned out on card-board backing as if the wearers have suddenly become invisible halfway through a jaunty ballet performance. Fanned out beneath them, as an afterthought, are three balls of tomato-red wool. Featherstone's Ladies' Fashions has somehow survived and in its large glass frontage stand two mannequins with matt-beige skin, staring haughtily out at passers-by, static in their Crimplene pleated skirts, pussy-bow blouses and fitted jackets, each with a patent black handbag hooked over a mummified arm. I notice that the tips of their patent court shoes are faintly speckled with dust.

Past all this I go, pulling my suitcase-on-wheels as if I am crossing the anonymous space of an airport foyer. I walk briskly, for, though I know it is ludicrous to imagine that anyone might recognise me after all this time, I feel exposed here, want to realign myself in the safety of the house as soon as possible. I come to my father's old surgery next, which looks much as I remember it, a squat dark-bricked building, though the space in front of it has been tarmacked and divided up by fresh white lines with several of the spaces reserved for the doctors' vehicles. Opposite the surgery, Kentons is no longer Kentons but has been taken over by one of the larger supermarket chains. I recall how much my mother despised Kentons and how she would have welcomed this change when we still lived here.

Where the wasteground used to be, a new estate has been built. Looking down the side road that runs off from this part of the High Street, I can still make out the spire of the Catholic church, and the priest's house, the presbytery, but a curve of detached houses with their own driveways now blocks most of the view. Fronting the High Street itself are more houses, built of the same rust-red brick but pushed closer together, each with its own strip of grass at the front divided by a neat concrete pathway. Beyond these, and built in the same brick again, is a square block of flats, three storeys high, each flat having two small windows facing the road and a narrow balcony. Washing hangs on short lines, flapping in the breeze, and here and there a pot plant or a window-box brightens a window. Beyond the flats I can see a patch of grass where a solitary plastic football sits.

In my mind, the old house is farther along the road, and I am still looking across at the new estate – thinking about the trees and the old orchard and how long it must have taken to scrape the ground down to a bare canvas, wondering whether the new residents realise that snaking beneath their living-rooms and neatly laid patios is a nest of great tree roots – when I come upon it. Here it stands, the same faded pink and yellow crazy paving leading up to the front door, though my mother's cottage plants are gone, replaced by what estate agents call a low-maintenance garden, which amounts to a dwarf hedge and the twigs of a few unremarkable shrubs poking up through some gravel. I walk up the pathway and take the key from my pocket.

Pushing the door to behind me, I step inside and walk along the echoing hallway into the kitchen first. Then I realise that I am not the only person with a key to this house because there are two cardboard boxes sitting on the table. In the first of these, I find a loaf of bread, some eggs, tea, a carton of milk, some butter, a bottle of wine, and a note, which I open.

Dear Katie,

Thought you might need these to get you started. Your mother asked me to have the place cleaned (again!) and to replace the mattresses, crockery, cutlery, etc. – which has all been done. Couple of new duvets and some pillows in the airing cupboard too. (Afraid the garden's still a mess though.) The notebook by the boiler explains the central heating, hot water, etc. The other box is from your mother.

Love Harry

I smile at the note, grateful for Harry's thoughtfulness, though I hope he will understand that I have come here to learn how to be alone again. I am well enough now to be shamed by my months of dependence on others, and it is disconcerting to realise that I am still considered incapable of making such arrangements for myself (though it is true that I have given them no thought until now, have launched myself towards the sea in a vague trusting way, taking little notice of my mother's chatter about practical matters).

In a kitchen drawer, I find a knife, which I use to slice through the tape on the second box. Inside are sheets, pillowcases and several duvet covers, all in thick creamy-white cotton. I pull them out, layer by beautifully folded layer, smiling when I find that my mother has included a linen tablecloth and six napkins, as if she imagines I will be entertaining here. As I lift each piece from the box, the scent of her rises up at me, a mixture I have always known, of clean laundry, soap and old-fashioned French perfume, and I find myself gathering up great armfuls of the heavy material and burying my face in its cool comforting depths.

I leave the boxes where they are, and my suitcase beside them, while I explore the house. All the rooms downstairs have been painted white and each has the same speckled cream carpet, except the kitchen where there is pale grey vinyl on the floor and where the yellow, knotted pine I remember has been stripped out and replaced with functional white units. I try to remember how everything used to be and find that I cannot recall very much in detail, though I remember the soft crunch of newly washed scatter rugs beneath bare feet and my mother's fondness for soft furnishings – the splashes of pure colour from the cushion covers and bright curtains that she made herself in those days, sitting at her sewing machine at the kitchen table, her foot working at the grey, ridged pedal, hands guiding lengths of material beneath the hammering needle. But the house is blank and clean – I can smell the damp, soapy smell of carpet shampoo lingering in the air – and I am relieved to realise, almost immediately, that I will be able to breathe freely here.

I go out into the hallway again, eager to explore upstairs, and it is then, when I lay my hand on the rounded, grooved wood of the banister, that I am suddenly jolted by the past, feel it emanating from the scratched varnished wood as if it had absorbed something of each of us back then – a little warmth from our young hands perhaps, some essence of who we were – and retained it all these years. I look up to the top of the stairs, to the carved finial which still adorns the banister and which is peculiarly grandiose for what is, after all, little more than a seaside cottage, and for just a moment I could be ten years old again and flying towards these stairs, with Lottie in pursuit.

Once I have actually ascended the stairs I find little else to remind me of my childhood. In my old bedroom, I stand still and hold my breath, listening for the pulse of the past within these bare walls, but though the architecture of those window frames – the side window with the metal lever and the top casement window with the paint thickening and crusting around the edges of the glass – seems deeply familiar to me, like examining a part of my own body, nothing comes, and the view from the window has changed because the lawn and the garden that my mother made are gone, darkened by heavy, overhanging tree boughs and a mad tangle of dried weeds and interwoven shrubs that thrust upwards, fighting for the new light and air of spring. In the distance I can see where the sky turns darker blue, taking up the tints of the invisible sea like blotting paper.

I decide that I will sleep in my mother's old room since it is the only bedroom with curtains. Other than the metal bedstead, it is free of furniture and, like the rest of the rooms in the house, is painted and carpeted in white and cream. I find the new pillows and a duvet in the airing cupboard, then run back down to the kitchen to fetch the box of linen. I make up the bed, smoothing over the pillows and the sheets in my mother's way. I am pleased with the look of the bed when I am done, but it is only when I come back upstairs with my suitcase with the intention of hanging my clothes in the built-in cupboard, that I look around the room and realise that I have found my clean white space.

I follow the instructions in the notebook and manage to heat enough water for a bath. Then I cook a quick supper, which I eat in the kitchen, thinking that tomorrow I will shop at the new supermarket for anything I need. There is a moment when the silence here frightens me – the metal clink of my knife and fork returning to me from the blank walls, unmodified – and I consider whether I should buy a radio or a portable television, but almost immediately I realise that I do not want clamour and confusion disturbing this air. In the living-room, I sit on the sofa and drink half of the bottle of wine that Harry left for me, and then I slide the door bolts into place and turn out the lights, trying to memorise the positions of switches as I do so. Lying naked in my new bed, I wonder how it is that I found my way here without even trying.

A party going on nearby awakes me. I am accustomed to the noise of a city at night, but once I have registered the sound of voices and music carrying on the air, it seems harder than usual to push them to the edges of my consciousness. I could shut the window but in recent months I have become almost obsessive about the need for air while I sleep. The moon is almost full tonight and it blazes through the window and across my crumpled bed linen. I lie, half-awake, for what seems like an hour, beginning to panic myself by thinking that I have not done this for months now, not since those weeks in the flat before everything crumbled. The memory of this makes me impatient with myself and I get out of bed and reach for the thick cardigan I took off earlier. I wrap it around me, tying the belt loosely around my waist and, without switching on any lights, begin to pad around the house again in the shadows, feeling my way along the walls and then down the stairs.

There is something that I am trying to find here as I slink, cat-like, between the moonlight and the shadows, from room to room, something that almost exists here in the living-room, in the dark bulk of that sofa and the two chairs that could, in this light, be our old furniture, might still bear the imprints and the warmth of our bodies. I wonder if Daniel left anything of himself here and, trying to spook myself, if he ever comes looking for it. But there is no fear to be had here in the dark. I make tea for myself in the kitchen and sit and drink it until I begin to long for the warmth of bed again. I go back upstairs and read for an hour or so and then car doors start to slam and laughter and goodbyes puncture the air and silence falls.

I awake again, some time later, with the covers kicked loose and the moon shining down on to my body, giving my skin an unearthly glow. Nothing disturbs the night now and when I go to the window and look out I can see no signs of life near by. Then, just across the street, a square of brightness flashes up, someone switching on the light in one of the flats. The high thin wail of a very young baby, the sound that must have awoken me this time, finds its way across the darkness to me. I listen, thinking that the cries will soon cease, because the tiny creature producing them must surely use up its energy soon, but instead of dying away they escalate and after a few minutes one furious scream is rolling into another. I pull on my cardigan and bundle up my duvet and a pillow, then make my way down the landing to my old room, at the back of the house, where I spread out the bedding on the single bed. I cross to the window, to open it, but the catch is stiff and I have to jiggle at it for a moment. A flake of paint falls, and it squeaks, then suddenly gives, swinging wide as the breeze catches it. I feel the cool night air sliding languorously in, give a little shiver and pull the cardigan more tightly around me. Then I lean out of the window and breathe deeply, listening for the sound I have been waiting for. It comes from beyond the black trees: the soft hush-hush of the unchanging sea.

CHAPTER 15

The thudding bounces off the walls of the house and makes me stiffen, but it is only Harry at the door, come to tell me that the telephone engineer will call this afternoon to reconnect the line. He is thinner than when I last saw him but at least he has lost that shrunken look he had at Daniel's funeral. He waits on the doorstep expectantly so I suggest going somewhere for coffee, which makes him laugh because this is Broadgate, not London, and it is only just gone eight o' clock. I understand then that the thing to do would be to invite him in, so I make tea because there is no coffee and we sit at the kitchen table and discover how to talk to each other again, now that he is almost an old man and I am no longer a child.

The years between then and now are dense mazes, too full of dead ends and diversions to be turned into easy narrative, so we wander around the edges of things: how Lottie is doing these days, whether there is anything I require seeing to in the house, where to buy any extra furniture I might want. I am at pains to assure Harry that I am quite capable of seeking out what little I need (and, though I do not say this, I have no intention of sullying these clean spaces with clutter). Then I ask him about his shop and he tells me about it, and the new one he's about to open in Canterbury. Out of politeness, I say that I must come and see the shop soon and he looks pleased about this and says he'll be there all day today, if I want to drop by. He glances at his watch and says he ought to be there now, in fact, so I see him to the door and he thanks me for the tea. As I watch him go, away towards the centre of town, I see what it is about him that has changed: although Harry's manner and his voice are as spirited as ever, he has lost that exuberant quality in his movement, the way he used to spring through a door as if sure that something good and exciting was waiting for him on the other side.

Later that morning, I leave the house to itself and step out into the Saturday Broadgate of my childhood: a tabby cat blinking at me from a backdrop of net curtain and china figurines, the air smugly undisturbed other than by the faint squawk of a children's television programme coming from the window of one of the flats. Farther along the High Street there is movement though: a boy in a long white apron is washing down the pavement in front of one of the bistros, his broom swishing the sudded water into the gutter and outside the butcher's a man is shouldering half a pig from the back of a van, where a row of carcasses display the clean red arches of their abdominal cavities. The boy in the apron says good-morning to me and the man with the carcasses nods as I pass and I am reminded of how far I am from London where there are none of these neighbourly little incursions into your day that, inconsequential though they may be in their own right, can add up to some kind of diminishment of your privacy. In the Market Square, I stop to look at the Anglican church, which has now had the hole in its tower filled in with putty-coloured stone, and then steer a path among the vans and cars which line the square and browse around beneath the blue-striped awnings. There are the usual fruit and vegetable stalls, a fishmonger's and the warm bloody smell of a butcher's, together with stalls selling local cheeses and olives and preserves and another where great bundles of fresh herbs – coriander, basil and flat-leaf parsley, purple sage and sorrel – are being set out, still damp from their plastic wrapping.

I recognise Harry's pictures instantly: a view of Broadgate beach; sailing boats in the marina. And I remember how I used to love watching the definite strokes of his brush, pulling familiar scenes out of blank canvas like magic. It is a mistake that I am here though. My promise to visit the shop had been a mere courtesy and, imagining it to be much farther along this stretch of the High Street than this, I had intended to turn back well before I reached it. I am about to walk away, when Harry himself nips out of the door, looking delighted to see me, and before I can do anything about it, I am inside the shop, having to be interested, and he is putting the kettle on to make coffee.

Other than the two pictures in the window, the remainder of the work on display on the ground floor (for there is a set of wooden steps leading up to another gallery) is clearly the product of other hands. While he washes out two mugs, Harry explains that the main part of his business is selling on behalf of other artists, all of them local and many, he adds with a wry smile, younger than him.

'Some of these are rather beautiful,' I say, eyeing a painting of a female torso on the wall above me.

'Yes,' says Harry, coming across to look. 'Our customers have rather more sophisticated tastes these days . . . ' He glances at his own pictures in the window with open disdain. 'Still manage to flog a few of these from time to time though, when the coach tours pull in for a rest stop. Not that they sit very well with everything else.'

'But it's good that you're still painting,' I say, trying to sound encouraging, though I can see exactly why he feels so little affection for these lifeless exercises.

'That's old work, as it happens. I've a stockpile of 'em through there.' He points through to a darkened backroom where I can see stacks of frames. 'I've hardly painted anything myself in the last few years.'

'Oh?' I say because I can't think of anything better.

'I suppose I just woke up one day and decided that I was sick of churning out second-rate tourist fodder,' says Harry with a shrug.

'That's a shame,' I say. Harry raises his eyebrows, laughs at my dissemblance.

'Not really. Have you decided how long you're staying?' he says, suddenly changing tack. I cannot help recoiling a little at this sudden enquiry, aware that Harry and I are not, after all, casual acquaintances. My mother may well have told him why I am here, in which case he must view me as some kind of feeble, recuperating creature, unable to function in its own environment.

'I don't know yet,' I say coldly, accepting the coffee he hands me and walking around the shop for a second time in order to avoid his eye. 'For the summer at most. I really will have to get back to work again after that,' I add, in case he fails to grasp the gaping hole that my absence has left in the London employment market. I try to think of a good reason for my being here, some solid plans for the weeks ahead of me, but everything that comes into my head sounds like nothing and when I try to visualise myself walking on the beach or reading in the garden, I see myself as a nothingness too, a gossamer creature, and I wonder what is left of me when you take away the structure of work and the shapes into which other people have tried to mould me.

Ashamed of my lack of substance, I speak without thinking, trying to breathe a life into myself by adopting a hearty tone: 'Of course, I'm going to tackle the garden,' I say. 'It badly needs it.'

'That would please your mother,' replies Harry, and then says that it's a pity it's been allowed to get into that kind of state, but the tenants were only ever bound to keep it tidy, and the last tenant couldn't even manage that. I am about to say that the old garden must still be there beneath all that chaos, waiting to be found again, when the door opens and Cheryl, the woman who manages the shop for Harry, comes in and he is caught up straight away in yesterday's business and a customer who wants a picture shipped to the States. I wait for a pause in the conversation so that I can tell him I should be going, but he is picking up the phone, and he and Cheryl are discussing packaging while he waits to be connected, so I take my coffee and go up the stairs to the little gallery on the first floor, wondering if I ought to buy something while I am here.

The gallery has two windows, almost the height of the room, and light is streaming in through them. I wander around, stop to look at a piece of twisted, bubbled blue-green glass, which has been polished until it gleams and which wouldn't take up too much space in the house, and then I notice a small oil painting at the far end of the room. I go to it, bending over to look more closely. It is entitled 'Storm Coming' and depicts a bay that may or may not be Broadgate, with a string of black rocks running out, dominating the bay. Beneath the rocks is a flat sea, a deep, unhealthy shade of green and with some ominous quality about its glassy surface. Above the shoreline is a strip of blue, but a heavy sky presses down on the horizon, streaked with purple and brown like a bruise, and a black cloud jags over the end of the rocks, looking as though it might clamp down at any moment, like the top half of a jaw, on the small figure of a fisherman who sits at the heart of the painting, unaware of his vulnerability, spotlit by a single ray of sun that has penetrated the cloud. There is something oppressive about the whole painting and it is less than comfortable to look at, but at the same time, compelling. The fisherman has blond hair.

'Cheery, don't you think?' says Harry, coming up behind me.

'This is yours, isn't it?' I say, though I know the answer.

'Yes, I wasn't being entirely truthful earlier. I painted this one, and few others in a similar vein, a couple of months ago, just after Dan died. Not sure if it will sell though.'

I nod, understanding what he means, because it is not

the sort of picture you might buy when you are in holiday mood and, small as it is, I can see how it might dominate any room in which it was placed. Then I say something about shopping and organising the house and Harry follows me downstairs, chatting on to me and to Cheryl, and I remember then something my mother said once, about Harry being friends with everyone, and can see how this might be, because it is easy to warm to his quick laughter and the way he speaks so easily, as if conversation is something organic to him. I hesitate at the doorway, because I have been moved by the painting and I feel I have not said enough. The words that come have nothing to do with it.

'It's funny to think you could have been my stepfather,' I say. 'Once, I mean.'

Harry gives a wry grin, lifts a hand in greeting to the driver of a van which has just pulled up and says: 'Lucky escape for you then!' and wanders off to help unload the delivery.

*   *   *

The house and I grow used to one another. I have bought a few items for the kitchen and the bathroom, and visited the bookshop where I select some new fiction, some classics to reread and, on a whim, a copy of *Swallows and Amazons*. These are sitting in a pile beside the sofa and I am beginning to work my way through them. The telephone line has been connected now and I receive a couple of calls from my mother and one from Lottie who, though I have not invited her, promises to visit, but I make no calls myself. The weather has turned unseasonably warm and I get up early each morning and run along the beach because this seems to be the sort of thing that people do when they are by the sea – indeed, there are usually at least a couple of other joggers out at the same time each day, mostly elderly men in tracksuits, moving their limbs cautiously out of a slow walk, as though wary of breaking them, who have started to greet me as we pass. I return to the house, shower, make breakfast and settle down to read for the rest of the morning.

Later in the day, I walk for miles, down to the marina and then along the new coastal trail that starts from here; or, if I am feeling particularly lazy, back along the length of Broadgate beach. One day I take the pathway across the rocks and walk right round to the beach in Moreland Bay, where I look for the entrance to the caves where Josie took us that day. I cannot see it at first and then I spot it, a darkness in the cliff-face, and I walk away from the water's edge and stand at the entrance, peering into the darkness for some minutes. Then I walk on, keeping up a rhythmic, fast pace, enough to feel my heart beating, all the way to the end of Moreland Bay itself and then home again. In the early evenings, I buy food and, because the supermarket always seems to have run out of newspapers by that time, go next door to the little newsagent's. This is how I learn that Harry has been talking to people because the elderly lady behind the counter looks closely at me one day and says that I must be Dr Matheson's girl, starts telling me what a good doctor he was and what a shame it was, and that I look just like my mother did, and I pretend to have some vague memory of who she is and excuse myself as quickly as possible before she starts asking questions. I return home, eat alone at the kitchen table (the tablecloth and six napkins are sitting in neat folds in the airing cupboard) and read in bed until I fall asleep.

Though he is busy with the new shop, Harry finds time to drop in once or twice to see if anything needs doing, and sometimes we bump into one another in town. Thus by a gradual process I learn more about his life here: that he has a house of his own now, at the far end of town overlooking the recreation ground, that he lives there alone, although it is clear that he shared it with someone else at one time. I wonder about Cheryl, the manager at the shop, but when I hint at it, Harry tells me she is recently divorced and determinedly single, though I cannot help suspecting there is some history between them. We are talking outside the butcher's one day when a young woman passes and just for a moment I mistake her for Gina, old Mrs Harvey's daughter, and then realise that she cannot possibly be. She is, Harry tells me, Gina's eldest daughter, the child who was swelling Gina's stomach that last summer we were here. Then he says that Gina is dead – from eclampsia with her second child – that she is buried in the churchyard where her husband still lays flowers every Sunday. That night in bed, I imagine her lying there, swathed in her purple maternity dress, her ripe body falling away to nothing. Except for Harry, no one else comes to my door.

*   *   *

I have been happy, in an unobtrusive way, these past two weeks, waking to silence and spring sunshine turning the bare walls of the house to primrose, so I do not know why it is that today should feel any different, except perhaps that I did not sleep well last night with the baby in the flats crying for longer than usual. Or maybe it is some niggling awareness that it is a Monday morning, the start of the week, and all the weekend visitors are gone, back to their purposeful lives. Elsewhere cities are stirring and people are moving through the morning with a sense of purpose; other existences, rich and vigorous beside mine. Overnight, I have somehow become uncomfortable with this invalid kind of life and I lie between the heavy sheets, a sense of panic beginning to accumulate in the pit of my stomach as the questions I have been avoiding for weeks come at me with a new determination: What will I do? Where will I go?

The unsettled feeling persists after I return from my run. I try to read but I cannot concentrate on my book and eventually I put it aside, pull on my trainers again and walk back down to the beach, hoping that more activity will help to shake the uneasiness out of my bones. But the day feels wrong all round: the air on the beach is static and too hot for the time of year, and the sky above me is high and empty. A small fishing boat has been pulled up on the shingle, farther down the beach, and it lies there immobile, blue paint flaking in the sun. Even the sea seems at odds with itself, slapping against the shore in enervated little waves and flattening out completely a yard or two from the shore. An elderly couple are perched on a rock at the back of the beach, their faces turned up to the sun. They do not move, brown skin coarsened by age, fossilised bones.

I step out along the shore, trying to invest myself with some energy. The turnstones stop fussing at the water's edge as I approach and the shingle crackles beneath my feet, proving that my body has mass, but still I have a sense of disappearing, of walking out of myself almost, becoming less real as I move between this wedge of land, this wedge of sky. I see myself through the eyes of the old people on the rock, becoming smaller and smaller as I move away along the water's edge. I try to breathe deeply, but the air is liquid and warm, does not shock my lungs to life in the way that it does when I run in the early morning. And it is as well that I am quite alone because suddenly I find myself giving a little moan of panic and sinking down on to the shingle, as if trying to reconnect myself with something relatively solid.

The little girl does not hear my moan or the slow deep breaths I am taking in order to calm myself. She is too intent on reaching the water, pounding past me on legs that have just started to elongate out of toddler chubbiness, slithering over the shingle and sand. When she gets to the water's edge she does not care about the half-heartedness of the waves, just hops out of her shoes, rolls off her short white socks and runs straight in with a gleeful yell. The cold green water closes around her feet as she splashes away from the beach and I check over my shoulder, sure that she cannot be alone. A young woman with long tawny-brown hair stands on the shingle at the back of the beach. Two pink legs project like chicken wings from the baby sling she is wearing.

'Daisy! That's far enough now!' calls the girl. Her voice is low, only reaches us because the air is so still, but the child has stopped wading out now and is bending down, hair, a good few shades lighter than her mother's, falling forwards over her shoulders, peering into the shallow water. She hovers, quite still, and then her hand darts down into the water and she lifts something up to the sunlight in a shower of glittering drops – a shell. She holds it in the palm of her hand, turning it over as she examines it, and then she is gazing down into the water again, searching for another, her little hand plunging down through the surface when she finds what she is looking for, and all the time keeping up a running commentary to herself which I cannot quite make out from where I am sitting, can just hear the rise and fall of her voice, the lilt of delight when she finds something worthwhile.

Soon she wades back towards the beach, the hem of her pink T-shirt (the front of which is stained with what looks like chocolate) held out to form a hammock. As she reaches the edge, a wave, slighter stronger than the others, hits the back of her calves just as she is trying to toss her thick curling hair out of her eyes. She sways for a moment, trying to hold her balance and then a stream of shells and shining pebbles slithers out of one side of the T-shirt hammock, sliding over her cotton skirt and plopping back down into the water.

'Oh, you pests!' she berates them in a strange, chirping little voice. She feels my eyes on her then.

'Hello,' I say and two grave eyes stay fixed on me. I try a smile, but a breath of wind ruffles her hair and she springs to life, not, I think, fearful of me, just intent on scrambling back over the shingle towards her mother who is on her feet, beckoning now. I watch her go, her feet planting into the shingle as she runs, leaving dips like little shovel marks on the surface of the beach. She joins her mother and the baby, whose legs are kicking in the sling now, and I wonder if they have come from one of the glossily painted huts that line the back of the beach and have crisp curtains in gingham or sea-blue and wooden verandas with plants growing in olive-oil cans.

I sit for a few minutes longer, remembering the child's bare, shoe-pale feet stepping confidently out into the water, her small, sure hands feeling among the pebbles and the shells, think how perfectly she seemed to fit between the sea and the sky and whether this is how I might have appeared to an observer when I was a child and this same beach was my playground. And then I think that it is not surprising that I have felt myself disappearing because I never touch anything, have just walked across surfaces without connecting to anything, and then the unease with which I awoke suddenly engulfs me and I am sickened by my pallid, bloodless excuse for a life.

I must do something, *anything*, rather than sit here with myself, and I find myself on my feet again, walking swiftly back along the beach, up on to to the pathway behind the beach huts. All the way home I do not drop my pace, pushed on by something outside of myself, and when I reach the house, I go in the front door and walk straight to the far end of the hallway, where I unbolt the back door and step outside again. Out on the patio, I look around, properly this time, searching for a spade or some kind of garden implement that I can use. I can see none and there is no shed where something of the sort might be stored, but I step off the patio anyway and wade through the long rough grass towards one of the walls, where, I recall, there was once a flower border. When I reach it, I drop to my knees, breathing hard, and start to scrabble through the brambles and the tangled blanket of last year's weeds until my hands meet the rough earth. I dig my nails in then, push my fingers hard into the damp earth, tearing through the undergrowth, jamming them downwards and then round until I have a good handful, which I ease up slowly: a flaking, misshapen clod, the same rich black earth which my mother nurtured so carefully, digging in sackfuls of compost, year after year. I hold it up to the sunlight. A shiny pink worm glints, tries to bend its raw looking flesh back into the darkness.

CHAPTER 16

Lottie wants me to send photographs of all things, certain that she will be able to lift something of our past from them, though I insist that there is little here she would recognise. She runs through a list of names next, people she thinks might still be living here and whom, she assures me, I must remember. I tell her briefly about Harry, and about Gina, then invent a knock at the door. I replace the receiver and listen to the silence that comes.

I no longer run on the beach in the mornings. Instead I go straight out into the garden where I hack at the roots of weeds, grasp their dew-slimy stalks and twist their tough fibres till I can wrench them up from the earth. In the corner of the patio, a great pile of them accumulates, ready to be put into rubbish sacks. I am using the tools I found at the back of the cupboard under the stairs: a large spade, a fork and a bluntish hoe, and I have supplemented them with a sharp new pair of secateurs and some shears which I bought, along with a thick pair of gardening gloves which I always forget to wear, from the DIY shop in Braxtable. Harry, practical as ever, has pitched in with an old-fashioned rotary lawnmower.

I garden brutally for this is all I know – and, fortunately, it is what is required right now – slashing back or heaving out anything that gets in my way: leggy shrubs that have fallen across the patio or crossed the vague line where I think the edge of the lawn might once have been, brambles which snag around my feet or tear my skin, clumps of rough-textured grass that have embedded themselves in the soil and which cut the flesh of my palms when I pull them up. I work fast once I have started on a particular project, not resting until I have finished, sweat running down my temples and into my eyes. The joints in my arms, shoulders and wrists have been jarred by the constant digging and the earth dries on me, sucking the moisture from my skin, so that by the end of the day my hands are parched and lined, like an old woman's.

When, eventually, I have cleared enough space, I heave the lawnmower through the long grass, backwards and forwards, up and down, until something like a lawn runs down the middle of the garden again, a bare green surprise like a newly shaven face. The grass looks rather odd, bent and whorled in places, and there are vivid green patches of moss here and there, springy like new carpet.

Towards the back of the garden, where the larger trees have been left to their own devices, my task becomes more difficult. Here there are pliant young branches which snap back behind me as I pass and great patches of nettles. I ease my way round thorny shrubs and step on dark, rotting things which collapse and squidge beneath my feet and might be the remains of last year's fruit or fungi. There is no foliage on the trees yet – just furred buds fattening themselves in readiness – but some of the branches are so intertwined above my head that they cut out the light and muffle sound so that you could be in a cave or in the depths of a forest.

I move around this part of the garden without method, just going where my eye draws me, and it is here that I like working best, for though the rest of the garden is private enough (my only neighbour being the old man next door, who, I am told by the lady in the newsagent's, is virtually bedridden and whose daughter has to come once a day to see to him), there is something hushed and secretive about this spot. I like to crouch down as I work, quietly taking in the woody, earthy smells of last year's leaves and the clean scent that rises from the damp chocolatey soil as it gives beneath my boots. When I need to stretch my legs, I stand and lean against the oak tree, pressing my cheek against its thick trunk, against the rough comfort of its bark.

One day I scrape back wet leaves and find the corner of the concrete base where my father's greenhouse once stood and where my mother used to arrange her pots, and I set about clearing this. It takes me a good hour to hack my way through the snarled grasses and a vicious bramble that covers it, but finally the flat grey surface is exposed, like a smooth gravestone in a wooded vault. I have a sudden urge to lie down upon it, to spread my arms across its width and point my toes towards its base and gaze up through the tangle of branches above. I think then that I will have to hire a tree surgeon at some point because I cannot deal with all these thick boughs jutting out in the wrong directions, and if anything is to grow here again, I will need to let some light in. But it seems a pity to hurry this and for now I content myself with creating pathways and clearings around the bases of the trees.

Every day I work like this, moving from task to task without thinking, and stopping only to eat, or when evening begins to sharpen the air and the light starts to fade. Then I go inside, strip off my dirty clothes, run a bath and ease myself down into it so that it comes right up to my chin and steam dampens my face. Later I eat, read a little, but my body is unused to the kind of sustained effort I have been demanding of it and fatigue rolls over me at an early hour. I drop into bed with a new gratitude, knowing that sleep will fall like an axe. Sometimes I awake in the night, hearing the baby crying across the way, but it is a momentary coming to. I close my eyes again, anaesthetised almost immediately. Dream of nothing.

*   *   *

Spring has been swallowed up today. A stinging rain beats down on the windows of the house and the temperature has dropped overnight. I think of the shoots I found yesterday, pushing up through the soil at the edge of the border I was starting to clear: tender, pinkish-green tips, pointing hopefully towards the sky. I had been ridiculously delighted to find something other than weeds and unruly shrubs growing in this garden and keener than ever to continue with my work. Today is not a day to work outside, however, so I put aside the old jeans that I have been wearing for days now and dress myself in smarter clothes, then step out into the rain and the wind and walk to the station.

Even in this short space of time I must have started to forget the pleasures of urban life, for though Canterbury is a compact little city, there are coffee shops and department stores, restaurants and bookshops aplenty within its stone walls, and I walk among them gladly. I save the cathedral for last and wander around the narrow side streets, among the chattering school parties, the Japanese and American tourists, the students and the buskers, feeling my spirits rising despite the persisting rain. I like this about cities: the way that they seem to absorb all the activity that takes place within them until they reach a certain pitch, a certain level of energy that perpetuates itself quite independently of any minor comings and goings, and how you find yourself being pulled out of your own particular velocities just by being there. I realise too how much I am at the mercy of myself when I am alone in the house in Broadgate and that perhaps this is not necessarily a good thing.

I eat lunch in a tapas bar, then spend a few hours making my way around the clothes and shoe shops, trying things on that I don't really need, though this does not stop me buying a pair of Italian boots, high-heeled and sharp-toed and too beautiful to be left in the shop. Thinking about the garden, I find a bookshop and look for something that will help me identify plants. I find a guide with colour plates in it and a book about pruning, because the garden is reaching the stage where my ignorant assaults on it will not do any longer. I have thought about asking my mother for advice, but, though she would undoubtedly be touched by my efforts to rediscover her garden, she might want to know why I am bothering when the house will probably be sold in the autumn, and I do not want to field questions like this when the answers aren't even formed in my head yet. I pay for my books, then, dodging a gibbering beggar demanding change outside Christ Church Gate, hand over the entrance fee for the cathedral.

The building looks implacable in the afternoon light and as I cross the precincts towards it I am in half a mind not to go in after all. It is only when I enter that its beauty catches at me and I stand, hand at my throat, gazing up at its soaring gothic arches. Given the number of tourists thronging the little streets just outside, the cathedral is surprisingly empty. I add my footsteps to the few that echo here and seek out the spot where Thomas à Becket lost half his skull and wet the ground with his blood, then the crypt and the tomb of the Black Prince. I am about to approach the cathederal quire when I stop, realising that people are being ushered in. The attendant catches my eye.

'For evensong?' he asks and I find myself nodding because it seems rude to refuse his invitation, as good as admitting that I have only entered this place of worship for my own aesthetic gratification. He shows me to a wooden bench at the far end of the quire, where I find myself alongside a small party of American tourists, talking quietly together in mid-Western accents. The man beside me nods in a friendly way as I take my seat. I do not return his smile, but I feel more at ease knowing that I am not the only stranger here. A hasty glance at the service sheet

shows that there isn't much in the way of audience partici-
pation required either.

The members of the choir enter then and their voices rise
up, sacred and unblemished, marking the beginning of the
service. I close my eyes and listen and thus it is only when
the first reading begins that I notice the tramp who ac-
costed me outside Christ Church Gate sitting directly
opposite me. After that it is hard to concentrate because I
keep expecting him to leap up and shout out some lunatic
abuse or start babbling to himself. He shows little sign of
agitation, however, other than a tendency to glance over his
shoulder rapidly from time to time, as if expecting to catch
the person sitting behind him trying to pick his pocket, or
ridiculing him in some way. I notice that he is well dressed
for a beggar; his status is only given away by the matted
condition of his long black hair and a certain wild look in his
eyes. He catches me looking at him and returns the scrutiny
with a glare so fierce that I wonder if he recognises me as
the tourist laden with shopping bags who refused to give
him any change.

By the time we emerge, evening has fallen. I walk back
to the station and wait on a wet platform for my train to
come, thinking that it is as well that I have the garden to
return to and my new books under my arm or I might be
tempted to take the train in the other direction, away from
the bleak rain of Broadgate and back towards London and
all its consolations.

I want to face the emptiness of the house quickly, before I
make it into something more than it is, so I hurry along the
High Street, dodging the puddles. But Harry, who is talking
to a very elderly lady on the other side of the street, spots
me and beckons me over. I have no choice but to join him,
and the old lady, who turns out to be Mrs Harvey, whose
disabled husband has, apparently, also managed to stay
alive all these years. I remember disliking her when I was

a child, but I am disposed to be sympathetic towards her because of Gina and because she is so very old now. She soon uses up my limited resources of this emotion, though, with her questions about what, exactly, I am doing here and how long I intend to stay and wasn't it funny, my mother just up and leaving like that all those years ago and me looking just like her, and wasn't she just the opposite of my father who had the time of day for everyone? Harry signals a silent apology to me and then makes some excuse about having a table booked and leads me off in the direction of the wine bar.

'Sorry about that,' he says with a smile. 'There's no stopping her once she gets started. I *was* going to grab something to eat as it happens, so it wasn't a total fabrication.' He motions at the window of the wine bar where, even at this hour, most of the tables are taken. 'The food here's not bad if you want to join me.'

I am about to say no, but the supermarket will be closed by now and, despite the casual tone, Harry looks so hopeful of my company.

'Sure,' I agree.

I encourage Harry to talk over dinner because it means that I don't have to. The food is a long time coming and we drink a good deal of wine while we are waiting which has the affect of tingeing Harry's usual loquacity with melancholy. To begin with he talks about business, but soon we are on to the old times – the day we all went sailing, a trip to the zoo we once had, a birthday picnic we planned for Lottie. He talks about these things as if they are precious objects, preserved in glass cases, and it occurs to me that it is my mother that he really wants to talk about, though he rarely refers to her directly. I wonder, but do not ask, just how often they have been in touch over the years.

'Sorry,' he says, when our main courses finally arrive, 'I seem to be monopolising the conversation.' And I think then that Harry, who is friends with everyone and on first-name terms with the staff here, might be lonely, might come here because it is bright and bustling and full of noise. Later, he talks about Daniel, about how he regrets not having seen more of him, that he should have made more of an effort to know who he was, 'the usual stuff,' he says, with a shake of his head. I risk a question about Josie.

'Ah Josie,' he says with a sigh. And he tells me – as if I didn't know – what a difficult child she was, how, even before she came to stay with us, she'd been having a hard time at school, had actually been moved twice, and that his relationship with her has always been troubled.

'She's never really forgiven me for leaving her mother, you see,' says Harry, refilling our glasses. 'Blames me for everything, which is right really because I was young and stupid at the time and when things started to go wrong between Theresa and me I took it personally and made everything much worse than it actually was. Theresa says it was more laziness than anything else, that I fancy myself so much as a romantic that I simply couldn't bring myself to make the effort once things became less than perfect.' He laughs at this, a little ruefully, and I remember a day long ago, Josie and I adrift in the treetops and her stories about Harry doing it with everyone. Then he tells me he and Josie quarrelled years ago, something to do with her wedding, and that they haven't spoken since, that he has tried to put things right once or twice, but with no success.

'What about the funeral though?' I ask. 'Wouldn't that have been the time?'

'Probably,' he says. 'But she didn't look open to . . . ' He shrugs and for the first time I see that Harry is a man who lets things happen to him, that his easy nature is not always a blessing. I change the subject then, ask him about tree surgeons and where I can hire a skip for all the rubbish I have cleared from the garden, because I think I can trust Harry by now not to trouble me with questions about why I am bothering in the first place. I refuse dessert and Harry's offer to walk me home and leave him with a promise to drop into the shop next time I am passing.

*　　*　　*

The rain has stopped now and the sky is high and clear. Away from the main stretch of the High Street, Broadgate is closing up for the night – curtains are being pulled, lights switched on. I think of Harry returning to his own darkened home, how he has allowed life to put him there. The stars are bright over the bay tonight and the only sound is the clipping of my heels on the wet pavement as I head back towards the house. I am reminded of the last night I walked back to Helena's flat and how, looking up into the same clear sky, I felt overwhelmed with loneliness. And it comes to me that that moment of absolute vulnerability, just before everything imploded, was probably the truest emotion I have experienced in years. I hold this thought for a moment, turn it over, like the little girl with her seashells and her pebbles, while it retains its clarity, then push it away again because such an insight is of little use to me when there is nothing I can do about it. There is something unyielding in me now, something intractable about the shape I have chosen. I let myself in and flick on the hall light. Then I close the door behind me and push the bolts into place.

CHAPTER 17

On Friday the men arrive to cut back the trees at the rear of the garden. I make tea, then hurry them out of the house into the garden where we discuss the details of what is to be done – enough pruning to untangle the densest areas and allow some light through but no more than that. I ask them to have a look at the plum tree too, because I think it may be dying, then leave them as they begin securing one of the boughs of the oak tree with loops of rope. But even from my bedroom at front of the house I can hear their banter and the high-pitched scream of the saw cutting into the flesh of the tree and if I stay around long enough they will be wanting more tea. I abandon the book I was trying to read and, for the first time since the day I felt it trying to spit me back out again, take a walk down to the beach.

This morning it does not resist my presence, perhaps because it is already busy with people arriving for the weekend. Cars are pulled up outside a number of the beach huts, some with boat trailers attached. A couple dressed in rolled-up jeans and wearing matching sunglasses are unloading bags of groceries and a box full of clinking bottles from the back of their Range Rover as I pass. They look up at me and the man says a cheery hello, as if the word is a holiday novelty, and I smile and walk quickly away, down to the water's edge, where the wind is flicking up hurried little waves which slap down on the shore in quick succession. In the distance, three children have managed to construct a vast sandcastle, presumably by carrying bucket-loads of sand from the edge of the water up on to the shingle, and now they are busy digging a moat around it. Behind where they play, a man and a woman are setting out beach chairs in front of one of the huts, and even farther down the beach a mother stops pushing a buggy along the shoreline and leans over to check on her child, or perhaps to pick up something it has dropped. An elderly couple, dressed in waterproof jackets despite the sun and the clear sky, say good-morning to me. They are holding hands. My aloneness has become fact to me since the night I walked home from dinner with Harry, and, now that I have had time to ponder it, I have come to see that it is not wholly right. Still I cannot envy the togetherness of others. The truth is that I would not know what to do with other people's lives, would take them and turn them into something cooler and altogether more friable.

The children are busy with their moat and do not notice me approaching. Two of the girls are dark-haired and must be about seven or eight years old, hipless and long-limbed in cut-off jeans and floral T-shirts. The third child is smaller and fairer and I recognise her as the girl I saw playing on the beach before. I have been half-watching the three of them, simply because they are in my eye-line as I walk down the beach, but as I draw nearer, something about the youngest girl troubles me. I watch more closely, see that she is no longer crouching down, patting at the shingle with a spade, but has stepped back from the moat and is standing with her head drooped and something frozen about her stance. The smaller of the dark-haired girls is standing almost in front of her, leaning in towards her, too close. The third girl is digging and taking no notice of the other two. I quicken my pace then, until I am almost upon them, and it is then that I understand what is happening.

'I *said*, go away!' hisses the dark-haired girl.

The small child looks up at her, a world of incomprehension in her serious eyes. 'Why?' she asks simply.

'I told you. We don't want to play with you.'

'Can't I help dig?'

'No!'

'Why not?'

'Because,' says the dark-haired girl, her thin, wavy hair catching in the wind, 'you stink.'

The younger child flinches and I too am shocked by these words. Childish as they are, they are invested with real viciousness.

'No, I don't,' says the small girl forlornly, looking over her shoulder towards the woman with the buggy, who has stopped farther down the beach and is staring out to sea.

'Yes, you do.' And once again, she leans over, pushing her face into the other child's. 'Stinky! Stinky! Stinky!' It should be nothing more than a playground chant and had the words been spoken out loud they would have had little power to wound. But they are delivered in a whisper, and the dark-haired girl uses them like a knife. The small girl's face flushes deeper still and her eyes suddenly fill with tears. For a moment I do nothing, unnerved to hear words with such malicious intent issuing from that tiny mouth, where I can see little teeth gleaming in pink gums, like embedded pearls. Then I spring to life, reaching them in a few strides.

'What do you think you're doing?' I demand. The dark-haired child looks up at me, alarmed by my sudden presence, the hand that has encircled the top of her thin arm. Her older sister (for so she must be, because of the resemblance) looks up from her digging for a second, then, catching my eye, thinks better of it and pretends not to have noticed anything amiss. 'What do you think you're doing?' I repeat, giving the girl a push, which is more violent than I had intended, nearly knocking her off her feet. 'Don't you know that it's wrong to bully someone younger than yourself? To bully anyone?' She stares up at me, and nods, a nervous twitch of a movement. 'How would you like it if I did that to you?' I continue, pushing my face into hers and mirroring her own behaviour. 'If I spoke to you in that way?' She has a mean, pretty face and I have an urge to slap it.

'We didn't want her to play with us,' explains her sister in a neutral voice. She doesn't look up from her work as she speaks. 'She keeps messing up the moat.'

'I'm not interested,' I say, my grip tightening on the girl's arm. 'I'm just telling you that if I *ever* catch you talking to her or anyone else like that . . . '

'Is everything all right?' comes a voice from behind me. I whip round to find a tall sandy-haired man standing a few feet away. He looks at the girls questioningly. 'Sarah? Lorna?' The younger of the girls jerks her head in affirmation.

'No, it is *not*!' I say, rage wobbling through my voice. 'I've just caught your daughters bullying this little girl, she's nearly in tears!' I release my grip on the dark-haired girl's arm and point to the younger child who has not moved in all this time, is just looking up at us with her grave eyes which are, however, no longer filled with tears. 'You should think about teaching them a few lessons about how to behave! If *I* ever catch them doing that again I'll be tempted to do it myself!'

The man turns to the girls. 'Go back to the hut,' he orders quietly. The eldest girl looks up from her digging, challenges him with eyes. 'Right now!' he barks suddenly and both girls grab their buckets and spades and scramble up the beach towards the hut where a woman stands, shading her eyes and looking down towards us.

'I'm terribly sorry, I had no idea,' says the man, 'I thought they were playing nicely down here.' He looks at the remaining child with concern. 'Are you all right, sweetheart?'

She says nothing, just stares for a moment. Then, seeing the woman with the buggy coming in our direction now, darts down the beach to her. The young woman looks down blankly at the child clinging to her legs, doesn't reach for her.

'Are you her mother?' I call. My voice carries across the beach, querulous, shrill. Their relationship is obvious but I want to hear her confess it. She looks at me, nothing registering on her face. A bundle of blankets twitches within the buggy.

'I said, are you her mother?' I repeat, when she is close. She is younger than I had thought, has a pale oval face and the same serious expression as her daughter. She nods, though still appears uncomprehending. Her dullness serves only to infuriate me more.

'Don't you thinks she's a little young to be left playing while you wander off down the beach?' I demand. The girl pushes her long wavy hair out of her eyes and blinks at me.

'But she was . . . ' she says in a voice so soft that the wind almost carries it away. She motions towards the two dark-haired girls who are now crouched down in front of the beach hut, busy with some new game.

'Oh? And you know those children, do you?' She shakes her head, pushes her eyebrows into a frown of concentration. 'Don't you think you should be a little more discerning about whom she plays with?' Again, the uncomprehending look and a flare of anger in my chest because I need her to understand and suddenly words are coming out my mouth of their own accord and I am making her see that anything might have happened to her child while her back was turned, that she could have drowned or been injured or someone might have tried to abduct her and if any of these things had happened the blame would lie with her, and she is looking scared now, is finally getting it.

I take a breath, slow myself. The sandy-haired man is looking at me with alarm dawning in his eyes, the way people look when they realise they are in the company of a mad person. My legs feel as if all the strength has gone out of them and I have a strange weak sensation in my stomach.

'As I said,' he intervenes (and he is speaking to the mother rather than me, clearly judging her to be the more rational of the two of us), 'I am terribly sorry and you can be sure it won't happen again. I really had no idea they were misbehaving . . . '

She nods.

'Well perhaps you could try supervising them properly in future!' I shoot out, aware now that my behaviour is overwrought but unable to let it go, wanting, for some reason, to extract further payment from these two. The man looks at me wearily. He is about my own age, perhaps a few years older.

'They're my sister's girls, as it happens, but I'll make sure their mother speaks to them.' He looks over to the beach hut, to the woman who is watering pot plants on the veranda. He meets my glare and gives up on me. 'Look, I only came down to check on them, that's all.' He turns to go. 'I really am very sorry,' he adds to the girl's mother. I watch him leave, then spin on my heel and stride back down the beach. As I reach the path, the thin wail of a baby carries down the beach.

When I reach home the men are still working in the garden, so I keep walking, beyond the house and down to the marina, where I find a sheltered spot against the wall and sit for a time, watching a man teaching his son to rig a small dinghy and letting the gentleness of the spring sun quieten me. Lottie maintains that I was hot-tempered as a child, but I have always been puzzled by lack of self-control in others, the way people allow their feelings to get snagged up in the affairs of others. I cannot remember the last time rage crashed through me like that, sweeping away everything before it, and I do not like the feeling of exposure it has left me with, am out of kilter and strangely vulnerable now, crouching here against the solid warmth of the wall. I push the thought of it away, concentrate instead on the sailing lesson taking place before me.

*   *   *

The plum tree is not dead after all, though the tree men think it may only have a few seasons left in it. After they have gone, I examine the wound on the oak tree where the bough has been removed and check the remainder of the pruning, pleased to see that they have taken notice of my wishes and not destroyed the air of secrecy at the far end of the garden. I stand on what I persist in thinking of as my father's gravestone and look around me, then up into the newly revealed blue, and remind myself that I ought to visit his real grave at some point because it is years since Mummy has been able to tend it. As children, Lottie and I always enjoyed these visits: the trips backwards and forwards to the tall taps that stood at intervals along the pathways, like a series of periscopes, each of us holding a plastic container with the top cut off; the squeak of the tap as it resisted your hand and then a hollow, metallic whine, like a voice from the dead, before it coughed up water; then back to Mummy to water in the new plants she brought twice a year to redecorate Daddy. We used to wander off after a while, leaving Mummy digging vigorously with her little trowel, a line of pots waiting beside her, inevitably drawn to the little rows of children's graves at the back of the cemetery, where we would read out the inscriptions in suitably doleful and momentous tones and gaze at rain-sodden teddy bears and plastic windmills in cartoon colours whirring eerily in the breeze, spooking ourselves with plans for our own sad passings. Lottie wanted a black and gold carriage and horses with plumes and everyone sobbing into handkerchiefs, whereas I preferred something altogether simpler, saw myself in a white dress, looking pale and composed, and only muted tears because everyone would know that I had never really been of this world.

Now that the heavier work has been completed, I need to begin pruning the larger shrubs that form the skeleton of the garden. In the evenings I study the books I bought in Canterbury, teach myself about soil types and aspects and planting schemes (wonder too what my London acquaint-ances would think if they could see me engaged in such a middle-aged activity) and, now that spring is beginning to unfurl leaves here and there, I am delighted to find that I can identify at least some of the plants in the garden. Some of their names come to me in my mother's voice and I remember then how she used to talk to me as she worked.

This afternoon, armed with my manual and the new secateurs, I busy myself with cutting back what I think is a philadelphus. I am timid to begin with, wary of doing damage to the plant, but the work imposes a rhythm of its own after a time, slow, yet deliberate, and I move from this to a cotoneaster which has sprouted out in all directions at the back of a border, overshadowing all the intriguing shoots that are beginning to ease themselves out of the earth beneath it. Sunshine falls on my back and my shoulders as I work and this, together with the breathing verdancy all around me – for I am sure I can hear the garden reawakening when I crouch down among the fattening buds and the damp, living earth – begins to soothe me. By evening, a new pile of prunings sits on the patio and I use the secateurs to cut these down into smaller pieces and fill three more rubbish sacks. I look around me, my eye falling on a rose bush just beyond the patio which has grown tangled and leggy, but the light is beginning to fade and it must wait until tomorrow.

I drink more wine than usual after dinner and it may be this, or the surge of excitement I am experiencing as the garden begins to reveal itself, that prompts me to tell my mother what I have been doing when she telephones. She is surprised to begin with – understandably so, since I have never before expressed any interest in gardening – then animation begins to gather in her voice, as, between us, we begin to put together the puzzle of her old garden. She supplies pieces as they come to her: yes, the old-fashioned rose would be there, right by the patio, she remembers that because it had the most exquisite quartered flowers; the philadelphus – if that's what it is – must be a more recent addition, because she can't recall planting one and she's sure she would remember – she has one now, of course, the plant with the white, scented flowers that grows just by the door of the flat. She is very fond of her small city garden, she tells me, but craves trees around her. We talk practicalities (me stumblingly, because I am still speaking a new language): dogwoods can be taken right back to ground level; roses don't need as much finesse as you are led to believe – and then, out of nowhere, she asks if she can visit sometime, something she has never suggested before, even when the idea of me taking the house was first voiced. I say nothing for a moment and, sensing my hesitation, she explains that she would like to help me. I answer ambivalently, not because I dislike the idea of my mother working alongside me in the garden, but because my instinct is, as always, to draw back whenever I sense someone moving towards me. I change the subject to Lottie and her children and we say no more, for now, of visits.

Someone is knocking on my door though it is only seven in the morning and I am not yet dressed. I consider ignoring it because I am not expecting anyone, but it comes again, louder this time and, before I am halfway down the stairs, once more. I unbolt the door, frowning to myself, and then pull it open with a sharp tug. If any thoughts of who might be on the other side ran through my mind as I crossed the hallway, the three people that await me were not included among the possibilities. Looking out into the new day, I see the young mother from the beach standing there, the baby, in a pale-blue sleepsuit, curled up on her shoulder, squirrel-like. Beside her, in pink pyjamas and Magic Roundabout slippers, is her little daughter. I say nothing, just stare at them, unable even to pretend that I understand what they are doing outside my house, how they knew to find me here, and, more than anything, why they would want to do so in the first place. The mother looks at me with something in her eyes that I don't quite understand, and then she puts her hand on the shoulder of her elder child and pushes her towards me.

'Take her,' she says, never dropping her gaze from mine.

'What?' I say. I hear her words perfectly clearly, just cannot absorb their meaning.

'Take her,' she repeats. Her voice is barely audible, but now I realise that what is emanating from her eyes – which are as grave as her daughter's – is pure aggression.

'What are you talking about, exactly?' I say, reaching for the door with my hand because though the girl is holding a baby and looks even younger than she did when I first saw her, I have a sudden urge to protect myself.

'If you know so bloody much about looking after children,' she says, and her voice is beginning to shatter now, breaking up into shards, 'you try doing it!' And then her face twists and she bursts into tears, right there on my doorstep.

CHAPTER 18

I have put them in the living-room. As a rule, I would prefer not to have strangers falling to pieces inside my house, but my instinct is to contain these three before this grows into something bigger and even less controllable outside, under the high blue sky and the inquisitive eyes of next door's daughter, who regards our little grouping with curiosity as she walks up the pathway to her father's house. I go into the kitchen and take a long time making tea in the hope that by the time I take it through there will no longer be sobbing, and that the small girl will have stopped stroking her mother's arm and exhorting her not to cry, like a solemn little mother herself.

Another sound reaches me as I put the tea things on a tray: the baby has started to cry now. I wonder whether it might be easier if we all sat down and wept and had done with it, but when I go through with the tray, the girl has stopped crying, has her sweatshirt tugged up on one side now, with the baby feeding at her breast. Her daughter is kneeling up on the sofa, looking out at a blackbird, which keeps fluttering down on to the window-sill and looking in with a bright beady eye.

I put a cup and a bowl of sugar on the low table in front of the girl, trying not to notice the folds of her exposed belly, which are chalk-white and loose, though the rest of her body has the narrow lines of the very young. She twists in her chair and shifts the baby, trying to find a better position for feeding, then pushes her sweatshirt up further. She is not wearing a bra and though the baby covers one breast, I can see the other in its pale, blue-veined entirety. I sit down on the other side of the room, because this girl, barely more than a teenager, is making me more uncomfortable than I would care to admit: there is something about her willingness to expose herself to a stranger in this way that shocks me, and yet I feel the braveness of it too, and the tenderness of the moment.

Something has to be said and since it is obvious that my words on the beach yesterday have done more damage than I could have realised, I start towards some kind of apology. To my dismay, the moment I begin to speak, the girl's face collapses again. Her daughter is busy at the window, rearranging my books and chattering to herself under her breath and she does not notice her mother's renewed distress. The baby too is oblivious, continues to feed in loud, smacking sucks as silent tears course down the girl's face, dripping on to the downy scalp at her breast.

'What is it?' I ask. I must not leave the room, though every impulse directs me to do so. At that moment, the baby loses its grip on its mother's breast, or rather, jerks back and wilfully throws itself off. I wait for it to open its mouth and clamp itself back on, but instead it rears back its head, arches its tiny body and screams.

The girl's face contorts and the tears begin to fall faster. 'Oh please, don't,' she begs the baby in her whisper of a voice, and she drags her heavy sweatshirt up still further, uses her chin to hold it in place, then with her free hand she squeezes her breast and tries to push her nipple back into the baby's mouth. The baby lunges at it, tries to take it, but finding only the very tip in its mouth, pushes itself off again and writhes in fury, its head worming from side to side and its mouth stretching wide like some kind of maddened alien life form. The girl tries again, fails again; and sweat is rising on her brow, will mingle with her tears any moment now. Her sweatshirt falls from where it has been wedged beneath her chin and covers the baby's head before she can stop it. The screams reach a new level of intensity.

'Oh, God . . . ' moans the girl and she is rocking backwards and forwards on her seat now, her eyes closed against this, even as she pulls up her sweatshirt again and tries once more to reposition the baby. 'Please do it,' she says, to herself or to the baby, as she tries to push her dark nipple into its gaping mouth. 'Please.' I feel I should be helping, that if I could hold the sweatshirt in place for her, or indeed the writhing baby, that she would then have both hands free, could help the child to take the breast. But I cannot do it. I cannot make myself cross the room to someone who is already so exposed to me, so vulnerable, can only watch in horror.

'I think Kieran needs a cuddle from me, Mummy,' announces her daughter getting down from the window-sill and eyeing the scene with sagacity. And she goes to take the baby in her arms, just as her mother is attempting, yet again, to make it take the whole of her nipple into its mouth.

'Please, Daisy, no,' whispers her mother, pulling the baby away weakly. 'Just leave him, please . . . '

'I'll just give him a nice cuddle. *That* will make him feel better,' continues the little girl, and she reaches for her little brother, tries to drag her mother's arm out of her way: the baby's head flops back, alarmingly loose like a rag doll's, and he gives another bellow of rage. His mother's hand shoots out to rescue his unsupported head.

'Daisy!' What did I say? What have I told you?' The little girl quickly retreats to the doorway, looks at her mother, big-eyed. 'Can't you see how difficult this is? Why don't you ever listen to me?' demands her mother. 'Why?' Then she gives another moan, shakes her head as if trying to dislodge something bad within it. 'Sorry,' she says, 'sorry,' and she holds a hand out to her daughter then collapses back on the seat, lets the tears run past her ears, on to her shoulders and the chair, where they land like dark raindrops. 'I don't know why he won't do it,' she whispers to me between the baby's outraged wails. 'Daisy always did.'

I breathe slowly, try to think what to do with the madness that has come in here, right into this house, which is bare and clean and quiet, where I am half-dressed and just beginning my day. I would like to sweep them all out of here, on to the street, let them disperse like dust, but I do not know how to do this without creating more mess, so I just keep breathing, in and out. And the only thing that comes to me is that the little girl should not be witnessing her mother's distress, that the proper thing to do would be to distract her in some way, though there can be nothing in this house that might interest a child. I search for the instincts of a normal person within me, think about Lottie's children and try to remember what they were like when they were small. Then I stand up and cross to the little girl, putting myself between her and her mother.

'Would you like to bounce on my bed?' I say. She looks at me warily, waits for a second as if expecting intervention from her mother. Then she nods, unsmilingly. 'It's Daisy, isn't it?' I say. She nods again.

'Well, come on then!' I say too loudly, in a children's-TV-presenter voice, jolly and solicitous, that does not belong to me. 'My name's Kate, by the way.' I lead her out into the hallway and point towards the stairs but she just stands there, looking at me expectantly.

'Would you like me to show you where it is?' I say, then I jog lightly up the stairs, as if to show her what fun all this is, stop at the top and beckon to her. To my relief, she follows me up and I take her along the landing and show her my bedroom, the bed I made only half an hour ago – that fast fading memory of peace – with its fat, smooth pillows. 'All yours!' I announce in my new stupid voice. She hesitates again, then scrambles up on to the bed, tries a small bounce. A gleeful smile transforms her face for an instant, but she is still watching me carefully and I realise my presence is restraining her now. 'Leave you to it!' I say. As I reach the top of the stairs I hear the double thump of pillows landing on the floor, then the metal twang of springs. I imagine those small feet digging up the white expanse of quilt and stand still for a moment in the space between the mess up here and the mess waiting for me downstairs. Then the phone rings.

'Have you got a baby there?' demands Lottie a few minutes later, breaking off from her litany of vague woes.

'Yes . . . Someone else's,' I finish nonsensically. The baby's cries, which ceased while I was upstairs with Daisy, are building up in a crescendo, and it is my guess that the stupid creature has thrown himself off his mother's breast again. 'Look, I have to go, Lottie, call me another time.' I put down the receiver, but go into the kitchen, rather than the living-room, where I switch on the kettle again and listen to the thud, thud over my head and the wailing that winds itself around the door. I wonder how this can be happening.

By the time I have made more tea, the cries have stopped and when I go back into the living-room, the baby is asleep, stretched out on his mother's lap with his arms raised up in the air, as if warding off her attempts to nurture him even while he rests. His face is no longer puce and his amphibian-like eyelids are flickering and translucent. The girl has also stopped crying but she is sitting rigidly and she has the same blank look about her that she had yesterday on the beach, which I now realise is not a manifestation of vacancy but of utter defeat. I notice that her wrist is encircled by a series of heavily beaded knotted bracelets that make her pale arm look thinner and somehow vulnerable. I put the tea in front of her, though her first cup remains untouched.

'Asleep?' I whisper, motioning to the baby, and then wonder how many more moronic words can pass my lips today. She nods and her mouth trembles. I take in the whiteness of her face, her youth, and the dark shadows beneath her eyes and I know that without meaning to I have added to the stock of her misery. I also know that if I am worth anything in this world I must try to comfort her, though I do not know how. I sit on the edge of my chair, force myself to begin. I ask questions, try to sound like someone who wants to help, but my exertions are of little use.

'I'm just so tired,' is all the girl keeps saying, in that whisper of a voice, grimacing as if the effort to speak, to impose some kind of order on her thoughts is almost too much. 'So tired.' And for all my attempts, I can extract little more from her except that the baby is colicky – which means little to me – and won't feed properly and that none of them seem to get any sleep at night. I look at the child, sleeping in her arms now, and find it hard to accept that this is the same enraged creature whose cries were bouncing off the walls of my house only minutes ago.

'But why don't you sleep during the day? When he does?' I ask.

She shakes off the suggestion. 'I have to look after Daisy,' she says.

'Well, she seems very well-behaved . . . '

'She is . . . but she's only five, I can't just leave her . . . '

And then she looks at me, right at me and into me, and I remember her words as she stood on my doorstep less than an hour ago. Still I refuse to believe that she intended, with any seriousness, to hand over her child into the care of a stranger.

'There must be people who could help you,' I insist. She shakes her head. 'What about your mother?' I try.

'She's dead,' she says, still gazing at me.

'Well, then you must have friends, other mothers, with children that Daisy could play with?' I say firmly.

'I don't know anyone. We only moved here a few weeks ago.'

'Well, I can't take her!' I blurt out suddenly.

She says nothing.

'You don't know me!' I say. 'I don't understand how you even managed to find me here! You must realise that I don't know the first thing about children. And I'm very busy here too.'

She gives me a look then, a stripping kind of look that makes me forget how young she is and makes me ashamed of the lie. In desperation, I try to think about Lottie again, how things worked with her children.

'What about school? Or some kind of childcare?'

'She's too young for school. They won't take her till September. I can't afford a childminder and the nursery places are all full.' She recites this in a flat voice, as though she has rehearsed the words.

'This is ludicrous,' I say. 'You must have a doctor or a midwife or someone who could help you. Oh, please, I'm sorry.'

Her face is collapsing again, mouth buckling. She leans forward over the baby, whispers something in a broken voice.

'What?' Her shoulders heave painfully. 'Please don't cry again,' I beg, though still I cannot bring myself to cross to her, touch her. 'I didn't hear what you said, that's all.'

She lifts her face, tries to speak, steadies herself, then in the strongest voice she has used since she stepped through my doorway says, 'If you don't help me they will take her away from me.'

'What about clothes?' I say. I am not so much panicking as dazed, unable to believe what I have just agreed to do. 'She has pyjamas on at the moment.'

'I'll fetch some from the flat. We are just across the road.'

'Yes,' I say.

Daisy's feet are still thudding persistently on the bed upstairs as I sit without moving for the few minutes it takes her to go to her flat and return with a plastic carrier bag, the baby still asleep on her shoulder. She puts the bag down by my feet.

'Hadn't you better . . . ?' I motion towards the stairs, meaning that her daughter is still playing up there, oblivious of her mother's plans for her. She disappears and then comes down again shortly.

'She's fine,' she says. 'She's made a cave out of your bedding though,' she adds, with a small smile of apology.

I realise that I have just enough time to stop this.

'Look, I don't think I can do this. I know I took Daisy off to play earlier but don't . . . I don't know anything about children! How do you know that I can . . . ? I don't even know your *name*.'

'Marie.' She is calm now, blinkered by the promise of sleep and anxious to return home before the baby wakes. Even as I speak I see that my words will roll right over her.

'And you're coming back to fetch her this afternoon, aren't you? And if she cries for you, I'll have to bring her to you, even if it means waking you. You do understand that, don't you? I can't possibly . . . ' Don't trust me, is what I want to say. I do not trust myself.

'Yes.'

She is walking towards the door. I am right behind her.

'Just a few hours,' I am saying as she walks down my pathway. 'That's all I can do and you must promise that you will speak to your midwife or whoever . . . '

She turns, grave eyes looking right into me again. 'Yes,' she says quietly.

The other question comes to me only when she has reached the gate, when it is too late to call her back again. 'How did you know where to find me?'

She looks over her shoulder, smiles faintly through her fatigue. 'We've been hoping for you.'

Then just a dark head moving behind the hedge and a strange child waiting for me upstairs.

*   *   *

'Hello,' I say, standing tentatively at the doorway of my bedroom. The little girl is standing on the bed looking out of the window. She must have watched her mother go. 'Are you OK?' I ask, knowing that if she shows the least sign of distress, I will not be able to do this, will have to march her straight out of my house and back to her flat. She looks at me and nods. 'Your Mummy brought some clothes for you. They're in a bag downstairs. Shall we get you dressed?' I cannot think of anything else to suggest, have no knowledge of how to entertain a five-year-old who has wearied of bouncing on beds. I do not know what I will do if she says no, if she insists on staying in her pyjamas, because it seems to me that she would be perfectly reasonable in rejecting my authority. But the suggestion seems to catch her attention and she bounces down from the bed, her feet planting themselves on the floor with a thump.

'I can get dressed myself,' she announces and sets off downstairs. I follow her down into the living-room and we take the clothes from the carrier bag. With a critical eye Daisy examines them: a pair of jeans, a long-sleeved T-shirt with a pink heart on the front of it, pink ankle socks, white knickers and a pair of scuffed trainers. Satisfied, she strips off her pyjamas and stands naked in front of me, pink as a prawn and unashamed.

'Shall I help?'

She shakes her head and so I let her do as she wishes and while she is struggling into the jeans and dragging the neck of the top down over her curly head, I am already looking at my watch, calculating how much time must pass before I can justify thinking that I have done enough, already hungry for the moment when I will have this house to myself again, for the wonderful silence which will wrap itself around me when she is gone. Then I will have time to work out how to ensure that Marie and her children do not find their way on to my doorstep again. For now, I must find a way to entertain this little girl who has finished dressing herself and is looking at me expectantly. There is another knock at the door and I fly to it, in the belief that Marie must have changed her mind. When I open it, it is only Harry standing there, but I usher him in all the same, deeply thankful for the presence of anyone who might dilute the mixture of me and this child.

'Hello,' he says to me, then 'Hello!' again as he spots Daisy, in the doorway of the living-room, watching him. He squats down in front of her, holds out his hand. 'What's your name, sweetie?'

'Daisy Annabel McClean,' she says solemnly, not taking his hand.

'Of course it is,' he says, smiling at her. 'I know your Mummy.' He stands up again. 'I've brought the van,' he says. 'I thought we could run some of your garden rubbish to the tip. It'll save you hiring a skip.'

'Oh, thanks, Harry,' I say, gratitude saturating my words because he is here, and because he talks to Daisy as if he knows just what to say to a child, and because, suddenly, I feel a little safer. 'I don't know how much I can help though . . . I've said I'll look after Daisy for a few hours . . . ' I look at him, try to signal my difficulty.

'Are you any good at picking up sticks, young lady?' enquires Harry. 'You look as if you might be.'

Daisy looks up at him. 'Yes,' she says proudly.

'Then we'll be needing your help in the garden,' he announces, taking her by the hand and leading her down the hallway towards the back door. He opens it and a slab of sunshine falls diagonally across the mat. I pull on my boots, hurry after them.

I do most of the work because Harry is too busy helping Daisy who, in that strange chirp of a voice, has insisted that her pile must contain precisely one hundred sticks and that she and Harry must break off from time to time to search for caterpillars. I am more than happy with this arrangement because I can lose myself in the cutting and bagging up of the prunings knowing that the morning is moving past, can almost, at times, forget that the two of them have anything to do with me. I think that Daisy must sense my unease in her presence because she says little to me, but she is clearly enamoured of Harry, and he, in turn, seems delighted with her company, enters into her schemes for trapping woodlice as if he can think of no finer way to spend a morning. I watch him with her, remembering what he said to me in the wine bar the other evening, about not expecting to see much of Daniel's children now that Daniel is gone, and I am struck by the waste of Harry, how he seems oddly powerless in the face of his own life. I think, too, that it is as well he possesses such easy charm, such kindness, and that you always sense him opening all of himself to you when you are in his company, because otherwise you might come to despise him.

Daisy has spotted next door's overfed cat at the bottom of the garden and she tears off towards it, abandoning her woodlice project.

Harry grins at her as she goes, then at me. 'How come the little visitor, then?' he asks.

'I have no idea,' I whisper, though she is well out of hearing range. And, hurriedly, I tell him everything, about the trouble on the beach yesterday, about Daisy and her mother arriving here this morning and handing themselves over into my care. The words fly out of me because it is a relief to give this story to someone else, to make the problem of Marie and her children less my own.

'But you know them,' I say eventually. Harry looks puzzled. 'You told Daisy that you know her Mummy,' I remind him.

'Oh, I see,' he says, 'well, yes, by sight. In the way that

you know anyone new who arrives in a small town. They moved into the new flats across the road a month or so ago.'

I nod. 'And they're on their own?' I check.

Harry thinks for a moment, and then explains his hesitation. 'Sorry, I was just trying to remember how I knew . . . ' he says. 'And it's because of Cheryl. Her sister's daughter – I think that's who she said – is their health visitor. I remember Cheryl saying something to me about Daisy's mum bringing the kids here to get away from a violent husband. Or boyfriend or something, I can't remember the exact . . . '

'Ssssh,' I say, because Daisy is hurtling back up the garden, pursuing a rather alarmed looking cat.

Harry says we can't all drive to the tip together because there is no child-seat in his van – something I would never have thought of – and anyway it is midday so what about lunch? This makes me panic again, since I have no idea what to feed a small child, but Harry solves the problem by suggesting we go to the Italian café near his shop for pizza. Daisy is excited by the outing to begin with, hardly glances towards the flats as we walk past them on the opposite side of the road, and when we reach the café, she chooses a table by the window and allocates seats to each of us. But halfway through the meal, which she eats methodically and without fuss, she begins to quieten and soon she is staring out of the window at the weekend traffic, oblivious of Harry and me.

'Tired out,' says Harry, and I agree with his diagnosis because it is as good as any. More than anything I am relieved that the morning has passed, and now that I know it is drawing to a close, find myself able to address a few questions to Daisy. When the bill comes I will not allow Harry to pay, though he insists he should.

Harry leaves us outside the flats and goes back to the house to begin loading up the rubbish sacks. I press the button on the intercom. 'It's us,' I say clumsily.

'Mumm–eeeee!' calls Daisy from beside me, skipping up and down. 'We're home!' The door buzzes and I push it open on to a narrow stairwell with two doors leading off it. Daisy ignores these and bounds up the stairs. I follow her, my footsteps echoing thinly. Marie is standing at the top of the second flight of stairs, looking down at us as we ascend. When Daisy reaches her she drops down on to one knee, catches the child to her, then buries her face in her hair as if she wants to breathe her in.

'She's been fine,' I say as I reach them, my voice bright with relief. Daisy is pulling at her mother's sweatshirt and bombarding her with cats and caterpillars and pizza and Mummy, Mummy, Mummy.

'Ssshh,' she admonishes her, pushing her away gently and closing her eyes for a second as if the onslaught pains her.

'Did you get some rest?' I ask.

'A little,' says Marie. 'I got some ironing done though. Kieran's still asleep in his cot.' She has a little more colour in her face than earlier, but her expression is flat and this rankles with me: I want there to be more to show for the sacrifice of my morning.

'Good,' I say uncertainly. Daisy pushes open the door to the flat and runs inside. I glimpse a small room, divided into two areas by a breakfast bar, neat and sparsely furnished. A clothes-horse draped with babygros takes up almost the entire floor space of the kitchen area, which looks spotlessly clean. There is a baby's plastic play-gym in the centre of the carpet, and in the window several jewel-coloured glass mobiles of the kind you see in New Age shops are twisting and chiming against each other in the breeze. Marie is rubbing her eyes, raking her hands through her hair, and though she is looking in my direction, I am not sure that she sees me.

'Thanks,' she says then, remembering that I am still here.

'You're welcome,' I say and then I go back down the stairs and home again.

CHAPTER 19

I came here to be safe, but when I wake up this morning, I no longer feel it. I have slept at the back of the house, in my childhood bedroom, because last night the walls of my mother's room seemed too far away and I felt adrift and vulnerable, lying on that great raft of a bed with the darkened flats across the street looming up at me. I lay rigidly for an hour or so – as if fearing any movement might betray my whereabouts – then gave up and came to sleep in this little white box of a room.

Spring sunshine breaks through the window, flooding the white walls and my bed linen with clean yellow light, but I do not stretch out and bathe in it like a cat, I get straight out of bed, because if people come knocking at my door again, I must be ready for them. My whole body is tense, as if anticipating the need to deflect some aggressor, and I wonder if I should go for a run before breakfast to shake the tightness out of my muscles. Then I reject the idea and shower and dress instead; I would have to pass the flats on my way there and back, and, what's more, the wide open beach where they walk and play is no place to be. After breakfast, I try reading but something has been breached and I cannot concentrate; scheme after scheme comes to mind, pushing all the sense out of the words before me, so that they become meaningless scratchings, a procession of ants across a page. I could leave today, go back to London and find a flat and some work earlier than I had planned. After all, there is nothing to tie me to this place. Or I could go abroad for a week or so, a holiday from a holiday, put a distance between myself and yesterday. Or I could speak to Cheryl's sister's daughter or whoever it is and make her do something, or simply tell Marie that she and her children are not my responsibility, that it is preposterous for them to hand themselves over into my care. I envisage myself enmeshed in the sticky web of other people's lives and it makes my throat constrict. Then I pull myself up, remind myself how risible this is: a grown woman hiding in her house, waiting for a knock at the door, almost sick with fear.

I drop my book and go to the back window. The garden glitters, fresh and dewy in the morning sunlight, and I go out into the hallway, pull on the boots which sit permanently beside the back door and step outside, wanting to be among all that green and gold brilliance and thinking that steady work and the perfect smell of the earth will soothe me. Plans have started to formulate, now that I have my books to consult in the evenings, and I am piecing together some little areas of knowledge – a border that ought to be made deeper and planted more luxuriantly, a gloomy corner at the back of the garden, where the surface of the soil is always slimy, which should be filled with lush green foliage, shiny, secretive leaves gleaming out of the darkness. I may or may not hear a knock at the door from here, or the telephone ringing, and this uncertainty calms me too because people may have been waiting for me but that does not mean I have to let them find me.

*   *   *

By lunchtime I am hot and happier. I go back into the house where I find my eye drawn to the other end of the hallway. A sheet of paper lies on the doormat, blank side up, and claustrophobia squeezes at my windpipe again. In trepidation, I approach it, but when I pick up the flimsy sheet and turn it over I see that is only a cheaply produced flyer from a replacement-window company. I take it through to the kitchen and throw it in the bin, then drink two glasses of cold water straight down. There is French bread in the cupboard, and some cheese, and I eat these because I am hungry, yet barely notice the taste, for in my mind I am still surveying the garden, the contours that are beginning to emerge as years of neglect are put right and an exuberant spring does its own work. On my way out again, I glance at myself in the mirror that hangs in the hallway, see that my unmade-up face is flushed from the sun and from the morning's work and that my hair has worked itself loose from the clip I use to hold it back and is now strewn over my shoulders in messy clumps. I hear Eleanor, in our university days, telling me that when she looks at me she thinks of a mannequin, because I am always perfectly dressed and groomed, even when I am ill or drunk or unhappy. The words have a pejorative edge that I did not perceive at the time, when I was merely irritated by her unerring admiration of me. I smooth my hair back and refasten it with the clip, thinking that I will have to learn to contain myself again when it is time to return to work.

The day is over and no one has come. By evening, I can be in the house again without that choking feeling pushing up inside my chest and as I strip off my muddy clothes and bathe, I find myself ridiculously high-spirited. I open a bottle of wine and cook dinner. Sing to myself in celebration of solitude.

The baby's cries pull me up out of sleep like a rope. I cross to the window with caution, as if I am fully expecting Marie and Daisy to be standing on the balcony of their flat, beckoning to me. The light in their living-room is on, and I think I see a shadow moving within the room, behind the curtains. I get back into bed and pull the duvet around my nakedness and lie there feeling my muscles beginning to stiffen. After a few minutes, the crying ceases.

*   *   *

I work in the garden, eat and read and no one knocks on the door or telephones me except my mother, and she is happy to talk about the work I have been doing and not about me. She does not even enquire why I am expending so much energy trying to help her suffocated garden breathe again. (Once, feeling obliged to justify myself, I attempt some kind of explanation but she just brushes over my words and says that there is no why with a garden, which surprises me because my mother is not the kind of woman to indulge in whimsy.) By Thursday I have rearranged what happened earlier in the week into another form and am brave enough to walk right past the flat and into town, telling myself that Marie and I did nothing more than glance off one another for a moment, that, contrary to her portentous (and, in retrospect, faintly silly) pronouncement on my doorstep, there is no intrinsic connection between us. The renewed lack of responsibility makes me reckless and I spend much more money than I had intended, seeking out scented candles and books and expensive notepaper, cut flowers and two vases to put them in, before thinking about food for the weekend.

Harry spots me and strides back down the supermarket aisle to say hello. Soon I wish I hadn't waved at him because after he has asked about the garden, he wants to know if I've seen Daisy's mum and when I say no he just keeps going, says he's found out a bit more about her, that strictly speaking, anything the health visitor knows is supposed to remain confidential, but you know . . .

'Yes, yes,' I say, impatient with him.

'According to Cheryl – it's her sister's daughter who . . . '

'You said.'

'It's a difficult case because the girl is not really coping too well, but other than taking the flat – the council pay for that, it seems – she won't accept any help or join in with any of the mothers' groups where she might find some support.'

'Oh?' I say, deliberately let my eyes wander away from his face to signal my lack of interest.

'Apparently she's convinced that anyone in authority is out to get her and the children.'

And I see her then, sitting opposite me in my living-room: *If you don't help me they will take her away from me.*

'Are they?' I ask.

Harry shrugs. 'Who knows? But I wouldn't have thought so. They don't take children away these days just because mothers have post-natal depression or whatever it is that's wrong with her, but – so Denise says – this Marie spent most of her childhood in and out of care herself, so I guess she's pretty wary. Understandable, I suppose. Poor kid looks so young, she could do with a bit of looking after herself, I would imagine.'

'Yes, well,' I find myself saying in a hardening voice, 'she'll just have to learn to trust people, won't she? That's the only way she's going to get better.' Harry looks taken aback by my tone but I don't care, am resentful of him for making me stand here in this supermarket aisle while we rip open somebody's life like a pair of vicious housewives. I follow him to the ten-item checkout and wait while he chats to the bony-faced woman on the till, who has hard new moons for eyebrows. She is friendly, albeit in a weary kind of way, as if the effort of conversing taxes her to her limits. As she scans each item, she pushes it down the metal slope towards him with an angry little movement.

Something about her looks familiar and when Harry is done he says, 'I've just realised that you probably knew Samantha when you were little,' smiling at first me, and then her, as if he is giving us something precious.

She looks at me, sharp eyes sizing me up.

'Really?' I say and then, only because Harry has made it impossible to do otherwise, add: 'What's your surname?'

'It's Barratt now, but I would have been Jones back then. I remember you and your sister. And your mum. You lived up at one of the big cottages, didn't you?' It seems more of an accusation than a question but I nod. 'Up near where the estate is now,' she clarifies for me. The connection is forming in my mind: I remember a girl with thin plaits and the sound of wedge heels on cobblestones, and the time that Josie dared to take on Samantha Jones and her cronies. 'You're back then?' she questions.

'For a while. I think I remember you too,' I say, because thanks to Harry something has to be said. 'You must have been about the same age as my sister, Lottie.' She thrusts the last of my shopping away from her – an expensive bottle of red wine – and it rolls down the slope at an angle and smacks into the edge of the counter.

'Yeah, but we didn't really play together.' She raises the new moons at me. 'You were a bit posh for us.' She laughs as she says this, but still makes me feel as if she is seeking some kind of apology.

'Oh, really?' I say icily.

'Nice to see you again anyway,' she sighs as I hand her a twenty-pound note. I take the change with a cold smile and bid her the tersest of goodbyes and as I do so I can almost hear the words that were once spoken about my mother following me.

'Snooty.'

Recalling the contents of Harry's basket: a couple of heat-and-serve meals for one, a small container of milk and a plastic bag containing two apples, I regret my earlier brusqueness.

'Come over for dinner one night,' I suggest and he says yes and looks pleased that I have asked.

It is wrong to blame Harry but the cries seem louder tonight and some irrational part of me cannot help thinking he has forced me to become more sensitive to them. I lie in bed, waiting for them to stop, and after a time they do, but then

I am awake again and only an hour has passed on my bedside clock and the cries are coming once more. The third time I am dragged up from sleep, the screams show no sign of abating, just keep winding up to a higher and higher pitch. I turn my back to the window, think about moving into the other bedroom, then try to force sleep on myself, but there is a puppet show behind my eyes that will not stop: Kieran, a writhing red ball of rage; Marie, with sweat dampening her dark hair as she tries to keep her patience, with him and herself, coaxing him on to a breast he does not want to recognise; and Daisy, unable to sleep, trying to help her mother and only making things worse. And I am suddenly cold with fear that something bad may happen in the middle of this night when Marie is alone and it is too dark for her to see a way out of this. I think of myself, how I have hidden from these three, locked myself away with my books and my good wine and my easy work and, though the thought of inviting in everything that is happening across the road horrifies me, I cannot stop myself from getting out of bed and reaching for my clothes.

'Who is it?' says Marie.

'Me'. She recognises my voice and buzzes me in. I find her waiting for me at the top of the stairs, her long pale legs protruding from a short dressing-gown. The door to her flat is pulled to behind her.

'Hi,' she says softly. Kieran is asleep in her arms.

'I heard him . . . I thought I should come and see . . . ' I whisper.

'Yes,' says Marie. She looks down at the baby who is twisting his body in discomfort even as he sleeps. 'He can't sleep properly because he's hardly fed at all tonight.'

'Is there a reason why?' I am struggling because I do not want to sound as though I am insulting the child. 'I thought babies naturally . . . '

'Not this one,' says Marie and she laughs, a desperate

attempt at light heartedness that threatens to break half-way through. 'They say he has a poor suck reflex because he was premature.'

'Daisy's asleep?'

'She went back just a minute ago. I shouted at her again so she's been crying too.' She rubs at her eyes angrily. 'And I don't know what we're going to do because one of the neighbours has started to moan about the noise and I'm sure she's going to complain to the council.' She looks down at the baby, fury and love in her eyes. 'It's not as if he does it on purpose!' I gather myself up, make the words fit together.

'Shall I come for her tomorrow?' Marie looks at me, weighing up what I have said. Though her eyes are dry, I can see that she has been crying. Then she just whispers a yes, turns to go.

*   *   *

'We have to go to church first,' Marie informs me when I arrive the next morning.

'Oh.' It has taken all my courage to bring myself back here, now that it is daylight and last night's fears have reduced to size. 'I thought of taking Daisy to the bookshop on the High Street, if it's open on a Sunday, so she could choose a couple of things for us to read together.' Daisy herself is busy in the bedroom, which leads directly off the living area, lining up some battered looking dolls on the edge of the bed and taking no notice of us. Marie carries on changing Kieran's nappy, on a mat on the carpet, cleaning between his splayed, frail legs with a wodge of baby wipes. I had expected her to be limp with defeat this morning, but instead she is agitated, scrabbling with a free hand to find a fresh nappy in a bag beside her and flicking her long hair back impatiently when the baby reaches for it. 'Perhaps you could just take Kieran with you today,' I suggest, looking around the room and taking in the sparseness of it, just a sofa and an armchair and a child's table-and-chair set made of red plastic, with some felt-tips and scrawled-upon paper strewn across it. The rest of the room is bare, except for a wooden crucifix on the wall, and a few books on the window-sill which are all children's, except for an oversized astrology guide with a lurid orange and purple cover. On the breakfast bar is a china representation of the Virgin Mary holding baby Jesus.

'Daisy must go as well,' she says, sealing the tabs of the nappy with a deft hand. Kieran's little body looks engulfed by the white bulk of it and I can see deltas of veins branching out beneath the thin, mottled skin of his abdomen and his chest. He stares up at his mother and flexes his feet. 'You could come with us.'

'Where?' I say, though her meaning is clear. 'To church?' She nods. 'Oh, I don't think I can,' I begin hurriedly. 'It's not something that I do – well, very rarely.' I look at the crucifix, at the Virgin Mary on the breakfast bar. 'And you must be Catholic, aren't you . . . '

'Everyone stares at us,' says Marie interrupting me.

'Oh, surely not! Why would they?' She says nothing. 'Or if they do,' I reason, 'it's simply that you're new faces in town.' She takes no notice of me.

'It's nearly Easter so we all have to go and we've hardly managed to get out of this bloody flat all bloody week!' She sits back on her heels and stares down at the blue velour sleepsuit in which she is about to dress the baby, her fingers working at the material. 'Sometimes I don't know why we came here,' she says bleakly.

'Why did you?' I ask, sensing there is little to be gained from trying to quell her paranoia or to dissuade her from taking the children to church today. She shakes her head.

'I don't know. Because my mother brought me here for a holiday once, just before she died. Stupid of me. I thought I might find something of her here but she's nowhere any more.' She looks at the crucifix. 'Nowhere I can find, anyway.'

Daisy runs ahead, past the driveways of the large detached houses, bounding over an imaginary skipping rope. Marie carries a sleeping Kieran in her arms and I have Susan tucked under my arm – a baby doll with blonde curls, unfeasibly long black eyelashes and a dirty smudge on one cheek – because Daisy insisted that she must come. At the entrance to the church, Daisy stops to wait for us. As we reach her I allow Marie to go ahead of me and she goes straight inside, to a stone font in the vestibule. She runs her finger over the surface of the water and then crosses herself.

'Would you lift Daisy?' she asks, turning to me. I pause, for I have never picked up a child before, not even one of Lottie's, but Daisy comes to me and holds out her arms so I lift her as best I can and when I have her in my arms I am surprised by the muscular solidity of her little body. I carry her across to the font where, slipping one arm around my neck to secure herself, she leans over and dips her finger into the water, then crosses herself solemnly, in exact imitation of her mother. Then she slithers out of my arms and down to the ground again, quick as an eel.

'Am I supposed to . . . ?' I look at Marie for direction.

'Only if you want to.' And I don't because I am not sure how and because already I feel I am trespassing here.

An elderly lady greets us then and she says hello to Daisy and takes her by the hand. Daisy goes with her, towards a group of children standing on one side of the church, without protest or a goodbye. Then she stops and suddenly darts back to us and I think that she is going to refuse to leave her mother, but she has only come to wrestle Susan out of my arms. She skips back to the group of children and the elderly lady lines them up in pairs and leads them off through a wooden doorway.

I turn to ask Marie where we should go, but I find that she is down on one knee, facing the altar and crossing herself again, with Kieran still cradled in the crook of her arm. There is something so dramatic and yet somehow self-effacing about her stance that I am reminded of Josie, down on her knees in prayer at Daniel's funeral, and am self-conscious on her behalf. Then she is up again, leading the way to an empty pew.

I will not make the mistake of leaving my seat for communion this time. Marie pays no attention to me or the rest of the congregation or the sleeping Kieran, just stares at the altar, at Jesus's tautened muscles on the cross or at the priest, and I wonder why it was she needed me to come here with her. I watch her as she takes communion, and as she walks back towards me, notice that her pale face has an unworldly quality in the half-light. Then I register someone's eyes resting on *me* and see a man who seems familiar to me, just behind her in the aisle. He lifts a hand and, just for a second, gives me a big unholy grin. I return the smile uncertainly, before realising that he is the man from the beach hut, whom I berated just days ago. I look away, turn the pages of my hymn book.

'I need to get him home,' says Marie as soon as we are outside again. Kieran is beginning to twist in her arms and though his eyes have not yet flickered open, his mouth is turning towards her breast, already rooting for his next feed. We hurry down the road, away from the little groups that have stopped to talk as they emerge from the church door. Daisy is skipping, and waving over her shoulder to another child, and chirping away about Sunday school and naughty men who stuck Jesus on a cross until he was dead but he woke up again and walked off, and Marie is not really listening because she is anticipating Kieran's wrath if he wakes before she is back at home. At the entrance door to the flats, she crouches down in front of Daisy. I walk a few paces away.

'But I want to stay with you and Kieran today!' I hear Daisy saying, and though Kieran's head is butting at her now, Marie's voice remains even, telling her that it's just for today, that Mummy is not feeling too good and that she needs Daisy to be a big, grown-up girl for her, and Daisy is still protesting, defiance entering her voice, and I see a flush suffusing Marie's face as she loses her composure.

'You have to, you just have to!' she says in a despairing voice, her face starting to crumple, and I go to them and kneel down on the pavement in front of Daisy, offering myself up to her.

'Daisy. Would you like to come to the bookshop with me?' I ask in my children's-television voice, which is beginning to come far too naturally to me now. 'I thought we could go to the bookshop together and choose some lovely new books for you, while Mummy has a little rest.'

Marie and I wait as Daisy considers this, considers me.

'Yes, please,' she decides.

Marie seizes the opportunity, giving Daisy a hug and dropping a kiss on her hair, then letting herself into the flats with a quick goodbye. The door slams behind her, muffling Kieran's first cry, and then it is just me, Daisy, Susan and an imaginary skipping rope.

CHAPTER 20

If I do not fill the silence, Daisy may start to fill it herself, with questions about what is wrong with her mother or, worse, tears. I keep her at bay with staccato questions – favourite colour? book? television programme? What does she like to eat best? When is her birthday? Shall we draw or does she like to paint, though I haven't any paints so we'd have to buy some, or would she prefer to read, or go for a walk on the beach? All the way to the bookshop I fire desperately, occasionally hitting the target but more often than not eliciting one word answers or, once or twice, no response at all, though this seems to arise from the little girl's self-absorption (she chatters to herself beneath her breath as we walk along the High Street) rather than a deliberate attempt to rebuff me. When we reach the shop she skips off ahead of me to the children's section and heaves a hardback book with colour plates of the solar system from a display table, insisting that this is exactly what she wants. I have no idea whether it is suitable for a child of her age but we take it anyway, together with a couple of storybooks, which I select randomly from the five-to-eight-year-old fiction section.

'Can I dig up your garden again?' asks Daisy on the way home, rescuing me from my seemingly unstoppable stream of words.

'Well, not all of it,' I say, hiding a smile as I unlock the front door and guide her inside.

Daisy's project involves digging earth from one of the borders and transporting it, in the plastic bowl I have found for her in the kitchen cupboard, to the patio, where she pours it into a heap and smoothes and moulds it with her hands and walks around it, surveying her work, until it matches some template she has in her mind. Then she begins adorning it with pebbles, grass and prunings, leaving off from time to time to collect more soil, or to direct me to do so, when she decides her earthen castle requires a new wing. Knowing that I will be unable to concentrate on any real work while she is in my care and relieved that she seems happy enough for now, I give myself up to assisting her and we squat down together in the sunshine, two muddy-handed savages considering design options.

Now that she has found something for us to do, I am less apprehensive, and as soon as I stop closing down on her with my questions, she becomes easier with me. Initially she limits herself to a commentary on the work in progress, and, though she rarely glances up from what she is doing, I can feel her assessing my responses. Then she tells me that Kieran was sick in Mummy's face the other day and I say poor Mummy, and I must have passed whatever test she has set for me, because suddenly she is off, in that chirp of a voice, hardly pausing to draw breath, wanting to know if everyone gets up again like Jesus did or do you stay killed and did I know that her granny's a skeleton; telling me that her star is Aries and Mummy says that's why she's bossy and can we build a tree-house next and then make a boat and sail it in the hole we have dug which we could fill with water from the garden tap and what is bossy? I soon learn that if my answers are too ponderous she will not hesitate to cut me off in mid-flow and I bristle at this to start with, unused to a child's candour, and then sometimes she surprises me by seizing upon something small that I have said, as if she has spotted a penny glittering in the grass, and then she wants to turn my words over and discover every detail of how, when I was a little girl myself, I used to collect plums from that tree over there and what colour the plums were and if my Mummy told me off for picking them.

'What would you like to eat, Daisy?' I ask, when the sun is overhead and she is beginning to lose interest in the castle. Anxiety gnaws at me again because I had not thought to ask Marie about such practical matters. I picture what is in my kitchen cupboards and try to think whether anything is suitable for a five-year-old to eat. 'I could make you some scrambled eggs. Or some soup, or we could go to the supermarket and buy some sausages or . . . '

'Do you have any pasta or ice cream?' says Daisy, regarding me solemnly.

'Oh, yes,' I say in relief. 'Well, no ice-cream I'm afraid, but we could go for a walk later and buy some.'

'Hurray!' She stabs at the air with the trowel I have given her.

'How does Mummy do your pasta for you?'

Daisy considers for a moment and I am just about to start rattling off options again, when she asks: 'Do you have ham and cheese?'

'Yes, I do.'

'I'll have pasta in a bowl with ham and cheese, please,' she says decisively, then puts down the trowel and makes for the back door.

Daisy looks at the meal I place before her, requests more cheese be sprinkled on top, then, apparently satisfied, says no more and begins to eat, breaking off from time to time to drink noisily from a glass of water. My kitchen chairs are too low for her, so she is sitting, somewhat precariously, atop two of the cushions from the sofa, her legs hanging down like a rag doll's. I eat quickly, stupidly nervous of her response to my culinary effort, and finish before she does. Someone knocks at the door and I leave her in the kitchen while I answer it. A woman of about fifty, with hair like black nylon, is standing on the doorstep. It is hard not to stare because she is dressed in such an exotic jumble of clothing: a cerise skirt of Indian cotton clinging to the mountain of her stomach, a lime-green crinkle-cotton blouse straining over her large breasts and a wisp of yellow chiffon wound round her waist.

'Oh hello, dear,' she begins in a breathy voice. 'Sorry to disturb you but I'm Pat from across the road, come to give you this.' She thrusts a key at me, jingling the gold bangles on her wrist, and rushes on. 'Only the little boy's been taken sick and they've rushed him into Braxtable and his mother said that you were looking after the other little one, asked me if I'd give it to you and let you know that she's got to go with him . . . '

'Just a moment,' I say, holding up my hand. 'What's happened? What did you say was the matter with Kieran?'

'Had enough!' calls Daisy from the kitchen.

'Well, she was in a terrible way because he'd been sick everywhere but he wasn't crying any more, he was just lying there, looking all funny and cold, and then she saw the rash and she came knocking at my door because they haven't had a telephone line put in.' She pauses too late for breath, has to suck the air in before she can continue. 'Anyway so I rang the doctor for her because she was hysterical and they said she was to take him straight to Braxtable General.'

'Did they send an ambulance?' I say, glancing over my shoulder into the kitchen where, through the half-open door, I can see Daisy fitting pasta tubes on to the ends of her fingers.

Pat-from-across-the-road shakes her head and the gold hoops in her ears shiver. 'No, they told her to get a taxi because it's quicker . . . '

'She can't afford a bloody taxi!' I say.

'Finished!' calls Daisy.

'Well I lent her my lottery money because there's plenty of time to pay me back when the little boy's better.' Her small olive eyes look kind enough and I'm just about to thank her when it occurs to me that she is probably the neighbour who has complained about the noise. She is edging her feet forwards, calloused toes curling out from a pair of delicate thonged sandals, trying to see past me into the house. Her legs are bare beneath the cotton skirt and, I notice, speckled pink with a shaving rash.

'Thank you for your help,' I say. I go to my bag, which is hanging over the banister, find a ten-pound note in my purse and push it towards her. Her hand, small and wrinkled, darts out to take it.

'Everything OK?' I ask Daisy, popping my head round the door. She smiles impishly, wiggles her pasta fingers at me and giggles. Her drinking glass is filmed with cheese-grease and smeary fingerprints. 'I just have to make a quick phone-call and then we'll go and buy ice-cream,' I say, closing the door behind me.

'McClean, Kieran,' I say into the phone. 'A little boy – a baby – and his mother, Marie. They would have come in about an hour ago, I think. It's imperative that I speak to her.'

'Just a moment,' the nurse says and then I hear her covering the mouthpiece and a muffled conversation.

'Hello?' someone whispers.

'Marie, it's Kate.'

'Hi . . . ' Her voice is out of control already.

'It's OK,' I say, though, clearly, it isn't.

'They think it might be meningitis.'

'Oh, Christ . . . '

'They've taken him away into another room and they won't let me be there because they've got to stick a needle into his spine, to draw off fluid. And they have to hold him down because it's dangerous if he moves, but he's so little . . .

oh God.' She cannot speak any more. I search for something within me that I can give to her.

'So you're saying that it's not definite yet? It may not be meningitis at all.'

'No.' But she does not believe it.

'Listen to me,' I say, with as much authority as I can muster. 'You have to stay strong. For Kieran's sake. He needs you to.'

'I'm trying,' she whispers.

'Of course you are. It's probably not meningitis at all and if it *is* anything to be concerned about then he's in exactly the right place. You have to trust these people, Marie.' There is silence at the other end. 'OK?'

'OK,' she says in a voice that seems to come from very far way. 'Did Mrs Fields find you? My neighbour.'

'Yes, I have the key right here,' I say, clutching it as if I might be able to absorb some of its strength. I pull together the last of my resources, because I have no choice but to do so. 'And Daisy can stay here. Unless you think I should bring her to the hospital.'

'No, no, I don't think she should come. I really couldn't . . . '

'I know. Marie?'

'Yes?'

'Call me as soon as there's any news.' I give her the number and wait as she writes it down.

'Why were you talking to my Mummy?'

Daisy is standing behind me, staring at me. Now I don't have even a minute to take hold of this thing and compose it into something innocuous. I fiddle with the phone on the cradle for a second, playing for time.

'How would you like,' I say, sitting down on the bottom of the stairs so that I am at eye level with her, 'to stay here tonight? As a special treat? You could have my old room, where I used to sleep when I was your age.' I am praying that she will not sense the edge of desperation

229

around the bright core of my words. She looks at me, unsmiling.

'Why? Where will Mummy be?'

'Well,' I hold out a hand to her, draw her near. She does not resist, but looks down at my hand covering hers as if she wonders what it is doing there. 'Mummy and Kieran had to pop down to the hospital for a little while and the doctors might want them to stay there, probably just for one night.' I am waiting for her to ask why, still not knowing what I will say if she does.

'Will Mummy come in the morning?' she asks instead, in a slow voice. I can see her weighing it up: the thrill of sleeping somewhere new, her mother's absence.

'Oh yes!' I say in my jolliest voice. 'As long as the doctors say so.' She takes this in.

'Will I be able to clean my teeth?'

I brandish the key triumphantly. 'Mummy's left me this, so we'll go across and fetch all the things you need and you can bring Susan if you want to. I expect she'd like to sleep in a new room with you.' She nods in agreement, but doesn't move. 'Why don't you come and take a look at it?' I coax. 'See what you think. Did you know that you can hear the sea from there?' This swings it. She gives a whoop then slithers past me, and races up the stairs.

Daisy is restless after lunch, doesn't want to play in the garden any more, or read or draw, and my old trick of allowing her to bounce on my bed occupies her for less than five minutes before she is back downstairs again, asking me whether we can make some cakes. I suggest that we go to the beach instead because I don't have any cake tins or flour and I am relieved to see her looking animated by this idea. She runs to fetch her trainers, insists on struggling with the Velcro fasteners herself, before pointing a foot at me and requesting my assistance a minute later.

A light wind is coming off the water, and Daisy launches herself into it, tearing off ahead of me and whirling around at the water's edge with helicopter arms, dipping down to snatch at shells and sea-shiny pebbles and chirping to herself whenever a stronger gust of wind catches at her clothes. I am glad that we came because out here, under the sky, it is easier not to think about the phone ringing or about white coats gathered around a tiny bed and hands pushing down on spindly limbs.

Daisy zips backwards and forwards to and from the shoreline, pointing out a boat on the horizon, wanting me to throw pebbles in the water. When she tires of running about, we sit on the shingle and she chatters about mermaids and whales and dinosaurs and do they really exist. Suddenly she gives an acquisitive shriek and pounces on a crab claw, which she has spotted lying nearby, like a curve of fibreglass, spray-painted orange. She turns it over, examining the pincers carefully, then jabs it at me and growls. I know enough by now to pretend to be scared, so I scramble to my feet and let her chase me up the beach, dropping to the ground and letting her catch me just in front of the beach huts. It is only as I am begging for mercy and fending her off as she strangles me a little too vigorously with one arm that I realise we are being observed.

The man who smiled in church is sitting outside his beach hut, with his feet up on the veranda rail. He has stopped writing or drawing in the notebook that is propped up on his knees, has his pen poised in the air as he watches Daisy and me tumbling about on the shingle. I sit up straight, tell Daisy that's enough, though she continues to giggle and lunge at me as I get to my feet.

'Hello,' I look directly at him, wanting him to know that I have registered him watching us and to feel my resentment. He is wearing jeans and a navy-blue oversized fisherman's jumper – the kind that people seem compelled to purchase the minute they come within a twenty-mile radius of the sea. 'I'm sorry if we disturbed you,' I say coldly.

'Not at all,' he says with a wave of his hand, and then he looks down at his notebook again, crosses something through.

'What are you doing?' Daisy asks him.

'Time to collect your things,' I say, taking her hand.

'Writing,' says the man, looking up and smiling at her. She resists my pull.

'What kind of writing?'

'Stories, I suppose,'

'What kind of stories?'

'Daisy!' I interject, tugging at her again.

'Rubbish ones,' confides the man with a wrinkle of his nose. Then he grins widely at her and closes the book. Lets it slide off his lap.

'We built a mud castle in her garden,' announces Daisy, and then, in a second, loses interest in him and scampers away across the shingle.

I stand there for a moment. 'Her mother's in hospital today,' I say because I can't think of anything else and because, for some reason, I feel compelled to justify why Daisy is in my care.

'Nothing serious, I hope?' he says, politely.

'No.' It has hardly anything to do with me, let alone him. I motion towards Daisy, who is halfway towards the pathway, then follow her down the beach.

We stop at the supermarket because Daisy wants 'food of the sea' for dinner – which turns out to mean prawns – and then we go to the flat and she collects an armful of essential things which keeps being added to until I have to remind her that she is only staying for one night and that the bedroom is a small one. I can hear the phone ringing even before we are through the door of the cottage and I send Daisy to wash her hands upstairs before snatching it up.

232

'It's not meningitis,' says Marie.

'Thank God.'

'They're running some other tests – blood and urine and things – but they think he's just badly dehydrated. They've put him on a drip – he's got this enormous great tube thing attached to his little hand and he keeps trying to bat it off because he can't work out what it is, the poor mite.' Tearfulness threads through her voice but I can hear relief too. 'Is Daisy all right? She hasn't cried for me, has she?' she asks and I cannot help a little pride entering my voice when I tell her that her daughter has been perfectly happy with me all day. I offer to bring her to the phone but she says no, Daisy doesn't like telephones, that she will see her tomorrow.

'Not tonight then? They're sure about that?' There is a pause at the other end.

'No. I have to come back in the morning though, to collect some things for me and Kieran. They've said Daisy can stay here too if she wants to . . . but I *have* to be here all the time because of feeding . . . They want me to bottle feed him for now as he's so weak, but I don't want to give up completely, not yet . . . '

I am not listening to the details.

'How long?' I say.

'What?'

'Have they told you how long Kieran might have to stay?' I cannot help the urgency of my tone pushing its way past politeness.

'No, well, a few days at the least so they can monitor him. Just till he's stronger.' I wait for my throat to constrict. The panic that is flaring up within me wavers, then subsides.

'Daisy can stay here,' I say. 'If she will.'

'What time's your bedtime?' I ask Daisy.

'Nine o'clock,' she says, looking at me hopefully. I narrow my eyes at this and affect sternness. 'Eight o'clock?' she tries.

'Half-past seven,' I decide and again I feel a little twinge of pride, or something like it, when she gives a melodramatic sigh but does not argue.

'What time's my bath?'

I eye the smear of mayonnaise around her mouth and the dirt that has collected beneath her wafer-thin fingernails.

'Now.'

'Oh, *man!*' she moans, and rolls her eyes heavenward.

'Why don't you have bubbles?' she demands when she is sitting, flushed and pink, up to her waist in warm water. Her clothes are in an untidy heap on the bathroom floor where she has thrown them. Following her instructions, I have put her pyjamas and a towel to warm on the radiator.

'Grown-ups don't,' I say. 'Shall we wash your hair?' She groans but slides back in the water anyway until only her face projects from the water, like a relief portrait. She closes her eyes, swishes her head around so that her hair lifts and floats in the water like a halo, then twists her torso from side to side and announces she's a mermaid. I have pulled up a chair next to the bath and when she rises up from the water I wash her hair, using my own shampoo and conditioner because we forgot to collect hers from the flat. Fear of hurting her makes me over-cautious but she yells out just once, when I am rinsing her hair under the shower, scolding me for allowing water to run in her eyes. Soon I am untangling wet curls with a wide-tooth comb, while she sings a tuneless little song to herself.

'Do you know how to wash yourself?' I say, handing her my sponge optimistically and sitting down in the chair again. She is moon-faced and very young with her wet hair swept flat to her skull like that.

'Yes,' she says grabbing it from my hand and tapping perfunctorily at her straight little body for a few minutes. She dabs under her arms and warbles away to herself, oblivious of my presence. The rising steam beneath the yellow light and the damp warmth of the bathroom combine to make me feel sleepy. A wave of fatigue washes over me and I realise how much I am longing for the time when Daisy is safely asleep and I can breathe freely again. I wonder how much more will be required of me today, try to dredge up what Lottie used to say about getting her children to bed at night.

It comes to me that she has stopped swishing about. The singing has stopped too. When I focus on her again, Daisy is sitting quite still, staring at the white tiles on the bathroom wall with a strange look in her eyes.

'What's the matter?' I ask.

'Is my Mummy going to die?'

'No!' I say, jerked back to full alertness. 'What on earth gave you that idea?'

'You said she had to go to the hospital,' she says, still staring straight ahead.

'Yes, but not for *her*, for Kieran, darling. And he's going to be better very, very soon.'

Her gaze does not change. 'That lady in the blue dress said there was something wrong with Mummy and Mummy got cross and said that was because she had to look after me as well as Kieran.'

'Which lady?'

'That nurse lady who comes with a bag of things but she's not a nurse.'

'You mean the health visitor?' Daisy nods, her eyes fixed on the tiles and her face beginning to flush.

'And now Mummy's in hospital,' she states, convinced by her own logic.

'Listen,' I say, getting down on my knees and leaning on the edge of the bath. 'I *promise* you that your Mummy is not going to die, Daisy. She's just been a little bit tired since Kieran was born and soon she's going to feel much, much better again.' She says nothing. 'I promise you,' I say again.

'But she will die one day.'

'Oh, Daisy . . . !'

I close my eyes for a second, feel the steam beading on my forehead and try to think my way out of this.

'We all die eventually,' I say, trying to invest my voice with some kind of calm sagacity, and then immediately regret my candour because I can see the alarm growing in her eyes and add quickly, 'but then we go up to heaven, which is lovely.' This is no time for a discussion about the multiplicity of beliefs, but still I feel I am cheating her with my pat answers, hate deceiving her more than I could have imagined.

'Will Mummy go there before me?' persists Daisy.

'Well, just a little bit before. And when you get there she'll be waiting for you.' The flush is spreading down Daisy's neck and across her chest.

'But she'll be a skeleton,' she says, her voice beginning to rise in despair. She turns to me now, her eyes seeking anything that might help.

'No, darling,' I say, casting around wildly for explanations. 'Our bodies don't go with us when we die. We don't need them any more, you see. We leave them behind, here on earth, and then we go up to heaven.' I hold her gaze for too long. The way people do when they are concealing a lie.

'Well, then . . . ' says Daisy accusingly, her features beginning to move, ' . . . then she won't have any hair!' and then it erupts out of her: a great wail that has no end, and her face is no longer a little girl's but a baby's and I am grabbing for that towel on the radiator and heaving her slippery body from the water and her legs are bumping against the edge of the bath. I hold her clumsily to me, in the chair, and her dripping arms are around my neck and she is telling me, over and over again in that broken little voice, that she won't be able to recognise Mummy when she sees her.

'It's all right, it's all right.' I keep rocking her to and fro and saying it over and over as grief shudders through that ribcage, which is small as a bird's against mine. She pushes her clammy face into my neck and her head is sleek like an otter's and smells of shampoo and I am telling her that everything will be all right, that Mummy and Kieran are going nowhere without her, and wanting her to trust my words because there is no one else right now.

I had not expected her to fall asleep so easily, though yawns began to intersperse her sobs long before I managed to quieten her completely. Once the crying is quite finished I dress her in her pyjamas, then blow-dry her hair and brush her teeth as best as I can. In the bedroom, she wants the window open because of what I had said about the sea. Then she asks me to stay with her until she is asleep and I sit on the edge of the bed, reading from one of the books we bought until her breathing begins to deepen and her lashes settle on to her cheeks. Then, I creep out, put on the landing light in case she wakes in the night, and go downstairs, straight to the kitchen where I pour myself a large glass of wine. When I check on her before going to bed, she does not appear to have moved.

I am dreaming of a voice calling to me, in a wood where the trees weave a thick green canopy above my head, but every time I turn to see who it is, they are gone, and yet the voice keeps coming and I am turning in circles, spinning round, then searching the ground with my hands like a blind person because the voice always seems to be behind me and below me, down in the undergrowth. The man from the beach is watching me, asks what I am doing and I say I thought I'd lost her but it is not my voice after all.

A hand is pulling at my nightdress. I come to, see Daisy's dark eyes looking into mine. She looks very small in her pink pyjamas and with that mass of hair around her face.

'I wanted Mummy,' she says.

'Oh,' I say, sliding my hand out from under the cover and taking her chilly fingers. 'What's wrong?'

'The sea is scary,' she says. 'It won't stop whispering at me.'

I ease myself up on to my elbow and push my hair out of my eyes. 'Shall I come and shut your window?'

She shakes her head. 'Can I come in with you?'

'OK,' I say after a moment. 'For a little while.' And I lift up to the duvet for her. She clambers in and turns her back to me, then folds herself into me as if she knows my shape already. Her hair tickles my face but I do not dare move for I can already feel her breathing slowing.

Sometime in the night she rolls away and then back towards me again, muttering something and then reaching out her arms to me. I inhale the faint sourness of her small breath and look at her waxen little features in repose, wonder if she knows where her father is or whether she thinks she has made him disappear too. Then, just as dawn begins to lighten the room and I am thinking that I might as well get up soon, go downstairs and read perhaps, I begin to drift off again and we sleep till morning, the two of us, heart to heart.

CHAPTER 21

Daisy has filled up my house with Susan and soft toys and the clutter of new felt-tips bleeding into the carpet, their lids lost under the sofa or between the cushions; with her scraps of paper with wavering lines of semi-intelligible writing scrawled across them, which get stuffed into keyholes and stuck on to doors or wrapped around banisters, and with duvets which are pulled from beds and draped over chairs, and pillows piled up or stuffed into drawers – that have been emptied of my troublesome clothes – to form the architecture of her imaginary world. Potions are made in the bathroom sink when my back is turned, mixtures of shampoo and toothpaste and more felt-tips, concoctions which, inevitably, are spilt when she tries to transport them to her bedroom or the airing cupboard.

She fills my head, too, with her need to be fed at regular intervals and washed and clothed and kept from thinking too much about her mother's absence; with her butterfly whims to make cakes or windmills and parachutes and paper pigs and aeroplanes and to visit that man with the funny grey hair who is Harry. All this leaves me physically exhausted – though I cannot understand why this should be, since no one task requires particular exertion – and turns my brain to white noise by the end of the day, so that there are times when I wonder if I can go on doing this till Marie comes back, or even until bedtime, and when I begin to regard this child's un-extraordinary mother with a new awe because, until now, she has managed to do it every single day of Daisy's life.

But I am learning new things: the way it feels when her little fingers automatically worm between mine when we walk along the pavement on our way to the beach or to the shops; how, paradoxically, lunatic energy animates her when she is truly exhausted; that though she has never been to school, Daisy has the ability to write, albeit haphazardly, because Nanna Sarah who is Daddy's mummy used to be a teacher and showed her how; and that she has a rare sense of humour and a gleeful laugh I find myself working harder and harder to elicit.

And then, after a week, her mother wants her back.

'Mummy!' Daisy erupts from the living-room and throws herself at Marie's legs, tries to shin up her. Marie sets down Kieran's car-seat and him in it and then she is down on her knees with Daisy in her arms and Kieran is blinking up at the two of them, bright eyed and curious.

'He looks like a different child!' I say, leaning over to wonder at the new curves of his cheeks.

'Doesn't he?' says Marie happily, looking up at me. 'He likes his bottles much more than anything Mummy has to offer, don't you, darling?' She looks at Kieran as she speaks, but her hand is stroking Daisy's face, running over it as if it were a talisman. Marie's face still lacks colour, but she has lost the extreme wan-ness that she had before she and Kieran went away and the darkness around her eyes has gone. It occurs to me only now how little we know about each other, we two who have shared a child for the past week, that I have no idea where she comes from, or anything about the father who put her into care, or the respectable sounding grandmother who taught Daisy her letters and whose son liked to smash his fists into the delicate bones of this pale face. Marie turns back to Daisy and buries her nose into the little girl's neck, breathes in the warmth that I know even in my sleep now.

'Oh, I've *missed* you!' she says, her voice fierce with emotion. Daisy wriggles, nods.

'Bad news, I'm afraid,' Daisy says, drawing back and shaking her head portentously. 'Susan's head fell off.'

We get the children past Mrs Fields, who pokes her head out of her front door the minute we enter the stairwell, the gold hoops in her ears quivering with anticipation, and back into Marie's flat. Daisy slips away from me immediately, races into the bedroom without a second glance. Marie takes Kieran out of his car-seat and lays him down on the carpet where he gurgles to himself and starts to kick his legs out riotously. Then she reaches into the side pocket of her rucksack and takes out a brown paper bag. She holds this out to me, not meeting my eye.

'I bought you these,' she says as I open the bag and take out a small purple box of chocolates. 'It's not much but the hospital shop didn't have anything very exciting . . . ' Her voice is louder than usual and I realise that she is unused to offering gifts.

'Thank you,' I say. I gesture towards the bedroom where I can hear Daisy berating Cloppy, the worn grey donkey who has usurped the decapitated Susan in the last day or so. 'But she's been lovely, you know.'

Marie nods. 'Still . . . ' she says.

'Mummy!' calls Daisy. 'Where's my pretty bracelet gone?' There is the sound of a toy box or something being upended in the bedroom and I am outside now, can feel the skin of family reforming around them already. I call a goodbye to Daisy, who does not appear to hear me. Then I go down the echoing stairs with my shrink-wrapped consolation prize under my arm.

*   *   *

You cannot take a child out of a house just like that. Not if you're expecting the rooms in that house to go back to being the way they were before, for the air within them to close around the space that has been left as if it had never been there in the first place. Even when you have cleared away all evidence of that child's presence – as I do all afternoon, cleaning the house with a dogged persistence as though the rhythms of my scrubbing and polishing and the flat blast of the vacuum cleaner will smooth over the jaggedness of my thoughts – their absence still yawns. There is a new quality to the silence that descends when I switch off the vacuum cleaner and it swallows its own roar: flecks of dust I have kicked up float through the sunlight and there is something hermetic about it, the sweet, dying air of an old people's home. Knowing that I cannot be shut up in here with just myself and this nothingness for a moment longer, I flee upstairs to change.

I run farther than I have ever done before: along the beach and up to the lower cliff-path, and then right round into Moreland Bay, beyond the entrance to the caves, pushing my muscles harder and harder until sweat is running into my eyes and my breath is coming in great lung-tearing gasps, until I cannot think about anything else. When I can go no farther I drop down at the water's edge and feel my heart crashing in my chest, trying to pump oxygen more quickly to my clamouring muscles. I lie back and stare up at the hard sky. A wave slaps over my foot and the chilly water finds its way through my trainer and my sock on to my skin. I do not move.

Exercise and the contents of most of a bottle of red wine do nothing to help me sleep. I lie for hours, fragments of thoughts falling like confetti, then whirling away as if the wind has caught at them: think of Josie, as a teenager and then down on her knees at the funeral, of my mother and her peculiarly upright stance and whether she has ever had a lover since she left Harry. I think of Adam and David, my

242

own most recent lovers, and then realise that I cannot imagine ever having sex again and that maybe it is as well because people never want just that from me, always think it is a road to something else. Eleanor enters my thoughts and I remember how she too wanted to get inside of my skin, tried to pull friendship out of me by persistence. I feel a twinge of guilt for her that would never have troubled me in daylight hours, push her away again. I run my hands over myself to pass the time, trying to remember a response, then cannot be bothered.

All this time I have been waiting for him to start crying. I do not know this until I hear him. Then I am up at the window in an instant, watching for the light to flick on in Marie's flat. I hold my breath, a still shadow at the window, as I hear Kieran beginning to work himself up. Then, after a few minutes, the cries stop. I stay at the window, waiting, reach for a cardigan as the cool air begins to chill my skin. My ears strain but there is no more crying and after half an hour the light across the road goes off again.

I hide from my disappointment downstairs in the living-room where I turn on the lamp, pick up the newspaper and try to concentrate on the crossword that I half completed earlier in the evening, willing the list of cryptic questions to block out all the other half-formed questions that are swarming around my head tonight. After an hour or so, sleepiness finally begins to roll over me and I get up from the sofa. As I do so I notice something on the carpet, just beneath the armchair. Crouching down I pull out one of Daisy's socks which I must have missed when I cleaned in here. It is balled-up and inside out and the candy pink cotton is grubby with dirt on the sole. As I go to stand up again I spot something else behind it, farther back. I reach beneath the chair and pick up a scrap of orange paper, then smile when I see what is on it: two stick figures, one taller than

243

the other, with matching grins, holding wonky buckets and spades in their hands. Wavy lines run across the top of the page, where a shark with vicious jaws hangs, seemingly in mid-air, beneath a pro forma sunshine.

*   *   *

I lie stiffly, stare up at the white expanse of ceiling, thinking about Daisy's grandmother who lost her one day and cannot teach her anything any more. How she must yearn for that small wriggling weight upon her knees. Then grief crashes into me, gets into every part of me in an instant, like salt into a small wound. My chest heaves, but I cannot cry, just hear myself whimpering, like an animal. I pull my knees up and clutch them to me, reducing my surface area as much as possible, then lie, heavy as a stone, and wait for dawn to come.

*   *   *

My head aches with agitation and self-loathing and too much coffee and then church solves the problem because Marie does not like going on her own. I find myself outside the flats, stepping back and looking up at their window, where, yes, the curtains are open. I buzz again, and then again, check my watch, sure that I cannot have missed them. The intercom does not crackle into life. I hover for another minute, thinking that if they have already gone ahead it will soon be too late to join them. I buzz one more time, then come to a decision, and set off down the side road, hurrying towards the church. When I get there, I go straight inside and begin looking up and down the rows of the people already seated. Still I cannot see them anywhere and I start to wonder if they might have gone for a walk first, perhaps trying to get Kieran off to sleep before the service. I make my way along the aisle and sit down in the middle of one of the pews, then twist round in my seat to check upon new arrivals. People trail in, in family groups, or couples, or alone. Eleven o' clock approaches and either end of my pew

244

has been filled. It would not be easy for me to leave without drawing attention to myself, and still they do not come

The clock strikes the hour and I understand then that I have been mistaken. The knowledge settles on me, smothering the ebullience that fizzed through my veins as I raced around the house trying to get ready in time and that now, in retrospect, seems like a manifestation of the madness I had thought was safely locked up inside my head. I stare at the dark wood of the confessional opposite the end of my pew, thinking that once again I am here when I should not be. The priest is at the altar, fretting about with things and glancing out over the congregation. He has grey thinning hair and kindness in his expression and I will stay because I am here now and because if anyone needs his help it is me.

There is nothing physically wrong with me. I keep telling myself this all the way through the service, this private incantation acting as a bulwark against the public ones that keep pushing in upon me from every direction. But I cannot help it, feel sure that some vital part of my internal structure has been torn out of me, like a backbone stripped from a fish, and that, at any moment, when we are listening to this grey-haired man talking on and on or standing to sing a hymn, I might collapse in upon myself, simply cease to be, and no priest or impassive Jesus on the cross will do a thing about it because I am nothing to them, not part of anything they recognise, here or anywhere else. And it is as well that I am surrounded on all sides and that some shred of propriety stops me from elbowing my way out of here. When the service finally ends I thank God for the first time that morning then push my way past the stupid dawdling people all the way down the aisle until I am out again beneath the fierce blue sky, feeling as if I have been expelled like a cork from a bottle.

'No little one today?' says a voice beside me as I try to

find a way through the confusion of chattering mothers and unleashed children outside. The man from the beach hut must be mad too because he is smiling at me as if everything beneath the sun was orderly and right.

'What? No. Her mother's taken her away,' I say, then check myself because I can see I have startled him, and because now I am beginning to talk like a mad person. 'The baby's better,' I add in a steadier tone.

Beach-hut man nods. I notice that the sun has bleached his sandy hair since I last saw him and that the skin on his forehead looks as though it has just escaped burning. 'Harry mentioned it.'

I try to make the connection and fail. 'I didn't know you knew each other,' I say. 'Do you paint?' I ask, trying to anchor myself to the surface of the day with formalities.

'Not so anyone would want to look,' he grins. 'I don't really know Harry – sorry, I should introduce myself first. I'm Aidan. Aidan Ford.' He holds out a hand to me.

'Kate,' I say. I try to smile but it dries on my teeth and I see myself through his eyes, madness written grotesquely across my face in the unforgiving sunshine. I drop his hand and turn to go.

'Yes, again Harry told me,' he says. 'As I say, we don't really know each other. I knew his son better. Daniel.'

'Daniel?' I say, stiffening and turning back. 'How could you have?' I pause, not knowing how to frame it. 'You know what happened to him?'

'Yes, poor guy. I didn't know him that well, but we used to play football together sometimes when we were kids.'

I am about to ask him how this can be, because all the beach huts seem to be owned by out-of-towners, when the priest walks past us and Aidan touches his arm and thanks him for today's service.

'I'm always relieved when it's Father Jones,' he says in an undertone, when the priest has passed by. 'I can't stomach Father O'Connell too often, the old curmudgeon.'

'I wouldn't know,' I say. 'I mean, I'm not actually a Catholic, so I shouldn't be here at all.' He makes the kind of face which means it's not important and I gesture back towards the church. 'Well, you're certainly made to feel that way.' I intend the words lightly, but something of my despair reaches my voice and he registers it.

I wait for him to speak, thinking that he will try to correct me, but instead he nods, and says apologetically, 'Yup, we're a pretty exclusive bunch at times,' and then looks at his watch. 'Do you think it's too early for a drink?' he says, wrinkling his nose as he pretends to ponder the idea. 'I always feel as if I deserve one for good behaviour.'

And, because I have lighted upon someone who might be able to give me something of Daniel, something which has eluded me till now, and since there will be plenty of time to fall apart later, when I am all alone in that blank of a house again, and, most of all, because a drink is possibly the only thing in this world that might numb me at this moment, I agree to go with him.

The Ropemaker's Arms has been refurbished since Harry used to drink in here when we were children, has made itself over as a dining pub with chalked-up menus and waitress service. Aidan orders food then we take our drinks outside on to the terrace and sit in the sunshine like normal people. I encourage him to talk so that I don't have to and he tells me that he lives in Canterbury now but grew up in Moreland Bay, that the beach hut belongs to his sister who uses it in the children's holidays. When his lunch arrives – I have refused any – I try to speak a little, which is easier now that half a sun-warmed glass of red wine is beginning to wing through my bloodstream, but I find he is aware already of my tenuous link to Harry and about the work I am doing at the cottage and I start to resent Harry for his garrulousness and, illogically, the man opposite me for his part in it. We talk about Daniel instead and he tells me what I know already: that he loved his football and motorbikes, that he was friendly and good-natured, that though he cannot quite visualise Daniel's face now, he remembers a gentleness about him.

By the time he has finished eating and returned from the bar with more drinks I am reaching the end of my social resources – which are more limited than ever today – and instead of dreading the empty house I am now longing to be there. I ask him why he returns here, though it comes out sounding like an accusation, and he tells me that he only visits at weekends, that he had a sudden whim to fill them with boyish pursuits because otherwise work invades every corner of his life, that when his sister mooted the idea he thought of sailing and walking and fishing and sitting out on the rocks, reading or writing. He pulls a self-deprecating face as he describes this romantic vision of himself, then tells me that the rest of the time he teaches history at a boys' school.

'Do you like it?' I ask, out of politeness rather than real curiosity and he says yes, he loves it – though he wouldn't normally admit to this, for fear of transmogrifying into some kind of Robin Williams character.

I finish my second glass of wine quickly and get up to go, half-expecting him to suggest a date since he is probably attractive enough to think that I might accept and because men do not normally allow me to walk away without leaving some kind of hook in me. I am already arming myself with excuses to deflect him, but he thanks me for joining him and leaves the pub with me, then heads off in the direction of the beach.

She cannons into the back of my knees, nearly knocking me to the ground, then clambers up into my arms. I swing her up and hold her tightly, feeling her little heart beating from the exertion of running.

'We were shouting at you!' she announces, patting at my cheeks with cold hands.

'I'm sorry, baby, I didn't hear you,' I say, smiling at her knitted eyebrows and reproachful manner.

'Silly billy,' she says, wagging a finger at me, then wriggles in my arms and slides down to the pavement again. 'I've been looking for crabs and I'm not a baby.' Marie comes up, pushing the buggy, with a child's orange fishing-net balanced across the canopy.

'Where on earth have you three been all day?' I say, mimicking Daisy's admonitory tone. It is easy to be light-hearted now.

'Down on the beach,' says Marie. There is colour in her cheeks today and even a touch of animation about her.

'No church then?' I say, casually.

'We went to the nine o clock. This one decided to wake us up very early this morning,' she looks down at Kieran with a wry smile. Then she tells me that at least he slept well during the night, which I know already.

'I'm going to try breastfeeding him again,' Marie informs me. 'The hospital said I shouldn't bother, now that he's taking to bottles so well, but I want to give it one last try. I did it for Daisy and I'm sure I can do it for Kieran.' Now that she is no longer exhausted, she gleams with the invincibility of youth.

We turn and begin to walk back towards the High Street, Daisy tugging at my skirt as we go. Something is formulating in my head even while Marie and I chat about small things. I could stop it, but I don't.

'I was thinking yesterday,' I say, then hesitate. 'About Kieran,' I continue. 'Clearly, he's a great deal better, of course, but you've still a lot to cope with, taking care of him as well as Daisy, and no family nearby to support you . . . ' Marie looks puzzled, cannot see where I am heading. 'I was wondering if you'd like me to help with Daisy on a more regular basis? I won't be staying here for ever –

obviously – probably no longer than this summer I should think, but it's not as if I have to work while I'm here . . . '

'I want to sleep in your little bedroom where the sea comes in,' chirps Daisy, tugging at me again. Marie shushes her and I plough on.

'It would mean you could just concentrate on Kieran for a few hours a day and catch up on some sleep when you need to and then you'd have more energy for Daisy and some time for yourself . . . ' I am gabbling now.

Marie has stopped pushing the buggy. 'Are you sure?' she asks, reaching for her daughter's hand.

'Yes. Mornings, afternoons – whatever would suit you best.' I smile munificently.

She looks down at the little girl. 'Did you hear what Kate said, Daisy? Would you like to go and play at her house sometimes? Just while Mummy gets a few things done at home? It's only if you want to, you know.'

'Yes, please,' says Daisy emphatically.

'Are you sure, darling?' Daisy is bored with the subject now, ignores her and then tries to pull her hand free so that she can pick up a piece of chalk she has spotted on the pavement. 'When would you be thinking . . . ?' Marie wavers, unwilling to set any terms, so I help her out, suggesting that Daisy comes first thing each morning and stays till lunch, or after lunch if that is easier, and we agree on this. Marie says little but her eyes are full of gratitude and, as we walk the rest of the way home, I am triumphant and at the same time sickened by myself, by my little act of treachery.

I give Daisy a kiss, tell her I will see her in the morning, then help Marie get the buggy through the door of the flats and Kieran out of the buggy while she collapses it.

When she has him back in her arms, she turns to me. 'I forgot to say,' she says, flushing slightly. 'The health visitor was asking me about Daisy, about who was looking after her while we were in hospital . . . '

'Yes?'

'I told her you were Daisy's auntie.'

'Oh.' I think about this for a second. 'Why?'

'Because she's always asking me questions,' she says, a defensive note coming into her voice. 'And to stop everyone around here talking about me all the time.'

'I'm sure they don't,' I say, not wanting to tell her that if they do, she will only have made things worse, because all they have to do is ask Harry to find out that she is lying.

'Do you mind?' asks Marie, looking shamefaced and very young all of a sudden.

'No,' I assure her.

'Auntie Katie, Auntie Katie!' chants Daisy over the banisters, then collapses into fits of giggles.

And so it is that Daisy comes to my house every morning when she is fresh from sleep and bubbling over with joyous energy, ready to tear about on the beach or at the recreation ground, to make fairy cakes with blue icing or paint or draw or stick things in or listen to me reading her stories. I find it easy now to let this grave-eyed little tyrant order our time just as she pleases and, after a while, even start to question why her mother finds it so difficult. We hunt for fossils and climb on the rocks or look for prawns in the rock-pools and one day I show her the entrance to the caves in Moreland Bay, though she shows little interest in going inside, just says they smell of the dark. I buy her things too – books, toys, jigsaws, clothes – just a few to begin with, then, when it becomes clear that Marie does not have the luxury of being able to turn them down, more and more, though I try not to be too blatant about it and keep some of them in a chest of drawers in my old bedroom.

And it is on a rainy morning in early summer, when we have stretched across the kitchen floor an old roll of wallpaper which I found in a cupboard – pinning it down with chair legs at the corners – and Daisy is painting what started out as a rainbow but has now become a great muddy swirl arching across the paper, that the doorbell rings. I rinse my hands quickly under the kitchen tap and rub them dry on my jeans as I walk to the door.

The thin-faced woman on the doorstep smiles nervously at me, goes to put her bony arms around me, then catches sight of Daisy through the kitchen door.

'Who's that?' she asks.

'Her name's Daisy. What are you doing here?' I ask my sister Lottie.

CHAPTER 22

With Lottie there is really no need to enquire. Even before she and her suitcase are through my front door it bursts out of her.

'I've left Brian!' she announces and she drops her suitcase in the hallway and gazes at me expectantly. She is almost vibrating – with some emotion that I can't yet identify.

'What?' I say blankly. 'Why?' Why now, is what I mean.

'Because of everything!' she says with a sweep of her hand and a triumphant flourish in her voice. And then I realise that what is pulsing through her is almost unbearable excitement. 'I can't believe I'm back here. It feels so strange after all these years!' she says, her eyes darting around the hallway, the staircase, through into the kitchen where Daisy sits on the floor, watching us. My sister is like a child on Christmas Eve, overwrought, breakable.

'Where are the children?' I ask.

'They're at his mother's this week,' she says with another wave of her hand. It is this, the dismissiveness of the gesture, that shocks me more than anything she has said about leaving Brian, because Lottie's life has always been swallowed up by her children. 'Once I'd decided I couldn't just sit there on my own. I had to come and tell someone!' She smiles at me, as if I should be flattered that she has parcelled up her feelings and brought them here to me.

'Brian,' I say. 'He's still at home?'

'Oh, I didn't *have* to leave – ' she says. 'Brian says he

should be the one to go but I thought of you here, all on your own, and it seemed the obvious place to come . . . So here I am!' She laughs, a little wildly, and I think of Daisy when she is giddy with fatigue.

Daisy herself is standing in the doorway now, eyeing Lottie warily. Lottie signals the questions to me again. Who is she? What is she doing here? I introduce the two of them and Daisy plucks up the courage to say hello. Then I explain as much as I can in Daisy's presence, hoping that for once Lottie will try to understand the unspoken things: that I am not, as she thought, on my own, that this little girl with the serious eyes uses up all of me and, most importantly, that there is no room for another child in this house.

Later, when Daisy has gone home and I have recovered from the shock of my sister's arrival, I begin to soften towards her. In the evening I cook dinner for us and we sit out on the patio, listening to a solitary bird singing in a tree near by, its voice cutting cleanly through the approaching dusk; breathe in the sweet heavy perfume of nicotiana drifting up from the border. Lottie is calmer, now that she has finished racing around the house peering into every cupboard and alcove and out of every window as if expecting to find our younger selves hiding away somewhere. Though she says she rarely drinks, we have already got through one bottle of wine, and I am beginning to relax, to overcome the panic that always seizes me when Lottie comes at me unexpectedly, holding out her needs like a beggar's cup. This evening I find room in me for love, and for guilt, because after all, Lottie cannot help herself: her unhappinesses have always been bigger than she is.

She sits back in her chair now, looking up at the sky, which is just beginning to darken, and she tells me how she has never been sure that Brian loves her as much as she loves him, how, these days, he seems unreachable.

And then, about how she has felt herself disappearing since the children have all been at school, that she has lots of friends in the same position but that none of them seem to feel the meagreness of their lives in the way that she does; she cannot explain it to them, how slight her existence feels to her.

'This week, when the children went to Jean's and Brian was working all the time or off playing football, I just couldn't stand it any more,' she says, turning to me.

'What will you do though?' I ask, refilling her glass for her. 'I mean, what is it that you want instead?'

'A job to begin with, I suppose,' says Lottie, sipping her wine. 'That's what other people do.' She sits forward. 'Do you realise that I've never worked, Kate? Not properly. Only the odd part-time thing here and there that hardly matters, unless you count those few months after secretarial college before I got married. I can't believe how I've managed it – never to do anything! I don't know how it's happened or how I haven't noticed before but I seem to have ended up living some kind of half-life.' She sees I am about to protest and stops me. 'It's different for you, Kate. I know you had a difficult time recently, for whatever reasons, but you've travelled and been to university and had lots of jobs and boyfriends and been to parties . . . ' She looks at me enviously.

'Yes,' I say slowly. 'But I'm not sure that I feel as if I have. That it makes any difference.'

'That's easy to say when you've done it,' says Lottie. 'Those things *are* a part of you, whether you feel it or not. People will always treat you differently from the way they treat me.'

'But why does this entail leaving Brian?' I ask. 'Would he really object if you went out to work or took some courses or whatever it is that you need to do? What does he say about all of it?'

'I don't know,' says Lottie in a voice that is suddenly small. 'I've never asked him. Not properly.'

'But why?' I try to keep my voice level, but Lottie senses my incredulity and defends herself.

'Because I just feel that he wouldn't approve! He's always loved me being at home with the children and looking after everything. It's what his mother did and he's always going on about how important that was for him and his brothers when they were growing up, which is fine for him because he has a whole life outside that house that has nothing to do with me or the children.' Lottie tries to maintain some composure and then her face suddenly crumples and once again I am reminded of Daisy. 'I'm just not going to do it any more, Kate! You know, ever since Daniel died I've been feeling like this and I can't! I can't just carry on saying everything's all right when it isn't!'

'OK, OK,' I say, seeing that with very little encouragement she will work herself back up to the feverish pitch she was at when she arrived here. Then I ask out of curiosity: 'What's Daniel got to do with it though?'

'Nothing really,' she says, her voice quietening now. 'It's just that you realise there's too little time. Or rather,' she frowns, confused by her own thoughts. 'There's too *much* time to be unhappy in. Unhappiness just goes on and on unless you make it stop.'

I take Lottie around the garden before darkness falls, showing her what I have done so far, and we talk about the house and Broadgate and what has changed and what is still the same. I tell her more about Daisy and Marie and Kieran. Lottie says she is surprised because I never showed the slightest interest in her children. I apologise and take her arm as we walk, though I am unable to explain why it is that their existence has hardly registered with me. Lottie wants to go everywhere tomorrow she says: into town because she didn't get a proper look when she drove in, to the beach, down to the harbour, to Daddy's grave, and I have to remind her that Daisy will be with us in the morning, that her little legs will soon tire if we attempt a Grand Tour. We could drop by at Harry's though, because Daisy loves going there.

Lottie stops by the plum tree, looks at me in alarm. 'Oh no, I can't see Harry! Not yet.'

'Why not?'

'Because he's in touch with Mummy, isn't he?'

'I think so. What of it?'

'She doesn't know yet. About me leaving Brian,' explains Lottie. The shadows of the leaves from the plum tree mottle her skin and she looks thinner and more insubstantial than ever, out here in the coming darkness.

'Well, she has to know sometime,' I reason, 'though I suppose it ought to come from you and not from Harry.'

'She'll be furious with me,' says Lottie forlornly, and I feel a surge of irritation, want to remind her that she is a mother with children of her own. I breathe deeply, force it away as we walk back towards the patio, and then fetch another bottle of wine from the kitchen and hunt for some cigarettes. I check if Lottie wants to come inside because it's getting cooler now. 'No, I'm fine out here,' she says. 'I shouldn't really keep drinking though. I'm not used to it.' She lets me refill her glass anyway, takes a deep gulp of wine and continues where we left off. 'I'm sorry, I know it sounds ridiculous, as if I'm scared of telling her . . . It's just I feel as if Mummy despairs of me sometimes. I can't help feeling that I'm some kind of burden to her.'

'I don't think that's it,' I say, lighting a cigarette. 'I think it's more that she doesn't always know what to make of you.' I draw in smoke, remembering Lottie's headlong flight into marriage at seventeen, her subsequent plunge into motherhood, and how, even as she approaches middle age, everything she thinks and feels thrums at the surface of her. 'You've always been so emotional, so . . . so absolute about everything, and Mummy just isn't. I don't think it's disapproval, you know. She's different, that's all.'

'Do you think so? I'd never thought of it that way,' says

257

Lottie, animated by the idea. 'I've always felt that she had more in common with you. It's almost as if she finds me . . . the way I behave sometimes . . . distasteful.'

'No, you're wrong,' I say emphatically. 'As I say, it's just a difference of character.' The light has almost gone now and I am growing sleepy with wine and too much talk. My eyes rest on a white rose that grows up the wall just here, its petals luminous, achingly white in the twilight, and I am not listening to Lottie any more because we are starting to go round in circles and she is talking about old times, and then something she is saying reaches me.

' . . . she's always used to say thank goodness it was you and not me with Daddy . . . '

'What?' I say, suddenly alert.

Lottie is slumped a little in her chair, gazing up at the sky again. She senses the change in my tone, glances at me quickly. 'Sorry,' she says, going to get up from the chair. 'I'm rambling now. Too much wine . . . ' She waves her glass at me apologetically.

'What does she say about Daddy and me?' My voice falls like a stone.

'Nothing . . . I shouldn't have . . . ' she begins, then stops and shakes her head as if she is trying to clear it.

'I know what happened, you know,' I say in a low voice. 'I've always known.'

Lottie stares at me. 'How could you? I was never allowed to . . . I wouldn't . . . '

'Josie told me. Years ago.'

'Oh my God.' Her hand goes to her mouth. 'Then . . . you've known all this time? You don't remember it yourself though? Surely not?'

'No.'

Lottie falls back in her chair and then her voice explodes from her. 'My *God*, Josie was a vicious cow! How *dare* she tell you! Mummy would have strangled her if she'd ever found out. And how did *she* know?'

'She was very good at discovering things you didn't want her to, I seem to remember,' I say.

Lottie is shaking her head again, in disbelief this time, and her hands twist round one another in agitation. 'Why would she do that to you? I can't imagine why she would. *Or* why I ever liked her so much!'

'It's OK,' I say in a voice that is beginning to tremble though my body is taut. 'She sort of compelled you to. Even me. Even when they had gone, after everything that happened, I can remember feeling that it was my fault, I mean, that it was only because she found out what a bad person I was that she hated me so much.'

'Well, it was hardly your fault, was it?' retorts Lottie. 'Any of it.'

'Her disliking me?'

'No, no, about Daddy I mean.'

It is my turn to stare. 'Of course it was. How can it have been anything but my fault?'

'But what could you have done?' says Lottie. 'You were only four years old.'

'Yes, but I could have fetched help, couldn't I?' I say, and my voice is beginning to crack with the relentless pressure of the truth. 'I wasn't too young for that, was I? I could have gone out into the garden and screamed and screamed until someone came and did something!'

Lottie is looking at me in wonder and pity.

'But you don't know then,' says Lottie, something gathering in her eyes. She stands up, comes to me, and says gently, 'You don't really know what happened, Katie.' And she is crouched in front of me reaching for my hands, pulling them to her and I am pushing her away, because I am barely human and no one, not even my sister, should have to touch me. 'Kate, listen to me! I only remember some of it myself, but what I do know is that you couldn't get out! Don't you know that? The door of that greenhouse was jammed!' I turn my head away, stare past her at one bloom on the rose bush that is starting to go brown around the edges, but she won't leave off now she has started. 'Listen! Daddy had been meaning to fix it for ages and he hadn't because he'd been so busy at the surgery and it was worse that day because it had been raining all week and the wood has swollen. You couldn't have saved him anyway, because the doctor who came said it was instant. So it wasn't your fault, you see. You were just too little, that's all!'

I cannot speak or move. Fierce white petals rise up out of the darkness and burn my eyes. There is something else. Something Lottie has said that cannot be right because it does not fit with the words that Josie poured inside me all those years ago.

'The rain . . . ' I say, brokenly. 'Josie said it was a heatwave. That Daddy . . . ' my breath shudders out of me, ' . . . that he was starting to rot.' Sourness fills my mouth then and I am up on my feet, wanting to deadhead that one overblown bloom that is spoiling the effect of the others, but as I cross to it, I trip on an uneven paving-stone or something because I am on my knees with the black soil coming up at me and Lottie is there with her arms around me, telling me that it wasn't possible, that she and Mummy had only left us there, potting up seeds, that morning, that it wasn't, could never have been.

After a minute I can see again and we get up off the ground, brush ourselves down and go back inside the house. In the living-room we light the lamps and pour the last of the wine and Lottie keeps shaking her head and saying she can't believe it, all these years, and she wants to tell me more, about how Mummy thought I was young enough to forget, that it would be better never to tell me, about how, when they found me, my hands were cut and swollen from hammering on the door – but I say can we stop now and we pretend to talk about ordinary things until we have finished the second bottle of wine and Lottie is yawning, ready for bed.

I say she can sleep in my old bedroom and we carry her suitcase upstairs and make up the bed together, then clean our teeth in the bathroom as we used to do when we were young – and all the time the voice in my head, telling me over and over that my entire life has been wrong.

I lie in bed listening to Kieran's second round of screams. Marie has been white-faced again, and quieter than ever, this last week or so. Kieran is putting on weight now that she has finally given up trying to breastfeed him, but the bottles make his colic worse than ever. She is counting the days, she tells me, because the health visitor says that there is nothing to be done, that everything will get easier once he is twelve weeks old. Marie thinks that maybe it was the same with Daisy though she can't honestly remember because everything seems like a fog right now. Eventually the crying stops and then I hear a noise across the landing and a tall silhouette appears in my doorway.

'Kate?'

'Yes?'

'I can't sleep.'

'Me neither.'

'Can I come in with you?'

I sit up, throw back the duvet on the far side of the bed and Lottie slips in beside me, lies on her back and pulls the duvet up to her chin. There is a gap between us but still I can feel the tension in her body.

'I keep thinking about the children,' she says, staring up at the ceiling. 'What they're going to say about it all.'

'It will be OK,' I lie.

'Do you think so? Really?' says Lottie in a scared little voice.

'We'll talk about it in the morning,' I say firmly and after a moment I reach across and take her thin hand in mine, try to send comfort into the long bones of her fingers.

Daisy bursts in the next morning and clatters over all our troubles, pushing them aside for later. We give her a second breakfast, then take her down to the beach. On our way I point out to Lottie all the changes that have taken place along the High Street. She seems disappointed to see the restaurants and wine bars and the new delicatessen, as though she was expecting nothing to have changed since she left, as if someone has deliberately taken something away from her. She doesn't join in with Daisy and me as we chase each up and down the shingle, just sits on a rock and watches us, though when we go for pizza at lunchtime, she chats to Daisy like a practised mother, asking her about her toys and her little brother and her favourite food in all the world.

In the afternoon, when we have taken Daisy home again, Lottie and I walk into town to the graveyard, to lay flowers on our father's grave. A sense of momentousness swells up in me as we walk towards the entrance with our offerings: everything ought to be different after what was said last night, out in the darkness of the garden, but when we arrive at the grave it is just me and Lottie and the sound of the wind catching at the plastic liner in the rubbish bin near by, and as we kneel down and arrange our flowers in the little urn at the base of our father's gravestone, we talk about mundane things. As we prepare to leave, a funeral cortège is arriving at the far gate. We pass by a hole in the ground that looks as if it might have been dug in the last day or so. Lottie looks down at the raw mouth of earth and gives a little shiver.

'I still can't get used to seeing that. I think that's what upset me so much at Daniel's funeral. Seeing him swallowed up by the ground like that.'

'We hardly knew him though,' I remind her. 'Sometimes I think there's something wrong – sham, I suppose – about making his death into something it wasn't.' She starts to look offended and I add hurriedly, 'I mean that about myself too. Because I couldn't stop thinking about him afterwards and I'm still not sure why.' Lottie nods, says nothing for a minute, as I close the iron gate behind us.

'He was a part of our childhood though, wasn't he?' she says, frowning as she tries to grasp at something difficult. 'There's something sacrosanct about that, isn't there? You always think of your childhood as something untouchable and then something gets hold of it and changes it.'

'I'm not sure that's possible,' I counter, thinking that what she told me last night should have done just that, and yet it doesn't feel as if anything has changed, not here, at my father's grave today, or anywhere else. 'And anyway, that has to be wrong, doesn't it? We can't reduce a grown man to the little part he played in *our* lives all that time ago!' I think for a moment. 'Except maybe that's what everyone does when someone leaves us. Maybe we never do see the whole person.'

Lottie, who usually defers to everyone, is not really listening.

'There's something terrible about it. Unbearable. Almost as though you're burying part of yourself.'

I don't bother to argue with her, take her arm instead and turn towards home.

He can't have been far behind us because we have only been back in the house for a few minutes, starting to unpack the shopping we bought from the supermarket, when the knock comes at the door. Then again, harder, just as I reach it.

'Brian!' I say. Then, 'How did you know to come here?'

'Lottie said this was where she would be,' he explains, and I feel stupid for asking, since Lottie never mentioned concealing her whereabouts. Brian has lost weight since I last saw him, a year or so back, and he looks younger for it. He hovers uncertainly on the doorstep. 'Would it be OK for me to see her? I don't want to bother her, but we really need to talk.' His voice is level but I can see how much of an effort it is for him to maintain this. His hair, which is normally brushed into a short, neat style, is unkempt today and his eyes look puffy, as if he hasn't slept. For the first time since I have known Brian I feel a rush of sympathy for him.

'I'll ask her,' is all I say, but there is no need because Lottie has shot out from the kitchen, a roll of foil still in her hand.

'What are you doing here?' she asks him in a kind of awed tone. He makes no move to step inside, just spreads his hands out to her and Lottie says nothing more. She just stares and stares at him and wonder keeps growing in her eyes.

'Well, you'd better come in,' I say.

The telephone rings and I think about leaving it. Lottie and Brian are in the living-room and I do not want them to think I might be listening. Then I remember that it may be Marie, needing me to help with Daisy this evening, and I run downstairs and snatch up the receiver.

'Hello?'

'Kate?' says a male voice I don't quite recognise.

'Yes?'

'It's Aidan here. Aidan Ford.'

'Oh. Hello.'

'I bothered Harry for your telephone number. I hope you don't mind.'

'No.'

It's just that I'm coming down to the beach hut tonight and I was wondering if you might like to come out for dinner. With me, that is.' Out of habit, I am about to say no. Normally I only ever bother with dating if I have decided to sleep with someone. But Lottie and Brian are showing no signs of going out or going home and if I have to creep around the house or sit in the kitchen for the entire evening it will be wearisome.

'OK,' I say. 'That would be nice.'

Before I have started back up the stairs, the phone rings a
second time and I pick it up expecting it to be Aidan calling
back. It is my mother, wanting to know how I am and
whether the babysitting is proving a success. I tell her what
Daisy has been doing but do not mention about my sister
being here because it is pointless to trouble her about Lottie
and Brian if they are going to resolve things. Then she asks
about the garden and says she thought of visiting next week.

'Next week?'

'Well, if I'm to sell the house in the autumn I ought to
take a look at it I should think. And I *would* like to see
what you've done with the garden.' She must sense my
hesitation, for she adds, 'Of course, if it's inconvenient I
can come another time . . . '

And I say no, next week will be fine, and if a note of
resignation echoes down the bare hallway, it is because it
seems there is nothing I can do to stop this house from
filling itself up with people.

CHAPTER 23

Lottie knocks on the bathroom door, then pokes her head round.

'Hello,' I say lightly, checking my make-up in the mirror.

'You look nice,' she says timidly. I fix her with a stern stare and for a second she looks at me in trepidation until she realises I am teasing.

'Oh don't!' she wails and then she balances herself on the edge of the bath, a thin shape in my mirror, and tells me that she thinks everything is going to be all right after all, how Brian says that after she had gone it felt as if something had been ripped out of him and the emptiness had terrified him in a way he'd never anticipated and he knew then that he had to do something, couldn't just let her vanish.

'I still can't believe he came for me,' she says, more to herself than to me now. She wraps her arms across her body, draws the thought close to her. 'I never imagined that he would, Kate. Never.'

And she says this bluff husband of hers hadn't realised how lonely she was, hadn't sensed her unhappiness, and I want to say that he must have been blind because doesn't she wave her emotions in people's faces like flags, but I stop myself because I do not want to take that shine out of my sister's eyes.

'And do you know, he says he's quite happy for me to get a job or go to college or whatever I decide to do! He thinks it would be better for all of us in many ways but he would never have suggested it because I do so much at home already, looking after the children and everything, and he didn't want me to feel that it wasn't enough – for me to feel pressured to do more than I do already.' She is like a child again, uncovering something wondrous.

I smile at her and say if they want to they better stay here tonight and Lottie says that they wanted to ask me something, were wondering if I would mind them staying for longer? Brian's mother is always happy to have the children and to take them into school so a few more days wouldn't matter, and it would be like a holiday being here, just the two of them. I hesitate, think of me and Daisy and our little world within these walls, then remind myself that Lottie – and, by extension, her husband – have as much right to be in this house as I have.

'You must have the front bedroom then,' I decide. 'I'll move my stuff into my old room tomorrow.'

'Oh no . . . ' begins Lottie. 'We don't want to cause you any trouble . . .

'It's absolutely fine,' I say. 'Just one thing you should know though . . . '

'What?'

'Mummy says she's coming next week.'

'Oh.' Lottie ponders this. 'There's no need to tell her, is there? About why we came?'

'Entirely up to you,' I say, with a shrug. 'But I can't see why she needs to know anything.'

I am already regretting accepting Aidan Ford's invitation, starting to panic to a ridiculous extent about what I have committed myself to, as if, during our short telephone conversation, I have somehow agreed to set up home with him rather than eat dinner. But now that Lottie and Brian have come out of the living-room at last and are roaming around the house, I am grateful for an excuse to be gone. Just as I am at the door, about to leave, Brian comes down to the hallway and thanks me for letting them stay. He promises they will take care of themselves and not trouble me – and looking at him, I realise that he has lost something more than the weight around his middle: it is the unwarranted air of smugness that always rankled with me. I tell him that they are welcome to stay as long as they wish and, as I walk along the pathway, away from the house, I wonder if, in time, I might even come to like my sister's newly crestfallen husband.

I meet Aidan in the Ropemaker's Arms (having turned down his offer to collect me from the house). I see that he is wearing a jacket and tie and I start to panic again, hoping that he has not dressed up for my benefit, and am relieved when he explains that he's come straight from London, from a meeting with an old university acquaintance who, he hopes, will commission a book. From the pub, we go to a new seafood bar by the marina and by the time we have ordered food and wine I am starting to calm down, remembering what I had forgotten about him from last time we met: that though he seems to enjoy my company and understands when he should laugh, he shows no signs of wanting to push down any barriers between us or even of an awareness that any might exist. I tell him about my sister coming and about Daisy and how she says she'll never forget me when I am dead and buried under the ground, and he cracks open lobster claws for both of us, pours more wine and I decide that he is not the kind of man that I sleep with: he is too open, too boyishly enthusiastic for anything more to be discovered by that particular route. (And in truth, I am not altogether sure that this is what he is seeking. Once or twice during dinner I find him looking at me for a second longer than necessary, but his expression is unreadable and I wonder if his mind is simply elsewhere for a moment.)

Later I ask him about the book and he tells me that this is his particular passion, the history of the early

Christians, that he has had articles published in the past and contributed to collections of essays, but that this would be his alone. I tell him – it only coming into my mind as I speak – of my childhood yearning for martyrdom, my secret wish to join a nunnery and how I planned to conceal the fact from my family and he laughs enough for me to know that I should be careful, yet I do not stop, still want to give him a little more of myself, a reward for not demanding it of me. So I confess that something draws me towards the altar even now, but that I cannot seem to get closer, that you'd think it would be easy to fill a vacuum but that nothingness is more stubborn than you'd imagine. It tries to hold its shape. And I say that I envy people like him and Marie, for whom it must be like breathing. He thinks about this, pours more wine as the waitress removes the wasteland of lobster and prawn shells between us, says that yes, the shadow of the crucifix was always present in his mother's house and the houses of his aunts when he was a boy, but that he's not sure it's as easy as that.

'But it has to be,' I insist, 'when it's always been there. It must get into the fabric of you . . . into your *bones* . . . '

He shrugs, accepts a cigarette from me and holds it between long fingers. 'Yes, but then you grow up and you question everything, reinvent bits of yourself, just as everyone else does . . . '

'But I'm not sure you ever lose it entirely. Particularly you Catholics, though I'm not sure why that should be. Some kind of atavistic pull towards ritual perhaps . . . '

'Yup, we're big on ritual,' he agrees with a grin. 'But you have to realise that a great deal of the time we're just following the script. Most of the time I'm in church I'm thinking to myself what a load of bollocks the whole thing is.'

The waitress comes over again and waves dessert menus at us, and we deliberate, then send her away for the bill instead. 'And I'm not sure I'm the exception to the rule,' continues Aidan when she has gone. ' I think that the gap between you and us, if you want to see it that way, is narrower than you might think.'

'Really? Then why bother with any of it?' The discursive tone is gone from my voice, has been replaced by bleakness because he seems to be saying that nothingness is all there is.

He looks down at the table, seeming to watch the smoke drifting up from his cigarette, then says quietly: 'Because when it does come to me I understand . . . something central. Only for a second though, like something catching the light. I think that's all we get. Any of us.'

Then he laughs and tells me, as he pays the bill, a story about his mother, how she and her sisters saved up to go on holiday to Rome and how, when she finally walked through the doors of St Peter's, she was appalled by its worldliness, its marble vulgarity.

'It was too much for my poor mother,' he says, as we get up from the table and make our way out on to the harbour-side. 'She'd grown up in this backwater, had never really travelled until then, and I think she felt that when she stepped inside St Peter's something momentous would take place within her, that she would find herself at the heart of her faith. It must really have been quite devastating for her.' And he relates how, in her distress, she left her sisters and walked into that great baroque nave, Bernini's massive cherubim, fat and opulent, on either side of her, and everything gilded and overblown, and that she was close to tears. Then suddenly she found herself in front of the Pietà, alone, and it was so still and sombre and tender that it was this quiet simplicity, and not all the manifestations of wealth and power around her, that finally made the tears come.

'And you think they are enough?' I say, as we walk back towards the cottage. 'These moments?'

'Sometimes,' he says. 'I'm not sure. Do you want another drink somewhere?'

'No,' I reply. I say nothing more the rest of the way home

and when we stop outside the cottage Aidan turns to me and looks at me searchingly.

'I'm sorry, Kate, I haven't upset you, have I? You must realise that my little theories are as pointless as anyone else's . . . '

'Oh no,' I say, and then, because he looks so serious, so concerned for my welfare, something playful rises in me. 'I was just trying to decide whether to sleep with you or not.'

He opens his eyes wide in mock horror at this, then laughs out loud. 'OK, OK, I'm going!' he says, backing away. 'I don't think I can bear to stand here waiting while you come to a decision: the outcome might be too wounding. I'll call you when my courage is up again.'

Then he is gone, off down the road and disappearing into the darkness, and I smile to myself before going inside, realising that I wasn't entirely lying.

Samantha Jones or whatever she calls herself now stares at Daisy, who is waiting at the end of the checkout, holding the plastic bag I have given her.

'How's her mum now? And the little one,' she asks in a loud voice, addressing me as if Daisy wasn't here at all. 'Coping better?'

'Fine,' I say, busying myself with my wallet. I hand over my debit card and Samantha swipes the card, waits for the authorisation code to come through.

'She doesn't look like you, does she?' she says, looking at Daisy again, then at me, probing us with hard, black-lined eyes. I am blank for a second, then I remember Marie's lie. 'I mean, you wouldn't know you were her auntie. Not to look at you.'

'No,' I say in as even a tone as I can manage. The woman on the checkout behind Samantha's has no customers and she is listening with interest. Our till churns to itself and I lean over the counter to sign the scrap of paper Samantha hands me.

'But if she's not your *sister's* girl . . . ?' she persists. Daisy appears at my side, her head bobbing up next to the conveyor belt. 'Only someone mentioned she was back as well.'

'She's not *that* sort of auntie,' says Daisy, drawing herself up in a dignified fashion and regarding Samantha Jones with fine contempt. I take my card and receipt, pick up our bags of shopping, and then Daisy and I leave.

Lottie and Brian have driven into Canterbury and won't be back till this evening. On our way home from the supermarket, warm summer rain starts to fall, so we abandon our plans to weed the garden and make ourselves comfortable on the sofa together, Daisy tucked perfectly into the curve of my hip and waist with her head resting on my shoulder. We have finished all our books so I decide to try her on *Swallows and Amazons*, though I suspect that the narrative will be too complex for a child of her age. I am wrong. After a page or two she stops wriggling and grabbing at her toes, and by the end of the first chapter she is listening avidly. She demands another chapter and then another and we keep on reading until my voice is growing hoarse and we are immersed in a world of camping and explorers and firelight, of pirates and sailing dinghies and open expanses of water. I sense her watching me as I read, though I pretend not to notice. Once she reaches out a hand and strokes my lips, feeling the shape of my voice. I finish another chapter and glance down at her, see her just about to push an experimental finger into her nostril.

'Yuck!' I say. 'Don't do that.' Then I glance outside. 'Oh look, it's stopped raining,'

'Hurray!' She rolls across my lap and on to her feet, then flies to the window.

Bright sunshine has burned through the rain clouds and everything outside is shimmering and green. 'Time to explore!' she orders, then dashes out into the hallway, starts murmuring lists to herself – 'We need our boots, coats on, chocolate . . . ' I manage to persuade her that we will not be needing torches or a tent today and we hurry out, past the flats where Marie and Kieran must be sleeping, since the curtains are drawn, then down to the beach, where we stride out, across the wet shingle which glitters in the sunlight, towards an exuberant rain-washed sea.

But the beach is not big enough to contain Daisy today: she is full of vast adventures that override her normal capacity for walking, and she insists that we must march onwards, round into Moreland Bay and then to the little cove beyond because you never know there might be a wreck there. I do not argue, knowing that she will tire long before we get that far and we walk to the end of the beach and make our way up on to the lower cliff-path. Halfway along it, Daisy spots another path, smaller and rougher than this one, leading up through the rocks towards the crag of Moreland Point.

'Come on!' she orders, and we climb up, around slippery rocks and over wet grass, cutting across the higher path to Moreland Bay and around more rocks until we are up on the Point itself, standing on gravel, because you can actually drive all the way up to this viewing place if you are approaching from town. Beyond the gravel and the wooden bench facing out to sea, there is a small fence. On our left-hand side, down towards Moreland Bay, the cliff is sheer.

Daisy is giddy with excitement when she realises how high we are, leaping up and down and running around without any fear. I grab hold of her arm firmly, terrified that the air at the cliff's edge may suddenly empty itself of her. I manage to persuade her to come to the safety of the bench with me. Seated, I put my arm around her shoulders, keeping her close, and we gaze out to a sharp horizon, screw up our eyes to see if we can spot a skull and crossbones on the ship that is being drawn slowly along it.

'Where do we live?' asks Daisy, wriggling out from beneath my arm and kneeling up on the bench.

'Just down there,' I say, looping my arm around her waist. 'Look down at the beach, and the beach huts behind it, and keep going back from there. Can you see the church spire? Not your church, the one in the Market Square.'

'Where, where?' she says, bobbing up and down and craning her neck. 'I can't see it!'

I point again. 'There. And I can't quite make out your flat, but if you look over there,' I move my finger, 'you can just see the houses next to where you live. See that patch of red behind the trees?'

'Yes,' she says, standing up on tiptoe on the bench; she pauses. 'No.' I take her hand and point it in the right direction and this time she does. 'Oh, wow!' she squeals, then slides back down beside me on the bench and looks warily at an angry looking seagull which has landed rather too close to the bench for her liking.

'Why is it so small?' she asks after a minute.

'What?' I say.

'That country where we live,' she says, pointing down towards Broadgate again.

'Town, you mean,' I correct her, and I am about to explain to her about distance and how it makes things look smaller than they really are, but I can see she has lost interest already, is watching the seagull wheeling over our heads.

'It just is,' I say. 'Did I tell you that I used to read *Swallows and Amazons* when I was a little girl? It was my favourite book ever.'

'In the olden days, you mean?' she says, slipping off the bench.

'Yes.' I agree.

Then we make the town grow bigger again by going back

274

down the pathway and following the higher path inland until we are among the houses.

Aidan Ford calls me again, the day before my mother is due to arrive. We drive to the cinema in Braxtable and watch a dreadful film, which unites us in vituperation in the pub afterwards. We drink too much and don't get round to eating in the end, have to leave the car in town and take a taxi home. Our driver is in a hurry, keeps barking his location into the radio, and as we swing round one particularly sharp bend on the way into Broadgate, I am thrown against Aidan for a moment. I laugh, being a little drunk, and, just for a second, before we straighten ourselves up, think about kissing him. At the cottage, he gets out of the taxi with me and we say a chaste goodnight and I watch him start to leave. Then I call him back and ask him whether he is going to church tomorrow. He says no, that he's going to Canterbury at the crack of dawn because he has stupidly promised to help his sister decorate. He waves a finger at me and says he hopes I'm not just using him for his religion.

*   *   *

My mother arrives, stepping smartly out of the taxi and walking up the pathway with her little black case in her hand as if she had never left. I have told her about Lottie and Brian being here – concealing the real reason for their presence – and so she greets them without surprise and asks them how they are enjoying their break. Next she turns to me and nods approvingly at my appearance.

'You look decidedly better,' she announces, kissing me on the cheek and then entering the house.

We show her around the kitchen and the living-room downstairs, talk about her journey down and other small things, and then I send Lottie upstairs with her to settle her into Lottie's old room, where this morning I made up the bed. I stay in the kitchen, needing to concentrate on cooking because I had forgotten how much organisation is required when there are just a few extra people around a table. It did occur to me to invite Harry too, but in the end I decided against it, unsure how either he or my mother would feel about being in this house together again. Marie shrank away immediately when I suggested she come, the thought of strange company and perhaps more questions deterring her. I came close to saying just Daisy then – nearly justified it to myself, for after all the space beside me at the table is always there now: the cushions ready on the chair, the table legs waiting to be kicked – but stopped myself in time. I had no intention of asking Aidan to join us until last night, when I found myself leading towards it with the question about church, and now I am glad that it was not possible, because I am already damp-faced and vaguely panicky in the heat of the morning.

My mother comes into the kitchen to thank me for the vase of flowers I have put by her bed. I take a bottle of white wine from the fridge and open it while she says that she had forgotten how charming the cottage is, that she still has some of the rugs that used to cover the floors here if I would like her to bring them down for me, next time she comes. The front door slams and Lottie appears to say that Brian's gone into Braxtable to fill the car with petrol. The hot air in the kitchen makes her gasp and she bats it away with her hand, and says Mummy should come out to the garden with her where, at least, the air is moving.

'Oh, but you're not to look at it without me!' I say, from where I am crouched in front of the oven basting a chicken which bubbles and hisses in its own juices. 'Not properly, anyway,' I plead. My mother smiles at my agitation and promises me that she will wait till after lunch for the full tour.

Later, when the chicken is resting under a blanket of foil and the potatoes are crisping in the oven, I come to the back door for a breath of air myself, and a glass of the cold wine. Brian is back, sitting in the shadow of the house reading the newspaper, and my mother and Lottie are halfway down the garden, walking arm in arm. Lottie is talking earnestly and my mother is nodding at intervals and looking solemn and I shake my head in amusement, knowing that for all her avowals to the contrary, my sister will find it impossible to resist telling our mother everything.

*   *   *

Lunch has long been cleared away and my mother has slept upstairs in the cool of her room for an hour and is sitting out on the patio now, in the shade of an umbrella. The heat of the day begins to be drawn down into the earth again and Lottie takes Brian off for a walk along the coastal path.

'Let me see this garden of yours, then, darling,' says my mother, putting down the travel section of the newspaper. 'I've tried my very best not to take too much notice until now.'

'It's still yours, you know,' I say. 'I've planted some new perennials at the front of the borders because they were so bare – I think most things had been suffocated – but a lot of the framework is yours. And it *feels* the same somehow.'

'Yes,' considers my mother, her eye travelling over the borders on either side of us as we make our way down the lawn, 'though of course it's hard to be sure after all these years. But I understand what you mean: I think you do leave a bit of yourself in every garden you make.' And as we go, my mother bends down to examine a particular plant, cradles a flower in the palm of her hand or draws a rose down and inhales its scent. Occasionally she gives a little cry of recognition when she finds something that was hers but has long been forgotten, as if she has, indeed, rediscovered a missing piece of herself.

I describe the hard work in the early weeks – the digging and pruning and clearing – and how the garden slowly started to reveal itself again. I show her the plum tree that is still living and capable of producing fruit after all this time and we run our hands over its bark admiring its fortitude; then look at the trees which the men cut back and those which were allowed to stay as they were, in the natural arch they had formed at the far end of the garden. I am childishly excited, showing my mother all this, and she rewards me with detailed questions about my work, with her memories of the garden as it was and with practical advice. I tell her about the little colour schemes and arrangements of contrasting foliage I am trying to create, or which I can visualise in my mind, and when she comments that I have a natural aptitude for this kind of work, an artistic eye, I am on the point of blurting out the idea that came to me one morning when I stepped outside and the grass was still wet with dew beneath my bare feet, the thought – which has no practical conclusion yet – that now I have had my hands in the earth, I can never go back to tapping away at the surface of life again.

'Lottie and I talked this morning,' says my mother suddenly.

'Yes, I saw you,' I say, with a knowing smile.

'And now I need to talk to you.'

We are in the shade of the trees, beside the smooth concrete oblong where my father's greenhouse stood, and when I see the way my mother is looking at me I understand that Lottie has said nothing about nearly leaving Brian.

'Oh,' I say, looking down at the ground. I watch as an ant ascends a blade of grass, clings on as the thin green road on which it travels begins to bend under its weight.

'Darling . . . ' It is the first time I have ever heard my mother falter and I stare down at the ground, my hands clenched by my sides. If this is to be spoken of, I want it to be over with, quickly. My mother turns to me. 'Darling, I

278

had absolutely no idea that you knew! You must understand that I thought I was doing the best thing at the time because you were so little and you'd be sure to forget if we let you, and now I find out . . . ' She grimaces and her hands twist together. 'Such a terrible thing for a child to witness, you see. You must understand that if I had known . . . that you knew, or the ideas that had been put into your head . . . '

I take her arm, make her walk with me again, willing her to understand that it would be a far more terrible thing if she were to break now, right here in front of me. 'It doesn't matter,' I say. 'I was shocked when Lottie first told me everything, but I've hardly thought about it since. I promise you.'

'What I don't understand,' she says a little later, when I have made tea for us and we are sitting on the patio again, just as Lottie and I sat the night she came, 'is why you never told me what Josie said? Why you never came to me at the time? I feel terrible about that. As if you didn't trust me!' I think back, try to get at it, but though I can still feel the sting – the shameful wrongness of me – I can go no further. 'And yet . . . It doesn't altogether surprise me,' muses my mother. 'You were such a strange little girl, you know. A dear little thing, of course – and very loving – but so self-sufficient, so contained even when you were tiny. When we found you that day, you'd obviously been distraught – your poor hands were bruised . . . '

'Lottie said.'

'But you were sitting there so calmly, just holding Peter's hand . . . ' She turns away from me for a moment, then gathers herself up again. 'You see, I've never worried about you in the way I do about Lottie. People used to say your father was highly-strung – that's what they called it in those days – and Lottie's just like him, of course. That's why it was such a shock to me when you were ill. I'd always thought your sister . . . '

'Lottie's OK,' I say, thinking about Brian and how he has been fussing round her in recent days, attending to every need she makes known. 'She's more of an Amazon than we give her credit for.'

'When I think what that child did to you . . . ' says my mother and it takes me a second to realise that she is not talking about Lottie any more.

I think about Josie, down on her knees at the funeral, imagine penitence for a moment and then dismiss the image because the adult Josie has nothing to do with me. I try again, think of her as the child I knew but still she is unreachable, locked as she should be in the past with the child that was me, like a snapshot taken from a distance.

'Please,' I say, touching my mother's arm. 'It's finished now.'

CHAPTER 24

'He slept through the night!' announces Marie, arriving with Daisy the next morning. 'Can you believe it?' Kieran is bright eyed and curious, his head against her shoulder but twisting to follow the flutterings of a pigeon in a tree. Oh, bye-bye, sweetheart,' says Marie, as Daisy, straining at her hand, breaks loose and shoots inside the house. 'I even had time to have a shower before they both got up!' She shakes her still-damp hair joyously, to demonstrate. In her newly ironed clothes she is as fresh and green as spring, though rain is beginning to stipple the path on which she stands.

'Good news!' I say. 'So what are you two up to today?'

'Well, the children's grandmother sent some money through an old friend from home – she still doesn't know where we are,' she adds, seeing the look of concern on my face, ' – and Kieran could do with some new clothes, so I thought I'd be brave and take him into Braxtable on the bus.' In my mind's eye I see that cheque, inscribed in schoolteacher's ink, hope restrained behind carefully formed letters. A message sent into nothingness. Marie's face has clouded a little and I wonder if she sees something similar or whether it is just the past reaching out for her.

'Well, we were going to have a picnic,' I say, looking up at the sky, which is a uniform grey. 'But I don't think that's going to happen.' My mother comes to the door then and holds out her hand to Marie, says what a beautiful baby Kieran is – which is true because this morning he is round-eyed and blinking and alert, as if the switch of consciousness has been turned up overnight. I can tell that Marie finds my mother's brisk manner intimidating though: her voice drops to a whisper again and she can't come in because there is a bus leaving any minute now. We wave them off from the doorstep, then go inside and shut out the niggling rain.

The weather sets into a pattern over the next few days: rain starting at dawn and continuing through till early afternoon, and then the sun breaking through and turning the afternoons hot and humid, just when it is time for Daisy to leave. Brian checks the forecast and informs us that it will be fine again by the end of the week, so we postpone any thoughts of a picnic until then. Our household also settles into a new routine: in the mornings, when Lottie and Brian are still reading the newspapers over a late breakfast, or have gone off for one of their drives along the coast, Mummy and I join forces to keep Daisy busy with reading and writing and drawing and games.

I had been concerned about how Daisy would react to yet another stranger in the house, but she has accepted my mother at once, hardly registering her arrival and attaching herself to her almost as if she considers her an extension of me. She is more wary of Brian (whose voice, now that he has recovered from the shock of nearly losing his wife, booms cheerily through the house in a way that makes Daisy jump out of her little reveries) and, less explicably, of Lottie.

This surprises me since I have always thought of Lottie as someone who immerses herself in children and I begin to watch her, wanting to see if there is anything Daisy is doing to keep her at bay. And I realise that, without being in any way unkind, Lottie holds herself aloof from Daisy, from the little coterie that is made up of me, Daisy and Mummy. I realise something else too: that she, in turn, is watching me.

In the afternoons, I take my mother into town and show her all the newness of Broadgate. She looks hungrily at the restaurants, at the delicatessen and the bookshop, says if only when we'd lived here . . . We drop in to see Harry when we are passing (he has already visited us twice since she arrived) and Mummy finds the gallery delightful, looks carefully at each new picture or piece of sculpture that arrives and makes Harry promise to take her to the Canterbury shop next time he goes.

It is while my mother and Harry are in the upstairs gallery one day, looking at a picture Harry has just hung for display, that an idea comes to me, an idea which has grown into a resolution even before I hear their footsteps creaking down the stairs again. I tackle Harry about it the minute they come down.

'Harry, do you know anybody who has a boat? A little sailing dinghy, suitable for a child to sail in?' Harry leans on the little desk where Cheryl normally sits when she is in and looks at me questioningly. 'It's just that if the weather clears we're all going for a picnic on Friday . . . ' I glance at my mother and pull myself up, 'Oh, you will join us, won't you? It's Lottie and Brian's last few days here . . . '

'Your mother's already invited me,' says Harry with a grin.

'Good,' I rush on. 'You see, I've been reading *Swallows and Amazons* to Daisy – you remember how I used to love it when I was little? – and she's obsessed with the idea of sailing, but there doesn't seem to be anywhere you can hire a boat locally and I'm not sure that I remember enough about sailing myself . . . I just wondered . . . '

Harry considers my question for a moment, then says: 'Paul Makepeace – the chap who owns the seafood place down by the harbour . . . '

'Oh yes, I've been there . . . '

'He has a little dinghy. I could have a word with him, if you like. I gave him a hefty discount on a job lot of paintings for the restaurant, so I guess he owes me a favour.'

'Would you, Harry? Oh thank you!' I say and I am so

excited by the thought of Daisy's face when her pirate ship sails in to shore to collect her, that I give him a rare hug.

*   *   *

It is not overt, her observation – indeed, if I catch Lottie's eye she looks away and busies herself with something – but once I have become aware of it I feel it more and more and there is something in her eyes which she cannot mask quickly enough when I meet her gaze, something which I cannot quite read yet but which, nevertheless, makes me feel uncomfortable. Casually, I mention Lottie's reserve when she is around Daisy to my mother, but she is untroubled by it, says that maybe Lottie has filled herself up with her own children, that there is no room for any others. And as if to prove her right, Lottie and Brian announce over dinner that they will be going home on Saturday morning instead of staying for lunch on Sunday, that they've missed the children more than they could have imagined.

Harry telephones in the morning, just before Daisy arrives, to say that everything is arranged for Friday. That evening, I go to my wardrobe and fetch an old but favourite black shirt of mine and cut a large triangle out of the back of it. Then I go to the drawer in the kitchen, take out a white tea-towel and sketch the rough shape of a skull and crossbones on it, then carefully cut it out. With some white thread, I tack this on to the black triangle. My sewing skills are too rudimentary to produce a proper pennant, one that might be raised on the rigging of a boat, so I go outside and find a garden cane, then, using some of Daisy's craft glue, attach the flag to one end of it. The cut-out pieces of tea-towel are heavier than the light material of the shirt and when I stand the cane up against a chair, my Jolly Roger flops over on itself in a rather sorry fashion, but I am hoping that once the cane has been wedged into the boat's decking and the wind is pulling at the material, the whole thing will begin to look rather more splendid.

'Do you mind if she doesn't come tomorrow?' says Marie, standing at the front door as I try to coax Daisy into her sandals. 'I forgot to say before.' I let go of Daisy's foot and she giggles and scampers off down the hallway.

'But . . .' I say, 'we're going for a picnic. It's all planned. I was going to ask if you and Kieran wanted to come too.'

'Oh,' says Marie, looking embarrassed. 'I don't think we can. I bumped into a girl who was in the hospital at the same time as us – her little girl has some kind of kidney problem that has to be monitored – and she's coming over for the day.'

'Couldn't you cancel?' I say, unable to prevent a chill entering my voice. 'Or see her without Daisy?'

'Well . . . not really. She's not on the phone, I don't think. And I thought it would be good for Daisy, having another child to play with. Mandy's got a boy too, a couple of months older than Kieran, and she's on her own like me, so she kind of understands . . .'

What she means is that she doesn't want to cancel, wouldn't even if she could. I feel the shock of untethered, unexpected hatred welling up inside me. I push it down again.

'Of course,' I say, as calmly as possible. There is nothing to be done about it, but still words come, hard as pebbles. 'But I'm just wondering if it could be postponed till another day? We had some nice things planned for Daisy tomorrow and it seems a shame for her to miss out on them.'

Marie shifts from one foot to another, looks panic-stricken by the realisation that she is going to have to repeat herself. Once again she tells me that she doesn't know if this new friend of hers is on the phone, and she is too young, too lacking in self-assurance to rebuke me for making her repeat it.

'Well, shouldn't we check in the phone book?' I say. I am

forcing her to twist on a hook in front of me, as punishment, and I don't care.

'I don't think I can,' she says desperately, looking at the ground. 'Not now. I feel I owe Daisy some time as well. She's hardly seen me recently, what with Kieran being ill and none of us sleeping properly.'

'Well, it's a shame about the picnic.'

I would like to remind her of something she once said to me, about how the three of them, she, Daisy and Kieran, had been hoping for me or waiting for me or whatever it was she said to me as she turned to me on the pathway that day. Did God, or the horoscopes – or whatever the source of her convictions was – get it wrong, after all?

'A shame for Daisy, of course.'

And then I pull myself up and force myself to smile and tell her that it doesn't matter because we can picnic another day, and all the time a voice inside me accuses me over and over again: not for Daisy, for you.

Lottie comes to me in the kitchen.

'What are you doing?' she asks. Her voice is low, presumably so that my mother, who is arranging some roses in a vase in the hallway, cannot hear.

'Making breakfast,' I say shortly.

'No. What are you doing?' she says more emphatically. 'You know what I mean.'

I put down the knife I have been using to cut a loaf of bread and look quizzical. 'What?'

'Daisy's not yours, you know.'

'I'm sorry?' I frown at her to convey my bewilderment more effectively.

'Stop it, Kate,' she says quietly, 'I heard you. You made that girl feel guilty just because she wants to spend some time with her own child.'

'I did not!' I protest lightly. 'She can have Daisy whenever . . .'

My mother walks into the kitchen, takes some scissors from a drawer and trims some leaves from a spray of blooms.

'Yes, you did,' says Lottie, as soon she goes out of the room again. 'You implied it anyway. That she was doing something wrong.'

'That simply isn't true,' I say in a high, unassailable voice, which is supposed to reduce my sister's views to frippery, though I feel as if I should be backing away, fending off her quiet but unstoppable words. Then my eye is caught by the skull-and-crossbones pennant, propped up in the corner of the room. Disappointment and bitterness engulf me again and I look at my sister defiantly. 'Well, I'm sorry, but I can't help it if Daisy has a better time when she's here with me. I must say, I find it hard to fathom why Marie finds it so impossible to look after her. She's hardly a difficult child if you take some time to . . . '

'Stop it!' Lottie seizes my arm, her thin fingers enclosing my wrist tightly, bone on bone. I stare at her, amazed at my normally tremulous sister. 'I knew that's what you were thinking, Kate, and you have no idea how wrong you are. You really think that because you entertain Daisy for a few hours a day it qualifies you in some way? That it makes you a better mother than Marie?'

'I'm not saying that exactly . . . '

'Yes, you are! That's precisely what you're saying! Has it ever occurred to you that Marie has another child to take care of? Have you even noticed that? The poor girl looks absolutely exhausted most of the time – I remember just what it was like myself, how *desperate* you feel – and she's worse off than I ever was because she's on her own and she has no money or family . . . '

'Yes, I understand that . . . '

'No, Kate, I don't think you do,' says Lottie, dropping her grip on my arm. 'Look, I'm sorry,' she says, appearing to be as startled by her outburst as I am. 'I don't want to do this to you because you've had bad times recently and you've done everything for me since I came here – you've *always* done everything – '

'I have?'

'But I've watched you with that child and I've seen this kind of . . . of proprietorial way you have with her and it worries me. And now you're talking about her like this, as if you see something in her that her own mother misses!' She sighs, wanting me to understand. 'Any child is easy if you can devote every minute of the day to entertaining it. Don't you see that every mother would like to do that, if she only had the time, but mostly her life is too cluttered up by everything else . . . '

She runs out of words suddenly. Those already spoken hang in the air between us.

'And you're saying that mine is empty,' I say slowly.

'No!' she says, taking my arm again, more gently this time. 'I just want you to be careful, that's all. For your own sake as well as Marie and Daisy's.' There is love in her eyes, as well as concern, and I want to thank her for it, but then she smashes something else against me. 'I bumped into Samantha Jones yesterday. Do you remember her? She works in the . . . '

'I know,' I interrupt sharply. 'What did she say?'

'Oh, she was just puzzled I think, but apparently there's some story going around about you being Daisy's *auntie* or something?' Lottie looks at me questioningly and I am angry then, want to scream at her for caring and point out to her that little pedantries like that only matter in places that don't, like here, or the Toytown where Lottie lives.

'Samantha Jones has too much time on her hands,' I say, affecting indifference. I look out of the window, say I might go for a run before breakfast now that the weather has changed, and I pretend that it is this and not anger or anything else that drives me out of the house, past the Jolly Roger, grinning viciously in the corner of the kitchen, and my mother, with her clouds of roses in the hallway, away from the sound of nothingness closing in on me again.

*   *   *

Nothingness should be painless, numbing, a pleasurable blank. But it has teeth as sharp and as devastating as that line of black rocks out there, where Harry painted Daniel waiting for the jaws of heaven to snap down on him. I wonder how it would feel to fall from those rocks, whether you could just let the water swallow you whole or whether some hidden will to survive would send you scrabbling back, up towards that green canopy above your head, exploding through the surface and pulling the blue air into your lungs again. I twist round and look at the town rising up behind me: mean little houses straggling up and down the hillside beneath a static sky.

'What's up?' says Aidan Ford, dropping down beside me.

'Nothing,' I say, turning back round, startled by his sudden appearance. 'I came down for a run then couldn't summon up the energy. I didn't know you were here. In town, I mean.'

'Spur of the moment,' he says. 'Actually I only came to pick up some test papers I need for this afternoon. Got to dash in a minute.'

'Right.'

'Do you want to do something tonight? I'm coming back down again after work. Tomorrow is sports day and I rather thought of skiving off and starting the weekend early.'

I shake my head miserably. 'Not really.'

Aidan nods, looks out over the water. 'I could cook for you,' he says. 'And, just to lure you in, you understand, one of my colleagues has been over to France and brought me back a good vineyard's worth of wine.'

I pretend to hesitate, but I am already persuaded. 'Well, all right then.'

*   *   *

'Bad day?' says Aidan eventually, when pasta and salad and wine and the cosiness of the lamp-lit beach hut have failed to haul me to the surface again.

'Yes,' I say, and because he doesn't press me, I tell him that it feels as if this town is starting to tighten around me like a snake, that I have been oblivious of it until this morning. And I tell him what Lottie said to me in the kitchen this morning and in the process of doing so, I find myself making us change places, my sister and I, so that it is she whose behaviour has been reprehensible.

'She made me feel as though I'm some kind of child snatcher!' I say, running my hands through my hair in agitation. Aidan smiles but says nothing, so I change tack, become an urbane observer, mocking my sister's deluded beliefs and the stupidity of Samantha Jones and her kind. 'I mean, I had thought – mistakenly, of course – that I was *helping* in some way!'

'You love her, don't you?' says Aidan suddenly, cutting across my dissembling.

My ears start to ring with panic. 'Daisy?' I say, ordering my voice to stay steady.

'Yes.'

There is no sound except the wash of the sea outside and the faint hum of the candle Aidan has placed on the table between us, which bends and flickers in unseen currents of air.

I try to find the right words. 'Yes. Yes, I do.'

He asks nothing more of me, just acknowledges what I have said with a look and starts to pour more wine for both of us, but something is lifting inside of me, wrenching itself free and rising to the surface, and there is nothing I can do to stop it finding its way out of me. 'It is that . . . but it's more too . . .'

He waits, letting me draw back or continue as I choose. I breathe deeply. 'You see, I lost a child once. A baby. Not that long ago.' I cannot look at him, feel as if I am buckling inside, can only stare past him, at the tongue-and-groove panelling on the wall opposite me, at the grain of the wood beneath the blue gloss. But still it will not do. I am thinking of Lottie and what she said, about living a half-life, and realising that the story I am telling is a half-truth, that it is worth nothing without the rest of it being pulled out into the light. 'No,' I say, frowning, shaking my head, almost distracted by the effort of making the words come. 'That's not it. Not all of it, I mean. I didn't lose a baby. I got rid of one. It was my fault.' And I drag my eyes up to meet his, thinking that, because I have seen that casual gesture of his, that crossing of himself before the altar as though he is hardly aware of the shape his body makes – which, when I first saw it, the day he showed me the tiny Catholic church in Braxtable, had the odd effect of making me want to go to bed with him – that those blue eyes might turn black now, the wrath of God channelling through them. Still he says nothing. Then he puts down his wine glass, pushes the candle to one side and stretches a hand across the table to me. Lifts it and cups my cheek.

'I'm not sure you fancy me,' I say, petulantly, as we walk home.

Aidan raises his eyebrows in surprise. 'What makes you say that?'

'Well, shouldn't you be making more effort to get me into bed? It's starting to feel insulting.'

'Would you have done? Tonight?' He looks at me doubtfully.

'No,' I say primly. I have already given him far more of myself than I should have done.

'I thought not.'

'Nevertheless . . . ' I say, and pull a face at him, 'rude not to try.'

This time we kiss and it is just starting to become a prelude to something fiercer and I am thinking that here, in front of the house, might not be the best place (but not stopping), when Aidan pulls away from me.

'I wanted to ask you something tonight,' he says.

'You don't want me to dress up in your fisherman's jumper, do you?' I giggle at my own joke, exuberant from French wine and his kiss.

'I wanted to ask if you'd come to Rome with me.'

'What?' I say, sliding out of his arms, which are sitting loosely around my waist. *'When?'*

'July. When term finishes.'

'Why?'

'Why am I going, or why am I asking you?'

'Well, both.'

'I need to do some research for this book.' He spreads his hands. 'Actually, I don't need to go at all, but I want to. I haven't been to Rome since I was a student and I feel as though I only scratched the surface then. I've been meaning to go back for years and spend some time there and never got round to it.' He pauses. 'And I want you to come because I think you'd like it – the spirit of the place would suit you, the . . . ' he searches for a suitable description, then gives up, ' . . . the bigness of it.'

'Well, thank you for asking but I don't think I can,' I say, stepping back from him, my ears starting to ring again. 'I'm needed here.' We both know this isn't true and so I stumble on, 'And you'll get much more work done if you haven't got someone trailing around with you . . . '

'Oh, I'm not going if you don't come,' he says in unconcerned tones.

'But that's not fair!' I protest. 'You're putting me under an obligation now. If I don't agree to go, your research doesn't get done.'

'No, no,' he says. 'I told you, I don't *need* to go. And if I can't persuade you to come with me, I'll probably slope off somewhere else for a month or two. My sister will be wanting the beach hut soon. It's just that when I thought about Rome, I could see you there.' He pauses again. 'And I couldn't think of anyone I'd rather be with.' He smiles, gestures at my feet. 'Besides, those boots are wasted on

Broadgate.'

'Give me some time,' I say, backing away from him, away from arms that might close around me, close on empty air. 'But I think the answer's probably going to be no, I'm afraid. I can't see a way . . . '

'Think about it,' he says, then says good-night from where he is standing. I watch him for a moment before I go in, disappearing between the street-lights.

The next morning I find my mother standing at the stove in a shaft of yellow sunlight, scrambling eggs for Lottie and Brian. On the table is a basket already packed with a stack of foil parcels and, laid across the top of it, three elegant *ficelles* wrapped in paper. I make coffee for both of us and sit up on the worktop, looking out at a day full of perfect blue sky, perfect sunshine, and Lottie and Brian laughing about something round the corner on the patio – and all of it hollow as a shell without Daisy in it. I must try though, make some sort of effort to enjoy a picnic that was my idea. I remember that I should ring Harry, to tell him not to bother about the sailing dinghy.

'He knows,' says my mother, when I mention it. 'I spoke to him last night.' She peers into the pan, assessing the eggs, then continues to stir, this time more rapidly.

'You and Lottie haven't fallen out, have you?' she asks, as she scrapes the eggs over the slices of toast she has laid out on two plates. 'I'm afraid I couldn't help overhearing a little of your discussion yesterday, when I was in the hallway.'

'No, of course not,' I say, slipping off the worktop and taking the plates from her. 'I'll take these out, shall I?'

'Thank you, darling.'

My mother is counting out linen napkins – which she insists will be necessary – when I come in again.

'I do empathise with young Marie, you know,' she says, glancing up at me. 'I was just thinking how very hard it is to bring up children on your own.'

'I'm sure it is,' I say shortly, folding up the picnic rug that someone has draped over a chair and wondering if she and Lottie have been discussing me. I am starting to feel as if this house is edging me out, as if the air within is expanding and I am on the outside, being pushed away.

'It's the responsibility of it all that's so terrifying,' continues my mother, ignoring my terse tone. 'I know I used to feel utterly overwhelmed by it sometimes. Those times in the middle of the night when everything seems much worse than it really is.'

'Did you?' I say, startled to hear that my mother's self-assurance has ever wavered, even for a moment. 'I never knew.'

'Well, you wouldn't, darling. That's all part of the responsibility. And Marie seems dreadfully young to be carrying all that weight, don't you think?'

'Yes, I suppose so,' I concede, looking round for a beach bag for the picnic rug, then seeing a striped one on one of the hooks by the door. 'At least you had Harry to help you when we were young. For a time, anyway.'

My mother sighs at this, shakes her head. 'Even more responsibility.' Then, seeing that I don't understand her meaning, explains: 'Harry was a darling. He still is, of course, but I remember being quite panic-stricken when he and the children arrived here all at once like that. I felt I had enough to cope with, looking after two of my own.' She crosses to the cutlery drawer and begins counting out forks. 'And I'd never wanted to come here in the first place, only agreed to because your grandfather wanted Daddy to take over the practice, so I suppose I began to feel pinned down here even more firmly at that time.'

I have stopped what I am doing, with the picnic rug only halfway inside the beach bag, the top of it spilling out like a fat plaid slug.

'So you didn't leave here – and Harry – because of me?'

My mother looks bemused. 'You and Josie?'

'Yes.'

'Of course not. Whatever gave you that idea? Obviously, I would have had to think what we were going to do about Josie if things had continued, had to have Harry make some effort to . . . civilise her, I suppose, but these things happen with children and people find ways . . . ' She gives another sigh and gathers up more cutlery from the drawer. 'I simply didn't want the responsibility of more people at that time in my life. I don't think I really trusted myself in that way. Perhaps I thought I wasn't up to it.' She smiles. 'And, of course, when you are younger you're sure that opportunities will keep arriving on your doorstep, should you change your mind at a later date.'

'I can't believe you haven't had other opportunities,' I say, looking at her still regal profile.

'Oh yes,' she smiles, and she is all matter of factness again, no trace of regret in her voice now. 'But once you make yourself into a certain sort of person, it can be rather difficult to unmake yourself again, you know. One gets set.'

Lottie and Brian come traipsing through then, with their empty plates and teacups.

' . . . While you're all here, I should probably tell you . . . '

Lottie stops clattering plates in the washing-up water and looks scared, as she always does when she feels anything new descending on her.

'What?'

'I've decided not to sell the house after all,' says my mother.

'Why not?' asks Brian, and my mother starts to say something about keeping it for weekends and how it ought to have been used for holidays with the children all these years, and it comes to me that the house has been waiting for her, has drawn her back in spite of herself, and I understand now that my job was merely to prepare it for her arrival. Aidan's invitation flicks into my mind again, as it has done intermittently since last night, and a sharp memory stabs at me, of leaning against my mother's legs on a warm summer's evening, listening to the undulations of her voice, and I wonder if she and Harry will ever take that trip to Florence that they imagined among the dark foliage and the sweet perfumes of my mother's garden.

*   *   *

Harry takes the lead, setting off down the pathway with a foldaway chair under each arm, a clumsy grey bird, faintly comical in his skew-whiff straw hat. A portlier figure follows, Brian with two similar chairs under his right arm and another under his left, together with a beach umbrella. He is already sweating through his shirt in this heat. Lottie is carrying the beach bag with the rug and a bag of clinking bottles and she too looks bird-like, her small head wrapped in a headscarf and her thin body hopping along beside her husband's, trying to keep up. Mummy and I bring up the rear, she looking composed in linen trousers and a cool white blouse, carrying the basket containing the bread and cheese and pâtés, and me with a jumble of everything else we need crammed into two carrier bags because at the last minute we couldn't find anything more suitable.

I look straight ahead as we walk, watching Lottie's sharp shoulder bones moving beneath her cotton dress and feeling the heat striking up from the pavement. 'I'll catch you up in a minute,' I say suddenly, just as Harry turns off from the High Street, down towards the beach. I have started back the way we came before anyone has a chance to ask me where I am going, though my sister's soft moan, which has more to do with the heat than anything else, reaches me: 'Oh, *Kate!*'

I keep going, the plastic of the carrier bags cutting into my palms and making my hands sweat, walking faster and faster, until I am opposite the flats. I stop and look up at Marie's window but the sun is glaring off it, blinding me with its dazzle, so I cross the road and stand outside. I put my bags down and am about to press the buzzer when I notice an empty pushchair – green, not like Kieran's blue one – parked in the stairwell. I stand here, undecided, not even knowing what I have come here to do. Then I hear a noise, a child's voice, and something floats down the stairwell. I push my face up against the glass and see what looks like a piece of plastic material lying at the foot of the stairs. Attached to it, by pipe cleaners, is a pocket-sized doll. Then something else drops, doesn't float this time but plummets straight to the ground with a smack. Another piece of material, this time with a headless naked Susan attached. Giggles come from above and then a little girl whom I don't recognise scoots down into the stairwell, her red hair secured into two high bunches by green bobbles. She picks up the pocket-sized doll and parachute, then, sensing someone observing her, looks at me. I watch her weighing me up, deciding whether or not to smile, and then there is another movement on the stairs and the red-haired girl turns towards it, says something, her finger starting to stretch out in my direction. I jerk away from the door, out of sight, then cross back over the road and set off towards the beach at speed, the bags bouncing off my legs as I go.

The beach is busier than usual today and there is a holiday feeling in the air, with people spilling out from the verandas of the beach huts in little knots of umbrellas and chairs and children and buckets and spades and fishing-nets. I spot our party easily enough though, my mother sitting straight-backed on the rug beneath the striped beach umbrella, with the picnic basket beside her, while Harry arranges the chairs, his straw hat bobbing up and down. I can almost hear her ordering their various positions, though I am well out of earshot. Lottie and Brian are standing just in front of them, Brian leaning down to take off his shoes, with one arm on Lottie's shoulder to steady himself. A light breeze is playing with Lottie's hair, which has turned lank in this heat, and she brushes it out of her eyes with an agitated little flick. The intense sun will soon bring shadows under her eyes and a headache throbbing at the delicate skin of her temples.

The heat of the day has yet to turn the light hazy and they are delineated sharply against the background of shingle and cliffs and sea. They become for a second, before one of them moves, statuary. I walk towards them thinking that, in a strange sort of way, I have put them all here, arranged them like figures in a happy tableau I'd imagined. Then I remind myself that the good things that have come about as a result of my being here have mostly been inadvertent, accidents of fate. But, in that case, perhaps the bad things that I did once, or thought I had done, which feels like the same thing, were nothing more than accidents too. All but one of them, that is. One of them I must claim as my own. A small, small child that tried to be mine. And I do, now, suddenly fearless beneath the wide blue sky. And I am still here, breathing self-consciously in and out, my feet still moving forward over the hot, bleached shingle.

I see Aidan's car outside his beach hut, see his profile moving about in the shade of the veranda, dodging the sun's rays and sports day, and something sharp and tender blooms in me, like blood billowing in water, and I change direction, away from the picnic party, something in me beginning to take flight as I walk straight towards him, faster now, my bags still banging clumsily against my legs and my feet pushing back the shingle and sand behind them into little troughs that start to slide in upon themselves, erasing my tracks.

Karen Powell was brought up in Rochester and studied English at Lucy Cavendish College, Cambridge. She now lives in York. This is her first novel.